Weres and Witchery

A SPICY SMALL TOWN PARANORMAL ROMANCE

AK NEVERMORE

Cover design by BookMojo

Paperback ISBN: 978-1-964466-32-3

Digital ISBN: 978-1-964466-22-4

To everyone who was hanging out in the shadows during those high school keg parties. I see you—Cheers!

CONTENTS

This book explores themes which some readers may find uncomfortable and/or offensive to include:

- **Spice -** Open door sex scenes with spanking, biting, and knotting.
- **Violence -** blood, guts, and references to sacrifice (both human and animal) and postmortem desecration
- **Language -** some variation of the "F" word is used 183 times and other salty language abounds.
- **Generally unsavory behavior -** my bad guys / girls aren't good people. They do bad things and aren't sorry, but I promise they get what they deserve.

If any of the above are triggers for you, please put this novel down and back away slowly.

Still here? Awesome. Just remember, it's a fantasy, people. Don't try this stuff at home.

Senior Year, High School

JENA NURSED HER WARM BEER, trying to melt into the shifting shadows at the edge of the bonfire's flickering light. These stupid parties were totally not her scene. She leaned back against a tumbled stone wall, roots digging into her backside and sighed. Around her, the majority of Havers High and its recent alumni mobbed the late autumn field and stood in clusters beneath the trees surrounding it. Everyone was either having a great time in their cliques, making out with someone, or standing around the kegs waiting to fill up their red plastic cups.

The next crappy song started up, and Jena frowned into her beer, all by her lonesome. Not that she wasn't used to that, but why she let Felix talk her into these things…Okay, she knew why, but the off chance she'd see Chase Montgomery here—

Ugh. What was the point? He was four years older and didn't even know she existed. He probably had a girlfriend at college, and if he did, she definitely wasn't five-two and chubby. Jena raised her cup, chugged half of it, then grimaced. *You're not drinking it for the taste, Jena.* And so what if he'd smiled at her—okay, more like had smiled in her general direction, like, twice, maybe.

God, she was an idiot, but those frickin' dimples of his…

Coming here was just asking for trouble. Too bad town was a good five-mile hike, and she was stuck here for the duration. Still, if she'd been smart, she'd have started walking back as soon as she saw Felix talking to Liam. That boy seriously scrambled Felix's brain.

Jena finished her beer, scowling. He probably didn't even remember she was here, which didn't bode well for her catching a ride back into town. Damn it. The last thing she wanted to do was call Aggie. Her aunt had practically thrown her out the door. She had a very clear vision of what she thought almost eighteen-year-olds should be doing with their weekends, and it was not studying for advanced economics placement.

Which Jena really needed to get if she wanted that scholarship.

She set the cup aside and pulled a flask from her bag. If she was forced to be here, she might as well drink something worth the hangover.

She glanced at her phone. *Come on, Felix…* How long could it possibly take to hook-up?

Nope. Never mind. The reminder of her own inexperience didn't improve her mood. Chase wasn't the only one who didn't know she existed. She was a frickin' pariah, and Felix saying he'd date her if he were straight didn't help. She'd seen the dudes he'd hooked up with, and most of them were a far cry from Liam. No wonder he was taking his time.

Jena sighed and tipped back her flask, downed a hefty mouthful, then buzzed her lips at the burn. Whatever. Being abandoned by Felix was actually preferable to listening to Aggie complain about her staying home every Friday night. He'd be what? Another hour? Then they could leave.

A nearby gaggle of jocks and their dates laughed, and Jena's hackles rose at Crystal's saccharine giggle cutting through it. Jena didn't doubt that whatever the bitch had said was about her, given the way Becky and Sue glanced in her direction. Stupid Westside weres. It was like they'd made it their goal to make Jena's life hell.

Mission accomplished. She couldn't wait to get out of this stupid town.

Which meant she really needed to study.

The group laughed again, and Jena looked away, slouching down behind her bent knees as she tried to ignore them. She picked at her frayed jeans. God, the way the three of them stood around in their slutty little cheerleading outfits with the boys in varsity jackets drooling over them—Jena flicked a leaf off her concert tee. Whatever. It wasn't like she cared.

Much.

Crystal swept her long blonde hair over her shoulder, everything about her too perfect. Like she and the rest of them were better than anyone else. Jena's fingers started to tingle, and she shook the influx of magic away, getting a hold on her temper.

Deep breath, Jena. I will not hex…I will not hex…

But damn, a gnarly zit right on the tip of Crystal's nose would go a long way to making Jena feel better. She smiled imagining it, then swallowed it quick as she felt someone's gaze on her. Her eyes flicked around the field, the skunky reek of pot and clove cigarettes riding heavy on the wind. Ugh, this was so not her thing.

Just past Crystal's gaggle, a bunch of Haver's alumni sat in a line of folding chairs with a cooler, back from college for Thanksgiving break. Nope, no piss-warm swill for them. Their bottles clinked as they played cards and laughed, popular girls hanging over their shoulders or on their laps. Must be nice. *Drink up guys, because this is the best your pathetic lives are gonna get,* Jena thought uncharitably, raising her flask again—

Her roaming gaze stalled on Chase Montgomery sitting at

the far end of their group, his ball cap pulled low over his eyes as he played his hand. Oh God, he was here. Her stomach gave a little flip, and her palms started sweating. Damn it. Felix had told her to wear the shirt that showed off her boobs—wait. Was Chase looking in this direction? You never could tell with that stupid hat of his…

Jena snorted. *Stop it.* If he was, it wasn't at her. She pressed her knees together, shrinking in on herself. It was probably to check out Crystal flashing her ass. That's what was holding everyone else's attention. Jena took another swallow of liquor, trying not to drool over him and failing miserably.

Of all the boys in Havers-by-the-Sea to have a hopeless crush on—but God, he was hot, with those caramel waves spilling out around his hat and stubbly square jaw—and he'd definitely bulked up while he was away. Weres had a tendency to do that, but damn, the boy was stacked. Was it weird that he had sexy forearms? Because they were definitely sexy.

Too bad he was the heir presumptive to a pack of assholes that hated her guts.

Yeah, that kind of killed it. It was never gonna happen. Jena sighed. Right, she'd gotten her glimpse, and the last thing she needed to do was to get caught checking him out. The rest of the pack would have a fit.

She glanced at her phone again. *Come on, Felix…no, you know what? Fuck it.* She'd wait by the car—oh God. Unless Felix and Liam were *in* the car. She'd get the play-by-play later, but it was not something she needed to see IRL.

The crowd around Crystal laughed again, and the mood around the fire changed from laid back to anticipatory. Shit. Jena capped her flask and stood, gritting her teeth as she started cutting through the crowd toward the cars. Whatever was about to happen she didn't want any part of—

"Jena!" Becky called. "You're not leaving already, are you?"

Double shit. Everyone in the immediate vicinity stopped yapping to watch what was about to go down. That it was going to be something to humiliate her, Jena had no doubt. Damn it. "Yeah. My ride's ready to go," she lied.

"That's so weird, Mark was just telling us he saw Felix and Liam in the woods, and they seemed pretty busy." The group laughed again, and Jena's temper spiked at their sniggers.

"Well, then I guess Liam's a minute man," Jena gritted out, pushing past—

Her foot caught on something, and she went down hard, her chin clipping a stone and a sharp pain at her throat. Her teeth clashed together, and stars burst across her vision. She cried out, the air knocked from her lungs and a weird warmth blooming from her chin to her collar bone. Jena groaned, struggling to get up, and her body not cooperating.

"Shit, is that blood?" one of the jocks asked.

The group edged away from her. Jena tried to push herself up—her vision grayed, and someone screamed. Why couldn't she—tears burned her eyes. Oh God, it hurt...

"The fuck did you do?" someone growled, the sound of running feet around her as people fled the scene.

"I didn't—she just fell, man, it wasn't me, I swear!"

Strong hands were on her, gently turning her over— "Damn," Chase murmured, pushing her hair back. "Shhh... it's okay, I got you. Lemme see..." He pulled Jena into his lap, and tilted her head back, growling, his palm pressed to throat. She whimpered, her pulse against it wrong. "I'm gonna fucking kill him."

Her thoughts fuzzed in and out. Of course. Of course it would be Chase, that he would see her like this—she couldn't catch a frickin' break. But she supposed there were worse things than dying in his arms. Her head lolled, and he steadied it, cupping the back of her head.

"Hey, relax. I'll take care of you."

Jena bit back a sob, and he frowned, then lowered his face to hers, and put his mouth over the wound. She froze as his lips touched her skin, the tingle of his saliva immediate as it worked to heal her. Over his broad shoulder, Felix stared at them wide-eyed, his face white, and the rest of the party running for their cars, engines starting in the distance.

"Assholes," Chase murmured, running his tongue down the line of her throat, trailing over the wound. The musk of his cologne rolled over her. Jena bit back a gasp, her fingers curling in his hair, and her body heating in response. He shifted her in his lap, his body definitely doing something, too.

"Okay. Umm...I-I'm gonna pull up the car," Felix said, darting away.

Jena moved to get up, and Chase's arms tightened around her. "Not yet," he murmured. "I'm not done."

Oh God. Jena's eyes closed as he lapped around her chin, a rumble growing in his chest. She swallowed, her breath shallow. The long swipes of his tongue changed to soft kisses peppering her jawline, and her breath caught. He was kissing her. Chase Montgomery was kissing her, taking care of her like she mattered—

"Are you hurt anywhere else?" he rumbled, sweeping his hand over her.

Yes. *No—damn it. Bad, Jena.* That throbbing definitely did not count. "I'm-I'm okay."

"You're not. That's gonna leave a scar," he frowned, holding her closer as she went to get up again. His lap! She was sitting in his lap—He brushed her hair back again, his gaze roaming over her face. "Give it a minute. Felix still has to bring up the car. You need to go easy, or that gash will open back up. I stopped the bleeding, but it was really deep. It's gonna take time to knit together. You should probably get stitches."

She raised her eyes to the shadows beneath the brim of his cap. "Um. Okay, thanks, but I-I really should—"

"No, you shouldn't. Let me take care of you, Jena," he murmured, dipping his head to lap at her throat again.

He knew her name. Holy crap, Chase Montgomery knew her name, and he was *licking* her! Fireworks went off in her brain, blowing rational thought out of the water—

He started to pull away, and she kissed him.

A pleased rumble went through his chest as he returned it, open frickin' mouth, his tongue sliding between her lips to tangle with hers.

Jena moaned into his mouth. He was kissing her! *French frickin' kissing her*. God, she should've almost died sooner, because this was heaven—

"You're so damned beautiful." His fingers tightened in her hair as he teased his lips over hers. "I knew you'd taste sweet."

And she was officially dead. She must be. Was this real?

His lips were back on hers, and they parted again with a gasp. He groaned, sweeping his tongue through her mouth. His other hand kneaded her hip, then slowly traveling upwards to cup her breast—

"Ew! Are you freaking kidding me?" Crystal's squeal shattered the moment, and Chase pulled away, dumping Jena on the ground. Crystal stood there gawking with Becky and Sue. Jesus, when had they come back? "Were you seriously making out with her?"

"What?" Chase forced a laugh, pulling the brim of his hat low as he stood. He ran the back of his hand over his mouth. "No. We would've been screwed if someone got hurt out here, and Boyd dared me to see how far I could get with her. Two birds, one stone. I probably could've bent her over if you hadn't showed up," he said, adjusting himself.

Jena's heart shattered into a million pieces as she rolled to sit, vomit searing the back of her throat. She fought back tears. It'd been a dare?

Headlights bumped across the field, and Felix pulled up. He left the car running and jumped out of the driver's seat. He froze at Crystal and her friends laughing and stupid Chase standing there looking like the piece of shit he was with his hands shoved into his pockets.

"You should take her home," he muttered at Felix. "She doesn't belong here."

The tattered remains of Jena's self-worth crashed and burned. She ducked her head, tears rolling down her cheeks. Felix opened his mouth then closed it with a frown, going to Jena's side to help her up. She meekly let him guide her to the car, shaking. A joke. Kissing her had been—*she*—was a joke.

Chase was right. She didn't belong here at all.

Twelve Years Later

IN AN OCEAN OF SMALL TOWNS, Havers-by-the-Sea was rock bottom, and Jena was drowning.

She closed her eyes and fought to steady her breath, 1970s elevator music and the frequent beeps of the other cashiers' scanners too loud in her ears. Jesus take the wheel. Paper or fricking plastic. That's all she'd wanted to know.

But instead of answering the damned question so she could bag the twelve-pound Sunday roast with all the fixings, the eminent Ms. Mary Montgomery of the Westside Montgomery pack—absolutely not the Eastside, bless your heart—had taken it as an opportunity to launch into yet another sermon categorizing Jena's many failings. The third? No—fourth one this week, which was two more than Adelene Pritchett had given her, and three less than Martin Kind, who was not, in fact, kind at all.

This. This was why Jena had left.

Well, that and Ms. Montgomery's stupid son, Chase. The hulking prick leaning against the neighboring register's divider, staring in her direction from beneath the curled brim of his ratty ball cap, his caramel waves spilling out around its sides. People edged away from him as a muscle in his square, stubbled jaw twitched. Looked like he had something to add to the conversation, and it was killing him to not open his mouth.

Good. She hoped he dropped dead along with the rest of them.

He crossed his arms over his massive chest, and she swore she could hear the fabric of his t-shirt scream as his muscles flexed. How he'd gotten even bigger than that last night she'd seen him at the bonfire… A wash of rage went through her. Whatever. Fricking weres. God, she hated him.

The checkout line behind Havers's royalty had grown three deep. Clevis Blackford stood behind them with a six pack of beer and nail fungus cream. Then came Sherri-Lynn Page. She failed to hide a pregnancy test beneath the latest edition of *Starr Magazine*. Brenda Spitz brought up the rear with an economy-sized box of diapers and three pounds of ground chuck on clearance that should've been thrown away at the beginning of the week.

There were other checkouts, sure, but as far as entertainment value? Jena's line had the rest beat. All of them listened to Ms. Montgomery's diatribe, rapt, as though they hadn't had front row seats to the dumpster fire that'd been Jena's formative years.

As if they hadn't sat back with popcorn and watched her family die, one by frickin' one.

Jena pulled out a paper bag and snapped it open. The shrew blinked hard and took a step back, one hand rising to clutch her dollar-store pearls. The real ones were just for church because apparently our Lord and Savior appreciated that kind of thing, but a pink tweed pants-suit and kitten heels could be worn anytime. Before nine a.m. on a Saturday morning certainly didn't seem to be an exception.

"I prefer plastic." Ms. Montgomery huffed, taking a big breath and diving right back in where she'd left off, despite having stated her preference for paper this past Tuesday.

"My mistake." Jena smiled, and it was. Coming back had been a huge—

"There a problem here?" Sal, the store manager asked, sauntering over like he hadn't seen everything play out closed-caption style from the comfort of his office. God, he was a troll. Literally and figuratively. He hiked up his waistband, his flopping gut doing more to hold up his sagging chinos than the tired belt strapped somewhere south of his non-existent waist.

"No, sir," Jena forced her smile wider and shoved a bag of vegetables at the bitch. "Ms. Montgomery was just reminding me that despite my Bachelors degree in business and an MBA in finance, I'm still townie trash not fit to lick her shoes."

Clevis brayed out a laugh, and a .02 oz. blob of phlegm spattered onto Jena's cash register scale. Behind him, Sherri-Lynn went green and dry-heaved. Girl was definitely in the family way.

Ms. Montgomery gasped and looked between Jena and her manager. "Well, I never—what kind of an establishment are you running here, Salvator? Are you going to let her speak to me like that?"

"Ah, I—No, no, of course not Ms. Montgomery!" He wet his blubbery green lips, and Jena pulled the tie of her apron in anticipation, her fingertips tingling with intent. *Say it, say it, say it…* Sal took a deep breath. "You're fired."

Thank God.

Jena ripped the bundle of cheap fabric up, over her head, tossed it at him, and was out the sliding door before it'd opened halfway, already texting Felix.

I owe u nachos

FR?

What did it? NM who?

Montgomery

Which one?

Head bitch

Hah. Called it. Tournament ends @ 2. Meet u @ Snaps

Jena gave the last message a thumbs up and pocketed her phone as she headed down the picturesque, tree-lined street. She rubbed her arms in the early autumn chill. Damn it, she'd forgotten to grab her sweater. Oh well. No way was she going back for it now. Hopefully it would be in the lost-and-found when she picked up her last check.

Worst case, the town was small enough she'd see it on whoever stole it and could hex them. The karma she'd burn would be a wash if they did something to deserve it, and theft definitely qualified.

She sighed, tucking a pin-straight lock of raven hair behind her ear and looked up through the changing leaves at the bright, sidhe-blue sky above Main Street. Havers-by-the-Sea—Havers, to the locals—might be rock-bottom for her, but she had to admit it was pretty, in a Norman Rockwell with pixies kind of way.

Too bad everyone in it thought she was spit. Well, not the pixies. The little idiots had always liked her for some reason, which equated to the same amount of bragging rights as the neighborhood stray not hissing at her.

Damn it. She'd been lucky to get hired at Sal's. His grocery was the preeminent establishment on the main drag with its white clapboard and dark green trim. Crates of produce lined the front, priced exorbitantly for the normy tourists that came to gawk at the selkies and merfolk down at the shore. They had a whole thing down there—or so Jena had been told. Thanks to her father, the docks, and the entire surrounding neighborhood, were completely off-limits.

That was only marginally worse than the "not particularly

welcome" she was getting from the rest of the town. At least she couldn't hear what they were saying about her down there.

Jena sighed, rubbing her arms again at a cool breeze and reluctantly deciding to forgo a coffee. Cups, the peachy-pink stuccoed café, was just across the way, all bougie with its white wrought iron outdoor seating. They made great coffee, but it was a hater hotspot, especially at this time of the morning.

Yep. It would be a pretty idyllic town for anyone without her last name.

She kept walking, glancing at windows as she passed. Farther down the block stood ReRun, the baby blue second-hand shop, and then there was Ollie's Pizza Palace at the corner.

None of which were looking for help in the off-season, and neither were any of the other, smaller businesses. Okay, that wasn't entirely true. Coach Gray, her ex-gym teacher turned photographer, had been eager to hire her for the front desk until she'd told him she wasn't interested in "modeling" after hours. Felix had called that one, too, but not for nothing, the dude had always been a perv.

Jena sighed as she turned the corner from Main to Cross, the waterfront sparkling in the distance. There would be work there, but the last time she'd attempted to set foot on the docks, it hadn't ended well. Granted, that'd been ten years ago, but Selkies had longer memories than most—especially the ones with skins that'd been hexed.

Yeah, that'd been removed, but Jena got it. It was the principle of the thing, and what her father's shitty use of power had done to public sentiment had been the one sin her mother couldn't eat.

She jammed her hands deeper into her pockets—pointedly not making eye contact with the town's early morning pedestrian traffic and resisting the urge to trip the odd jogger. Life was difficult enough if that was their chosen form of recreation.

She kicked at a scattering of russet leaves and buzzed her lips, the reality of her unemployment settling in. It'd been a shit paycheck, but it'd been a paycheck, and now her only option was to drive the hour to Fayet and look for something there. Also a dicey prospect thanks to dear old dad. No one was jumping at the chance to hire a delinquent warlock's daughter.

Jena sighed again, stopping short in front of The Witchery as a harem of giggling pixies zipped around her, already high on dust.

"Jena-Jena-Jena! You're-back-you're-back-you're-back!" they chanted in a rapid-fire falsetto before careening down the block. Her gaze went past the tiny, winged humanoids to run over the gothic brownstone. If only taking a break from reality could be as easy for her. Too bad the universe seemed to delight in slapping her upside the head with a healthy dose of "this is your shitty life" lately.

The heavy purple curtains were still pulled across the front window, and Jena's reflection stared back at her—Morticia Adams after one too many meatball subs. That's what happened when you ate your feelings. Or so her lying, cheating, piece-of-shit ex had said. Whatever. Screw him. It was just winter weight, right? Practical, really. She'd need it to keep her warm since there was no way she could splurge on propane.

Damn it. Jena frowned. She should've gone back for her sweater.

Her fingers closed around the heavy bronze key in her pocket, and she whispered the spell to deactivate the cantrip just inside. She unlocked the shop's door, licking the tingle of magic from her lips, and the bell above the door tinged as she opened it.

Amber, frankincense, and the scent of palo santo

surrounded her, clearing her head. She stepped over the line of salt and padded through the darkened shop to the back counter. Aggie would still be sleeping. That last round of chemo had been really rough on her.

Which was why Jena had come back.

She moved about the cramped shop, gathering the next batch of items to take photos of. Tourist season wasn't what it had been, and with Aggie so sick, it cost more to keep the doors open than closed. Online sales were the only thing keeping the shop her mother had started with her best friend afloat.

That and the paycheck Jena wasn't getting anymore.

She scowled. The smart thing to do would be to sell off the inventory and the building. They could use the proceeds to pay the back taxes and settle Aggie's medical bills. It was a historical property, and if they hit the market right, there might even be enough capital to get her some decent hospice care.

Yeah, the smart thing. Jena's scowl deepened. She'd been here for the past two weeks with that intent. Instead, she'd been bagging groceries to buy time for the miracle to happen. What exactly that was, she hadn't a clue, but every time she went to dial a realtor she felt like she was gonna throw up.

Jena sighed, arranging tinctures against a makeshift backdrop. Whatever. It would be what it would be until it wasn't anymore. She pulled her phone to snap a pic and upload it to the website, then cross posted to their storefront on a bespoke crafter's site and The Witchery's socials.

And as of right now, what it was definitely wasn't smart.

CHASE HEFTED the roast into the back of his mother's SUV and closed the hatch, trying to control his wolf. How Jena Seymore was even better looking than he remembered…

she'd always been pretty, but all her curves from high school had filled out and blossomed into something he seriously wanted to sink his teeth into. And damn, those bright green eyes. He raised his ball cap just long enough to wipe the sweat from his brow.

What a firecracker. The way she'd sashayed out the door after putting his mother in her place? That sass was just the gravy on top.

His mother had more than deserved it. He'd been rightfully suspicious when he'd heard she'd been doing the grocery shopping herself these past two weeks. He'd also known he should keep his distance from the curvy little witch, but curiosity had finally won out, and offering to help his mother pick up the roast had just solidified her motives. Now that she'd gotten Jena fired, he knew damned well Ginny would be the one picking up vegetables.

God, his mother was a bitch. Why she couldn't leave Jena alone—Christ, he wasn't gonna be able to leave her alone after seeing her. Knowing she was back in town had been making his wolf crazy enough, but now? His urge to protect her—Jesus, just to be near her—had blown into overdrive. The last time he'd seen her…He needed to apologize—for everything—and make sure she was okay. Thankfully, she'd left her sweater behind. It'd give him the perfect opening to talk to her.

Hopefully she'd talk to him after that fucking stunt he'd pulled.

He closed the trunk, his mind made up as it thunked. "I'll catch up with you later."

Mary Montgomery turned to look at him like he'd just sworn in church. "What do you mean you'll catch up with me later? Who's going to help me unload these groceries?"

Chase shook his head. Unbelievable. Because she didn't have a house full of servants waiting upon her every whim and his two younger brothers to muscle this crap inside. "I dunno, ask Patrick or Luke. I've got some stuff to do at the office."

"But it's Saturday! I don't understand why you—" His mother's eyes narrowed, then flicked to Cups at an abrupt chorus of feminine laughter. She swallowed a smile that was far too lupine. "Oh. Of course, dear. I'll see you tomorrow. Don't be late for dinner…and you know, there's always room at the table for one more."

His inner wolf growled at the suggestion, and he curved a palm around the brim of his cap, pulling it lower as his mother got in her SUV and drove away. The way his parents had been harping on that lately was gonna push him over the edge. If he heard about his damned responsibility to mate and contribute to the pack one more time…

"Chase!"

He slowly turned, already knowing what he was gonna see. Crystal, Becky, and his younger sister, Sue, decked out like this was Aspen. They sat around one of the little round tables in front of Cups with their frapa-whats-its. Christ. Dealing with their mean girl squad this early was gonna be straight-up painful. He blew out his cheeks and crossed the street without looking, praying he'd get hit.

No such luck, and he was pretty sure it wasn't gonna improve as he pulled out a chair and flipped it around to sit. Last thing he needed was for Crystal to take it as an invitation to crawl into his lap, or his bed.

Again.

He pinched the bridge of his nose, glad he didn't remember most of that. "Ladies."

"It's so funny that you're here, we were just talking about you," Crystal bubbled, fondling her straw. She wet her bubblegum pink lips, eyeing him like breakfast.

Hard pass, and there wasn't a goddamned thing funny about any of this.

"Yeah?" he drawled. "How so?" Chase stared at his sister,

and she didn't return it. Pack dynamics aside, why she was always sucking up to Crystal... Sue had actually been a decent person at one point, but lately that'd gone out the window. The little conniver had set him up. She'd known he was gonna be here with their mother.

"The Samhain festival this Friday...are you going?" Becky asked, her eyes flicking to Crystal patting her blonde updo with a smug smile on her face.

Shit.

"Isn't everyone?" he asked, picking at a chip of white paint peeling from the table. He knew exactly where this was going and wasn't about to jump on board.

Becky blinked at him. "Well, yeah, but, Shaun is taking me, and Kenny is—"

"I'll probably head over with the guys," Chase said, pointedly not looking at Crystal as he stood. "I've gotta meet a contractor at the office," he lied. "See you at dinner tomorrow, Sue."

She cringed and gave a little nod. Smart girl. She knew she'd stepped in it, and they were gonna have words later. What the hell was up with her lately? She knew damned well there was no way he was taking Crystal Chambers anywhere —especially not anywhere it'd be construed that they were a thing. That drunken hook-up had set enough tongues wagging, and he sure as hell hadn't been the one to broadcast it.

Especially not to his goddamned mother.

Crystal moued at him. "Will I see you later, too?"

"Probably, it's a small town," he said, putting the chair back where he'd gotten it from.

Their heated whispers followed him across the street, and he rolled his eyes. Yep. He was a prick, and nope, he wasn't gonna realize she was perfect for him. Chase gritted his teeth as he stepped through the grocer's sliding glass doors and made a beeline to the register Jena had been working at. Nice, her sweater was still there. He picked up the bright blue bundle, fighting the urge to bury his nose in it as he turned to leave—

"Ah, Chase, a moment?"

Sal. Chase sighed as the troll came over to him.

"I just wanted to say I'm sorry." Sal wrung his hands, the sweat on his brow glistening in the overhead florescent lighting. "But I didn't know what else to do. Your mother—"

"Yeah, I know. Don't worry about it. I appreciate you doing me a favor and hiring Jena."

The grocer took a deep breath, his shoulders relaxing. "Honestly, I'm surprised she lasted as long as she did. This town doesn't forget."

Chase grunted, but that was a load of shit. It forgot everything that didn't fit the damned narrative, and Jena had been as much of a victim as the rest of them. She hadn't done anything to deserve the way people treated her, then or now.

Especially him.

He clapped Sal on the shoulder and used the side door to leave, picking up the faint trail of Jena's scent down Main. Granted, Chase didn't know all the details, but he did know that her father had been into some shady shit and ruined Jena's family name. Before the warlock had come into town, they'd been guardians of the node of magic outside of town and were as prominent as the Montgomerys—Eastside or West.

Then people's memories got fuzzy, and who the hell knew what really happened. But it'd resulted in the smoldering ruins of their manor and the node falling to shit without someone maintaining it. Everyone was still up in arms about Jena leaving instead of shackling herself to the thing, but Chase couldn't blame her. Not after how they treated her when her mom died. He bit back a growl remembering Jena as a little girl with tears streaking her face, glaring around Aggie Wright's skirts.

He ran a hand over his stubble as he turned onto Cross Street. He couldn't have been more than seven when it'd happened, but the visual still hit him like a fist. Christ, all he'd wanted to do was tear the throat out of whoever had made Jena cry, and the urge had never left him. He raised the sweater to his nose, and bit back a groan, her scent triggering his mating pheromones. Letting that fly was dangerous for them both, but damn, his wolf wanted to roll around in it.

Chase wanted to do a hell of a lot more than roll.

Jena was his—had always been his—though she didn't know it, thanks to this town's stupid vendetta against her family. The only way he'd been able to keep Jena safe from his pack when they were younger was by keeping his distance and standing down. He swore, thinking about that night that'd almost outed him—God, he'd been a fucking asshole— but if they'd gotten even an inkling that she was his mate… Chase ran a heavy hand over his face, not looking forward to the shit show brewing, but he'd be damned before they kept her from him for another goddamned minute.

He'd deserved it, but her leaving the first time had almost killed him, and now that she was back, he wasn't gonna let her go.

Chapter Two

JENA PULLED BACK the front window's curtains, the air shimmering with dust as light streamed in. She doubted they'd get any customers this early—or at all—but sitting in the dark wasn't exactly her idea of a good time, and there was plenty to do.

She sighed, her gaze sweeping over the smattering of odd-shaped tables crowded with crystals and the overflowing built-in bookcases lining the dark-papered walls. Once upon a time, this had been a sitting room in the old Victorian brownstone. In fact, she was pretty sure the worst of the drafts were coming from the fireplace hidden by that central transplant of shelves against the far wall.

Jena considered moving the damned bookcase for all of point three seconds before remembering the flying squirrel infestation junior year of high school. There was no way the chimney behind it was up to code. Still…eh, worst case scenario, she put a pin in that idea in case she ever needed to commit insurance fraud.

It was a distinct possibility.

She frowned, wending through oddities and mismatched stacks to the very small corner of the room that'd been put to rights as she'd photographed and inventoried stock. Not for the first time, the theme to *The Sorcerer's Apprentice* plinked through her mind. Too bad magic didn't work that way, and hiring a brownie was way out of her budget. They didn't exactly work for bread and milk anymore. She shivered. Ugh. The draft was definitely worse over here. *Nope. not turning on the heat yet. It's your own fault you forgot your stupid sweater—*

The bell above the door rang as someone came in. She turned, and her stomach dropped beneath a wave of rage and longing that just pissed her off more.

Chase Montgomery was in The Witchery.

Chase fricking Montgomery was in her store after everything he'd done and his goddamned mother had gotten her fired, *and* the son of a bitch was smiling at her. Her stomach flipped. Ugh! Damn his stupid handsome face. Well, the half she could see under that hat, but the rest of it could go to hell too, along with the rest of him.

"Hey. You forgot your—"

"Get out."

He flinched, dipping his head with a little nod, then opened his mouth like he was going to say something.

"I said, get out!"

"Yeah, I just—I got your sweater." He held it out like a peace offering.

Jena stared at it and then at him, her hands fisting at her sides.

He took a step toward her, then another, and she closed her eyes. *I will not hex him, I will not hex him…*

"Here," he said, his breath teasing across her skin, too close.

The sweater's weight settled around her shoulders with a wave of musk, and a tremor went through her, her knees threatening to buckle. His cologne…damn, it did things to her. She put a hand on a table to steady herself, light-headed, gritting her teeth as her lady bits sat up and took notice. Guess she hadn't outgrown that reaction to the jerk—a flood of memories from high school washed over her. Nope. Nooo. Not going there again. He was a Montgomery, and she was a

Seymore. *Stay in your own lane Jena, lest you get run over a second time.*

The back of his hand grazed over her cheek, and she trembled, every hair on her body standing at attention. "You're shivering," he murmured, his voice like melty chocolate.

Her eyes snapped open at his uninvited touch, the divot between his collar bones front and center. She raised her eyes to his, shadowed beneath the brim of his stupid hat and glared at him. "Touch me again, and I swear to God, I will hex your pathetic pencil dick until it shrivels up and falls off."

His smile widened and dimples studded his cheeks. "It's good to see you too, Jena, and you're welcome." He tipped his hat and made his way to the door, far too silently for a man of his size.

Her knees gave out as it closed in his wake, and she sat heavily on the floor. What the hell had that been about? His entire freaking pack had made her life miserable growing up, and her senior year had been hell thanks to him. Her fingers rose to the scar beneath her chin before she could shake the memory away.

She pulled the sweater off and held it up to the light. Had he done something to it? It didn't look ruined, didn't smell— her nose wrinkled. Ugh. Yes it did. Or maybe that was just his damned cologne still stinking up the shop. Meh, she couldn't get the smell out of her nose. It wasn't horrible—far from it unfortunately—but it was definitely him...which made it horrible on principle.

She ran a hand over her face. Why would he have brought it to her? Whatever. Weres, dogs, maybe he felt the need to fetch and retrieve. Jena shook her head, sure the reason would bite her in the ass soon enough. She carried her sweater behind the counter and tossed it over the chair. It would just have to sit there and stink until she was ready to go to the laundromat again.

Something thunked on the coffered ceiling above, and her eyes rose at the sound. Aggie was up, and she shouldn't be out of bed. Jena bit back a curse and pushed through the curtained staircase at the back of the shop, then took the steps two at a time to the landing leading to the living space above.

Architecturally, the building hadn't been changed much, if at all, from when it'd been built sometime in the 1890s, but the previous owners had decided to "modernize" the rooms above the store in the 60s. The results were unfortunate and so very, very rust and avocado.

Aggie had always talked about restoring it, but money had been tight. What they had done was piecemeal, as evidenced by the half-stripped woodwork around the living room. Gorgeous oak grain peeked out from beneath odd intervals of chippy, yellowed paint. Raising Jena, running the shop, and then her cancer diagnosis, had derailed Aggie's plans to bring it back to its former glory and been hell on the maintenance, too. The place needed some serious repairs, and it wasn't happening anytime soon.

Which is why seeing Aggie sitting by one of the floor-to-ceiling windows with a dental pick working white paint out of the acanthus leaves carved into the trim was a punch to Jena's gut.

"Aggie…"

The older woman flipped her off and kept working.

Jena sighed. "You want your tea?"

"Why, so I can puke it up?"

"You need to stay hydrated," Jena said, going to the connected kitchen to put water on to boil.

"My earlier question stands."

"I ordered some more peppermint."

Aggie snorted. "Stupid expense," she muttered.

"No, it was a necessary expense. Most of your herbs in storage went moldy. Next year I'll get the greenhouse going—"

"Next year I'll be dead."

"You keep being such a bitch, and I can guarantee it."

Aggie cackled, and it devolved into a wracking cough. Jena hurried in with a glass of water and held the woman's frail shoulders until it passed.

"You know that paint's probably full of lead."

"Somehow, I don't think that's what's gonna kill me," Aggie muttered, taking the glass of water and sipping it.

"The new scarf looks good. You're getting better at wrapping them." Jena tucked in an end of the peacock print silk covering Aggie's bald scalp, missing her thick gray braids. Chemo was awful, and that wasn't the only unwelcome change it'd wrought. The tie-dye caftan swamping Aggie's frame was easily three sizes too big now, and she'd been slender to begin with.

"Stop standing there feeling sorry for me. I do enough of that myself."

"I wasn't."

"Lies." Aggie sniffed, and her azure-blue eyes flicked to the clock above the boxed-in fireplace. It looked like someone had shoved a shipping crate against the wall, but at least there wasn't a draft. "Why are you here? I thought you had to work this morning."

"I did, until her eminent highness Mrs. Mary Montgomery got me fired."

"I'm not surprised. A dog with a bone, that one, and she hated your mother. Always was a venomous bitch, and she's done a fine job of poisoning her entire pack—so explain to me why you smell like you've been marked by one of them."

Marked by…Ew! Jena sniffed her shirt. "Is that what that smell is? Ugh! I'm going to kill him!"

"Kill who?"

"Chase. He was just here returning the sweater I'd left at Sal's."

Aggie's brow rose. "Was he?"

"Yeah, and now I know why; the jerk wanted to mess with me. God, what does he think I am, a fire hydrant?" Jena's temper spiked. Oooh! That asshole had no idea—wolfsbane. That'd been one of the few herbs she'd been able to salvage from storage, and she could spell a charm. Those didn't have active intent, so she wouldn't get whacked with karma. Jena didn't quite rub her hands together—

"Wasn't he your first crush?" Aggie asked, pulling herself off the floor to sit in one of the overstuffed armchairs ringing the room.

No, he'd been her only crush, and her stupid stomach still got butterflies when he was around. Jena pinched her nose and sniffed. God, that stank. "Absolutely not."

Aggie eyed her like she knew she was lying, resuming her architectural dentistry from a different angle. "You know they can't just pull those pheromones out of a hat, right? It only comes out around their mate, well, unless they're going through puberty, but he's what? Thirty, thirty-five?"

"Thirty-six," Jena murmured, grabbing a notepad to scratch out a list of spell ingredients. He was a senior when his sister Sue and Jena were freshmen, and she was definitely not his mate. She snorted, the idea laughable after the way he'd treated her. "Would his hand count? Because he's always smelled like that."

"Huh. I wonder if the rumors about him going feral were true…"

Jena looked up at that. "I'm sorry, what?"

Aggie tensed, a sheen of opalescence flitting over her irises. She shuttered, and Jena rushed to her side as she crumpled in on herself.

"What was it? What did you see?" Damn it, the last thing Aggie needed right now was a barrage of visions. They always took a toll on her, and she didn't have the strength to spare.

The older woman waved her away. "N-nothing…"

"Bullshit." Jena glowered. "Come on, back into bed." She hauled her up and helped her into the next room. "What was it?" she asked again as she got Aggie settled.

"Me going to take a crap and ending up in the basement," she snapped. "The floor in my bathroom's soft, and the plywood over it's not cutting the mustard anymore."

Anymore? That bathroom had been a death trap well before Jena had left. "I thought you were using the one down the hall."

"I was but…" Aggie coughed, her jaw working like she'd tasted something bad. "That one's closer. Do—do you think we could find someone to fix it on the cheap?"

What Jena was about to say died on her tongue. "Yeah, I'll go make some calls now."

Aggie nodded, and the teapot began to scream in the other room. Jena turned away from the frail woman, willing herself not to cry. However she had to do it, she'd get the bathroom repaired. It wasn't going to cost her nearly as much as it'd just cost Aggie to admit she needed it.

CHASE STOMPED THROUGH CALDWICK AND SONS' bustling lumberyard far past the time he should've been at his desk, workers scattering from his path. Business was booming and the yard at full capacity. They were slammed now that it was the off season, and he'd had to move everyone to a six-day work week to keep up.

He riffled a hand over his stubble, cursing his father yet again for screwing up relations with the pack in Fayet. The power-hungry bastard had been eyeing their territory for years. In his mind, co-existing wasn't an option, but they weren't about to bend a knee.

And the situation was spiraling. Just last week, one of the Havers's pack had been attacked on his way through Fayet.

The neighboring town had officially become off limits, and both packs were patrolling borders. Like not being able to access the east side of town wasn't bad enough. Now they had pissed off packs sandwiching them in.

It sucked. Chase wasn't privy to the details and had no desire to be—his brother Patrick had stepped up and stayed there after Chase's little lapse in humanity—but Fayet had a perfect location for him to expand to, with twice as much space as this one.

Unfortunately, they refused to deal with anyone from his pack. Didn't matter that Chase had more than enough capital to get it off the ground, or that he easily could hire a dozen plus locals to start. And the worst part was, he couldn't blame them for stonewalling. Making any kind of deal with Wallace Montgomery always felt like putting on a leash then handing him the other end, and Chase's father was not a man you wanted to be beholden to.

Which was why the east side of town was also off limits.

But at the moment, Chase could give a flying fuck about any of it. He ripped open the door to his work trailer and stormed inside, muttering as he tipped up his hat to run a hand through his messy waves.

Goddamn it.

The look on Jena's face when he'd walked into her store had made his wolf want to curl up and die. God, he'd wanted to curl up and die. She really hated him. Not that she didn't have just cause to feel that way, but how the hell was he gonna prove himself to her?

"So who is she?"

He stopped to look at Lucy, his office manager. She was one of the few people in this town who didn't care who his family was, or flinch every time he raised his voice. Probably because she wasn't from around here. He was sure she'd heard about him losing his shit, but she hadn't been here for it. The little tattooed were had transferred from a pack across the bay after a messy divorce a couple of months ago. "Pardon?"

She brushed her brunette bob from her eyes and sat back in her chair, failing to hide a smile. "You're a half hour late, and smell like a serious case of unrequited love."

Double fuck.

He slipped his hat back on, pulling it low. "I dunno what you're talking about," he muttered. "Messages?"

She just looked at him, waiting for it. Goddamn it. He'd hired her because she didn't buy into people's bullshit, but he sure as hell didn't appreciate the trait right now, and she wasn't gonna let it go.

He sighed. "It's complicated."

"Usually." She handed him a pink slip of paper. "This came in fifteen minutes ago, but I doubt you'll be interested. That witch everyone hates wants a quote on a bathroom remodel."

Chase perked up and snagged the slip. "She does?"

Lucy narrowed her eyes, abruptly way too interested in his reaction. "She does."

He grunted, looking over the brief rundown of what Jena thought she needed. Without even seeing it, he could tell it was going to be a bigger project than she thought—or could probably afford after losing her job, especially with the rush she'd requested. Christ, on a building that age? Pulling the permits alone was gonna take months without seriously greasing some wheels, and every contractor in the area would add a hefty charge on top of it for the headache. Gorman Howe, the town's building inspector, was a dick...but he just happened to owe Chase a favor...

God, this was perfect.

He slapped the message back onto Lucy's desk. "Set up a consultation for later today."

"Are you serious? You're booked out for consults until after Thanksgiving—"

"I am, but you're not."

She sat up straighter, her brown eyes wide behind her glasses "Me?"

"You've been wanting to get in on the sales side of things, here's your chance," he said, hoping he sounded nonchalant about it. Internally, his wolf was doing cartwheels.

Lucy tapped a pen against the corner of her mouth. "Why do I think you have an ulterior motive?"

"Because I do. This building is a historical property. Restoring it is exactly the kind of press we've been looking for." And it was, which should be enough to keep his family off his back when they found out he'd taken the job. He needed to buy time to win over Jena before they caught wind of anything, or they'd ruin it. "I want this project, and you're gonna get it for me, but under no circumstances are you to use my name or mention the Montgomerys."

Her brow rose. "That the only reason you want this job?"

"Does there need to be another one?" he deadpanned.

"Seems shady."

Jesus Christ. "So? You got a problem with that?"

"Nope." She shook her head. "You're the boss."

Chase grunted. "Take measurements, pictures. Write up a report. I want them all on my desk by end of day."

"End of day?" Her eyes bugged out. "Are you crazy?"

Not anymore—at least he didn't think so. "No, I'm the boss, and if someone else poaches this, I'm gonna be pissed." The chance of that happening was slim to none, but Lucy seemed to buy it. She spun around in her chair and picked up the phone, then paused with her hand over the receiver. "Just out of curiosity, what do I say when she asks who's going to do the work? Historical reno is your thing."

Shit. "Ah…tell her we've got a pool of skilled craftsmen to draw from."

"What, like a kiddie pool?" Lucy cocked her brow.

"There's you and Nuno. Everyone else just slaps up sheetrock."

"Yeah, like I said, skilled crafts*men*. There's two of us."

She rolled her eyes and started dialing.

Chase went into his office and made himself sit at his desk, his wolf pacing. Despite the big window looking over the lumberyard, his eyes went to the light signaling line one was in use. Everything he'd built, taking over Caldwick and Sons', it was all so that he could take care of Jena when she came back. That dream he'd had, the one that had pulled from his madness…he shook his head. That'd been real. He had to believe it.

God. But what if Jena changed her mind, or had hired someone else? She was smart enough to call around—No. No way was a job like this coming in under fifty K, and no one would be able to get out there any time soon. Besides, it was Saturday. Who else was open right now? Right? Yeah, right. He was good. She just needed to say yes.

Come on Jena…say yes…

The light went out, and Lucy was at his door a moment later. Her brow furrowed. "Are you okay?"

"Hmm? Yeah, why?" he asked, wiping his brow.

"You're sweating. Like, a lot."

Chase opened his mouth then closed it again. "You get the appointment?"

"I did, but she's already meeting someone at two—" A growl rose in his throat, and Lucy pulled back. "Dude."

Shit. "Sorry. I'm just—"

"Head over heels for this witch, that everyone, especially your family, hates." She crossed her arms over her breasts and cocked a brow. "I'm assuming the feeling's mutual, which is why you're having me meet her. Yeah, I'd say that's pretty complicated."

Triple fuck.

His throat bobbed, and she laughed.

"Damn, boy. People are gonna freak."

"Not if you don't tell them," he growled.

She held up her hands. "I'm not gonna say a word, but you might wanna rein it in a bit. Your wolf was about to take someone out."

He lifted his hat to run a hand through his damp hair, then snugged it back on. "You know who she's meeting with?" Tryson Corp. was slimy enough to try and sneak someone in there with a lowball price they wouldn't honor…

"No, but I do know it's at Snaps."

Chase's stomach lurched as he white knuckled the arms of his chair. "She's going out with someone—to a bar? Like, on a date?" If some asshole thought they could get her drunk—

"Umm…" Lucy's eyes flicked to his hands. Shit, he'd started to shift. He made a concerted effort to breathe. *Calm down. She's ours. She's ours…*

But maybe he should stop by just to check things out.

"Okay then." Lucy clucked her tongue. "Our meeting's for eleven. I was just coming to tell you I gotta beat feet to get there."

He nodded. "Do it, and if she asks for a ballpark, tell her twenty grand. I don't care how much it's actually gonna cost." He'd gladly eat the overhead to make things right with her.

"You're the boss." Lucy gave him a half-assed salute and closed the door after herself.

Christ. Chase pinched across his temples. Lucy had no idea how right she was.

Freak? Best case scenario his pack would disown him. Worst case…he bit back a growl. Worst case wasn't gonna happen. Especially not to Jena.

Chapter Three

"TWENTY THOUSAND DOLLARS," Jena groaned into her margarita.

"Are you getting other quotes?" Felix asked, chomping nachos. The lunch hour rush at Snaps had passed, but it was still packed, and it wasn't for the ambiance. The tiny restaurant was basically a shack with multicolored paper lanterns and flags hanging from the rafters, and the floor was bare concrete. Still, they'd been lucky to get a booth. The cantina's Tex-Mex was to die for, and their drinks were on point.

"I'm trying," Jena sighed, "but I had to leave messages at most of them, and the other one that picked up the phone can't look at it for another three weeks."

Felix flicked a lock of curly red hair from his eyes, the collar of his teal golf shirt popped. It clashed horribly with his olive and orange plaid shorts, but that was Felix. He always looked like he got dressed in the dark and was way too proud of that fact. "Maybe this Caldwick place is hurting for business."

"Maybe. The portfolio she showed me seemed to say otherwise, though. They've done a ton of work around the area, and it's really top-notch. They've got some guy on staff that actually specializes in historical restoration. The chick that came out said he can carve pieces to replace the ones around the sill that busted off the last time Aggie was hell-bent on chipping paint."

"Does he now? Any idea what kind of wood he prefers to work with?" Felix asked. Jena rolled her eyes, and he laughed. "Either way, sounds like the kind of outfit you're looking for. Maybe your luck is changing."

"Doubtful." Jena took another sip of her margarita. "Is town hall hiring?"

Felix snorted. "Yes, but trust me, you do not want to work in government, and I can't see you filing building permits. Gorman Howe goes through assistants like toilet paper. The man is misery personified, and the bureaucracy is awful."

"Can't be that bad—and aren't you fucking the mayor?"

"Oh, it is, and technically, he's fucking me, along with the town's mill rates. The man's not exactly a champion of fiscal responsibility, but the granite curbing does look nice."

Jena sighed. That job at the photographer's was looking better and better. Her savings was only going to take her so far, and shelling out twenty grand would tap it completely.

"How's the online store?" Felix asked, munching another chip.

"Not bad. I sold a bunch of tinctures today and one of those robes…which I need to get dry cleaned before it ships. God, you should've seen Aggie's face looking through the photos of what this contractor has done…"

Felix huffed. "You already know you're going to hire them. You just need to get more of the store's inventory listed to pay for it. There's a market for Aggie's stuff—and yours— if you ever get out of your damned head about it."

Jena sighed, sure he was right, but after her father had cursed the majority of the populace with blackmarket hexes and skipped town, she wasn't particularly eager to sell hers, even if they were legal. And there wasn't a chance in hell she was taking up sin-eating. She didn't really even know how to use that portion of her power, and it always made her feel gross. The stuff in the store, though, she could be more proactive listing that. "I know, and time's not an issue, considering I don't have a job anymo—shit."

Felix turned to see what Jena was looking at and did a double take. "Shit doesn't cover it. That's an 'oh fuck,' but it was only a matter of time. Might as well get it out of the way when we've got alcohol at hand." He raised his margarita and took a hefty swallow.

Jena wished he was kidding, but he wasn't. She might be on the local pack's most hated list, but Crystal Chambers, Becky Swann, and Sue Montgomery had been her biggest tormenters. They sauntered through the crowd to the bar wearing their coordinating off-the-shoulder sweaters and micro-minis. Jena wanted to melt into the booth with her not-so-skinny jeans and concert tee as they ordered their drinks.

"How in God's name have they stayed the same size as high school?"

"I'm pretty positive it's lypo," Felix murmured.

"Or some weird were thing."

"What, like they can shift belly fat to their boobs?" He leaned forward all conspiratorial. "Can you imagine? I'd have such a bubble butt—"

Jena slapped a hand over her mouth to muffle her snort. "Oh my God, shut up!"

"Jena? Jena Seymore? Is that really you?"

Oh fuck.

The noise from the crowd died down as people turned to watch, and Crystal's face lit up like it was Christmas. The other two were definitely sharing in the joy.

Jena gave a little wave. They were adults now. Well, she was an adult. Jury was still out on them. "Hey, Crystal. It's been a while."

She grabbed her drink from the bar and minced over with her minions in tow, the cantina going even quieter. Great. An audience, and Lord knew the bitch loved to perform.

"It has. Wow, I almost didn't recognize you." She eyed Jena up and down, the "you got fat" more than implied. Crystal's gaze slid to Felix, and her plastic smile curdled. "Felix. I hear you're working for my dad."

"Mostly under him. He's a real ball buster."

Jesus. Jena kicked him beneath the table. Felix batted his lashes and raised his glass again.

Crystal turned back to Jena, twirling a lock of golden hair around her finger. "Someone said you came back, but you know how rumors in this town are. I didn't think you were that dumb, but here you are." She grinned as snickers came from the crowd.

Felix started coughing, the word "cunt" definitely somewhere in the middle of it. Crystal narrowed her eyes at him. And just like that they were back in high school. Energy prickled at the tips of Jena's fingers, so damned tired of this shit.

I will not hex, I will not hex…

"Honey, you don't need that karma," Felix said, the hair on his arms rising in response to Jena's gathering power.

No, she didn't, and her intent was definitely ill.

"Is there something you actually wanted," Jena asked her, "or did you just come over here to be a bitch?"

"Mmm…" Crystal raised her glass and slowly poured her drink into Jena's lap. "Just to be a bitch." She grinned as the other two laughed—

"Why the fuck would you do that?"

Everyone in the cantina turned to the door, then edged away from it as one. Chase stood in the entryway, looking like he was ready to rip someone's head off.

Crystal paled, then forced a smile. "Oh. Hey, Chase-y…I didn't think I'd see you—"

"Shut the fuck up," he growled. "Sue. Home. Now."

His sister's head bobbed, and she took off at a run, scooting past his hulking form and abandoning the other two.

Becky glanced between Crystal and Chase and slowly slunk into the crowd as he stalked over.

"You need to apologize," he gritted out. Crystal opened her mouth to argue, and he jabbed his finger at her. "Don't. I saw the whole fucking thing and so did everyone else in here. You engaged. You walked over. You were a bitch."

"What the hell has gotten into you?" she shot back. "Since when do you give a crap about goth girl and the gay wonder?"

"Uh oh, trouble in paradise," Felix murmured.

They were a couple? Jena rolled her eyes. Duh. Of course they were a couple.

"Since when is it okay to assault someone and say shit like that? I don't give a fuck who your father is, it was a shitty thing to do in high school, and it's a shitty thing to do now. You're thirty-two fucking years old, Crystal. Grow up."

He pushed past her and her dangling jaw to come over to the table. "Are you guys okay?"

Jena stared at him. Did he have absolutely zero concept of how much he'd screwed them just now? Crystal was the kind of bully that if you took your lumps, she moved on, but if you tried to stand up to her, she made it her mission to make your life hell. And if you did it in public?

They were fucked.

Been there, done that, had the t-shirt, and the fact that her boyfriend was coming to their defense in front of the entire town was going to make what they'd gone through in high school seem like fun.

Jena shook her head and glanced at Felix. He looked as dumbfounded as she felt. "Un-fucking believable..." She threw her last twenty bucks on the table and pushed out of the booth, her sodden pants chafing—

No, you know what? Screw this.

"Mind your own fucking business," she growled up at Chase. Her fingers tingled as she drew a glyph in the air and energy surged. The pomegranate margarita Crystal had poured on Jena rebounded and splattered all over the bitch. She screeched, holding her dripping sweater away from her.

"Oooh…" Felix sucked air in through his teeth as he stood to join Jena. "Boomerang hex?"

"Yeah," she gritted out, making for the door.

"Nice. Careful, sweetie," Felix said on his way past Crystal. "Karma's an even bigger bitch than you." He reached out to finger her ruined sweater. "Ouch. Cashmere. You're never gonna get the stain out of that."

CHASE STARED AFTER JENA. How the hell had he screwed that up? He frowned, squeezing the brim of his hat lower, the gleeful whispers of the crowd about to send him through the goddamned roof.

"I can't believe you just did that," Crystal said from behind him.

He snorted, turning back to her. She looked like an extra from a slasher film. "Did what? Called you on your shit?"

"Took their side! How do you think it makes me feel that my boyfriend—"

"Your what?" His sputter became a laugh. "I'm not your boyfriend."

She huffed, eyeing the still-listening crowd. "Look, I know it's not official, but everyone knows—"

"Then everyone is wrong." He growled, struggling to contain his wolf. "We are not, nor have we ever been, together, and we're not gonna be."

Her eyes welled up with crocodile tears. "But you…that night…"

"No, *you* that night. If I'd been sober, I would've thrown you out. It was a mistake, and I wish to God it'd never happened."

She reared back like he'd slapped her. "A mistake?! It was not a mistake!" Her bottom lip trembled. "Oh God…is this you losing it again? Are you feeling okay?"

"What? No! I'm not—" Chase gritted his teeth as the crowd edged farther away from him. Goddamn it, she would throw that in his face. "Crystal, fucking you is number one on the highlight reel of shit I regret most in life, and it's never happening again. Move on. I have."

Her eyes narrowed. "With who? Jena?"

His stomach dropped. "What?"

"After we met for coffee. Brenda Spitz said you got Jena's sweater—"

"Okay, first of all, I didn't meet you for coffee, and second —" He pinched the bridge of his nose. "No—you know what? I've got work to do, and don't have time to play into whatever the fucking delusion you've got going on."

He turned on his heel, the whispering crowd giving him a wide berth as he stalked out. God, he hated this town sometimes. It was no wonder why Jena had left.

The cantina door slammed behind him as he stormed out to the street and down the sidewalk toward the center of town. Goddamn it! Fucking Brenda. The last thing he needed was to give people a reason to think he was going feral again or to give Crystal one to go after Jena. Fuck. He damned well knew she would. He scrubbed a hand over his face—

"You know, that probably wasn't the best time to make your move."

Chase stopped and looked to his left. Felix was sitting on a bench outside of city hall, his arms spread out over its back and one ankle crossed over his knee.

"I wasn't making a move."

Felix rolled his eyes. "Oh, please. Ever since I can remember, you've been making puppy dog eyes at Jena. I mean *I* appreciate the whole macho white knight thing, but she's not that kind of girl. She doesn't want to be saved, never has."

Chase's wolf growled. "Puppy dog eyes?"

"Oh, sorry." Felix winced. "Is that a slur?"

"Not in the way you mean," Chase grumbled, jamming his hands into his pockets. He rocked back on his heels. Screw it. "Then what does she want?"

The slim warlock's face lit up. "Are you asking for my help?"

"No." Yes. Maybe. He sure as hell wasn't getting anywhere on his own. "I just—never mind." Chase shook his head and kept walking.

"No, wait." Felix bound up from the bench to keep pace with him. "Look, I might not know all the ins and outs of were culture, but I've always had a sneaking suspicion—"

"Keep it to yourself." Chase growled. "And if you say one word to her or anyone else about it, I'll kill you."

"Annnd that's what I thought." Felix grinned. "For the record, I didn't say boo about you owning Caldwick's. I figured there was a reason you sent in your office manager who, by the way, somehow managed not to mention your name and still hype the hell out of you."

"She did?" Chase's heart leapt as he stopped to look at him.

"Mmm hmm." Felix dusted his nails across his shirt, then blew on them. "So, magical maestro of reno, what's the plan? Get Jena to sign a contract with a massive penalty clause, so when you show up, she has to suffer through you doing the work?"

"Something like that," Chase muttered.

"That's awfully *Hallmark* of you, but it's not going to be enough. You've got to get in good with Aggie, or you'll never get past the front door."

"Aggie—her aunt? I heard she was sick."

"Pancreatic cancer." Felix sighed. "They thought they

caught it early enough, but it's not looking good, and the last round of chemo almost killed her. Jena came back to settle her affairs, but you didn't hear that from me."

Chase palmed the brim of his hat, tugging it lower. Damn. He'd heard her coming home had something to do with the business. With all her degrees that had made sense, but he hadn't realized her aunt was that sick. Jesus. Aggie was all the family Jena had left. "That sucks."

Felix nodded. "It does…which is why I'm willing to help you woo her. Don't think I don't know about all the little things you used to do for her when you thought no one noticed."

"You do?" Shit. Who else had?

He rolled his eyes. "I'm gay, not visually impaired, and she's going to need someone sooner than she wants to admit. I'm assuming you're playing for keeps?"

"Yeah. I—" Chase glanced around. If there was anyone in this town he could trust when it came to Jena, it was Felix. He'd rather chop off his own arm than see her hurt. "S-she's my mate." Christ, that was weird to say out loud. Felt good, but definitely weird.

Felix pumped a fist. "I knew there was a reason Havers-by-the-Sea's heir to the pack royale's been holding out!"

"Dude, calm down. If anyone finds out before she does—"

"Oh, you'll be toast, and she'll have an even bigger axe over her head."

"To put it mildly, and Crystal's already suspicious."

Felix looked at him like he was an idiot. "No kidding. Refer back to my earlier comment about that being the wrong time and place to make your move, and if Crystal didn't have Jena in her sights before, she does now."

"Yeah, I know." Chase sighed, kicking the seam in the sidewalk. "So what do I do?"

"Don't worry about Crystal. Jena's tough, and that boomerang hex has more power behind it than people think."

"Boomerang hex?"

Felix rolled his eyes. "I'm rubber, you're glue, whatever you say bounces off me and sticks to you. That hex rebounds intent and apparently margaritas. FYI, I don't know anyone else that can physically manifest karma like that. Jena is more than capable of dealing with Crystal, it's you that's the problem."

"Me?"

"Mmm. Jena hates you. That party senior year really messed her up."

Chase rocked back on his heels, still feeling like a major asshole about that. He'd panicked when Crystal and her friends had caught them making out. Saying it'd been a dare to see how far he could get with Jena had seemed like a good idea at the time.

It wasn't, and everyone at Havers High had taken the ball and run with it.

"...but you know what they say about that thin line between love and hate..." Felix tapped a finger over his lips. "Sunday's supposed to be a scorcher. I'd suggest you go to the falls."

"The falls?"

"Yep, and bring some friends. Able's still in town, isn't he?"

Chase blew out his cheeks and nodded. "Yeah, until the end of the month, but—"

"But, but, but—no buts." Felix tsked.

"Fine. I guess I can do that. Why?"

Felix grinned at him and started walking away. "No reason, but if I were you, I'd shoot for eleven."

JENA THREW the last few spell components into the cauldron and set the egg timer. She pushed back from the kitchen island with a huff of satisfaction. Done! She was done! God, this stupid town, stupid weres…for a brief moment she actually missed the city. Not that there weren't supes there, but they tended to keep a lower profile when there were more normys around. You never knew how a non-powered human was going to react when they found out their roommate could hex someone with acne or bad teeth.

"Ask me how I know…" Jena murmured, laying out a silver talisman engraved with the phases of the moon along the knife-scarred counter.

"How do you know what?" Aggie asked, her shuffling feet rasping against linoleum. She plopped onto one of the narrow kitchen chairs, out of breath, then frowned, tapping her fingers on the worn tabletop as she sniffed the air. "Wolfsbane? Tell me there's not a heliotrope in that cauldron."

"There's not a heliotrope in this cauldron." There totally was, along with obsidian and amber. "You should be using your cane."

"Don't tell me how to live my life," Aggie scoffed, picking at the papers littering the table. "So what happened that you feel the need to whip up a batch of were-b-gone?"

"Crystal was being Crystal, and stupid Chase decided to ride to Felix's and my rescue." Jena frowned, sweeping some loose herbs off the butcher block and into her palm to toss into the garbage by the door. Aggie's supply of herbs was questionable to say the least and more threadbare than Jena liked.

Aggie grunted. "You got amber in there?"

"I do."

"Don't forget to add salt."

Jena hadn't, but put in an extra pinch anyway. "I got the quote for the bathroom."

"And?"

"Twenty grand, just like she said. It's there on the table if you want to look at it."

Aggie waved it away with a cough, and Jena's gaze went to the plastic covered windows behind the older woman, hoping there wasn't another draft. "You know I don't understand half of that stuff," Aggie said. "If I did, I might actually have a nest egg to help pay for it."

"You do, but it's in retail form." The timer binged, and Jena cut the gas to the stove.

"Stir it widdershins."

"I'm aware," Jena said, doing just that. Energy rose around her, condensing to prickle her fingertips and her lips as she spoke the incantation.

"*Ahaashi*, not *Ahahshi*," Aggie murmured.

"Do you want to do this?"

The older woman held up her hand and let Jena finish, the cauldron flaring violet as the magic took root. "Not bad," she said.

Jena dipped the talisman into the rapidly cooling liquid. "Thanks. I had a mediocre teacher."

Aggie snorted and pulled a scarlet envelope from her caftan. "This came for you."

"What does it say?"

"I didn't open it." Jena just looked at her until Aggie relented. "*But*…I'm assuming it's the coven wanting to know when you're officially joining and taking guardianship of the node."

Jena frowned, not about to have that argument again, but it wasn't like she hadn't expected them to make contact. Especially after she'd invoked that boomerang hex on Crystal. Too many people had seen her practicing, and without coven approval, that was a big fat no-no.

"Can't I just say I'm visiting?"

Aggie's brow quirked. "Are you just visiting?"

That'd been the plan, but…Jena's brow furrowed as she hung the talisman on a cabinet pull to dry. The charm spun, glints of light pinging off the backsplash's avocado tiles. All that was left to activate it was the light of the full moon—though the waxing gibbous would do in a pinch. "I don't know."

"Well, you should probably figure things out." Aggie coughed into her handkerchief, then tapped the contract for the bathroom renovation. "Starting with this. It's your building, what do you want to do with it?"

Jena huffed. It was, but she really didn't want to deal with that right now, either. She'd gotten her mother's percentage when she turned eighteen, and Aggie had 'sold' Jena the rest, along with the business, when they'd got her diagnosis. It was the only way to keep any of it when the medical bills started pouring in. As far as the state was concerned, Aggie was destitute.

Which honestly wasn't that far from the truth.

"Fixing it up to sell isn't the worst idea, and that Caldwick operation certainly sounds like they'd do right by the old girl," Aggie said, her eyes on the raised tin ceiling, the framework for the crappy suspended tiles the old owners had installed still crisscrossing the space. Thank God they hadn't replaced it with popcorn. "And if you're not keen to sell, you could always rent it out."

Yeah, Jena could, but neither option was particularly appealing. Nor was spending the rest of her life dealing with Crystal and the Montgomerys...but being here with Aggie and having Felix to hang out with again more than made up for—

Wait a minute. "Felix never said anything about the coven sending me a letter." And thanks to his mom, if there was one thing he was plugged into, it was witch politics. Jena dried her hands and checked her phone. Nope. Crickets on that front. Huh. She picked up the heavy envelope. Her name in golden gothic script was on one side, and a black wax seal with a raven on the other.

"At least they're not pretentious," she murmured.

Aggie snickered. "June Hill is secretary this year and took a calligraphy class. She got a fancy kit somewhere online. Pretty sure she does that with her shopping lists too. You gotta admit it's more impressive than Rick Kleppet's chicken scratch on the back of gas station receipts that used to get delivered."

She had a point. Jena cracked the seal and pulled out a photocopied application for membership and something printed on foiled cardstock. Wow. That had to be one heck of a kit...crap. "They're inviting me to the Samhain fire. Did you get one of these?"

"They know better," Aggie scowled.

Jena pulled out a chair and sat, tapping the invitation against her knee as she chewed her lip. Samhain was one of the four cross quarter days—the days that fell between the solstices—that all practitioners celebrated as high holidays. She'd never been to any of them, mainly because Aggie refused to go, even though she was a coven member. Something about the energy around the bonfire affecting her divination and making her squirrelly. Well, squirrellier. "Why would they invite me?"

"You know damned well we've been saving your mother's seat for you, much to Matilda Hanson's dismay. But even her sour puss can't dispute how strong your line is, and that node out on the tor hasn't had a guardian in far too long—despite them trying to get it to accept someone else. I'm assuming that invite's an olive branch to lure you back into the fold and get you to clean up the mess of magic out there."

"A trail of sweets leading to a candy cottage in the woods might be more effective." Jena snorted. Especially if it was made up of peanut butter cups and sour gummies. "And the strength of my line has zero to do with me."

"Just because you don't use it, doesn't mean you don't got it," Aggie said, bypassing their usual argument on the topic. "And joining might not be the worst thing. You'd have the coven's backing if a certain were gets uppity."

If? Crystal had already gotten some asshole to spray paint a slur across the sidewalk in front of The Witchery, but joining the coven wasn't happening. She'd heard more than enough about their shitty politics from Felix while she'd been in the city, and being a part of their stupid little sorority hadn't done a damned thing to save the rest of her family.

"Think about it." Aggie wheezed, struggling to her feet. "They could stand to have their feathers ruffled, and I'm certainly in no shape to do it."

Jena put down the invitation to help her. "Are you going to tell me to 'be the change' next?"

"No, I'm going to tell you to help me sit my ass on the john. That way if I fall in, I'll take you with me."

Jena laughed, steadying Aggie as she toddled down the hall. "And what a glorious end that would be."

"Maybe in my younger years, now it's as flat as a pancake. Flaunt it while you got it." Aggie leaned heavily against the sink, huffing as she pulled her caftan aside. "God, I fucking hate this."

Jena helped her sit down, agreeing. She fucking hated this, too.

~

CHASE SAT in his truck outside of the pack manor, drumming his fingers against the steering wheel. He'd expected a call after what'd gone down at the cantina, but not from his father. Wallace Montgomery might be head of the Westside pack, but he rarely involved himself in anything outside of golf and lining his pockets. He left the day-to-day operations and pack minutia to his beta, Malcom, or Chase's younger brother, Patrick.

The fact that the message had been from the old man and not through a proxy was troubling, to say the least.

Chase turned at a rap on his window, and rolled it down. Jesus. Speak of the devil, and Malcom was definitely in the same category. Something about the were chafed, and it wasn't just his shitty people skills.

The beta leaned in through the open window, his folded arms on the sill. "You planning on coming inside, or are you just gonna sit here?"

"You giving me a choice?"

"No."

Chase sighed and unbuckled his seatbelt, cutting the engine as the beta stepped back.

"You know what he wants?" Chase asked as he got out. The door closed behind him with a heavy *thunk*. It was a stupid question. The two were in lock-step. Malcom probably held his father's dick when he pissed.

"I do." The whip-thin older man hooked his thumbs into his belt loops. "And they've been waiting on you." He held out a hand for Chase to lead the way. "After you, son."

Great. The small hairs on his nape prickled as he started forward. He hated having that asshole behind him, and he wasn't his fucking son.

The pack's manor house was one of those newer McMansions in a neighborhood of postage stamp properties that'd started going up in the area a decade or so ago. Granted, its overly cultivated grounds and pristine lawn backed up to the state forest, but the bald hillside to the east with its stalled installation of three massive wind turbines screwed them out of any view they might've had. It was also screwing with the leyline if the coven in town was to be believed, though what that actually meant, Chase wasn't sure. The last meeting about the eyesores had devolved into everyone yelling over each other, and he'd left.

Too bad he couldn't exit here as easily.

He clomped up the front steps to the veranda, frowning at the cookie-cutter craftsmanship. For the amount of money they'd paid, the house was garbage. But his mother had gotten the sweeping front staircase and ballroom she'd wanted, and his father had gotten six months of peace and quiet before she was harping on the next way to beat the Joneses.

Chase didn't have to live in it, so he kept telling himself it was stupid to care, but when he thought of the pack manor, his mind always went to the group of log cabins deep in the western woods. That's where he and most of the other unmarried male members of the pack lived. His parents didn't like it, but they'd liked him going feral a lot less, and him being out there was a big part of what had kept him sane while waiting for Jena to come back.

Not that they knew the reason behind his breakdown.

"He in his office?" Another stupid question.

"Where else?"

Chase grunted, heading in that direction. Had his mother changed the wallpaper again? He swore last Sunday it'd been blue, not gold. Made the hallway even uglier than before. Chase shook his head. God, her taste was garbage, but what did you expect when you based an aesthetic on how much something cost, instead of how it looked?

The manor was suspiciously quiet, the servants absent. Usually he caught sight of a brownie or two when he was here, and the gnome typically answering the door hadn't. Luke was probably on his boat, and Sue out with friends, but the dread in Chase's gut got heavier with his wolf's pacing. Something was definitely not right.

Malcom stepped ahead of him to knock on the office door, opening it at a grunt from within. A billow of cigar smoke rolled out as they went inside.

Wallace Montgomery sat behind his lacquered cherry desk with a Cubano clamped between his teeth. Though it wasn't quite six p.m., the mountain of a man swirled a snifter of brandy. Chase was positive it wasn't his father's first, and it probably wasn't his second, either. In the chair across the desk from him, Mayor Chambers did the same, like they were celebrating.

Chase's eyes flicked to his brother Patrick, standing off to one side. He scowled back, rubbing the pack signet ring on his finger. Shit. Younger by less than a year, his brother only did that when he thought his toes were being stepped on. Whatever they were here for, it was pack business, and he wasn't happy Chase was being involved.

Spoiler, neither was he.

"Ah, Chase!" his father said like they were buddies. "Come, take a seat."

His chipper mood wasn't a good sign either. They'd never seen eye-to-eye, and that'd only become worse after Chase's breakdown. He had zero interest in becoming alpha and "taking his rightful spot" in the pack, whereas Patrick had a law degree and enough ambition for both of them. As far as Chase was concerned, Patrick could have it.

Too bad their father didn't see it that way.

Malcom shoved him forward when he hesitated, and Chase bit back a growl as he sat in the remaining chair, waiting for the other shoe to drop.

"I've had some disturbing rumors reach my ears today," his father began, ashing his cigar on the carpet. "What's this I hear about you and Crystal breaking up? Your mother's beside herself."

Seriously? "We were never together," Chase gritted out.

His father pursed his lips. "So you didn't fuck her?"

The mayor winced, and a low growl came from Patrick's direction.

Chase's eyes flicked from them back to his father. "Once. Trust me, it was enough."

"It's unfortunate you feel that way. Mayor Chambers and I have just come to an agreement." He tossed a portfolio at Chase and sat back, far too smug.

It landed at the far edge of the desk with an ominous thump. Chase didn't reach for it, already feeling sick.

"Your mother and I had hoped that you bedding the girl meant you'd come to your senses." His father's eyes glittered behind the striations of smoke across his desk. "However, after today's events, it's become clear that your refusal to step up and choose a suitable mate has reached an untenable juncture."

Chase palmed the brim of his cap, ripping it lower. *Jesus fucking Christ, here we go.* Asshole could never pass up the opportunity—"Don't. Don't fucking start on this again—"

"I am alpha of this pack, and you will respect me as such!" his father roared.

Chase's wolf surged to the forefront. "You keep pushing about this, and you might not be," he shouted back.

Patrick growled, taking a step forward, and his father raised a hand, forestalling him. His eyes narrowed, a grin slicked over his face. "Well. There it is. Finally. You want to challenge me, boy?"

He didn't, but if this was going the way he thought it was, he wouldn't have a choice. "Are you gonna make me?"

"How you react in any given situation is entirely upon you," his father drawled, spinning his snifter on the desk. "Tensions with the Fayet pack are coming to a head, and I'm not pleased with the increased presence of Eastsiders in town. Haver's leadership needs to present a strong, united front. As scions of the two most preeminent families in the Westside pack, your marriage to Crystal—"

"I'd rather go rogue," Chase growled.

His father shrugged. "Then I'll be forced to have Malcom take you in hand."

Chase paused at the threat. Wallace Montgomery held his position solely by blackmail and intimidation, but Malcom was another thing altogether. The rangy were was dangerous, and Chase had no illusions as to what that would entail. Malcom would hunt him down and drag him to the altar, or he'd kill him, and Chase's father sanctioning it was par for the course.

The sly smile on his brother's face wasn't giving him the warm fuzzies either. He knew damned well how much Chase hated Crystal, and Patrick had been sniffing after her for as long as Chase could remember. Asshole was probably betting on Malcom killing him. This scenario practically guaranteed to get Chase out of the way, permanently.

Unless he took alpha, but that meant he'd have to put Malcom down.

Chase ran a hand over his jaw, eyeing his father's beta and running his odds. Malcom returned his gaze and smirked like he knew exactly what Chase was thinking.

Shit. As much as he didn't want alpha, this bullshit ultimatum wasn't gonna give him a choice if he wanted to keep breathing. And if they knew how he felt about Jena, she'd be the one on Malcom's hit list. Leaving Havers with her wasn't an option, either. His father's goddamned pride would never allow it.

"Lemme think about it," Chase said as he stood, hoping that would buy him time to figure something out. Damn it. How the hell was he gonna—

"You have until the next full moon to put an engagement ring on Crystal's finger," his father said like it was already a done deal. "Your mother wants a November wedding."

Chase left the room swearing. The next full moon was in six days, on Samhain.

Chapter Five

JENA SHOVED another branch out of her way, huffing a lock of sweaty hair from her eyes. The tail-end of October should not be this hot, especially before noon. She slapped at a bug. Where was a harem of pixies to chow down on stupid things when you needed them? There'd been plenty of the little idiots in town, and them having the munchies was a given.

"Why did I let you talk me into this again?" she grumbled.

Felix laughed from farther up the trail. "Because you loooove me…"

She did, but this sucked, and she was pretty sure the shop's lack of air conditioning had more to do with her hoofing it through the woods to go swimming than anything else. Why didn't she remember the path to the falls being so steep? She looked around. Actually, come to think of it, she didn't remember this particular path at all. "How much farther is it?"

"A half mile or so," Felix said, stopping to take a sip from his water bottle and watch her huff to catch up. "Didn't you have to walk in the city?"

"Yeah, but it didn't have goat paths like this. It was all flat, beautiful pavement as far as the eye could see…" She wiped the sweat from her brow again. Everything there also had central air. "What possessed you to pick this way to come up? Did the river path wash away?"

He rolled his eyes. "No, but I figured after all that concrete you could stand to take in the majesty of the vista." He swept a hand at the autumn tree line like he was delivering it.

Beyond was a panoramic view of the valley, and okay, it was pretty, but not enough to justify the freaking incline—Her gaze landed on a ribbon of smoke below, the scent of roasting meat in the wind. "Are we cutting through pack territory?"

"Maybe," Felix drawled, failing to look innocent.

She narrowed her eyes at him.

"You know, you never used to be so uptight."

"I am not uptight." Okay, maybe she was, but she had enough on her plate without asking for more trouble.

"If you say so." He looked her up and down and cocked a brow. "Regardless, it's not going to be an issue. They moved their manor house to that new development over on Sunnyside a couple of years back."

Jena stopped in her tracks to tug the seam of her yoga pants. Her inner thighs were gonna be raw after this. "Ew. Where they're putting up those godawful turbine things?" She shook her head at Felix's nod. Who the hell would trade this for that? "That's crazy, and all that smoke down there says otherwise."

Felix shrugged. "It's more of a frat house arrangement now. I was at a party they threw a couple of months back." He got a wicked grin on his face, and Jena could only imagine what that had entailed. "The part of the pack left out here isn't like the one you remember, and we don't have to worry about big, bad Malcom lurking in the woods." He waggled his fingers all spooky.

"Ugh, don't joke about him." And definitely don't say his name three times into a mirror at midnight. He'd probably appear. Jena shivered, uncapping her own water bottle. She took a sip. Malcom had been the town boogie-man for as long as she could remember. Even Aggie had crossed to the other side of the street when she'd seen him.

"Me? Joke? Never. Come on," Felix said, jamming his water back into his pack and flipping the bag over a shoulder. "It's all downhill from here."

Jena snorted, glad the bent of his powers wasn't prophecy as she followed him. "So tell me about this invite I got from the coven."

"You got an invite?" he asked, glancing back far too coyly. She glared at him, and he laughed. "You have no idea how excited they are you're back—well, not Matilda, but she only gets excited when something catastrophic happens. The rest of them are positively slavering over the possibility of having thirteen members again. They haven't been able to do a proper working since your mother died, and with Aggie so sick…"

"You know, it's not like there aren't plenty of other witches in the world." Jena frowned.

"True, but there's only one line of sin-eaters."

Her feet rooted. "You know I don't do that."

"Don't isn't can't," he said over his shoulder, then stopped to face her. "And I get that you don't have a total handle on it, but if I could absorb someone else's karma and flip the power from it into my own spell—"

"You'd have such the bubble butt," Jena snarked, rubbing her arms at the unexplained chill that'd come over her. She hated talking about that aspect of her abilities. Hexes were bad enough, but at least they were commonplace. Sin-eating was a family specialty she'd never asked for and didn't want.

And like Felix had said, she also didn't totally know how to use it.

He rolled his eyes. "Well, duh, but that's entirely beside point. You know, if you figured out how it worked, you might be able to release your line from being tied to the node. It hasn't accepted a new guardian, and trust me, the coven has tried everything short of sacrificing someone's firstborn. Matilda's freaking out about it becoming an unseelie mound the way its magic has been leaking lately."

Jena snorted. Like that was gonna happen. There hadn't been a mound in this part of the country in forever. The grid of leylines wouldn't allow it. Granted, the peninsula the town called home was at the hairy edge of that, but seriously? Havers? "Maybe if they bulldozed the ruins up there, whatever evil fairies are hanging around would get the hint and find some other place to mess with," she muttered, the thought of the remains of the house she was born in making her skin prickle again.

"It doesn't work like that, and bulldozing it isn't going to change anything. Matilda's always going to make things out to be worse than they are, but it is a place of power, and that draws—" Felix gave a long-suffering sigh at her eye roll. "Jena, we both know you're ridiculously gifted; it's time you owned it. Don't think I don't know you ran away to the city trying to avoid who you are."

So he was right about that—okay, all of it—but screw him. She started walking again. "It doesn't matter who I am, they want me for who my mother was, and I'm not her. She's dead, and I'm not joining their crappy coven."

"Jena—" He raced to catch up with her. "Look, you're gonna do whatever you're gonna do, but I think you should consider it."

"You and Aggie both," she muttered, flicking a bug from her face. God, that was annoying. Stupid thing had the entire forest to fly around in.

"And that should tell you something right there."

Jena shot him an evil glare, but he was right about that too, damn him.

He'd also been right about everything going downhill. Twenty minutes later, she leaned against a bole of a tree, muttering an apology to the dryad for getting it all sweaty and sucking wind, her ankle on fire. The traitorous thing had twisted when a rock skittered out from under her.

"You gonna make it?" Felix asked.

"I'm fine. I just need to soak it." And lose like twenty—okay thirty—pounds. That wasn't gonna happen, but thankfully, they were close enough to hear the falls, even if they couldn't—

Felix's head jerked to the side like he'd heard something else, and he craned his neck to peer through the trees.

"What is—"

He held up a hand, cutting her off and crept farther off the path, into the woods. A prickle went over her skin as he pulled his power—distortion—and his form muddled into the surroundings. If she hadn't known he was there, she never would've noticed him. When he'd gotten about ten feet away from her, he crouched down behind a fallen tree and went still, totally disappearing. A handful of breaths later, he dropped his power and crooked a finger over his shoulder for her to join him.

Jena limped through the bracken, considerably more noticeable, and knelt beside him.

Felix put a finger to his lips before a grin split them, and he slowly lowered a branch.

Holy shit.

They weren't the only people who had decided to take advantage of the unseasonably warm weather and come to the falls. Half a dozen male weres lounged around the pool beneath the plunging stream, in and out of wolf form, and the ones sans fur were completely naked.

Jena felt her cheeks heat. "Felix!" she hissed. Nudity wasn't a big deal for weres, but peeping on them was still wrong.

"Shh! I'm busy…damn, would you look at the ass on the blond over there…"

Her eyes flicked to the were's admittedly impressive backside. "If they catch us here—"

"You're right. They might invite us to join them for a swim," he said, his voice laden with mock seriousness. He dropped his bag. "I volunteer as tribute."

"Felix! We shouldn't be here," she whisper-yelled—

And he was gone.

Shit. Freaking Felix. Jena chewed her lip as he strolled over to the group. She couldn't hear what they said, but a moment later, his shirt was off and his hands were at his belt. Damn it. Felix's pasty rear was not anything she wanted to see.

Jena sat back on her haunches and sighed. And now going out there after him would just be weird…not that being the only girl in a grotto full of naked dudes wouldn't be.

Whatever. She had plenty of work she could be doing back at the shop and hadn't wanted to come on this stupid hike anyways. She worked her way out of the bracken and back onto the path—

And bumped right into a very bare, very solid chest. Her eyes flicked down.

Sweet baby Jesus.

"Jena?"

She scrambled back at the voice. Fuck her life, fuck her life… "Chase!"

He stood on the path in all his naked glory except for that dumb hat, pulled low. His throat bobbed, and he whipped it off, covering his junk. "W-what are you doing here?"

Her mouth worked, but nothing came out. "Felix," she finally managed to squeak.

"Felix…" A slow smile spread over Chase's face as he glanced back at the falls, his messy caramel waves hiding his eyes.

Goddamn him, but he was beautiful. Why was it the jerks always were? Water glistened across his broad shoulders and a smattering of hair covered toned pecs he had no business having. Ugh. Why couldn't he be scraggly? She wrenched her gaze from the trail of tawny fuzz bisecting his lower abs and frowned. It was all disgustingly appealing.

So was what was under that hat.

Ugh! No, bad Jena…but maybe…ugh, no!

"I, uh…I should take you back…" He wet his lips. "Unless you wanted to…"

The suggestion snapped her out of her daze. "What? No. *No.* I'm good. And I can find my own way to the main road." She cinched her backpack and winced as she put weight on her—

Chase's arms were around her, and she was abruptly airborne, being carried like a baby.

"Put me down, you asshole!" Jena squealed. The frickin' nerve of him!

"You're hurt," he said, his stupid hat back on his head and his hands all over her. "And it's shorter if you cut through the compound."

"But you're naked!"

"Yeah." He grinned, starting down the path. "Guess you'll get a front row seat to my pencil dick shriveling up and falling off."

Jena slapped him, and she was abruptly pinned against a tree.

"Don't. Do that," he said with a low growl.

Her mouth went dry, a wave of his musk washing over her. She made herself stare into the shadows beneath the brim of his hat. "Or what? You'll leave me here? Boo-fricking-hoo."

He grinned, his canines a titch too long. "I won't leave you, but I will slap you back." His hand cracked down on her ass, and she yelped, springing forward and pressing against him.

Something definitely pressed back. She froze, staring up at him. "Y-you spanked me!"

"I did." His grin broadened as he ran his palm over the sting and squeezed her cheek.

The sensation was doing things to her nether regions it really shouldn't be doing. Her chest heaved as she glared at him. Because she was mad, not because she was turned on.

Shit. Keep telling yourself that, Jena.

"I hate you."

"I know. What do I need to do to change that?" he murmured, his lips too close to hers.

Her gaze flicked to them, her stupid breath catching. "I— What?" She slid her hands up his chest—trying to put distance between them, *not* to cop a feel—and it rumbled, his hand tightening on her stinging ass cheek and pulling her closer. Jena gave a little gasp as his head tilted like he was going to kiss her—Oh God, was he going to kiss her? Did she want him to?

Ugh, she so wanted him to.

No! Bad Jena!

"Lemme take you back before I forget that's what I said I was gonna do," he rumbled, his breath coming as fast as hers.

Jena just nodded and let him pick her up, threading her arms around his neck. She rested her head against his broad shoulder like it was where she was supposed to be, breathing him in as he strode through the bracken... Jesus. What the hell had just happened?

And a better question, why did she want more of it?

CHASE COULDN'T STOP SMILING. Jena was in his arms letting him take care of her. His wolf was doing backflips, and he wasn't far behind. She, on the other hand, was suspiciously silent; but considering his dick was still attached, he didn't think she was hexing him. Not yet anyway.

"You *groped* me," she said abruptly, pulling her head from his shoulder to glare at him as he slipped through the forest.

His smile widened. "You groped me back."

"I didn't mean to." Jena glowered. "I don't even like you. You *spanked* me!"

Hell yeah, he did, and he couldn't wait to do it again when he had a better view. "You slapped me."

"You have a girlfriend."

"No, I don't. I have a delusional stalker and a mandate," he muttered, scowling.

She opened her mouth like she was gonna ask him what he meant and then closed it again, huffing. Chase grinned. Damn, she was stubborn. They came out from the trees at the edge of the pack's compound, and he headed toward one of the cabins.

"I thought you said we were cutting through."

"We are, but I thought it might be a good idea to put on some clothes before I drive you back into town," he said, shouldering through the door of his cabin and into the neat little room.

"I don't need you to drive me anywhere."

"You're not walking."

She screwed up her face, her frustration obvious as she huffed. God, she was adorable. "You live here?"

More like it was where he slept. He spent most of his time at work. Since his breakdown, he wasn't good at being idle. He grunted and set her on the table. "Don't move, or this time you're going over my knee."

Jena's eyes narrowed. "You wish."

"I do." So, so fucking bad. He turned his back to her before she could see his cock at half-mast just thinking about it. The way her ass had jiggled beneath his palm—

And now he had a full-blown erection.

Pants. He needed to put on pants. Christ, it didn't help that he swore he could feel her eyes on him for the half-dozen steps it took to get to his dresser. His wolf whined, and Chase took a deep breath—

The scent of her arousal tinged the air.

Fucking kill me.

His Adam's apple bobbed as he pulled out a pair of jeans and stepped into them, his cock straining high above the waistband. He grabbed a t-shirt and pulled it on. Nope, that bulge wasn't suspicious at all. Damn it.

"Felix said you moved the pack house," she squeaked.

"My parents did. I stayed here." Chase kept his back to her as he went to grab the first aid kit. Most weres healed pretty quickly, but with all the parties the guys had been throwing with other supes, it didn't hurt to have supplies on hand. He turned around with it strategically placed in front of his bulge. A smile teased his lips to see her still on the table, her thighs squeezed together and a pained expression on her face. "Good girl."

Her eyes snapped to his. "What did you just say to me?"

He stepped in front of her and set the kit down, raising a hand to trace her jawline. "I called you a good girl for listening."

Her lips parted with breath and then she wet them. The pulse at her throat quickened. Christ, look at her, just waiting for him to tell her what to do…to submit…

His chest rumbled, leaning closer to her. "You like that? Being my good girl?"

She shook herself, backing away. "I—No. I'm not your anything."

Not yet, but she would be. Baby steps. Chase bit back a smile as he pulled over a chair. He sat in front of her and raised her foot into his lap. His wolf keened, desperate to bury his nose between her thick thighs.

"W-what are you doing?"

"Taking off your boot so I can wrap your ankle."

"Ew! No, I'm all sweaty—"

He raised an eyebrow, already setting her boot aside to peel off her sock. "I don't care."

Her toes were tiny with chipped, sparkly blue polish. She curled them like she didn't want him to see. "You don't need to do that."

Chase shrugged, pushing up her pant leg so he could get to her ankle. "I want to."

"No, don't." Jena ripped it back down, a blush staining her cheeks. "I-I haven't shaved."

He laughed, catching it and pulling it back into his lap. "I turn into a wolf. Body hair isn't an issue." Damn, her ankle was red and swollen. She'd really done a number on it. He flipped open the kit and took out a tube of muscle cream.

"You know, you're awfully bossy." She glowered.

He didn't bother to hide his smile. Woman had no idea, and he couldn't wait for her to find out. She huffed again, and his grin grew. He moved his thumbs along her instep and gingerly up her ankle. Damn, he loved touching her. "Where does it hurt?"

Jena bit her lip like she wasn't going to answer, then flinched. "There...but that—that feels good," she begrudgingly admitted as he rubbed around the spot. His tongue grazed over his bottom lip—

"Don't you dare lick me, Chase Montgomery."

He frowned. The compounds in his saliva would take care of that sprain in two seconds. "It'll heal faster."

"I don't care."

Chase popped his thumb in his mouth and wet it. "Then we'll do it this way," he said, smearing a gob of spit over the swelling. His smile turned to a full-blown grin at her little gasp of outrage. "What? I didn't lick you." He sure as hell wanted to, though.

"Why are you being so nice to me? Someone dare you to do it?"

Chase winced and gooped some muscle cream onto his

fingers. "No. I'm doing this because I like you. I've always liked you, Jena. That party—I owe you a huge apology. I-I lied about it being a dare. I wanted to kiss you, to—I thought if I admitted how I felt then, it would make things worse for you."

She snorted, her other leg swinging like she was agitated. "Gee thanks, being the laughing stock of the entire town was much better than just being a complete outcast."

"I know, I fucked up." He frowned, his hands massaging up her calf and then back down. "But it's different now. That's why I called Crystal out at Snaps. I'm not going to let that shit slide anymore." *You're mine.* The words caught on his tongue, she wasn't ready for them. Christ, he was shocked she was letting him touch her at all. Maybe it was his mating pheromones. The room was dense with them.

His fingers slipped, and he hit the sore spot on her ankle. Her other leg jerked forward and her toes brushed his semi. She gasped, pulling her foot back like she'd been burned.

Chase ducked his head, fighting not to moan and to rein in his wolf. "Sorry." Goddamn, her touching him—he'd bitten his cheek so hard he tasted blood.

"No. I am. I-I didn't mean to—" She'd gone beet red.

Right. It'd been an accident. She hadn't meant—her arousal teased his nose again, and his gaze rose to the darker shadow between her parted thighs. Her scent was driving his wolf insane. He bit back another moan, his cock throbbing at the thought of her being wet for him. What he wouldn't give to taste her right now…

"C-Chase?"

"Yeah, baby?" he rumbled.

"I think I should go home now."

His hands faltered, and he gave a reluctant nod, his wolf about dying as he reached for the bandage. He wrapped her ankle, then shoved her boot and sock into her pack and handed it to her. "I'm gonna pull the truck up, and I'll be right back to get you. Stay there, okay?"

She nodded, not looking at him.

The ride into town was loaded with silence. Jena stared out the window, thumb rubbing the strap of her pack. Chase chewed the inside of his lip, one hand on the wheel and the other squeezing the brim of his hat. Had he fucked up?

Christ, he didn't have time to fuck up. Five days. That's all he had before some major shit hit the fan, and she needed to know what was going on, how he felt…but if he told her now and rushed it…

Damn it. He couldn't lose her again.

"You can let me out here," she said, a full block from her shop.

"No."

She sighed. "Look, Chase. I appreciate you taking me home, but I don't want any more trouble than I already have. If someone sees you dropping me off—"

"You're hurt, and they can go fuck themselves," he growled as he pulled up to the front and killed the engine. Goddamn it, some asshole had spray painted a slur across the sidewalk in front of it. His temper flared as he unbuckled his seatbelt and stormed out of the truck. Fuck this town, and fuck his father. Jena was his, and his wolf—he—didn't give a flying fuck who knew it. He went over to the passenger side and threw her over his shoulder as she tried to get out herself.

"Put me down, you prick!" Her fists pummeled his back.

He slapped her ass, and she howled, reaching back to cover her rear. "You want another? Keep it up." He grabbed her backpack and slammed the door shut, then stomped into her store and up the back steps that he assumed led to her apartment.

"You're such an asshole! Ugh! Why are you doing this?!"

Fuck. He swung open the door at the top of the landing and strode into a long sitting room cramped with furniture.

He couldn't hold off anymore; he had to tell her, whether she was ready for it or not. Sweat slicked down the back of his shirt, his stomach a damned mess.

He dropped her bag and swung her onto a low couch, tenting his body over hers as she bounced against the cushions. "Why? Because you're my mate, and the sooner you accept that, the sooner we can figure out everything else."

She went pale, her pupils dilating. "No..."

"Yes," he growled. "Damn it, Jena, you feel it too, I know you do. That night at the party—I should've told you then. I should've—I should've done a lot of things differently, and I swear to Christ I will from here on out. You're mine, and I'm yours. Only yours."

Her brows furrowed, unsure, then she scowled, her eyes narrowing—Fuck that. He was done waiting.

Chase buried a hand in the hair at the nape of her neck, and kissed her. Softly. Sweetly. Shyly questing with his tongue as she gasped, then fisted his shirt, pulling him closer. Her leg wrapped around his thigh, and he groaned at her opening herself up to him.

Her lips were so fucking sweet...her skin...he nipped at her jaw and nosed behind her ear. She gave a low moan and shivered, her hands roaming towards his waistband. His cock went rock hard. Fuck, if she touched him, he was gonna lose it. His fangs lengthened, his wolf desperate to mark her as his, to claim her—*No. Not yet...*

He kissed her again, sweeping his tongue through her mouth and nibbling on her lip before going back for more, then propping up on an elbow and running a hand up her side to graze her breast. His throat bobbed, holding his breath as he swept a thumb over its peak, her nipple already pearled. She gave a low cry, and he cupped her softness, lightly pinching.

Jena arched into his touch, and he swallowed her moan,

tugging gently. Fuck, he wanted it in his mouth. He kissed down her throat and suckled her through her tee. Fucking sports bra needed to go. She curled her fingers in the hair at the nape of his neck, panting. Christ, that got him hot.

"That's it, baby," he murmured, kissing up her throat and rocking his hips against hers. She whimpered. Goddamn, he wanted her. "See? You feel it, too. I know you do. You're mine."

He lowered his lips to hers, and she bit him.

Her gaze narrowed. "I'm not."

Chase grinned at her, flicking his tongue over her bite. "You are, and I'm gonna prove it to you." He kissed her again, then pushed up to stand. Damn, she looked good all disheveled. He couldn't wait to get her absolutely filthy with his scent. "I'll see you tomorrow."

Confusion wrinkled her brow as she sat up. "Tomorrow? What's tomorrow?"

Chase palmed the brim of his hat and laughed, skipping down the steps.

Chapter Six

JENA STARED at the doorway Chase had disappeared through, desperately trying to regulate her breathing. That had not just happened. Chase Montgomery had not just smacked her ass, made out with her, and said she was his mate.

His. Mate.

She had to be dreaming. Or he was delusional.

Both?

She slapped a hand over her traitorous lips, still feeling his on them. God. Why had they felt so good? No. They hadn't. He was a terrible kisser, and this was a joke. It had to be a joke.

But…weres didn't screw around with that mate stuff, and his lips—his tongue—had been amazing. Had she ever been kissed like that? She raised her hand to fan herself.

The short answer was no, because his skills had definitely improved since high school. Damn. If he could kiss like that, what would it feel like if he—

No. *No.* Down girl. Jena pushed up to sit, scowling. It'd just been way too long since she'd been with someone. Christ, food truck tacos at 3 a.m. were fine dining after eating store-brand taquitos for, well, forever. That's all this was. She took a deep breath and cracked her palms against her thighs.

Her lady bits clenched at the sound.

How the hell he'd known she'd get off on—no. He didn't know. He was just being an asshole…which was another stupid thing she got off on. Jena ripped her hair back over an ear, frustrated. Looked like a date with her battery-operated boyfriend was in her future.

And she was so replaying Chase calling her his good girl in that growly voice of his.

Ugh! No, damnit, bad Jena! She shot to her feet and bit back a yelp as she collapsed back onto the couch. Christ. She'd forgotten about her freaking ankle.

Stupid Chase. God, what was she thinking! She hated him and all his muscly, domineering, too goddamned sexy kissing abilities. It was just another trick, it had to be.

Jena pulled her ankle onto her knee and traced a glyph over the swelling, trying to gauge the karmic price for healing herself. It was a lot lower than it should've been, thanks to Chase's stupid spit. And what the hell?! It was all his fault she hadn't thought to do this before. Ugh! Something about him had always scrambled her brain. That musk of his—she couldn't think straight when he was around.

Her fingertips tingled as a jolt of power left her, and the swelling receded along with the ache, leaving her karma at a deficit. She needed to do something to build it up if she wanted any hope of removing "BITCH" from the sidewalk in front of the shop. Fucking Crystal. Jena had zero doubt she'd put someone up to it.

Which was also Chase's fault.

Jena scowled as she stood. Her ankle wasn't one hundred percent, but it had healed enough to hobble into the kitchen and over to the Hoosier cabinet jammed into the corner. She pulled the bottle of whiskey off the top shelf.

Because alcohol made everything better.

She brought it over to the table along with a glass and sat, pulling out her phone to shoot Felix a text. Not surprisingly, he didn't answer. Jena tossed the phone aside and poured herself three fingers of liquor. Couldn't wait to hear about his waterfall escapades once he came up for air. That was guaranteed to put her in a better mood.

"There better not be ice in that glass." Aggie wheezed, shuffling in. "And I expect one poured for me by the time I get over there."

Jena took a sip. "You know you're not supposed to drink on your meds."

"Considering I don't plan on driving or operating heavy machinery anytime soon, you can make an exception."

"You can have a sip of mine."

"Hell no. You backwash."

"What?" Jena sputtered. "I do not!" She sighed at Aggie's "oh, please" expression and got her a glass, splashing a scant mouthful into it as the older witch sat.

"Don't go and waste it all on a dying woman," she muttered, picking it up and shooting it back before holding out her empty glass. "Please, sir, I want some more."

Jena frowned and poured her another measure. Aggie's *Oliver Twist* voice always got her. "Don't make me aim a blow at your head with a ladle." Jena held it out then pulled it away as the older woman reached for it. "This is it."

"Yes, Mom." Aggie sat back with a look on her face that usually meant she was plotting or about to say something scandalous. "So...what are we drinking to? You finally getting some?"

Jena rolled her eyes. "Hardly."

"Mmm. Must be why it stinks like pheromones in here again, and you're flushed. Is that beard burn all over your face?"

Jena put a hand to it, then scowled. "No." Maybe. Okay, probably, yes. She opened her mouth to make up an excuse—God. Whatever. "The jerk kissed me, okay? I don't get it. He —he said I was his mate. How is that even a thing? I didn't think it worked like that. Doesn't there have to be common genetics?"

Aggie shrugged. "A were's bond is a type of magic, and I'm pretty sure I remember your mother saying there was one or two somewhere in your family tree. Christ, you shake anybody's hard enough and all kinds of shit falls out. Think there's a jinn in mine."

"So you think it's possible?"

"Anything is possible. Probable is an entirely different wheel of cheese." She raised her glass then paused. "You hire that contractor yet?"

Jena took another sip of whiskey and frowned, pulling her laptop over. "Yeah. I signed the papers yesterday and emailed them right out. I didn't want someone else taking the slot they had. When I called to ask about the terms and conditions, she said they were booked solid until February. You're lucky they had a cancellation and can start tomorrow." She sighed, signing into one of the many job search apps she'd recently installed. Too bad they were all coming up with bupkis. "Now I just have to figure out how to pay for it."

"Terms and conditions?" Aggie asked around her glass.

"The contract is totally binding unless I want to pay double to get out of it. I mean, I guess I get that if they're so in demand, but it doesn't seem like a normal stipulation," she said, scrolling through nothing, nothing, and more nothing. "Granted, I know zip about historical renovations—"

"I wouldn't worry too much about it. I have a good feeling about this."

Jena cocked a brow at her. "The last time you said that, the dozen foster kittens you also had a good feeling about peed all over an entire shipment of bespoke silk robes."

Aggie shrugged, coughing into her handkerchief. "And I still maintain they must've been stitched with ill intent."

"That cost us five *thousand* dollars, Aggie."

"Saved us double that in the long run. Not to mention

accruing the bad karma for selling them," she said, taking another sip, totally unrepentant.

Jena shook her head, zeroing in on an actual possibility for employment. A shop in Fayet was looking for a bookkeeper. She shot off her resume and a quick cover letter. Couldn't quite tell what they did, but the salary was right.

"You answer the coven?" Aggie asked.

"No, but stupid Felix thinks I should consider it, too." Jena looked up at the pregnant silence that followed. "What?" Aggie shrugged, and Jena rolled her eyes. "You really think I should join?"

"I think you're as stubborn as your mother, and what I or Felix think doesn't equate to an ant's fart in a hurricane."

"But…" Jena prompted, knowing that wasn't the end of it.

"*But* you're an idiot if you piss on potential allies, and powerful ones at that. There's also the node to consider." She narrowed her eyes and waggled an arthritic finger at Jena's dismissive huff. "It needs to be taken in hand. All that wild magic leaking everywhere isn't good for anybody."

"Felix said Matilda thinks it's going to become an unseelie mound," Jena said, taking another sip.

"Unlikely," Aggie snorted, "but Lord only knows what it will attract, and it's already repelling the more conservative practitioners."

"Good, then maybe Matilda will leave," Jena muttered.

"And miss everything going to hell in a hand basket? I'd put money on the unseelie mound first." Aggie shook her head. "You know, just because you join doesn't mean you have to go to tea every Sunday. Hell, I don't."

"Yeah, but you're Aggie Wright, and the rules don't apply to you."

"And you're Jena Seymore. Your family used to be top of the food chain in this town, hell, in this entire county. No reason it can't be again, and then you make the rules."

Jena snorted, going back to her scrolling. "Pretty sure dear old dad screwed that pooch."

"He certainly did his damndest." Aggie sighed. "But that was William. Fun at parties but a shitty house guest and as vindictive as the day was long. Always pulling some stunt that made you wanna wring his neck, then gaslighting everyone with a perfectly plausible explanation. Son of a bitch was more charming than the devil himself and just as hell bent on staining souls. There's no way he was a pureblooded warlock for all he claimed to be." She took another swig of liquor. "Shit, for all I know, the bastard was unseelie…"

Jena shot Aggie a side-eye for maligning her genetics. "Gee, thanks for that."

"Fine. He could've been part demon. Regardless, by the time Rebecca'd had enough, she was already pregnant with you. He'd done a fine job of isolating her at the end, so I've no idea what went on between them, but I got the impression it wasn't good before he cleared out. I can't say anyone was sorry to see the backend of him. Weren't particularly surprised to hear he'd drained her bank accounts and pissed all over her assets on his way out, either."

How drunk was she? Aggie rarely spoke about what'd gone down between Jena's parents. She cocked her brow. "Hexing the majority of the town in the process will do that."

"It will at that." The older woman coughed. "And it backs up that he was less than pureblooded. No practitioner could accrue that much bad karma and keep their powers, but a demon? Unseelie? That shit's right up their alley."

Great. Just what Jena needed on top of all the other things she had going for her. Guess she was snagging one of those stupid mail-in genealogy kits from Ms. Pao at the library to rule out those fun developments. "I've always wondered if that last spell mom cast had something to do with him."

"You're not the only one, but he'd been gone for years at that point. Why he'd come back…" Aggie cracked her empty glass on the table. "And may I just mention, whatever her intent might've been, we'll never know because she was too damned stubborn to ask for help—mine included. Make no mistake, if she'd had the coven behind her, that spell wouldn't have rebounded, and the fire never would've happened."

Aggie paused, pursing her lips. "No, whatever went on that night, she took to the grave. All I can tell you is that she'd drawn a containment circle, the property was warded to the gills, and half of it was blown to shit. Whether she was summoning something or trying to send it back…" The older woman shrugged. "I couldn't say, and I've no idea why you were wandering out by the road instead of in bed where you should've been, but I thank God every day that you were."

She slapped a hand against the table and Jena jumped. "Now, since you got me drunk enough to spill shit I shouldn't, you can help me into bed before I slip and break a damned hip."

A containment circle? Jena had never heard that part of the story. She sat blinking for a breath before closing her laptop and getting up. An uncomfortable weight had developed in her stomach, and it didn't have anything to do with the whiskey.

Because if there was a circle, no matter which direction whatever it was had been going in, there was a very real possibility that what had killed her mother was still here.

CHASE SLOWLY CHEWED HIS MEAT, eyes focused on his plate. Around him, the top echelon of the pack sat around the manor's long, glass and brass dining room table for his mother's mandatory Sunday dinner. Her insistence that he take off his ball cap for the damned meals always guaranteed they were uncomfortable, but tonight's was particularly painful.

That he attributed entirely to Crystal sitting beside him, and the shit-eating grin on her face. She reached over to put her hand on his leg again, and he batted it away with a growl.

Christ, he didn't want to be here.

He shoved a forkful of potatoes into his mouth and grabbed his water to help choke them down with a quick glance through his messy locks at the sparkly, rhinestone clock on the mantle across the room. Damn it. Not even fifteen minutes had passed.

"Thank you so much again for inviting me to dinner, Ms. Montgomery," Crystal gushed, breaking into the too loud clink of golden utensils against china.

His mother waved a hand, the same damned smile on her face. "Of course! And please, call me Mom. We're practically family now, and I've been asking Chase to invite you to Sunday dinner for months." She beamed. "I'm so glad he finally came to his senses before you got away."

Chase coughed, a surge of bile rising in his throat. Crystal patted his back as he reached for his water again, and fur sprouted on his nape. "Don't fucking touch me."

"Chase!" His mother gasped, the rest of the table going still.

Crystal laughed like he was kidding. "Must've been a tough day at the office," she joked. A couple of people forced chuckles as he seethed, the room prickling with tension.

"So…I guess congratulations are in order?" his youngest brother, Luke, asked.

Patrick snorted. "More like condolences, but they should be directed at Crystal."

She failed to hide a smile behind her napkin. "You're so funny," she tittered.

Chase frowned around his bite. Patrick wasn't funny and never had been.

Their father cleared his throat and forks stilled. "Congratulations are yet to be determined, but I'm confident Chase will live up to expectations," he intoned from the head of the table. "Or not."

Chase clenched his jaw, not about to take the bait.

"Crystal is going to make a beautiful bride," his mother said into the uncomfortable silence that followed. "We've spent all day planning, and we've decided to have the wedding here. The ceremony can be out on the back lawn, and the foyer is perfect for pictures. Just imagine the banister swathed in silk and chrysanthemums, all done in shades of russet and peach—"

"And cream roses. I adore cream roses," Crystal added, clapping her hands. "It's going to be more expensive, but when I called the florist in Galleon Falls, they had a much better selection than the one here in town."

"You know money's no object, dear." His mother simpered. "You only get married once."

Chase pinched across his temples, a migraine brewing.

Crystal beamed at her, then turned to his sister. "We're going dress shopping Thursday. You have to come. I want your opinion on the bridesmaids' gowns. I'm thinking twelve, same color, different styles—"

"Twelve? Chase doesn't have that many friends," Sue snarked, then glanced at him like she regretted the comment.

"I've already taken care of that," their mother said breezily. "Patrick's offered to be best man, and then Luke and some of the other prominent pack members can make up the rest."

"Isn't it kind of early for all that? I mean, Chase hasn't even gotten her a ring..." Luke glanced at him. "Have you?"

"No," Chase spat. And he wasn't planning on it.

"But he will," his father said, his voice laden with finality.

"And it's never too soon to look for a dress...or to plan nursery decor." His mom smirked around her glass of rosé.

Chase bit back another growl. This was Hell. He was officially in Hell.

Crystal flipped a long blonde lock over her shoulder and eyed him up and down. "Guess you better start ring shopping, then," she said singsong, walking her fingers up his arm. "I left my size at Fynbender's and ordered in some options. They'll be here tomorrow."

Of course she had. Chase's water goblet threatened to crack in his grip. He was way too close to losing his shit. Christ, the entire fucking town must know about—

Jena.

He felt the blood drain from his face, and he put out his hand to steady himself. Fuck. If she thought he'd lied to get in her pants and was getting married after he'd told her Crystal wasn't his girlfriend—

"Sit. Down," his father's voice cracked through the room.

Chase's gaze snapped to the head of the table. Shit. He hadn't even realized he'd gotten up. He ducked his head, messy waves falling across his face. "I-I'm not...feeling well."

His father's expression didn't change, about as sympathetic as a reptile.

"Well, it certainly isn't the meal, you've hardly touched your plate." His mother huffed.

A hand caged Chase's shoulder with an iron grip. "I'll make sure he gets home all right," Malcom said from behind him, his raspy drawl raising Chase's hackles.

His father's eyes flicked to his beta's. Something passed between the two, and his father grunted. "Feel better," he murmured, cutting into the slab of bloody meat on his plate.

That wasn't happening any time soon. Chase pulled his cap out of his back pocket and snugged it on as Malcom goose-stepped him from the room and down the hall.

"I can make it home by myself," Chase said as they came into the foyer.

"Oh, I know," the slim man said, his grip unflinching. "I'm more concerned about you running off to see that whore witch you felt the need to manhandle through the middle of town today. You spent an awful long time in that shop of hers."

Chase tensed, and Malcom chuckled. "There is just something about that family draws you Montgomerys like flies to shit. The way your daddy used to drool over her mama was…unhealthy, especially for her. I'd suggest you keep your distance before her daughter ends up the same way."

"The hell are you talking about?" Chase turned to look at him.

The man grinned, and it wasn't friendly. "Now that would be telling, but I know you're smarter than you let on. I'm sure you'll figure it out." He slapped Chase's shoulder and sauntered back the way they'd just come.

"I've got a contract to do work at her shop," Chase called after him. "I can't keep my distance."

Malcom stopped. "Then I'd suggest you keep your hands to yourself and expedite the job. Put a leash on that wolf of yours while you do. I'll be watching."

He disappeared down the hall, and Chase shook himself like he was in wolf form before heading out to his truck. He got in and ran a hand over his scruffy jaw, staring at the house. Fuck. If Malcom knew about Jena…if he had any idea what she was to him…

He'd kill her.

Chase popped the truck into reverse and backed out of the driveway, kicking himself for letting his temper get the best of him and carrying Jena inside the way he had. After what Malcom said, Chase couldn't go there now, as much as his wolf was keening to, but maybe he could get her number—no. She'd hang up on him and never speak to him again. He had to explain in person. Luckily, the contract she'd signed stipulated work to begin tomorrow at eight a.m. sharp.

He prayed that would be soon enough.

Chapter Seven

JENA STARED AT THE CROOKED, wrought iron gates listing from the weed-choked drive at the side of the road. Visiting the ruins of the house she'd spent the first four years of her life in hadn't been on her bucket list, but after the rough night Aggie'd had, it was abruptly a priority.

The whiskey had not agreed with the older witch, and she'd been up all night. That cough she'd developed was deepening, and Jena really didn't like the sound of it. She'd hoped she could harvest the ingredients for a potion from the church grounds or around town, but it'd been slim pickings.

She wasn't about to ask the coven for charity, and Aggie would rather keel over than go back to the hospital. When Jena had suggested it, the older woman had pitched a fit worthy of a toddler that had only exacerbated her condition.

Which left magic, and unfortunately, the only other place that might have what she needed was through those gates. God, she hadn't set foot past them in almost twenty years. The last time she'd been here had freaked her out so badly she'd had nightmares for months. Something about the burned-out ruins on the hill—the tor—and the standing stones at its crown…

Jena shook the memory away. It didn't matter. She'd been a kid then, and she wasn't afraid of her own shadow anymore. Aggie needed her, and Jena wasn't about to let her down. She sighed and hefted her spellbag from the passenger seat. Dawn had already broken, and if she was going to do this, she needed to do it now.

The car door closed behind her with a thunk, washed-out sand from the drive crunching beneath her sneakers. She squeezed through the creaking gate, beneath the loose chain holding it closed. A faint prickle ran over her skin as magic rose up to meet her. Her brows furrowed at the remains of an old ward, twin to the one they had on the shop. This one wasn't going to keep anyone with ill intent out, but it was still strong enough to make them think twice about it.

She stood, re-shouldering her bag and started up the drive. A chill went through her, the spot between her shoulder blades pricking with the feeling of being watched. *It's your imagination, Jena. Big girl panties, let's go.*

Still…the autumn woods were too quiet, laden with a weird anticipation that only grew as she got farther in. The limbs of oaks, maples, and birch trees rustled, the sky still too dark to show their riot of color. The skittering of leaves filled the unnatural silence as the breeze picked up, then died away. She hopped over a rut where the drive had washed out, trying to remember what it'd looked like before, and failing.

She'd been so little when the fire had happened. Every now and again, she'd get a flash of memory. A room with pale yellow walls. Sunlight streaming through stained-glass. A big, shaggy dog…though Aggie swore they hadn't had one.

Jena frowned, remembering it clearly, unlike her mother. Aside from the distinct scent of her bergamot perfume, all of those memories were built around the photos in an album somewhere back at the shop, and her father had disappeared before she'd been born. She wasn't even sure what he'd looked like, not that she particularly cared.

He was gone, like everything else.

She passed between two cairns of stones, and the prickle

of another ward raised the small hairs at the nape of her neck, its power even fainter than the first. Seven. There would be seven wards to match the seven standing stones in the garden, protecting the node deep below, their power raised and rooted in the earth, nourished by wind and water—

And all of it razed by flame.

Jena closed her eyes and paused, her breathing stuttered. Aggie. This was for Aggie.

By the fifth ward, there was only the barest sigh of magic. The sixth and seventh were only discernible by their physical remains, whatever power had been harnessed to them long gone.

Blasted to shit.

Then the trees dropped away, and a fielded-hilltop opened up, the tor thick with goldenrod, black-eyed susan, and coneflower. Jena's gaze fell from the tumble of stones at its peak to scan the wildflowers. A reverberation teased her bones, the power in the earth so much stronger here where the leylines crossed to form a node than it was in town.

Felix was right—again, damn him—its power was dense, wilder than she remembered, and more intense. Turbulent tendrils bled out from the node and swirled around her, calling to her, recognizing the blood running through her veins and trying to embrace her. Wanting...

Her eyes squeezed shut. Knuckles white. God, it would be so easy to fall into it—*No. I'm only visiting, choose someone else...*

A sense of laughter and denial. Finality and ownership. Welcoming whispers she couldn't quite hear and a whisper of spicy citrus perfume...

Bergamot, like her mother had worn.

Enough. The node was screwing with her. She wasn't here for it and wasn't going to be. Jena slammed the door to her power closed and took the little crescent knife from her bag, the node scratching at the edges of her consciousness like a persistent stray. God, that was annoying—*Ignore it. You can ignore it for Aggie. This is for her.* Jena centered herself and gave thanks before bending to her task and gathering from the bounty before her.

Her path rambled, plant to plant as the sun rose in the sky. Dense clouds of sprites and pixies chased dragonflies through the field. She paused to watch them. Jeez, every harem from the western woods had to be congregating here. They zipped around her, their rapid little voices all blending together in an incessant chattering buzz as they flitted around, randomly dragging over whatever they thought would interest her.

She thanked them, putting odd pebbles, a rusted button, leaves, and blooms in her spell bag, but drew the line at the mouse skull, suggesting that it would make one of them a fine hat instead.

She slapped at a mosquito. Weren't there enough bugs to keep them busy? You'd think they'd be starving. Not that she'd suggest they find something to eat. Pixies would absolutely take a chunk out of you if they thought they could get away with it, and talking down to them was the quickest way to get bit.

She snorted. Yeah, that's what she needed, to be scratching at pixie bites on top of everything else she was dealing with. But, like Felix had said, places of power drew things, and there was certainly an abundance of magic here. No wonder Matilda was worried about this becoming a mound.

A whisper of the node's power skated over her psyche again, and she closed her eyes, fighting its seductive pull. No. There wasn't a chance she was going to shackle herself to it and spend the rest of her life rotting on a hilltop outside of Havers. *Find someone else!*

Bergamot teased her nose again. *But we've been waiting for you...*

Jena's heart jumped at the faint whisper. Shit, had she imagined that? She ran her arm across her brow. Delusional.

She was delusional, and that was bullshit. There were tons of other witches. Maybe she had sunstroke. It was already stupid hot—especially for October, but she suspected she was lucky the weather had been so weird this year. If they'd had a hard frost, she wouldn't be able to harvest half of what she was finding—

A long, rectangular stone pool abruptly stretched out before her.

She glanced up. Crap. She hadn't realized she'd gotten so close to the ruins, but there they were. Her mouth went dry, and she wet her lips.

Bittersweet and wild rose had covered the jagged remains of the house she couldn't remember living in, softening them. The remaining windows no longer looked like gaping maws, and she couldn't see down into the belly of the basement, though she clearly remembered the hole and the deep well of sidhe-blue at its center. Here on the north side, a grove of trees had grown close, and the scrap of shaded lawn had gone mossy, overgrowing the stone-lined path leading into the garden.

She pulled a mason jar from her bag and knelt at the rim of the pool to fish out a clump of duckweed with an eye out for any naiads lurking in its depths. Little jerks would pull her in if they could. She sighed, grabbing a soggy clump of green. Hopefully, she could figure out where the heck Aggie had shoved that dehydrator from a handful of Christmases ago.

Jena frowned and sat back, screwing on the top of the jar before adding it to the rest of her haul. A breeze from a sprite zipping by teased the fly-aways from her messy ponytail, and she absently tucked them behind her ear, looking east.

The hill the manor had been built on sloped away then butted up to a dense wood. Once upon a time, her family had owned all of it down to the river that was supposed to be somewhere out there. Now it, and the rest of the three-hundred and fifty acres surrounding the property, belonged to a private investment firm.

The handful of acres the ruins were on she supposed were technically hers, but she couldn't do anything with them. They were held in some kind of a convoluted trust with a list of contingencies and stipulations a mile long. Bottom line—she couldn't sell it, and at this point, when—not if—she died "without issue," it would go to the coven.

A small part of her wondered if trading that acreage for her college education had been worth it. But as Aggie would say, that cat had already fled the crime scene, and it was too late now. Jena was just glad they hadn't clearcut everything and put in condos or something equally ugly. What they were doing over on Sunnyside was tragic.

A natural breeze ruffled her hair, and she blew out a breath. Right. She needed to finish up and get back to the shop. What else did she need to look for while she was here? Pennyroyal wouldn't be in bloom, but if she could find some rootstock to take back with her, she might be able to force it.

Jena stood, stretching. A vague memory of a massive stone planter of the stuff teased her mind. Well, that would make sense, considering it was related to mint and would run rampant if given the chance. She meandered away from the reflecting pool toward the moss-covered path.

The garden was laid out in a concentric spiral. Jena entered and began to walk it deosil, following the clockwise path of the sun deeper into its heart. Unlike the hillside below, nothing stirred here, and the lack of lesser fae was stark. Tumbled urns and long stone planters of weeds spilled into the cobbled path's orbit. The twisted limbs of dwarf magnolias and flaming Japanese maples strained toward each other across the way.

She pushed their creaking branches aside, passing tiny, overgrown pocket gardens rife with the detritus of neglect. A crumbling stone bridge arched above the dry banks of a manufactured stream; the basin of the fountain ran thick with green sludge at the far end. At its center, a statue of the three forms of Hecate stood back-to-back, staring out over the garden with sightless stone eyes.

Jena shivered, the day abruptly not as warm as it had been. Going to the laundromat to get her stupid sweater cleaned jumped to the top of her to-do list as soon as she was finished here. The urn she'd been looking for was just across the way. She adjusted the strap of her spellbag and stepped from the bridge—

Sin, sin, sin, sin...

A wave of nausea went through her, and she stumbled back, falling onto her rear, the breath knocked out of her. She scrambled back. Oh God, that had to be the boundary of the containment circle and what was inside...

The rash of nightmares she'd had the last time she was here flashed before her mind's eye, and she forced herself to take slow, deep breaths. *Be rational Jena...there's nothing actually in there, there can't be, not after all this time. It's just the spell's residue...*

But damn, was it dank, and it called to her power like a beacon. No wonder she'd been scared out of her wits. She chewed her lip, running through all of the other herbs she'd harvested. Did she really need pennyroyal right this very second? Mmm...probably not.

Jena stood, dusting herself off. It was related to mint, right? They had plenty of that, and the substitution wouldn't throw off the magic too badly. She'd just toss in some of that goldenrod to compensate. Right? Right, yeah. It was a plan.

She turned with an awful certainty something was watching her, her skin crawling, and the small hairs raised up all over her body. *Walk, walk, walk, do not run...* It took all her willpower, and her steps were still faster leaving the garden than when she'd come in. *There's nothing there, there's nothing there...*

Crap. That was bullshit, and whatever her mother had put in that circle, it wanted out.

~

CHASE STEPPED through the door to The Witchery, the bell above him tinging. He'd never been able to get a good look at this place, though he'd been dying to for as long as he could remember. It was one of the few original buildings in town that hadn't been completely gutted, and damn, was it a beauty.

He gave a low whistle at the coffered ceilings and what he was pretty positive was the original globed central chandelier. Looked like it'd been outfitted for gas and electricity at one point. What were the chances the mechanism to lower it was still intact?

A smile bloomed across his face as he took in the rest of the room. Probably pretty good, considering the dark, arsenic green wallpaper peeking from behind a bookcase. Christ, this shit got his dick hard. He couldn't wait to get started.

Chase wiped his palms against his jeans and shrugged his tool bag higher onto his shoulder. The curtains were still pulled across the front bay windows, and the shop was silent. His nose twitched, picking up the subtle thread of his pheromones beneath the muddled scent of herbs and resin he'd always associated with Jena. But that wasn't her. Not really. She was the sharp jolt of ozone after a lightning strike refined by ambergris, hiding behind—

"Are you coming up, or are you casing the joint?" Aggie's acerbic wheeze called down the stairs. "If it's the latter, do me a favor and take out that bag of garbage by the door when you go."

"Uh, actually, I'm here for the bathroom? Second floor?" he called back.

"That's right. Stairs are straight ahead, but you already knew that, and you're late."

Late? Chase glanced at his watch. Eight-o-one. Great. Aggie was one of those. He wove through tables loaded with stuff he couldn't even begin to classify…damn, there was one hell of a draft at the back of the room. He made a mental note to take a look at that later as he headed up the steps.

Unfortunately, thanks to the pictures Lucy had taken and his previous visit, the second floor was exactly what he'd been expecting. The door on the landing at the top of the steps opened to one long room that'd been absolutely butchered. Crown molding, framing, all of it was slathered in white paint. Nail holes from mini blinds he could see from where he was standing, and he didn't even know what the hell to make of what they'd done to the fireplace. It looked like they'd crated it against the wall. Hopefully what was underneath was intact, but he wasn't gonna hold his breath.

A half-dozen mismatched armchairs, a couch, and two loveseats ringed the room, and above—Christ, they'd put in a shitty drop ceiling and the fucking floor was linoleum beneath the throw rugs.

But where the paint had been chipped away…he went to one of the floor-to-ceiling windows and ran a hand over the carved acanthus leaves and egg-in-cup borders along the trim. Tiger oak. Those dumbasses had painted over fucking tiger oak.

"If you're done gawking, I'm in the kitchen, first door to your right."

Chase pulled himself away from the window and stepped into the other room, his eyes going to the convex tin ceiling. Thank God they hadn't gotten rid of that, but the rest was definitely not original and a travesty of avocado and rust.

A nasty little mid-century kitchenette had been cobbled together on the far wall, half of which looked like it'd been chopped out with a hacksaw to make room for a Hoosier cabinet. That was loaded with implements like the ones he'd seen downstairs. All witch stuff, he guessed.

The butcher block island in front of it with the stainless-steel gas range was from this century, though the heavy iron cauldron taking up half of it could go either way. It was still a marked improvement from the baby-shit brown Formica and sickly green tiles around the sink.

Aggie cleared her throat, and he jumped, his brain on reno overload.

"Oh, sorry." He went over to the table in front of the long, inset plastic-covered windows and held out a hand for her to shake. "Chase Montgomery." Goddamn, were those stained-glass panels along the sides of the panes original? The plastic was so thick he couldn't really—

"I know who you are," Aggie snapped, waving his hand away. "And all I got to say is you're lucky your intentions are pure enough to cross my ward." She coughed, raising her scant brow at him. "Well, maybe not pure, but there's no ill intent about you, even if you did swindle your way in here."

His throat bobbed as he lowered his hand. "Ah, yeah. Sorry about that."

"No, you're not," she coughed, "and lying is only gonna compound your karma."

"Yes, ma'am." Shit. How the hell was he supposed to—

"Bathroom is on the other side of the apartment, off the green bedroom. You'll forgive me if I don't give you the grand tour. Feel free to poke around, but I catch you sniffing anything you wouldn't in church, you're out." She picked up a magazine, her dismissal plain.

"Um, thanks...is Jena here?"

Aggie glanced at him askance. "No." She coughed into a handkerchief. Damn. That didn't sound good—"You're safe for a couple hours. I'd suggest you get working and make enough progress to have to come back and finish it before she throws you out on your ass."

"Yes, ma'am. Thank you, ma'am." He tipped his cap at her.

She sniffed as he backed out of the door and into the hall. Jesus. Chase gave a huge sigh of relief—

"I heard that."

Fuck. What the hell had he gotten himself into?

Chapter Eight

JENA PARKED her car in front of The Witchery and let out a long sigh. Her impulsive decision to go into Fayet and check out the Spell Shop for ingredients had been a total waste of time and gas.

It might've been owned by legitimate practitioners ten years ago, but it'd since been bought out by some new-aged wannabe. No way was she buying herbs shipped in from halfway around the globe and treated with lord only knew what. For Christ's sake, they were selling them side-by-side with pink cartoon cat Tarot cards and penis-shaped incense holders…the latter of which she may or may not have gotten for Aggie's Christmas stocking.

But aside from that find, the trip had been seriously depressing. How was The Witchery failing so badly? The magic in this part of the county was deep, and the condition of the node wasn't nearly as dire as everyone was screaming about. Yeah, it was dense, but the wards constraining it were holding. Besides, there were at least a dozen established covens and three times as many practitioners between the two towns to stabilize the leylines if they got wonky. With the Spell Shop defunct, The Witchery should have a fricking line around the block waiting to get in.

Jena buzzed her lips, pretty certain that the reason why

they didn't had nothing to do with a certain mail order giant and everything to do with Mary Montgomery's slander. Without Aggie to stand up for herself, the bitch had done her damnedest to ruin the business, and everyone else had let it happen. Though where they were getting their supplies from…God, Jena hated this town.

She grabbed her bag, and headed into the shop, then up the steps. Her nose wrinkled. Ugh. The stink from her sweater had migrated to the second floor and beneath Chases's damned musk, it smelled like mildew and things best not disturbed had been. Guess the renovators had made an appearance. Lord only knew what they'd found.

She set her bag on the counter and went down the hall to Aggie's room. Soft, wheezy snores came from the curtained bed. Jena slipped into the room and poked her head into the bath. A fan had been set into the window blowing outwards, and a fresh piece of plywood was over the floor. Tubing to the sink, toilet, and tub snaked close to the wall where the older woman couldn't trip over it. Wow. There wasn't a speck of dust anywhere, either.

Something in Jena's chest loosened at the care the contractor had taken. The piles of construction mess she'd expected weren't there, and it looked like the little bath was functional. It was definitely cleaner than it'd been this morning. She'd made the right decision. Thank God. She didn't have twenty grand to spend on a thoughtless hack.

She backed out of the room, leaving Aggie to sleep. At least one of them would. Making that potion and processing all of the herbs she'd gathered was going to take the rest of the night. Jena didn't mind the work, but unfortunately, most of it was mindless, which left her brain free to spiral on stupid Chase Montgomery. And that was only marginally better than what'd happened in the garden.

She crossed herself and murmured a quick protection

spell. Her power hadn't screamed at her like that since she'd been unfortunate enough to stumble across a double murder scene back in the city, and this had been louder. Whatever was in there, she didn't want to call its attention. It'd already been far too interested in her. Jena chewed her lip. Why hadn't Aggie mentioned it though?

The easy answer was that she didn't know about it, but that didn't make sense either. Jena clearly remembered the months of nightmares she'd had after she'd gone up there the last time. Aggie had been with her then, and she'd been up with her after every horrible dream. There was no way she wouldn't have investigated, and most likely gotten the coven's help.

Which just solidified that whatever it was wasn't an echo or remnant of power, and if it was sentient and clever enough to hide…but then why out itself to her?

"Where were you all day?"

Jena yelped and almost dropped her strainer at Aggie's voice. "Don't do that! I thought you were sleeping! Are you feeling any better?"

Aggie shrugged, wheezing as she shuffled to the table. "Fair to middling. Make me some tea?"

"Only if you take this potion with it."

"What is it?"

"Disgusting. You'll love it." Aggie grunted, and Jena put the kettle on to heat. "I drove to Fayet to check out the Spell Shop."

"Waste of gas. You didn't get all that there."

"No. I went out to the ruins."

Aggie abruptly became more alert. "Did you now?"

"I did." Jena tapped off her strainer and capped the resulting liquid. "And whatever freaked me out as a kid is still there, just past the bridge, inside a containment circle. You have any insight into that?"

The older woman's brow furrowed, troubled. "No, and I

swear to you, I looked into it. Dragged the whole goddamned coven out there multiple times. None of us could pick up on anything…but it stands to reason you did. Whether you want to acknowledge it or not, your blood's keyed to that node and power calls to power. You're predisposed to be more sensitive to whatever happens out there, and if sin-eating was wrapped up in the spell, those echos would resonate even louder with you. What did you feel?"

Something a heck of a lot stronger than an echo. Jena frowned, but she guessed that made sense. "Sin and a sentient malevolence."

"Well, that's less than ideal," Aggie murmured.

"Ya think? But the circle is keeping whatever it is contained. The other wards are there too, except for the sixth and seventh." Damn it. It probably wouldn't be a bad idea to go and re-establish them. She wouldn't have to step foot on the hill to do that—and it absolutely would not mean she was agreeing to take her mother's place as guardian. It was just being responsible. If no one could banish it, whatever was in that circle needed to stay put. "And the node's not nearly as bad off as everyone says it is."

Aggie shot her a look. "Maybe not for you, but last time I was out there, I got hit with a jolt of power that made my teeth glow." She shook her finger. "And last month, June Hill about shit herself trying to reinforce the ward at the gate. Said it was like grabbing onto an electric fence. The hell it's not that bad. What you got out there is a bunch of pissed off magic with a sweet spot for you and no one else."

Jena rolled her eyes. "No, what's out there is a problem waiting to happen, and it's not the node, it's in the middle of that garden."

Aggie sighed and sat back. "I can't imagine anything being up there after all this time. Not anything the coven wouldn't have sensed…but your mother…" She shook her head. "I wish her grimoire hadn't gone up in flames with everything else. I've said it before, and I'll say it again, she was a next level witch. There's a reason your family was chosen to guard that node."

"There's also a reason our name is in the toilet," Jena muttered. "Speaking of which, I saw the contractor was here." She eyed the older woman over the herbs she was stripping. "Is he coming back to finish the job, or did you scare him off?"

"Says he's pulling permits tomorrow, so I'm assuming he'll be back. If not, I'm not gonna cry about it. He's got it set up so everything works, and I can use the shitter without fear of plummeting to my doom."

The kettle started to scream, and Jena paused her work to pour Aggie a cup of tea and a measure of potion. "Always a good thing, and I got an email from that job I applied for in Fayet, so I might even be able to pay for it. Looks like I'm going back for an interview."

"I hate that drive." Aggie scowled.

Jena sighed. So did she. The winding cliffside road was miserable in good weather, and it was supposed to pour for the next few days. The fact that her grandparents, uncle, his wife, and newborn had plummeted to their deaths around mile marker fifty-eight didn't help either. "Hey, do you know where that dehydrator ended up?"

Aggie coughed into her handkerchief and looked like she'd bitten into something sour. "It's probably upstairs with the rest of the junk I never use."

"Purist." Jena laughed, bringing over Aggie's tea and the potion. What the—

Jena set both down and picked up the paper. That son of a bitch. She stared at the front page headline, her blood pounding in her ears.

Montgomery-Chambers Wedding
Mr. and Ms. Wallace Montgomery are pleased to announce the

engagement of their son Chase Anthony Montgomery to Crystal Meghan Chambers…

"Are you fucking kidding me?" Jena gritted out, her teeth clenched so hard her temples throbbed. "That dirty, lying—"

"Who's this now?" Aggie asked, stirring her tea.

"Chase Montgomery!" Jena slapped the paper down onto the table. God, she was so fucking stupid! Of course it'd all been a lie. Why wouldn't it be? And she'd kissed him! Had let him—Ugh! Jesus, she felt gross—

"Oh." Aggie sipped her tea. "That."

Jena spun on the older woman, her eyes wide. "Oh, that?! That's all you have to say?"

"Eh, don't believe everything you read." Aggie wheezed, placing her cup back in its saucer and eyeing the potion. "Besides, I thought you didn't have a crush on him."

Jena scowled. She didn't, damn it. She just—"It's the frickin' Havers's Herald, not a supermarket tabloid!"

"I seem to remember an article they published where Milton Smith had died when his still exploded, exposing ten grand of gold bullion in his basement. Not only was Milton not dead, he was also less than impressed when he came back from visiting his mother in Persis to find excavators tearing up his foundation."

Jena stared at her, then shook her head. "That was a one off, and you better drink that."

Aggie met her eye and shot back the potion. She grimaced and glanced meaningfully at the paper. "And I'd talk to Chase before you get yourself all worked up."

"Too late. I'm already worked up, and I'd rather swallow my own teeth than talk to that jerk ever again."

"Then you better not act surprised when you go to get comfortable and something bites you in the ass."

～

CHASE PULLED into the compound and cut the engine to his truck. Damn, he was exhausted. A smile lit up his face, never having been happier about it. It sucked that he hadn't seen Jena, but the rest of the day had made up for it. If he'd known what an absolute hidden gem Aggie Wright was sitting on, he'd have offered to do the reno for free just to see the place shine the way it should. Shit, now there was an idea. God, never mind what restoring that would do for his portfolio, the sheer pleasure of bringing it back to life had him like a kid on Christmas.

Most of the shitty 60s upgrades he'd seen were just thrown over the original architectural elements. There was a freaking parquet floor with inlaid borders beneath the shag he'd flipped up in Aggie's room for Christ's sake. Yeah, it needed a ton of work, but it was gonna be heavy lifting and elbow grease more than anything else—

He stopped short as he went to close the driver's side door. The lights in his cabin were on and the drapes pulled. Fucking hell, what now? He grabbed his bag and stomped up the front porch, praying it wasn't who he thought it was.

No such luck. Crystal was in a sheer nighty on his bed with a glass of champagne, back arched and waiting for him. "Hey, Chase-y."

The hair on his nape rose at the stupid nickname. "Get out." He threw his bag on the table, then grabbed her sundress off the back of a chair and chucked it at her.

She didn't bother to catch it as it fell, her big brown eyes wide with innocence that she sure as hell didn't possess. "What do you mean, get out?"

"Exactly what I said. I don't want you here. I don't want anything to do with you, and I sure as hell don't want you on my dick. There's the door, use it."

She stared at him agape for a breath and then scowled. "How stupid are you?"

Chase laughed. "Excuse me?"

"This," she said, waggling a finger between them, "is happening. I don't know what kind of spell that witch has over you—"

His stomach dropped. "I don't know what you're talking about."

"Bullshit. I could smell how hot the two of you are for each other the second I opened the door, and I know you brought her home yesterday." Her face twisted. "*Everyone* knows. You're acting like she's your mate," Crystal spat.

"What?" Shit. In retrospect, he'd known carrying Jena in like that was asking for trouble, but at the time... Chase palmed the brim of his cap, ripping it lower. "No, I'm not. So what if I hauled her ass inside? She was being difficult. Stop making shit up, it didn't mean a goddamned thing," he said, his wolf snarling at the lie.

Crystal laughed. "God, you're an idiot. It means everything. Don't you get it? We're being handed the pack. We'll be the alpha couple, Chase. Do you have any idea how much power that is? I've worked far too long and far too hard sucking up to your family for you and that fat bitch to ruin this for me."

Chase's temper spiked, and he was across the room before he'd thought about it, his hand around Crystal's throat, pinning her to the mattress. "Don't fucking talk about her like that," he growled.

Her eyes glittered. "That's it, Chase-y, tell me what to do. You know how I like it."

"So does everyone else with a dick in this town." And he was pretty sure that included his brother, Patrick. He pushed away from her in disgust and crossed the room, grabbing a gym bag from the floor. Fuck this. He tore open his dresser drawers and shoved a bunch of clothes inside.

"What are you doing?" Crystal screeched.

"If you're gonna keep spewing bullshit and won't leave,

then I am." Before Chase's wolf did something to her he probably wouldn't regret.

"No, you're not." Her face contorted like she was fighting the same urge to shift. "Didn't you just hear anything I said?"

"That you're a gold-digging cunt who likes to crawl on top of guys when they're passed out drunk? Yeah, I already knew that. Hard pass on giving you the opportunity to do it again. This," he said waggling his finger between them, "is never fucking happening." He snagged his work bag from the table and stormed out, slamming the door on her protests. He'd sleep on the couch in his office. Wasn't ideal, but at least it didn't stink like conniving bitch.

Chase got back into his truck and gunned the engine. He peeled out of the compound and onto the dirt track leading to the main road. A shower. He needed a goddamned shower and a mind-wipe. That he'd actually been with that—

"Fuck!" he swore, smacking the steering wheel.

"You have no idea."

Chase jumped at the disembodied voice beside him, and he swerved, swearing again as he almost hit a tree. "Felix?"

The warlock grinned as he materialized in the passenger seat. "In the flesh," he said, plucking his collar, "and I'd like to keep it that way. My car's by the trailhead off Summit. Do me a solid and follow me back to town?"

Chase glanced at him and then back at the road. "What the hell were you doing at the compound?"

A smug grin lit up his face. "Well, I don't usually kiss and tell, but if you must know—"

"Dude. I don't care who you were hooking up with, why are you in my truck?"

"Oh, yeah, that. Long story short, I called in sick and was in the guest cabin next to yours. I couldn't help but overhear a certain bitchy blonde lose her shit about an hour ago."

Chase grunted. "Crystal said she smelled Jena there and thinks that I've been acting like she's my mate."

"You know, I leave you two alone for one day…" Felix tsked. "Tell me you sealed the deal."

"Not even close," Chase snorted, "but she didn't hex me, so that's progress."

"More than you might think," Felix murmured. "This is bad. I heard Crystal make a call, I've no idea who she spoke to, but not long after, Malcom showed up, and they got into it."

Chase turned onto the main road. "Into it like how?"

"Into it like a bunch of yelling—from her, not him. My God, she's a harpy. Anyway, she was screeching about how this wasn't what they'd talked about, and then it sounded like he slapped her," Felix said with no small amount of glee. He cleared his throat. "Don't get me wrong, I don't condone violence, but I can definitely understand the urge, and if anyone deserves to be slapped, it's her."

Chase grunted, on the same page. Crystal had the uncanny ability to bring the worst out in people. Felix took a breath and kept going.

"CliffsNotes, Crystal started crying, Malcom made some rather disparaging comments about her wiles, there was something in there I didn't catch about your brother, and then Jena's name was mentioned. Malcom said he would take care of it and left. If he suspects…"

Double fuck.

"He said he's watching me." Chase pulled his truck into the trailhead beside Felix's car. "You need to tell Jena what you heard. She wasn't there today, and if she's not there tomorrow—"

"I'll take care of it, but you need to do your part. I'm assuming all of this is related to the big nuptial announcement in the paper? It's all anyone at the compound could talk about. No one knows what to believe, but it's not true," he raised his brow, "is it?"

Christ, it was in the paper? "No. It's a bunch of bullshit

my father and your boss cooked up, and I've got no fucking clue how to get clear of it."

"Mmm. Something tells me they're not the only ones, and I'd recommend you play along until we can figure a way out of this mess. You didn't confirm anything about Jena did you?"

"What? No. I told Crystal she was delusional."

"Okay, so fingers crossed we have some wiggle room, but Malcom isn't someone I want to tangle with, and until I can convince Jena to join the coven, she's a sitting duck. They won't get involved unless they have a claim on her."

Chase blew out his cheeks. "My father wants me to give Crystal a ring. He said I have until Sunday to do it." He scowled. "My mother wants a November wedding."

"I'd speed up the ring thing if I were you. You need to sell that you're all in, and if you're going through the motions, it'll buy us time."

"After what I just said to Crystal? I doubt it."

Felix shrugged. "Tell her you thought about it, and that she was right. She's the type that'll lap it up, especially if you grovel. Buy her flowers or whatever men do to suck up when they're in the doghouse." His fingers flew to his lips. "Shit. Sorry was that a—"

"No, you're good," Chase muttered, chewing his lip.

"Make sure you are, too," Felix said as he got out of the truck. "The other thing I heard plenty of was speculation on your mental state."

Chase swore. Damn it. He knew that Crystal's remark at the cantina was going to start shit, and sucking up to her was the second to last thing he wanted to do.

But first on the list was getting Jena killed. Fucking A. He pulled onto the road behind Felix, following him back to town. Chase sighed, palming the brim of his cap. Playing along with this wedding bullshit was gonna be physically fucking painful, and if Felix couldn't convince Jena it was all a lie—cold sweat spiked over Chase's body. No. She'd listen. She had to. He didn't even want to consider the alternative.

Because Felix was right. There wasn't any other way to keep Jena safe until they figured a way out of this mess.

Motherfucker. Looked like tomorrow he was going to Fynbender's to pick out a goddamned ring.

JENA SWORE, struggling to get the heavy, bagged robe through the dry cleaner's door. This day just kept getting frickin' better and better, and she wasn't running on enough sleep to deal with it. She'd been up half the night with Aggie; her cough hadn't improved, and the stubborn witch refused to see a doctor. If it didn't start clearing by tomorrow, Jena was hog-tying her and hauling her bony ass in. She blew a hank of hair from her eyes and glared at Geri Diaz behind the counter. Geri blinked back at her, perfectly content to watch her struggle.

"You got it?" Geri drawled, once the door thumped behind Jena and she was halfway across the tiled entryway. The middle-aged woman wasn't actively anti-Jena, but she sure as hell had never lifted a finger to help her—or anyone else for that matter.

"Yeah, thanks," Jena said dryly, plopping the awkward load across the counter. Satin-lined, embroidered velvet was no joke. "I need this cleaned, and I don't know if you can do anything with this." She set her bagged-up cardigan on top of it. Despite washing it twice at the laundromat this morning, it still reeked of lying asshole.

Geri untied the knot, then pulled back like a snake was inside. "Whoo! What did you do, walk in on them?"

"Something like that," Jena gritted out.

Geri clucked her tongue and muttered something in Spanish. "Honestly, mating pheromones aren't meant to come out. The stuff bonds into the fibers, though the scent will fade," she raised a brow and glanced at Jena, "in a year or two."

Damn it. "So, it's ruined."

"Not necessarily..." The laundress sucked her teeth. "What a shame. It's hard to get this shade of sidhe-blue to take, especially with wool. Hang it up outside, and let it air out for a while, but I wouldn't walk around with it on, unless you want some serious problems."

"Got enough of those, thanks." Jena frowned.

Geri snorted, retying the bag and setting it aside. "This another one of those robes?"

"Yeah."

Geri pulled a pencil stub from behind her ear, wrote it up, and handed Jena a ticket stub. "Should be ready by next week."

"Next week?" Crap, the order was supposed to go out by Friday.

"Next week." Geri's thin lips tightened. "Right now I'm slammed with everyone's cross quarter day garb for the Samhain festival."

"Cross quarter day garb?" Jena sighed as the woman's brow knit. "I've never been. Aggie isn't a fan."

"Well, there's a surprise." Geri waved a hand at the racks behind her. "All of that's ceremonial robes, tuxes, and gowns that could put a quinceañera to shame. About five or six years ago, they decided to make it a big to-do. There's a huge carnival down at the waterfront, town hall opens up, there's a parade, and then huge party on the lawn. Hopefully that tropical depression rolling in rolls out just as quick. You have any idea what a pain grass stains on soggy silk tulle are to deal with?"

"Nope."

Geri shot her a look. "I'll take wet velvet any day. That's heavy as hell, but at least it doesn't shred."

"Then I guess next week it is," Jena muttered, already dreading writing that email. To say the man who'd bought the robe had been exacting was a serious understatement, but not having it cleaned wasn't an option. The must from Aggie's ruined herbs had made its way into storage and everything was coated with the funk.

Jena grabbed the bag with her cardigan and waved goodbye to Geri. It was time to meet Felix for coffee, which promised to be weird. Jena headed down the sidewalk toward town hall, chewing her lip. She'd expected him to be all fired up about his weekend exploits, but his texts this morning had been subdued. Something was going on. If whoever he'd hooked up with had turned out to be an asshole, she'd kill them. Felix deserved to be happy.

And damn it, so did she.

Which begged the question, why was she still in town again? Aggie. She was here for—

Chase Montgomery.

Jena froze as she saw him leaving the municipal building, then ducked behind a tree. She closed her eyes, swearing at herself. There's no way he hadn't seen her. Christ, how old was she? Screw this. She stepped back onto the sidewalk—

And he walked past her without a word, clenching a document tube in one hand and tugging his stupid hat brim lower with the other.

Jena's jaw dropped. *Are you fucking kidding me?* That sack of shit! She hadn't actually wanted to talk to him, but how the hell could he walk right past her without even one goddamned—Her fingertips tingled, a hex begging—*begging* —to roll off her tongue.

That lying son of a bitch.

Tears stung her eyes, and she dashed them away. He didn't fucking deserve them. She whipped her sweater into the first garbage can she passed, just wanting to be done with him and the rest of this shitty town—

"Oh, honey…what's wrong?"

She looked up to see Felix hurrying over in a salmon blazer and navy slacks. His button-down shirt had hotdogs all over it. Jena barked out a half-sob, half-laugh, and he put his arm around her.

"That sounds like you need a caramel latte with an extra shot and a double bacon, egg, and cheese with tomato and avocado on a croissant—stat."

Jena nodded. Yup. Time to eat her feelings. She wasn't going to argue, even if it was proving her stupid ex right. Felix handed her a magenta pocket square with an embroidered fish on it—because of course he did—and let her sniffle in silence all the way to Cups. He got her settled at a corner table inside and put their order in.

"You want to talk about it?" he asked when he got back to the table with their drinks. She shook her head, and he quirked a brow. "Jena—"

"What? There is no it." And it was true, damn it. Chase was officially dead to her. She forced a smile. "I want to hear about your weekend."

"Don't be so sure about that," he said, glancing at Kelsey Montgomery coming over with their order. Eastside—not west. She still looked the same, a smattering of freckles over her pug nose, braids the shade of cherry-cola, and overalls. Maybe she'd gotten a little heavier, but Christ, this town had to be in some weird time warp. Jena crossed her fingers that whatever wayback machine they had would do its magic on her so she could fit back into her favorite pair of jeans.

"Hey, Felix. Jena." She nodded at him as she set the tray between them and smiled at Jena. "I'm glad to see you back in town."

Well, that was one person. Jena forced a smile in return. Kelsey was flighty, but okay. They'd been study partners for a while, and her and the rest of the Eastside Montgomerys had always been cordial. Probably because they were wired to like anything the Westside Montgomerys hated. That wasn't to say Kelsey's pack had stuck up for Jena when she was being hazed, but that had something to do with were politics. Jena hadn't taken it personally. It was just one more of the fucked up things about this town everyone treated as normal.

"Thanks. I wish I could say it was good to be here."

Kelsey laughed, glancing around the café. "Don't I know that feeling. Give it time. It was weird when I started working in town, too. I mean, it's still weird, but things will settle down, and you're always welcome on the other side of the tracks. In fact, we'd love it if you came to this Saturday's pig roast. It's a Samhain tradition. Super low key and informal. My mom always sets out a spread so the pack can nosh away their hangovers."

"Thanks...I'll think about it," Jena said, surprised at the offer.

"You too, Felix. It'll be fun." Kelsey smiled at them again and went back to the kitchen.

Jena watched her go. "Well, that was unexpected."

Felix shrugged. "Things have changed since you've been gone. The Eastside pack isn't as reclusive as it used to be. They found some kind of mineral deposit in their territory, and they're not Havers's red-headed stepchildren anymore." He tugged one of his flaming curls and grinned. "I'm pretty sure they could give the Westside a run for their money if they wanted to."

"Huh." Jena bit into her sandwich, and it was pure bliss. "God, this is good."

"I'm glad, but at risk of ruining your appetite, we need to talk." He glanced around the café then drew a glyph on the tabletop.

Jena cocked a brow at the cone of silence he'd invoked. "Was the sex that outrageous?"

"Yes, but that's not what I want to talk to you about," he said, dead serious. "You need to know that this Chambers-Montgomery wedding is a total lie."

Jena started choking. "What?" she asked when she could breathe again.

"Look, I'm not clear on all the details, but Chase's father is forcing him into it, and while I was at the compound, I overheard Crystal and Malcom fighting. Your name came up."

"*My* name?" Jena squeaked.

Felix nodded, stirring granola into his yogurt. "Apparently your scent was all over Chase's cabin, and Crystal lost her shit."

"Oh, for the love of—you're right, this is ruining my appetite." Jena tossed her sandwich down. "He brought me home after I sprained my ankle, and you deserted me. There's nothing between the two of us, and there's not going to be. He's as much of a lying asshole now as he was in high school, and I don't want a damned thing to do with him."

Felix cocked a brow, deadpan, sucking yogurt off his spoon, and she squirmed.

"Okay. Let's go with that for now," he said. "Unfortunately, I don't think Malcom is on board, and I very clearly heard him say he'd 'take care of it,' and by 'it,' I'm almost positive he meant you."

Jena felt the blood leave her face. "He threatened me?"

"That's how I took it, and so did Chase when I hitched a ride from him back to my car."

"But you don't know for sure."

"No, but I think you need to take this seriously, Jena." Felix sighed, then jerked his chin at a paper someone had left at the next table with the pending nuptials splashed all over the front page. "Chase is going to play along with all that, and you need to join the coven."

She slumped back in her seat. "I don't believe it."

"Which part?"

"All of it." She crossed her arms over her chest. "This is just some bullshit story to fuck with me like he did senior year, and I'm not falling for it."

"Do you honestly believe Malcom would play along with something like that?"

"No, but…" Jena's brow furrowed. "You have no proof he was actually talking about me. There's a twist in this. There has to be. Why would Malcom give a shit about me? Chase Montgomery doesn't and never has."

Felix pursed his lips as he scooped more yogurt from the bowl. "That scar under your chin would say otherwise."

Her fingers went to it before she could stop herself. She scowled and shoved them back onto to her lap. "No, he didn't want to get in trouble—ugh, God, whatever. Maybe he just likes licking me."

"Oh, I'm sure he does." Felix chuckled at her glower. "He didn't have to close up that wound, and I was there. I saw how bad it was, Jena. He probably saved your life."

"Yeah, so he could keep tormenting me," she muttered.

…*"You feel it, too. I know you do. You're mine…"*

Ugh. She wasn't, damn it, and the only thing she felt was —Jena grabbed her sandwich and shoved a huge bite into her mouth. Never mind what she felt. Chase was a liar, and Malcom's threat or no, she wasn't joining the stupid coven.

CHASE GRITTED his teeth as he stormed down the street, people giving him a wide berth. Goddamn it! The look on Jena's face as he'd walked past her…a fist had settled in his chest, and it wasn't letting up. He knew he had to act like he was keeping his distance, but Jesus fucking Christ, why did it have to be so damned hard? Chase's wolf was snarling at him for hurting her again, and he wanted to kick his own goddamned ass.

What a perfect fucking mood to go shopping for a ring he didn't wanna buy.

He pushed through the door to Fynbender's, fighting the urge to smash something. God, the last time he'd been this damned pissed—

Chase blew out his cheeks. No. He wasn't gonna think about Jena leaving. She was his. When he'd gone to pull the permits this morning, he'd talked to Felix who said he was meeting Jena for coffee. He'd make it right. That's probably why Chase had run into her. He lifted his hat to swipe a hand over his brow. It was okay. It would be okay—

"Ah! Chase! I've been expecting you," Otis Fynbender said, coming out from the back.

Chase frowned. "So I've heard."

The spry, white-haired warlock laughed, opening a case. "I must say, Crystal's made your job easy, though they aren't anything I usually carry. I had to order them in on consignment from a shop in Galleon Falls. Here are the three she picked out. Two are good to go, but the third I'd have to size."

Chase sighed, crossing to the back case as Mr. Fynbender lifted out a square of black velvet. On it were three of the gaudiest engagement rings Chase had ever seen. Shit looked like costume jewelry.

"Are you kidding me?"

The old warlock pursed his lips. "No, I'm afraid not. She was very specific."

"Then she's going to be very disappointed." Unless his father was ponying up for that crap, there was no way Chase was shelling out for it. Jesus. One of them looked like a diamond daisy with spiky baguettes all around a central stone. "What else do you have?"

Mr. Fynbender's eyes sparkled as he waved a hand at the case to his left. Inside was a far more reasonable selection—

"What are those?" Chase asked, pointing to a set of rings off to one side.

"Ah, there they are. For some reason I keep losing track of that set…you have a good eye." Mr. Fynbender pulled them from the case and held them out. "This is an 1890s marquis cut, two carat, art deco engagement ring and wedding band."

Chase paused before he took them. "They're not silver, are they?" Man, the craftsmanship was top-notch.

"No, no. White gold, with a bit of rose in the filigree." Mr. Fynbender chuckled, handing them over. "Fair warning, it is one of the more expensive sets in the case. Naturally occurring blue diamonds with that color intensity aren't particularly common, nor is scrollwork that fine. I picked them up at an estate sale a few years back, and I'm surprised the set hasn't sold by now."

"It just has," Chase murmured, imagining it on Jena's hand. "Damn, it's perfect for her."

"Really? I-if you're sure…?" Mr. Fynbender stammered. "That I will have to size—"

"No." Chase said too quickly. "Ah. Can you do me a favor and hold onto it for me? I'll take….um, whichever one of those is cheaper," he said, pointing at two of the gaudier rings in the case. The difference between them and the set he'd chosen for Jena was night and day.

Mr. Fynbender pulled back, his shoulders straightening like he'd caught onto the ploy. "It's not any of my business, but—"

"No, it's not, and I'd appreciate it if it didn't become anyone else's either."

The warlock gave him a long look. "I hope you know what you're doing."

"Yeah." Chase blew out his cheeks. "That makes two of us."

Mr. Fynbender shook his head and muttered something about weres as he headed into the back. Chase pulled his wallet out and tapped his credit card on the counter, the day somehow rosier than it had been.

A half-hour later and thousands of dollars poorer, Chase opened the door to The Witchery and headed upstairs. The curtains were still drawn, and Jena was nowhere in sight, but Aggie was at the kitchen table working on a crossword. He heard her before he saw her, that cough of hers worse than it'd been yesterday. His brow furrowed as he set the document tube with the permits for the bathroom onto the table.

"How'd it go?" she asked, turning to cough into a handkerchief before he could ask her how she was.

"As expected." Even after he'd called in his favor, the building inspector, Gorman Howe, had bitched about Chase's plans, pointed out inconsistencies that weren't there, and then chewed him a new one just because he liked the taste of ass. "I have a temporary permit to start, and you can expect the approval to come through about six months, after the work's finished."

Aggie nodded with a humph, and reached up to tuck in a loose end of her paisley headscarf. "Manny always was a difficult son of a bitch. You didn't tell him it was for me, did you?"

Manny? Chase's brow furrowed. "I didn't use your name, but I had to give him the address."

"Well, I suppose that can't be helped…he's not coming here, though—" her eyes narrowed, "is he?"

"Ah…he has to inspect the work once it's completed and will probably stop by at some point unannounced to try to catch me cutting corners—which I won't do," Chase quickly said at her look.

"I should hope not."

"No, ma'am."

She sniffed, waving him away. "Well, then go on, get to it. That floor's not gonna rip itself up."

That it wasn't. Chase tipped his hat at her and headed down the hallway. His footsteps slowed as he passed by a cracked door, and Jena's scent washed over him. Damn. That had to be her bedroom.

A peek wouldn't hurt, right? Aggie had said he could look around. He'd stay in the hall and just poke his head in. He glanced back the way he'd come, his ears straining to hear if she'd gotten up, then pushed the door open, wincing at the subtle squeak of its hinges.

Jena's room was smaller than Aggie's but had the same layout, less an adjoining bathroom. Some idiot had tacked up sheetrock over the paneled walls he was positive were behind it. Two sets of inset windows faced the street with stained-glass borders like the ones in the kitchen, but didn't have the plastic wrap over them.

Unfortunately, the nasty crap made a difference. It was definitely chilly in there, which was probably why the sleigh bed was heaped with a tumble of quilts like Jena had just rolled out of them. He grinned, every last one some shade of blue. Those, her sweater, toe polish...he'd known that ring was perfect. Goddamn, he couldn't wait to give it to her.

The rest of the room was incongruously neat, just like his cabin. His grin got bigger, imagining their house, what it would be like living together...

"Wrong bedroom," Aggie wheezed at his elbow.

Chase jumped. Shit. "Ah, yeah. Sorry. The door was cracked, and the windows in here aren't covered. I was looking at the stained-glass insets."

Her brow cocked. "Sure you were."

"I was." His throat bobbed, and he wet his lips. "This building is amazing. I—thank you for giving me the opportunity to work on it. I—I've got a thing for antique architecture."

Her azure eyes narrowed at him again. "Is that so…"

"Yes, ma'am."

She clucked her tongue and pointed to a set of crappy composite double doors built out from the side of the hall. "Tell you what. Somewhere up on the third floor there's a dehydrator I need brought down to the kitchen. Should be new, in the box. It was heavy as hell, so it won't be too far in, but feel free to take a spin around while you're up there. I'd bring a flashlight. The electrical is wonky."

"Um. Now?" he asked when she kept looking at him.

"Yes, now, you think I'm gonna last much longer?" She coughed as if to underscore her poor health.

"No, ma'am." He winced. "I mean—"

"I know what you meant, now go." She shooed him.

He beat feet to the double doors. They'd been built out like that box in the living room. He pulled one side open, cringing at the way it dragged against the linoleum. Dark treaded steps curved out from the wall and headed up.

He clicked the flashlight from his belt on. Christ, were those walnut risers? The treads were a lighter wood, but they were so beat to shit he couldn't make out enough of the grain enough to identify it. He put a hand to the carved banister, thick with dust, his boot-falls echoing as he went up.

He came out at a railed landing, and then there was another step into what had to have been a ballroom. The ceiling was peeling and sagging in places, but at one point it'd been hand painted, and there were still places where the gilt shone. The room ran the length of the building, with long, floor-to-ceiling windows every few feet along the entire southern exposure.

Chase picked his way through the piles of crap and stacks of boxes. Holy shit, was that…He moved a pile of mouldering cardboard aside, cursing as the bottom fell out along with a tumble of books. He waved at the air, coughing, and piled them to one side.

Damn.

A deco-tiled fireplace with a lattice-worked, bronze surround as wide as his arm was long belled out above a cast iron coal bin. What a freaking find. He stared at for way longer than a normal person would, his brain pinging through all the steps to restore it before he moved on. More inlaid flooring, chandeliers like the one down in the shop. Jesus. What this must've looked like...

An arched, double doorway led to a hallway with two more empty rooms off it. A study and a morning room, if he had to guess by the built in bookcases in the first and the latter's exposure. Another door opened up to a stairway, then a small roof garden with a beleaguered leaded glass greenhouse, its copper struts blue green with patina. Christ, that had to weigh a ton.

He frowned, and it was probably why the ceiling below was sagging. The way the roof squishing under his weight stopped him before he could peek inside. Someone had laid down boards leading to it, but he didn't trust them. This was a disaster waiting to happen. If they got enough heavy snow, the entire thing would cave in. Damn it. That needed to be addressed sooner than not.

He headed back downstairs with the dehydrator in tow and set it on the kitchen table beside Aggie.

"Well, what'd you think?" she asked, turning away to cough.

"That your roof's about to cave in, and if that happens, it's gonna be a bitch to come back from." If they could at all.

Aggie pursed her lips, snapping up her crossword. "I'm assuming fixing it's going to cost more than twenty grand."

Chase barked out a laugh. "Yeah." He knocked his knuckles against the table. "Bare minimum, that greenhouse needs to come down before winter. The weight from all that leaded glass isn't doing you any favors."

Her eyes flicked to his. "Jena's not going to like that."

"She'll like it less if it ends up in her bedroom, and if it smashes, it's done for. We take it apart now, we can reassemble it after the repairs are complete. If I put up some scaffolding in the main room, we can probably buy another year. As is, I don't think the roof will last this one." He paused at the look on Aggie's face. "Don't worry about the money. We'll figure it out. One thing at a time, and I've heard that bathroom floor isn't gonna pull itself up."

She gave him a measuring look. "Nope. That it's not. Better hop to it."

He tipped his hat. "Yes, ma'am."

Chapter Ten

JENA CROUCHED over the steering wheel of her civic, struggling to see the road through the deluge of rain coming down. Some tropical depression bullshit—ugh! Why couldn't it have come through three days ago, so she'd never have gone with Felix on that stupid hike? She didn't care what he said. The papers this morning—every morning—her damned social media feeds, all of it was screaming about the event of the fricking century.

Chase was marrying Crystal.

Chase was marrying Crystal, and Jena had made out with him.

Worse, she'd made out with him and liked it.

A lot.

Damn it! Stupid, stupid, stupid…she smacked the steering wheel, tears pricking her eyes. How was she letting herself get pulled into this again? He was such a fucking liar. She wasn't his mate, and he was marrying—*marrying*—Crystal because of course he was. Why wouldn't he be? Granted, she was a shitty person, but she was gorgeous and her family was loaded. Wasn't that the exact same make and model of vapid bitch Jena's ex had dumped her for?

God, she was so dumb. You'd think after everything that'd happened the first time Chase had kissed her, she would've learned. But nooo. Screw his bullshit apology. It *had* been a dare to make out with her at that party. Hell, she'd bet he'd been the one egging on his stupid pack and all Crystal's bitchy friends to laugh Jena out of town. This was just more of the same. He probably got off on making her look like an idiot. A big, fat, gullible idiot.

Mission accomplished.

And now her roof was caving in. That was not the news she needed yesterday after spending the afternoon doing market research at the library.

As much as she hated to admit it, maybe there was something to what Aggie had said about the node repelling practitioners. Since Jena had been gone, the population of witches in the area had taken a nose dive, and the dozen covens she'd remembered had plummeted to a grand total of three with a smattering of actively practicing witches—none of which were in Fayet. No wonder that other couple had sold the Spell Shop and business at The Witchery sucked.

It didn't make sense. As powerful as it was, that node should be drawing practitioners to the area like a magnet, not chasing them away in droves. A little voice whispered that was because the magic was turning wild without a guardian, and she squashed it. The node might be ill-tempered, and maybe a little bloated, but it definitely wasn't wild. All the wards on it were holding, and if it was that important, it could pick someone else.

No. There had to be another reason practitioners were leaving.

Jena dashed a hand over her eyes, swearing. God, it was hard enough to see, and it was all Chase's goddamned fault she was out in this mess. If his stupid mother hadn't gotten her fired, she never would've applied for that job.

God, what a jackass.

Unfortunately, she wasn't just referring to Chase. The lone position in Fayet willing to pay enough to justify the travel had wanted to interview right away—which in retrospect, should've been a red flag—but she was desperate. She was not, however, desperate enough to sign onto a firm that she was pretty sure was laundering money.

What a waste of fricking time. That was four hours of her life and a half tank of gas she'd never get back for the second time that week. She was done with Fayet. Done! She smacked the steering wheel again, then swerved to miss a pothole. Christ, why was this so hard?

Bright side Jena, find the bright side...

Bright side, bright side...she'd just passed mile marker fifty-eight and hadn't plummeted to her doom.

Okay..good start, now maybe a little brighter?

Aggie was getting her bathroom. In fact, workmen should be there now. Hopefully they could stick to the budget they'd quoted, and she could pay for them to shore up the roof with unicorns and fairy dust. Both of which she was more likely to stumble upon than enough cash.

Jena sighed. A new roof. Damn it. "Can't wait for how much that's gonna cost," she muttered. Was selling your eggs still a thing? She had to have a couple decent ones left. If not, technically she was pretty sure you could live with only one kidney. Jena bit back a sob as the sign for Havers-by-the-Sea came into view. Twelve more miles. God, she just wanted to be home—

Home.

The unexpected emotion that came with the word made her pull back from the wheel. Those drafty rooms. The soggy floor. Aggie and Felix. That was home. Where she'd grown up. How was she going to sell the shop?

She couldn't. But how the hell was she going to pay to fix it?

Didn't matter, she had to. As much as it made sense on paper, it would be like cleaving off a part of herself to let it go. And when Aggie died, it would be all she had left of her. Jena had tried walking away once—had walked away for ten years

—and despite the fact that she hated certain parts of it, coming back to Havers was like being able to breathe again.

Havers-by-the-Sea was home.

Even with Chase fricking Montgomery, a.k.a. lying-sack-of-shit living there, and a needy node she was not signing up to babysit.

Goddamn it.

Twenty minutes later, she parked halfway down the block because for whatever reason, his big ass truck was in her spot. Not a freaking vehicle in sight from the contractor she'd hired —if that prick was screwing with her again and had sent them away...

She was gonna kill him.

Jena ripped up the parking brake and took a deep breath, her fingers tingling. Fuck Chase Montgomery and everyone else in this goddamned town—

No. I will not hex, I will not hex...

Jena killed the engine and sprinted for the shop, the rain hitting her like it hated her, too. She stomped over the damned spray-painted sidewalk, now declaring WITCH, and tore the door open. Jackass should've taken that as warning because she was gonna hex him with a perpetually limp dick—

Ugh! No. Bad Jena... She stood dripping in the entry way— not hyperventilating—for a hot minute trying to talk herself off that ledge before muttering to herself and slogging up the stairs. Christ, she'd taken drier showers.

Voices came from the kitchen. Not hammering, saws, or whatever construction sounds that should be happening on the opposite side of the apartment. Jena gritted her teeth and stormed into the other room. Whoever this asshole thought he was, he had another thing coming.

"You!"

Chase was sitting at her goddamned kitchen table having a cup of tea with Aggie like he had a right to be there. His head jerked up at Jena's exclamation, and the stupid smile slid off his face, his throat bobbing as he stared at her. A wave of that fucking musk hit her square, and she growled.

"So, how'd it go?" Aggie asked, cheerier than she'd been in days.

"What the fuck is he doing here?"

"Showing me tile samples," she said, waving a hand over the books spread out between them, then covering her mouth as she coughed.

The sound didn't improve Jena's mood. Damn it. She should've bailed on the interview and taken Aggie to the hospital. She'd already been halfway frickin' there driving out to Fayet. Tomorrow they were going. No more excuses.

"I like these little hexagons with the navy squares," Aggie said, pointing to a sample.

Jena pulled up short. "Tile samples?"

"Mmm, the lead time can run out six weeks or more on some of these, and Chase wants to have it on order ASAP." She tapped one of the pages. "See? This one right here. Pretty good match, don't you think?"

Jena attempted to breathe through the wave of fury incinerating the last thread of her patience. "You? You're the historical renovation expert? That's what the 'see you tomorrow' the other day was about?"

He just stared at her, his jaw clenched and his chest rising and falling like he'd run a marathon. The cloud of musk coming from him thickened.

"He is, and he's absolutely brilliant. Finished pulling up that floor today. You know they set those old pipes in mud? Not real mud, but that's what they call it. One of them had a crack as long as my finger and was pissing beneath the floor. We got water damage running behind the paneling in the room below right down to the basement. It's no wonder all those herbs went moldy. Sump pump failed and there was a quarter inch of standing water. Chase's already installed a new one for us and has it airing out."

Aggie beamed at him, and the top of Jena's head about blew off.

"I don't want him here," she seethed.

"And I don't want you fucking up the hardwood, but there you are, standing in a puddle," Aggie said, licking her finger to turn a page.

"I—" Jena glanced down. The floor was drenched, her white button-down totally transparent, and her bra wasn't leaving anything to the imagination. No wonder he was staring, she was giving the jerk an eyeful and then some. She turned on her heel, swearing. "Goddamn it! Get out of my fucking house!"

HOLY SHIT, *holy shit, holy shit…* Chase stared at the space Jena had just left, his cock throbbing and his wolf going apeshit. Aggie touched his arm, and he jumped.

"Guess she's read the paper."

His throat bobbed. "Um…yeah."

"It true?" He shook his head, and Aggie grunted like she'd suspected as much. "Then don't you dare leave."

"No, ma'am," he murmured, licking his lips. Leave? He couldn't have moved if he'd wanted to. Goddamn, Jena was gorgeous when she was all fired up, and with her clothes plastered to her like that… He swallowed, trying to rein in his wolf—

Want, want, want…

Chase bit back a keening howl, about to totally lose his shit.

Aggie smirked around her handkerchief as she coughed. "Well, I suspect that answers that question."

He glanced over at her. "Pardon?" his voice cracked.

"Don't play dumb with me. I saw you haul her ass in the other day, and you were staring into her bedroom like you'd found El Dorado." She wheezed, waving a hand in front of her face. "You know how hard it is to get pheromones out of the drapes?"

That wasn't the only thing that was hard.

Aggie chuckled, and it dribbled into another cough as she grabbed her cane and slowly stood. "I'm gonna go lie down. Don't let her bully you into leaving before you're ready to, and keep it down once you convince her to let you stay. I don't need to be privy to a porno."

He felt his face heat, not sure what to say as she toddled out. But she was right, he wasn't leaving. Not without Jena listening to him. He'd thought about shit a lot since he'd talked with Felix, and it was time to lay all his cards on the table. She needed to know why he'd done what he'd done all those years ago. Maybe then she'd forgive him and—

Jena stormed back into the room, her hair in a messy bun, wearing a baggy tee shirt—

And some asshole's boxers.

Chase's lip curled, and he was across the room, caging her against the refrigerator. "Who the fuck do those belong to?" he growled.

She looked at him wide-eyed. "What?"

"These," he gritted out, fisting the fabric. "Whose are they?

"I—" She slapped his hand, and he growled again, his fist tightening. Jena glowered back at him. "You don't get to ask me that, and don't you have a wedding to plan?"

"The fuck I don't, and I already told you, you're my mate. I'm not marrying Crystal. Now whose are they?!"

"The papers say otherwise." Her eyes narrowed, and a muscle in her jaw jumped. "And they're my ex's. He was a liar, too."

"I'm not lying," Chase's voice rumbled dangerously low, fighting not to shift at the thought of another man touching her, their scent on her—"Take them off."

"What?" She laughed. "No."

"Take them off," he growled, his wolf front and center, "before I take them off for you, then paddle your bare ass for disobeying."

Her pupils blew out, and she squirmed, the scent of her arousal thick in his nose. "You wouldn't."

He leaned closer, inhaling. "I would, and I think you want me to," he murmured in her ear. "In fact, I think you put those on just to piss me off. Did you want to punish me, baby? To make me jealous? It worked."

She bit her lip and shook her head, her thighs squeezing together. "O-of course not. Why would I—" She swallowed raggedly. "You're with Crystal—"

"Say her name again," he growled, encircling Jena's throat and gently pressing his thumb against her windpipe in warning. "I'd rather slit my own goddamned wrists than touch that toxic bitch."

Jena wet her lips, her breath stuttered as she squirmed. "Oh please, everyone knows—"

"Everyone's fucking wrong, and that's on me, but playing along with that shit in the papers—goddamn it, Jena. Everything I've ever done was to keep you safe. If my pack had any idea that you're my mate—what you mean to me— they would've put you down first and asked questions later. I couldn't—I can't—let that happen, and I can't let you go. Not again. You're mine."

"I—no." She stubbornly raised her chin, her eyes unsure as her throat shifting against his palm. "I'm not."

Chase chuckled. Christ she was adorable. "You keep defying me, and you're the one who's gonna get punished... or is that what you want?"

"I—No," she protested weakly, her body screaming yes as it melted against his.

"What a little, lying brat." He ran his nose along the shell of her ear, and she whimpered. "You want me to spank that ass, Jena? You need me to put you in your place?"

Her breath hitched, nipples pearling beneath her tee. She wet her lips. "I d-don't know what you're talking about."

Chase chuckled, tipping up her chin. "Oh baby, we both know exactly what I'm talking about." His nose grazed hers, her stuttered breath sweet against his stubble. "Admit it. You're mine, and you're dying to be my good girl. Show me you want it as bad as I do." He paused, his lips hovering above hers—

"God, I hate you." she whispered, closing the distance between them, her lips on his, ravenous.

She might, but her body didn't. Chase pulled her close. He deepened the kiss, groaning into her mouth as she ran her hands up his chest to fist his shirt. His thigh slid between hers, and she ground her heated core ground against him, her arousal thick in his nose.

"You gonna behave?" he murmured.

Her gaze drifted to his lips, and she gave the barest of nods.

Chase wet them. "Then take off those fucking boxers and bend over the counter."

Jena hesitated for a breath, and then they pooled around her ankles. She stepped out of that fucker's underpants and went to the kitchen island, glancing at him over her shoulder as she assumed the position. "Don't make me regret this."

"No. No regrets, baby," he rumbled, stepping behind her and kicking her feet wider apart. "Mmm. I like it when you behave. Now raise your t-shirt and bend forward, cheek on the counter."

She slowly complied, pressing the side of her face to the

butcher block. Chase's eyes hooded as he took in the round globes of her ass and white cotton panties. Jesus. He smoothed a hand over them and stepped close to her thigh so she could feel how hard she was making him.

"You get two. One for baiting me and another for lying." He spread his fingers over the small of her back, keeping her still. Damn, she was fine. "You ready, baby?"

"I…" Her eyes squeezed shut. "Yes?"

"Yes, sir," he corrected.

She tried to jerk up off the counter. "I'm not calling you—"

His other hand came down, and she yelped as it connected, his dick jumping with her gasp. He bit his lip at the ripple of her flesh and the pink handprint blooming over her skin, rubbing it to smooth away the sting. "What was that?"

"Yes, sir," she meeped.

He dipped his hand to brush his knuckles over the sodden scrap of fabric between her legs. Her hips tipped up, pressing back for more. "You want me to touch you, Jena?"

"Y-yes…"

"Mmm." He lightly traced a finger down her cloth-covered slit, his cock throbbing. "Good girl, getting so wet for me. You like being spanked?"

"M-maybe—"

His hand cracked down again, and she cried out, her eyes wide.

"Yes, I do! I do!"

"What about this?" He slipped a finger beneath the fabric, running it through her folds. She groaned. Jesus fuck, she was soaked. "You like that?"

"Yes." She groaned, turning her forehead to the counter and rocking to ride his finger as he slipped it inside.

He closed his eyes and wet his lips, his breathing ragged. "Damn, Jena. I wanna taste you so bad. You gonna let me?"

She stilled. "I—"

Chase held his breath waiting for her to answer.

"This isn't a dare, right?"

"No, baby." He dropped to his knees and kissed the backs of her thighs, the crease below her ass... "This is me wanting you to come apart on my tongue," he murmured, sliding his hands up her legs and parting her cheeks, her panties bunching into her crack. Damn, that was pretty. A thong. He needed to see her in a thong. Chase breathed her in, the scent of her arousal making his cock throb. Goddamn—

"Oh God, yes, stop teasing me, and just do it."

Wasn't exactly a ringing endorsement, but—she made an impatient huff, and he grinned, spinning his hat around and buried his nose in the wet spot, inhaling. She rose up on her tiptoes with a little strangled noise that made his wolf want to howl. Christ, she smelled so damned sweet...he tore the side seam of her panties, and they fluttered to the floor.

"Hey!" She gasped, and he slapped her ass again.

"Quiet. I'll buy you a new pair." Something lacy. A rumble ran through his chest as he spread her cheeks again and took in her swollen lips. "Mmm. So fucking pretty." He parted them with his thumbs. Her tight little hole dripped cream, and he leaned forward, lapping it up.

Jena bucked back against him. "Oh God, yes..."

Never mind God, this was fucking heaven. Her scent, the way she tasted...Chase groaned, his wolf howling with delight. He tongued her sweetness, sweeping around her clit and sucking, then going back for more. Adding one finger, then two...

She gripped the counter's edge as he feasted, his scruff dripping with her arousal. "I-I'm gonna—"

"Not until you say you're mine," he growled, slapping her ass before fixing his hat and standing to take off his belt.

Jena whimpered, her legs shaking. "Please, Chase..."

"Say it, Jena." He flicked her ass with the belt's leather tip, and she gasped. His jeans fell to his ankles. He stepped out of them, toeing off his boots and stroked a hand over his aching length. "Say it, or I'm gonna come all over your ass and let you suffer."

She glared over her shoulder at him. "You wouldn't."

He laughed. "You wanna find out? You're mine. Say it." Jena licked her lips and looked down at his dick as he pumped it. Fuck, he wanted to see her on her knees—"I'd suggest you hurry up." He grunted, the visual putting him way too close to the edge.

"Take your hat off first. I hate that thing."

His rhythm faltered. He didn't…he never…fuck. His wolf whined. She was his mate. He grimaced, then he slowly reached up and flipped it onto the counter. Jena turned and stared at him. He made himself meet her gaze.

She reached up and swept his hair aside. "Your eyes are blue?"

He frowned, looking away. Yeah, blue. Not like a wolf, like a fucking Husky.

Puppy dog eyes.

Damn it. This was a bad idea. He reached for his hat, and she stepped between him and it, weaving her arms around his neck.

"Stop it," she said, pulling him down to claim his lips. "Blue's my favorite color."

Jesus, this woman…Chase groaned into her mouth as he picked her up and set her on the counter. Her legs wrapped around his waist, her fingers curling around his dick. He went stone hard at her touch. Damnit, he wasn't gonna last. She guided him to her entrance, and he gritted his teeth, stopping at the brink, his wide crown pulsing against her folds.

"Not until you say it." He panted, eyes darting to meet hers again. "Tell me you're mine."

Her emerald gaze trapped his. "I'm yours—"

His hips thrust forward, her eyes widening as he speared into her, velvet heat choking his length. He groaned and she cried out, her nails digging into his shoulders, his wolf howling in triumph—

"—for now," she gasped.

Wait, what? "It doesn't work like that," he growled, stilling against her.

She ran her fingers through his hair, and kissed up under his jaw. "Shut up and fuck me, Chase."

"Oh, I'm gonna fuck you," he growled. "Here, on the couch, in your bed, and when you wake up in the morning, it's gonna be with my dick knotted inside you." He fisted her hair and pulled her head back as he pistoned between her thighs. "You're mine, Jena, and this is me claiming you. There is no now or later, it's forever."

"I-I thought you had to bite me for that," she panted, the cabinet below her banging as his kneecaps hit it.

"We got time." He grinned, and his canines elongated.

She went pale. "You're not biting me."

"Yeah, I am. Now shut up and take my dick."

"I hate you." Her rocking hips meeting his said otherwise, but who was he to judge? Women were confusing. Especially this woman.

"You lying to me again, baby?"

Jena gasped with his thrust. "No!"

"Good, hate me harder. It's hot as fuck."

She scowled, and he put those pouty lips of hers to better use, devouring her cries as he pounded into her. Goddamn, she felt so fucking good…

She broke away from him, panting. "Take off your shirt."

He ripped it over his head and then did the same to hers and the ratty sports bra she was wearing. Lace. He wanted to see her in lace. Black—no. Dark green, like her eyes. "How big are your tits?"

"What?"

"I wanna buy you something." He grabbed double handfuls, pressing her back so he could inhale between the mounds. "Fuck. I wanna buy you everything." He scooped her up off the counter and started down the hall.

He kicked the door to her room open and threw her onto the bed. Her vanity mirror faced it. Nice, he hadn't seen that from the doorway. She squealed as he pulled her to the edge of the mattress, positioning himself between her sticky thighs.

"You're gonna watch me eat this pussy, and you will come for me. I want you nice and wet for my knot."

"What are you—oh!" He buried his face against her mound. "Chase, I'm not on—oh God…" Her back arched, his fingers scissoring and curling against her slick walls. He sucked her clit into his mouth and flicked it with his tongue, working her hard.

Shit must've been the magic combo, because when she came apart, and it was so fucking beautiful, his chest ached.

"Mmm. That's my girl." He kissed her inner thigh, slowly bringing her back to earth. He got on the bed and settled her beside him, lightly running his fingers over her soft, soft skin.

"I'm not your girl," she murmured, then threw her hands over her face. "You're getting married, and I'm the other woman."

He slapped her pussy, and she cried out. "What did I tell you?"

"It was in the paper!"

"I don't care. It's a lie, Jena. The only woman I'm marrying is you." She opened her mouth like she was going to protest, and he kissed her until she softened against him again. His thumb slowly circled her clit, and she flinched, so damned sensitive. He batted her hands away. "Spread your legs."

"Chase, I can't—"

He kissed her. "Shhh…you can for me."

She reached up and hooked a lock of hair behind his ear, her brow furrowed. "Please don't do this to me. It's—this is just sex. Don't make me like you again. I can't—I'm not your mate—"

"Being with you is never going to be just anything. It's everything. You're everything, You *are* my mate, and I'm gonna prove it to you." He kissed her again softly, then with more passion, hands roaming over her sinful curves. He rolled her nipple between his fingers, pebbling it, then bent to take it in his mouth. She moaned, hooking her ankles behind his thighs as he covered her, sliding back into her body. Christ, she felt so good, so tight, so hot and wet.

And all his.

"You feel me, Jena? How we fit? That's where I belong. So damned deep inside you..." She whimpered as he bottomed out with a groan. Chase kissed her softly, his forearms framing her head, working his hips deep and slow against hers. "Shh...That's it, baby. Take my dick, what's yours. Good girl. Now touch yourself," he murmured, kissing along her jaw. "I wanna feel you come on my cock."

Her hand slipped between them. She rubbed herself in small circles, her breath speeding with his as he rocked in and out of her wetness. Tiny tremors caressed his dick, building, echoing the growing tingle at the base of his spine. He teased her lips with his. "That's it...come with me..."

"C-Chase!" Her inner walls clamped down, and he groaned, thrusting against them and giving into the sensation. He reared up, bottoming out inside her, the base of his cock expanding as he came, long ropes of desire spurting, light bursting across his vision—

Her legs tightened around his hips, nails digging into his triceps, her cunt milking every drop as she came again, and then a third time. "Oh God, oh God..."

He fell onto his forearms, panting, and kissed her, stupidly content. He'd heard knotting your mate gave her multiple orgasms, but hadn't been sure it was true.

"Mine," he said with a dumb smile, still fighting to catch

his breath and grinning. Damn. He was so fucking happy he could please her like that.

"Maybe." She glowered at him—kind of.

"You are," he said, his knot slowly abating. "And I'm not done proving it to you."

Chapter Eleven

JENA WOKE with a solid weight against her back, an arm over her waist, and a leg thrown over hers. Chase. A smile lit up her face, despite being sore in places she hadn't even known existed. God, he hadn't been kidding about claiming her. She'd never been so absolutely owned by a man, in or out of the bedroom.

And it'd been glorious.

It was also probably a one-time deal, despite what he'd said.

Jena shoved a biting sense of loss away. No. No regrets. She stretched, rolling onto her back, and he stirred, moving beside her, his hand sliding up to cup her breast as he nuzzled against her shoulder. His teeth lightly scored her skin, and she shivered. That they hadn't done, though him biting her didn't sound nearly as bad as it had yesterday.

"You want more of this?" he murmured, rubbing his hard cock against her leg.

"I do," she said, reaching down to stroke him, "but I also want to be able to walk today."

He laughed, raking a hand through his hair. "You sore, baby?"

"Very." God, his eyes were so beautiful; the clearest of azure blues. Why he felt like he had to hide them…

"Good." He brushed his fingers between her legs, and she

winced. "I want you to feel me when I'm not with you, so you know who you belong to."

Temporary or not, mission accomplished. She glanced at the clock. Crap. It was already nine. "Don't you have to go to the office or something?" Aggie would be up soon, if she wasn't already—Oh God, they'd left all their clothes strewn around the apartment...

He shrugged. "Usually, but I cleared my schedule to work here for the next week. Lucy knows how to get me if she needs me for anything...and I'd rather not leave you alone." He frowned.

"The chick that did the quote? I liked her," Jena said at his nod.

"My office manager. She's good people..." He chewed his lip. "I can have the floor reframed this afternoon, but I'm gonna have to remove the trim and strip the paneling from the walls. I was hoping to talk to you about a bunch of stuff first."

Great. "Like?" She scowled.

He kissed her. "You know that look on your face isn't nearly as off-putting as you think it is." She double scowled, and he grinned. "What I have to say will wait, you need to eat. What do you want from Cups?"

"You're feeding me?" That was new. Her ex had criticized every bite she put in her mouth. She ran a hand over her stomach, and Chase grabbed it, kissing her knuckles. He laced his fingers with hers and rolled on top of her, pinning her hands above her head.

His brow furrowed. "Is that a problem?"

"I don't exactly need the calories."

A growl rumbled through his chest, and her lady bits abruptly didn't seem so sore. God, he got her wet. "Stop. You're gorgeous. You think my dick would get this hard if I thought otherwise?" He slicked his fat crown against her entrance. "Christ Jena, all I wanna do is be inside you..."

She tipped her hips, welcoming it. Oh God, the way he made her stretch…

"That's it, baby. Take it all…good girl…" he murmured, pressing deep as he teased her lips with his. "My mate, so beautiful…touch your pussy for me. I need you to fall apart."

She did as she was told. Why did him being bossy turn her on so much? He worked her with slow, deep strokes, his lips at her jaw, her throat…his teeth gently raked over her skin, and she moaned.

"Jesus, I wanna bite you so damned bad…"

She arched her back, a weird part of her wanting him to, but—"Will it hurt?"

"Yeah, but it's supposed to feel good, too." He pulled back to look at her and ran his thumb over her bottom lip. "You want that, baby? You ready to be mine?"

"I don't—I don't know." She still couldn't believe this was really real. What if he took it back? If this was all some cruel trick—She sniffled, and he stilled his hips.

"Hey. I can wait. I've been waiting. When you left…" He shook his head. "I get why you did, but it almost broke me. Now that you're back, I'll do anything to keep you happy so you'll stay. If that's waiting, then that's what we do. I don't care how long it takes."

Her brow knit. "Aggie said something about you going feral."

Chase grunted. "I don't wanna talk about it. You're here now. With me. Just—just promise you won't leave. I don't think I can come back a second time."

She searched his eyes. God, they were so sincere, something deep inside him broken. It hurt to see that, to know it was because of her. "I promise…as long as you swear this is real."

"Oh, it's real, baby, and I swear I'm gonna spend the rest of my life proving it to you." He kissed her and began to move, sliding slow and deep, the exquisite stretch and drag of him tipping her into passion, her release triggering his, his knot expanding, increasing and extending her pleasure as he filled her with his in return.

"Does that happen every time?" she murmured, once she could form words again. God, she'd never come the way she did with him. She hadn't even known it was possible to have consecutive orgasms like that.

Chase wrapped her up in his arms. "I don't know. Weres only do that with their mates. It's a breeding thing."

Jena's eyes snapped open. Breeding? Shit. "I'm not on birth control."

"I know. I'd smell it if you were."

"But then why didn't you—"

"One, your cycle is at the wrong point, and two…" He ran his hand over her abdomen. "Weres aren't wired that way. You're my mate, Jena. The thought of knocking you up gets me hard as fuck."

She glared over her shoulder at him. "You're not knocking me up."

"Yeah, I am. Just like I'm gonna bite you and put a ring on your finger." He grazed his teeth over the crook of her neck, and she shivered, instinctually baring her throat for him. He nuzzled below her ear. "Mmm. I like it when you submit."

"Don't get used to it."

He chucked, kissing down her jugular. "I like it when you fight me, too. Makes this that much sweeter. Now tell me what you want to eat. I wanna take care of you, Jena. I need to. It makes me—my wolf—happy."

"Whatever you're having. I'm easy."

He laughed. "No, you're not, and I'm guessing whatever you drink isn't plain black coffee."

Her nose wrinkled. "Ew. No. Whatever they have that's caramel and hot with an extra shot of expresso."

"Done." Chase kissed her again and sat up. God, he was a beautiful man. "Let me grab my cell so I can get your number.

I'll text you whatever specials Cups has when I get there." He grabbed a pillow and held it in front of himself as he went to crack the door.

Jena smiled. Chases's ass definitely put that were's at the waterfall to shame. "I doubt Aggie's up yet, you're probably safe."

He tossed the pillow back on the bed before he slipped out —and was back in less time than she'd thought, beet red, with a stack of their folded clothes. "Not only was she up, she was waiting for me. She doesn't sound great."

Jena frowned as he stepped into his jeans. She'd deal with Aggie after he left. She was going to the hospital today, no arguments. "Tell me she didn't proposition you."

"No, but she had some pointers." Chase grinned, his dimples on display. He tossed over his phone and rattled off the code to unlock it. "Text yourself so you'll have my number."

Her brow quirked. "You want me to go into your phone?"

"Yeah, why wouldn't I? I don't have anything to hide."

She thumbed in the code and pulled up his texts, her heart expanding when she didn't see Crystal's name—wait. Her eyes narrowed. "Who's Monica?"

"Some girl I met last year on a job out of town." He pulled his shirt over his head and laughed. "Nothing happened, but I like your jealous face. Delete her."

"Can I?"

"Yeah. Just don't get rid of Lucy or Karena, no sorry, Katrina Simmons. She's my contact for architectural molding. I can't think of any other females who might be in there, other than my sister and my mom."

Jena bit her tongue, about to suggest they get the axe, too…she sighed. "You know this…us…it isn't gonna work."

"Yeah, it is." He sat down beside her and took her hands in his. "Look, I know there's a lot we need to figure out. Right now, it's important you understand this bullshit wedding is something my father and Chambers cooked up between them. Crystal's only in it for the status my position in the pack would bring her. I had zero say, and it's not happening…but there's about to be a major shitstorm, and I need you safe while I deal with it. Promise me you'll stay here, okay?"

She narrowed her eyes. "For how long?"

Chase scratched his jaw. "I dunno. A week?"

"What?" Jena laughed. That wasn't gonna happen. "No. If I could deal with Crystal in high school—"

"It's not just Crystal. Sunday night…" Chase chewed his lip. "He didn't come right out and say it, but I'm pretty sure Malcom threatened you."

She felt herself pale. "Felix told me he overheard something, but—what exactly did Malcom say?"

"Ah…something about my father liking your mom and suggesting I keep my distance unless I wanted you to end up the same way."

A wave of rage washed over Jena, and she scrambled out of bed, a sheet wrapped around her. "Aggie!" she cried, throwing her door open and shuffling down the hall to the kitchen.

The older woman glanced up from her paper. "Well, well, look at you all freshly fucked. You'd think it would've improved your attitude. You must be doing it wrong," she called over Jena's shoulder.

"Did Wallace Montgomery like my mom?" Jena asked, ignoring Chase's snort.

Aggie shrugged, coughing into her handkerchief. "Everyone liked your mom, well, except for his," she said nodding at Chase leaning in the doorway. She squinted up at the ceiling, thinking. "It's possible they dated back in the day…I'm not really sure. I didn't move into town until after your grandparents' accident. Rebecca had already graduated high school. I can't remember her and Wallace being particularly friendly. Quite the opposite, actually, but then Wallace is a flaming prick, so no surprise there."

Jena chewed her lip. "Chase said Malcom threatened me."

Aggie's eyes snapped to hers. "Did he now?"

Chase nodded.

The older woman pointed at the chair across from her. "You sit. You," she said to Chase, "go fetch that cup of tea you promised me."

"Yes, ma'am." He came over and kissed Jena's cheek before donning his hat. "I'll be back."

"The sidhe-blue eyes that man has…" Aggie sighed, ogling his butt as he left, then slapped the table. "I like him. He can stay."

"I'm so glad you approve," Jena said dryly.

Aggie sniffed. "You should be. Now—time for brass tacks. Malcom's not someone to fuck around with, and if he threatened you, we need to get the coven involved, and we need to do it now."

CHASE WALKED into Cups trying to swallow the stupid smile on his face and failing miserably. Greta Hornsby, the proprietress, glanced up as the bell above the door tinged behind him and did a double take. He flicked the rain from his hat and bellied up to the counter to snap a pic of the specials.

"Good morning." He grinned, texting it to Jena. "That a new bandana? It looks great."

She flushed and went to pat the scrap of purple fabric holding back her steel gray hair before catching herself and frowning at her floury hands. "Well, you're certainly in a good mood this morning," she said, wiping them on her apron. "It's nice to see those dimples. I must say, being engaged certainly agrees with you."

And his smile was gone.

He cleared his throat. "Large black coffee and whatever you have that's hot and caramel with an extra shot."

Her eyebrow rose. "You sure you don't mean a berry frap?"

"Positive."

She wet her lips as she turned to the coffee bar, her eyebrow rising higher. "Anything to eat with that?"

"My usual and…" he check his phone as it pinged. "A double bacon, egg, and cheese on a croissant with avocado and tomato…and a raisin scone with clotted cream. Huh… wouldn't have guessed that…oh, and I need a cup of Earl Grey tea with lavender foam. All of it to go."

Greta's lips had flattened when he looked up.

"There a problem?" he asked.

She tapped her book of meal tickets with her pen and slowly shook her head. "No…though it strikes me this isn't your fiancée's usual breakfast," she said, handing the ticket to Kelsey Montgomery—Eastside, not West—through the window to the kitchen.

Chase ran a hand over his jaw and laughed. Goddamn, this fucking town… "My fiancée, huh? That's weird, because as far as I know, I haven't proposed to anyone yet." A smile slid back over his face. But he was gonna.

Greta poured his coffee and handed it to him, her eyes flicking to a paper someone had left on one of the tables. "Well, then maybe you should take a gander at what everyone's been reading. Your order will be a couple of minutes." She sniffed and turned her back on him.

Damn it, what now?

Chase went over and flipped the paper open, his temper jumping. He'd avoided the news and socials for the past few days exactly for this reason. There it was, front page in black and white, the Montgomery-Chambers wedding was being touted as the event of the season. He snorted at the picture. It was from a charity thing his mom had made him attend last year. Crystal was front and center, full-on diva, and he was standing in the background, talking to his sister. He was so far away, that if it wasn't for his hat, you wouldn't even be able to tell it was him. If that didn't give people a heads up that this was a complete fucking farce…

The article went on to list his accomplishments, her connections, and apparently their honeymoon was already booked in Paris at the end of next month. Too bad he didn't have a passport and was phobic about flying.

God, what a shit show. He tossed the paper down and scrubbed a hand over his face. This was getting way out of hand, and he was tired of playing along. He wanted to put a real ring on Jena's finger, and he wanted to do it today. What time did Fynbender's open? He glanced at the clock. Not for another half hour, at least—

"Order up."

Chase went back to the counter, pulling out his wallet to pay. Greta had disappeared, off broadcasting his breakfast order no doubt, and Kelsey was at the register.

"It's not true?" she murmured, glancing toward the office as she took his card.

He looked at her in surprise, then over his shoulder to make sure she really was speaking to him. "No. Not one goddamned word."

She nodded, running it. "You should talk to Phil."

Chase fumbled the bag as she handed it to him. Phil was the alpha of the Eastside Montgomerys and technically his uncle, though he'd never met the man. He guessed that made Kelsey his cousin, though the two branches of the family didn't talk— ever. At least not in Chase's lifetime. "You got his number?"

She glanced at the office again, then scribbled something on the back of his receipt and slipped it onto his drink tray. "Have a nice day."

"Yeah…you, too."

Chase stepped back onto the drizzly street in a daze. The hell had that been about? Aside from Kelsey, the Eastside Montgomerys stayed clear of town and kept mostly to the forest track that ran along the river. They had zero dealings with the Westside, and the two packs pretended the other didn't exist.

As to the why, he wasn't really sure, but he'd heard once that his father and his brother had gotten into it over succession when the last alpha had passed. Splitting the pack had been the compromise. Chase didn't buy it. Wallace Montgomery didn't know the meaning of the word and would have zero issue putting his own flesh and blood down to further his ambition.

But Chase suspected the reasons didn't really matter at this point. The end result had been the formation of two completely autonomous packs, and he couldn't see that ever changing…but if he could swap his affiliation…

Shit. It could be the out he was looking for.

"Looks like you worked up quite an appetite," Malcom said, appearing at his side. The hair on Chase's nape rose, and the asshole chuckled. "I told you'd I'd be watching, though I must admit I did not expect that much of a show. You might want to clue in your whore on how the mirror in her room reflects everything that happens on the bed…against the bed…over the bed…" Malcom grinned at him. "Including how she just loves to take every inch."

Chase's temper jumped. "The fuck do you want?"

"You already know the answer to that, son. I told you to keep your distance. It's a shame you don't take direction as well as Jena does."

"I'm not your fucking son, and keep her name out of your mouth," Chase growled, his wolf howling for the man's blood.

Malcom's grin got bigger. "After that display, I might just put more of her in my mouth than that."

Chase went to lunge at him, and he was grabbed from behind. The hell?

"Yeah, that's what I thought," Malcom said as he struggled. "Think it's time for you to marinate while I get the rest of the meal ready." Something cracked down on the side of Chase's skull, and everything went black.

Chapter Twelve

FLAME WHOMPED up around the base of Jena's cauldron, and she turned to rummage around in the cabinet for spell ingredients. God, she was out of practice when it came to hooking up. Birth control made her seriously rage-y, and she was kicking herself for not asking Chase to wear a condom. Of course, the jerk hadn't offered, either.

Weres didn't get or transmit STDs, but had he been serious about getting her pregnant? God, probably. Add that to the list of things they needed to talk about. That item was not, nor had it ever been, on her bucket list, and it wasn't going on as an addendum. Not to mention she was still trying to wrap her head around everything else he'd said. He might be all systems go, but she still had some serious reservations.

You know, little things, like his entire pack hating her. In particular, his stupid mother.

Jena sighed, still not knowing what the heck she'd ever done to deserve it, and set aside the empty jar of pennyroyal to search for the blue cohosh.

"You sure you want to do that?" Aggie wheezed from behind her newspaper.

Jena's eyes flicked up, and she smirked at Crystal's stupid face beaming at her from the front page. *Bitch, I got your man...* "Why wouldn't I?"

"You're not getting any younger," Aggie said, turning a page.

Jena glared at her. "Says the woman who never had children. You need to get dressed. We're going to Klineville General after breakfast." Ah, there it was. She pulled out the bottle of herbs out and uncapped it to sniff. Jeez, how old was this? It smelled like the apartment after Chase had torn up Aggie's bathroom floor.

"The hell we are, and I had you."

Jena opened her mouth to say something and then closed it. Aggie had been in her early thirties when Jena had come to live with her. She vaguely recalled a steady progression of boyfriends, but couldn't remember anything serious. Was that because of her?

"Stop over thinking it," Aggie said. "Only man I had any interest in settling down with had zero interest in the same." She coughed. "The rest were a good time until they weren't. I have no regrets. Not about that at least."

"Well, I suppose it's a moot point if this is the only blue cohosh you have." Jena poked deeper into the cabinet, pulling out odds and ends. She guessed it wasn't the end of the world if Chase was right about her cycle. Not that she totally trusted him. She should probably start paying better attention to that. "And you're going, even if I have to spell you unconscious and carry you there on my back."

"Don't make me hex you with vaginal dryness."

Jena glared at her. Aggie would do it, too. "Whatever. You've been so miserable lately, you can't spare the karma. You're going," Jena muttered, flicking through bottles.

The paper crackled in Aggie's grip. "No, I'm not."

Jena ignored her. Most of these herbs were just bottled dust. Fixing the roof to get that greenhouse going was abruptly a necessity, especially if she was staying. There wasn't a chance she was going back to the ruins if she could help it, and taking a trip to the pharmacy for the morning after pill was just asking for trouble. "Who was it you used to get your seeds from?"

"Abinathy's." The bell downstairs chimed as someone came in. "If that's not Chase, ten bucks it's Sweets. Woman's first in line for everything."

Great. Jena smoothed her t-shirt and cut the heat to the cauldron. Aggie had sent out the all-hands-on-deck to the coven and everyone was meeting here. The last time Jena had seen all of them together she'd been what? Fifteen, sixteen? Hopefully this time she wouldn't get another stern talking to about using hexes.

She blew out her cheeks, not holding out much hope on that front.

"Aggie Wright, where you at?" Sweets's island patois filtered up the steps.

Damn. Jena had hoped to be caffeinated before anyone showed up. "Kitchen," she called, cleaning up her mess. Last thing she needed was them sussing out what she'd been about to do from the spell ingredients on the counter.

A very squat dark woman in a massive headscarf and jewel-colored caftan waddled into the kitchen. "Uh uh," she said, shaking her head at the chairs. "Not one of those will I be sitting on. You still got the wide chairs by the windows?"

"Forget your glasses again? You just walked right past them," Aggie said, weakly fluttering a hand at the other room as she coughed. "I'll be there when I get there—and keep your nose out of my grimoire!"

"I don't need my glasses to see a doctor should be looking at that cough, and as if I'm needing to snoop through your poor pages of spells." She squinted over at Jena like she was just noticing she was in the room. "That you, Jena girl? You got old."

"Thanks, Ms. Sweets. Aggie was just telling me the same

thing," she said to the woman's back as she disappeared into the other room. "See, even she thinks you should see a doctor."

Aggie brushed her off. "Of course she does. Woman goes to an orthopedist every time she stubs a toe."

"Umm...maybe because she's a diabetic, and it's the responsible thing to do?"

"More like paranoid. I'm fine. It's just the must from the work in the bathroom disagreeing with me." The older witch glowered at her, muffling another cough. "I suggest you stop playing mother hen and start boiling water for tea before the rest of them get here," Aggie said, her arms shaking as she pushed herself up to stand. Jena went to help her, and Aggie shooed her away, begrudgingly grabbing her cane.

Well, at least there was that.

Felix came in next and leaned against the island in a houndstooth suit and loosened his plaid tie. God, where did he find these things? It was in shades of bright teal and mustard. "So tell me everything..." he prompted, a sly smile on his face.

She eyed him over her shoulder before going back to washing teacups at the sink. "Not without margaritas and a cone of silence. Put the water on to boil for me?"

"It better be worth the wait." Felix rolled his eyes with an exaggerated sigh and brought the kettle over. "And you know this is seriously pushing my culinary ability."

He wasn't overstating it. Felix was a menace in the kitchen. "It is, and I'll make sure you don't set anything on fire. You here as proxy for your mom?"

"Yes." He frowned, somehow managing to get an entire sleeve wet filling the kettle. "She's got my sister's kids again, and one of the little urchins is sick. She didn't want to risk passing anything to Aggie with her compromised immune system."

"I appreciate that," Jena said, glancing toward the other room as more people arrived.

Hopefully the rest of them took the same into consideration, if it wasn't already too late. Dust from the renovation could be the culprit, but Chase was so clean and had all those fans set up…

Someone in the other room cackled, and Felix rolled his eyes. It sounded more like a reunion in there than a coven meeting, though she supposed Aggie had become reclusive since her diagnosis. Not without cause, but it was a shame. The older witch had always been the life of the party. Their meetings had to be boring as—

"Ahaha!" Sweets's laughter boomed above the hubbub. "Matilda's stuck outside. Sour old biddy can't get past your wards. You should see her face!" There was a general shuffle as everyone moved to the windows and more laughter.

"God, that's still a thing?" Jena asked.

Felix nodded, the two of them sharing a smile at the ongoing joke. Matilda Hanson was the most negative person Jena had ever met. Everything was doom and gloom and there wasn't an ill-intent ward she could pass within a hundred feet without setting off—

But Chase hadn't.

A lump rose in Jena's throat. If he'd been planning on tricking her—if his intentions hadn't been pure—he wouldn't have gotten past the front door of The Witchery. She steadied herself against the counter, her knees about to give.

"Are you okay?" Felix asked, putting a hand on her back.

Jena just nodded. It was real.

She was Chase Montgomery's mate. It wasn't a dare; he wanted to be with her. She bit back a watery laugh and put her fingers to her lips. Could everything he'd said really be true? How was that possible?

"You in there growing the tea or drying it?" Aggie wheezed from the other room.

Damn. Right, the coven. It was showtime. Jena wiped her eyes, shooed Felix from the kitchen, then took a deep breath and finished loading up the tea tray.

Just as she'd expected, everyone was at the window making faces down at the street below—Except for Sweets, who was twerking against the glass. Not bad for a woman who had to be in her late sixties. Felix lounged at one end of the couch, shaking his head at their antics.

Jena set the tray down on the coffee table. "I'll go let Ms. Matilda in."

She started down the steps with a weird sense of déjà vu...or maybe it was just nostalgia. When she was younger, Aggie had always sent her downstairs to let the sour witch in. Jena checked the line of salt at the threshold and stepped over it to open the door—

"It's about damned time." The tiny blonde woman sniffed, adjusting her cat's-eyed glasses and shouldering past Jena. "You know, you used to be a lot quicker."

"I guess that's what happens when you get old," Jena said, her gaze on the empty spot where Chase's truck had been. Why would he drive it around the corner to Cups? It was only drizzling out.

Matilda eyed her over her shoulder, removing her clear plastic rain bonnet and sending her platinum bob of pipe curls bouncing. "You did at that, now didn't you? You got fat, too."

For whatever reason that last comment didn't cut as much as it normally would have. Jena closed the door and trailed after the older witch. "Thanks," she murmured, checking her phone. Nothing from Chase since the thumbs up for her order. She shot him a quick text.

The older witch humphed and marched up the steps with her head held high. Jena blew out her cheeks and followed. When she got back up to the main room, any levity there'd been was gone. Six witches, five warlocks, and Felix sat around the perimeter of the room, staring at her from over the rims of their teacups.

Felix patted the couch cushion beside him. She gratefully sat. At least she'd have one ally.

"Jena." June Hill, the coven's secretary, greeted her with a wide smile. A smear of mauve lipstick marred the soccer mom's front teeth. "I was so happy to get your completed paperwork. It's so satisfying that you're finally stepping into your mother's position and bringing us back up to thirteen members."

"What it is, is well past time," Matilda groused. "And I still think we should've given it to the Cassidy girl. She didn't up and leave."

"She also didn't get accepted by the node," Sweets murmured.

Jena shot a look at Aggie, who shrugged back. Screw the node, what were they talking about? Her paperwork? Felix began whistling softly, damn him. "I appreciate you holding the spot for me," Jena made herself say. When the hell had he sent that in?

Matilda snorted. "What a load of crap—"

"Enough of your doom. I want to hear about this threat," Sweets said, crossing her arms over her wide bosom. "Why would the likes of Malcom be bothering himself with one of ours?"

Jena's gaze went around the circle, her mouth opening and closing as she started to speak and then stopped again—

"Chase Montgomery is her fated mate, and he's also late with my damned tea." Aggie glanced out the window, then muttered, "It's not like him." She coughed.

It wasn't, and his truck being gone was starting to really bother Jena.

Mr. Fynbender hummed from the loveseat across the room.

"Do you know something, Otis?" Ms. Hill asked, taking

out a fancy leather-bound notebook. Her pen was topped with a sparkly poof of feathers.

"Hmm? No. Not a thing," he said too quickly, then busied himself with his cup.

Sweets eyed him like she knew he was lying. "Then what in the devil's all this with the wedding?"

"He said it's his father…" Jena began, laying out what'd happened the past few days—well, not everything—then what Chase had said this morning. "…and that's when he told me about Malcom. I don't think they know about the mate thing."

"Like hell they don't," Matilda spat. "If Crystal pitched a fit about the two of you stinking up his cabin, and Malcom showed up there, he's well aware—which means Chase's father is, too. He should've put the kibosh on the whole circus."

"Agreed. I never liked that man," Sweets said, rocking back and forth with her mouth screwed up like she wanted to spit. "Malcom, Wallace, hell, I'll throw that wife of his under the bus, too. The troubles she caused for your mother after claiming to be her bosom friend…uh uh. No. Something here's not right. No one of sound mind's going out of their way to mess with fate, and now you think Chase is missing?"

Wait, they were friends? Jena went to open her mouth, and Matilda snorted. "Malcom's mind is about as far from sound as you can get, and he's had Wallace wrapped around his finger since the word go. I swear, nothing in this town has been right since Rebecca died. Your mother—we had our differences, but she kept the covens together. Without her maintaining the node everything's fallen to shit, and uppity weres are only part of the problem." Everyone in the room looked at her like she had two heads. "What?"

"Not that I don't agree, but I think that's the closest you've ever come to a compliment." Aggie coughed. "You feeling all right?"

Matilda glowered at her. "Are you?"

Mr. Fynbender cleared his throat. "Whether Chase is missing or not, the real question is, why is it so important for this wedding to happen? When he came in yesterday to pick out a ring—"

"Yesterday?" Sweets asked. "Then why've I been reading about this hullabaloo since Monday?"

"That's what I'm trying to say. Chase wasn't exactly invested." Mr. Fynbender's eyes flicked to Jena. "I got the feeling he was being strong-armed into it, and when Crystal came in prior to that, most of what she said didn't ring true. Whatever she's hoping to get out of this marriage, it isn't love. Quite frankly, I'm not even sure she likes him very much…she did, however, like picking out her own bling," he said, waggling his ring finger.

Well, that was on point, and the Fynbenders were truth-seers. Each of the coven members had an aspect of witchery they specialized in, and it was impossible to try to deceive him without pinging his power. If anyone would know Crystal was full of shit, it was Otis Fynbender.

"Have you seen anything, Aggie?" Ms. Hill asked.

The coven turned to her, and Aggie pursed her lips. "Flashes. The bit that worries me is going to happen at the seven standing stones behind the ruins the next time the moon is full."

"That's tomorrow," Sweets murmured, "and on Samhain, no less."

Matilda scowled. "Was the cauldron lit?"

"Blue flame." Aggie nodded, and ice went up Jena's spine.

"That's witchery," Sweets said. "But what would that have to do with a were wedding or Jena and Chase?"

"He told me his father said he had to give Crystal a ring by then," Felix offered.

"She picked it up yesterday and wore it out of the shop," Mr. Fynbender frowned. "And was none too pleased with

Chase's selection, I might add. Shoved it onto her finger and stormed out the door like it was an insult. I was surprised she didn't exchange it when I offered."

"Oh dear," Kressida Pao murmured from one of the overstuffed chairs. The mousy woman was almost lost in the cushions. "A token given, signaling devotion, binding troth, his life to hers. That has the potential to be problematic."

"Even if it's not real, and he didn't actually give it to her?" Jena asked.

"Oh, yes." Ms. Pao nodded, her eyes magnified to twice their size by her cloudy glasses. Her line's power was with talismans. "Him buying it and knowing what it represents is enough. That magic is very old and doesn't have modern-day nuancing. Arranged marriages via proxy have been the standard from time immemorial, personal proposals and marrying for love's quite modern."

Great. Jena glanced at the clock, seriously worried. Chase should've been back an hour ago.

"But again, that's witchery," Sweets said.

"Is it though?" Clint Rondo boomed from the chair beside her. The florid man tapped his blunt fingers against his beefy thigh. "I'll give you that it's magic, but we don't hold the patent. Merfolk, sidhe, demons, quiet folk, succubi, any one of them, and a dozen others use it—"

"So then who's Wallace Montgomery in bed with, and why is he needing to bind that first born son of his to that hag of a girl by the cross quarter day?" Sweets asked.

"And at the risk of pissing us and fate off," Matilda added. "Both he and Malcom know better than to threaten one of ours…and trying to separate fated mates is just asking for the universe to come down on you. This stinks like a power grab, and it has to a doozy."

"It does," Sweets nodded, "and dollar to a donut, if we can figure out who he's canoodling with, we'll get the why along with it."

"Chase said something…" Jena started, "Malcom told him to keep his distance from me unless he wanted me to end up like my mom. He made it sound like his dad and my mom had been more than friends?"

The coven went still.

"He said *what?*" Sweets snapped, halfway out of her chair.

"Well now, that's beating the carpets for all the old dust," Rick Kleppet said with a snort. He pinched his long nose and set his teacup down. "When was that, Max? Senior year?"

The tall warlock at the window with gray streaking his temples turned from the street to answer him. "Around then. It was right after Rebecca fell out with Mary and the Montgomery pack split, or thereabouts. For whatever reason Wallace started harassing Rebecca—"

"No mystery there. She was always tight with Phil, and Wallace couldn't stand anyone having something he didn't, especially his brother," Matilda spat. "He and Mary are two peas in a goddamned pod. I never trusted that woman—she was always jealous of Rebecca."

Max hummed. "Regardless, it was unseemly. He'd already graduated college when he started harassing her, and with the silence, Phil's hands were tied, so Greg and I stepped in."

A grizzled warlock across the room that looked way too much like a fictional gamekeeper in a kid's wizard book snickered. "You remember the pie cantrip?" Rick gave a full belly laugh and so did several of the others.

"Ah, that was a good one…" Max wiped an eye. "Anyway, a couple of stunts like that and Wallace got the hint. Pretty sure he started officially dating Mary not long after, but I've no idea why she and Rebecca fell out."

"She saw something," Aggie wheezed. "What, I don't know, but it was related to her power. She never talked about any of the sins she saw. Mark my words, Mary Montgomery's got one hell of a skeleton in her closet and wasn't happy Rebecca knew about it."

"Begging your pardon," Sweets interrupted, "but I'm still stewing over the first part of what Jena just told us. He used those words, 'end up like your mother?'"

Jena nodded, still trying to wrap her head around her mom and Mary Montgomery being friends. "Do you think it's possible he did something to her?"

Sweets sat back shaking her head. "No," the big woman said. "I think it's probable, and Malcom's the rat in this wheel of cheese."

~

CHASE GROANED and put a hand to his head as he came to. He winced, pulling his fingers away, sticky. What the hell had happened? He looked around, propped up against a curved concrete wall, sitting in at least three inches of water.

Where was he? Everything was a murky gray, and he was soaked. A weird thrum of energy pulsed around him from the walls. They curved around him to form a massive cylinder. It shot straight upward for at least a hundred feet and ended in a circle open to the clouds roiling through the sky. Rain splashed down with no sign of letting up.

He wobbled to his feet, dripping, and gripped his head, trying not to puke. Fuckers had definitely given him a concussion, damn them. He held an arm out, his balance screwed. Christ, it looked like he was in one of those massive precast concrete tubes they used for drainage on civil engineering jobs.

Except he'd never seen one so long, and this one sure wasn't doing its job. He kicked at the submerged gravel and wet his lips, blinking up into the rain coming from the round dot of sky above. Suddenly flying didn't seem so bad. There wasn't a chance in hell he was getting out of there any other way.

He wiped his sodden hair from his eyes and gingerly

explored the bump behind his ear—Christ, that hurt—what had…his thoughts muddled, trying to piece together what he remembered. Malcom. He'd been talking to Malcom…but then who had hit him?

Chase laughed, then winced at the spike of pain it sent through his head. Jesus. In a town where he couldn't scratch his own ass without it being on the front page, that asshole had abducted him off Main Street in broad fucking daylight. If that wasn't just par for the course.

He patted his pockets, taking inventory. His hat was missing. Wallet and phone were gone. No keys. He hadn't been wearing a jacket, and it was cold enough to see his breath down here.

And he was soaking wet.

Well, he supposed worst case he could shift if the chill got too bad, but that didn't strike him as the wisest idea until he knew what he was dealing with. Depending how bad they'd fucked him up, he might not be able to shift back.

Shit. Jena was going to freak when he didn't show up with breakfast. He groaned, stumbling back against the wall, his head throbbing. Please, please, sweet baby Jesus, do not let her come looking for him. She needed to stay at the shop where she was safe, especially after the shit Malcom had said. If that asshole had put him down here, it was for a reason, and needing Chase out of the way didn't bode well. Marinate. Well, he was definitely sitting in soup. Goddamn it, if Malcom hurt her…

Chase bit back a growl, his wolf frantic to warn her, and he couldn't do a damned thing about it stuck down here. He was positive that wherever he was, it wasn't some place she or any other good Samaritan would stumble across him.

Okay, think, think…Chase ran a shaky hand over his face. If the beta had wanted him dead, he would be. Sooner or later, Malcom would come back to fish him out. Chase slid back down the curved wall, splashing as he sat.

There wasn't anything to do but wait. For Malcom, for this headache to pass…but goddamn whatever that fucking hum making his teeth ache was. Jena would be okay. She was smart. He sent up another prayer she'd taken his warning to heart and would stay put until he could get back to her.

Chapter Thirteen

JENA STOOD at the sink washing teacups and trying very hard not to cry. Felix dried them and put them away, watching her out of the corner of his eye. It'd been hours since Chase had left, and he wasn't answering his texts. She'd even tried to call, but it'd gone straight to voicemail.

Something wasn't right. She knew it in her bones.

In the other room, Aggie was in deep conversation with Sweets, Matilda, and Ms. Pao. The four of them spoke in low tones interspersed with Aggie's hacking. They'd shot enough glances through the kitchen door that it wasn't a secret who they were discussing. Jena kept her back to them. She couldn't deal with anything else right now—

Another set of cups clattered next to the sink, and she glanced over at Ms. Pao. The town librarian smiled back at her, her magnified eyes kind. "Jena…is there anything that Chase may have given you, or left behind while he was here?"

She wiped her eyes. "Aside from the work he did Aggie's bathroom?" Chase was the tidiest man she'd ever met, and they hadn't—God, the only thing he'd ever given her was his number—and the sweater she'd thrown away, but that was more of a return… Jena shook her head, tearing up all over again. "No."

Ms. Pao frowned. "Darn it."

"Are you going to try and scry for him? What if we got something from his cabin?" Felix asked, tossing the dish towel over his shoulder.

She blinked at him, owl-like. "I don't think that's wise. We don't want to—"

The bell downstairs rang as someone came in, and Jena pushed past her to see who. *Let it be Chase. Please, please, please let it be Chase—*

She threw open the door, and Kelsey Montgomery stood on the landing, chewing a nail. Before Jena could say anything the woman started talking.

"I shouldn't be here, but I'm tired of letting messed up shit happen. I-I really am sorry I didn't do more when we were younger." She took a deep breath. "I couldn't get away until my shift at Cups was over, but I saw Malcom and a couple other Westsiders take Chase away in a van this morning."

Jena put a hand to her stomach. Goddamn it, she knew something had happened!

"W-what do you mean?" she asked, her voice trembling. Kelsey glanced over Jena's shoulder, and Jena stepped aside to let the slim were in. "Please. We're all worried about him."

"If that psycho's got him, you should be," Kelsey muttered, slinking onto the couch.

"So spill it," Aggie snapped. "What do you know?"

Kelsey wet her lips. "Greta lost it when Chase came in this morning and gave your order instead of Crystal's. She left me at the counter, and I'm pretty sure she disappeared into her office to tattle, because when I ran out to give him his credit card, Malcom was there with two other weres. They had words, then one of them hit Chase over the head, and they dragged him into a van."

"Did they see you?" Matilda asked.

"Are you fricking kidding me?" Jena asked at the same time, her temper spiking. What the hell was going on in this town?

"I-I don't think so, and there wasn't anyone else on the street." Kelsey fished something out of her back pocket and handed it to Jena. "And no, I'm not kidding. Here's his credit card."

Matilda was out of her chair in a flash and snatched it. "Perfect. Where's your scrying bowl?"

Jena brain skipped at the change in topic. "Um. Under the kitchen sink..."

The little witch was in the other room before all the words had left Jena's mouth and rummaging through the cabinet. "Ugh! This is disgusting! Who uses a silver basin to catch leaks? Don't you have plasticware?"

"Just wash it, it'll be fine," Aggie called back, a fit of coughing drowning out Matilda's bitching. "Then what?" she asked Kelsey when she'd caught her breath.

"Um..." The were's brows furrowed at the older woman, and Aggie scowled, gesturing at her to go on. "Well, like I said, we recognized Jena's order, and not for nothing, but he was smiling like an idiot and reeked like sex." She eyed Jena up and down. "High five for scoring that piece of tail, girl."

Jena felt her cheeks heat. "Um, thanks?"

"You know it. Anyway, that kind of took the guesswork out of why he was there at nine in the morning getting your breakfast to go...but I think I did something stupid." She chewed her lip for a second. "I told him to call my dad and gave him the number. If any of them saw that slip of paper, I'm in deep shit."

"Who's your dad?" Aggie asked. "All you Eastsiders look the same."

Kelsey laughed. "Yeah, we get that a lot, probably because so many of us are twins or trips. My dad's Phil Montgomery, Eastside's alpha."

"And why would you be wanting to have Chase call him after the long silence betwixt your packs?" Sweets asked.

Jena wanted to know that, too, especially if Phil had been

friends with her mom. She glanced toward the kitchen, shivering. Whatever Matilda was doing in there was deep magic—the kind that made your bones thrum.

Kelsey squirmed like she felt it, too and scrunched her freckled nose. "Yeah…that's kind of…look, all I can tell you is it has to do with this wedding. It's not gonna be good for anyone. Like, really not good." She looked at Jena. "Which is part of why my dad wanted me to invite you to the pig roast, but I think you should come—"

"Ah! Gotcha!" Matilda yelled from the kitchen.

Jena was out of her seat along with everyone else except Aggie, crowding into the room. The little blonde witch stood peering into a battered scrying bowl on the kitchen table, her eyes occluded with a shimmering mist. She beckoned Jena closer.

The bowl glowed with silver light, and deep within its still waters was an image of Chase. Wherever he was, it was murky with power, and he'd lost his hat. He sat in ankle-deep water against the curvature of a gray stone wall, soaked, one arm resting on his raised knee as he chucked stones. He frowned and looked up, his blue eyes unfocused, like he was hurt.

"Well, hello, gorgeous," Matilda murmured with an evil chuckle. "Not that we all haven't heard the rumors, but I've got zero doubts now that someone got cuckolded."

"What do you mean?" Jena asked her.

"Weres' eyes are always brown. No exceptions, unless there's some other supe in the mix. And with the clarity in the pair that boy has, I'm betting it was a recent addition to the genome."

"Well, it's not from Wallace's side," Ms. Pao said. "His mother made a right pest of herself at the library documenting the Montgomery family's purity—Eastside and West. Or she did before they shipped her off to assisted living—"

"I'm still calling foul on that. Woman was sharp as a tack," Matilda spat.

Sweets hummed, staring into the bowl. "Though it pains me to agree with you, that shade of blue isn't something regressive popping up. Which begs the questions, who's that boy's daddy, and why is Wallace flaunting him as his own?"

"Do you think that's what Rebecca saw?" Ms. Pao rubbed her fingers across her lips, her brow furrowed. "Having relations behind Wallace's back would certainly be a skeleton she'd want to keep hidden, but the timing's not right...they fell out years before Chase was born. Mary was a Duffy, wasn't she?"

Matilda snorted. "Duffy. Who the hell knows where her people came from?"

"My dad might," Kelsey said, chewing a nail.

"Or Mr. Brock might remember something," Felix added.

"He's still the town archivist?" Jena shook her head at their nods. The vampire was old enough to personally remember the town's founding. If he could stay on topic was a totally different matter. "Can you see where Chase is?" she asked, more concerned about him than his family tree.

The film over Matilda's eyes shimmered, and the image in the bowl pulled back...and then back again, like a camera sliding down a track. It blurred, then steadied, wobbled—

And was gone.

"Damn it." Matilda swore, collapsing onto a chair. "Wherever it is, there's magic involved. He's underground, and that hole is deep. All things considered, he's a little roughed up, but doesn't look too bad. I'm assuming that means they need him for something."

Great. Jena was pretty sure that something was going to fall on Samhain, which gave them all of twenty-four hours to figure it out and get him clear of it. She turned to Kelsey. "I know this whole mess involves the Westside pack, but do you think your dad would help us?"

"I-I think so…" She glanced at the rest of the room. "If this wedding happens…yeah. I think he would if there's a chance to stop it. That's why I gave Chase his number, and like I said, he wanted to talk to you…and I mean, the worst he can say is no." Jena pulled out her phone and Kelsey shook her head. "You need to do it in person."

"Then let's go," Felix said, snugging his tie.

Jena shoved her phone back into her pocket. "Don't you have to get back to work?"

He psh'd her. "Thursdays Mayor Chambers has a standing re-election committee meeting that eats the entire afternoon. Let's just say that's not going well after the wind-turbine debacle over on Sunnyside and usually ends in cocktails. I'm not worried about it."

"You should be," Matilda scowled from her seat. "That debacle's not just an eyesore, they planted the damned things smack dab in the middle of the leyline that runs through town. Mark my words, no good's going to come from those things stabbing into it."

Jena blinked at her. "Other than being ugly, why? The magic should just run through them like everything else."

"Mmm. But it isn't," Ms. Pao said. "And without 'science,'" she finger quoted, "backing up the coven's concerns, the powers-that-be did whatever the hell they pleased."

Sweets snorted. "As if there'd just be a study lying around on that."

"No, but there is a census," Matilda snapped, "and Fayet's population of practitioners is a big fat zero. Everyone in town with a hint of ability knows the line's not flowing the way it should, and I'd bet my eyeteeth those things are the reason."

Crap. Jena chewed her lip. The power in that leyline ran east to west. If the turbines were somehow blocking the flow of power, it would track that the node had felt so much stronger, and why it was leaking power. Maybe it wasn't wild. Maybe it was just constipated.

Jena bit back a laugh at that visual. "No wonder the node's pissy." And maybe that's why they were having so much trouble finding another guardian for it. It didn't sound like any of the other candidates had been very successful in the protection department.

The coven members all glanced at her like it was somehow her fault, and she blew out a big breath, forcing a smile. "Okay," she clapped her hands together, "give me a sec to get my spellbag."

She left the kitchen and hurried to her room before she really stepped in it. Stupid visual or not, it wasn't a laughing matter. The Havers's node drew raw power from the sea and funneled it into three separate leylines before it sent it west to the next node somewhere past Glidden, three counties over. All that power had to go somewhere. If the node couldn't hold it and let go, Havers-by-the-Sea would be on the bottom of it.

"Not my problem..." she muttered, trying to convince herself. But it wasn't, was it? God, she had enough on her plate. Her stomach churned. Okay, fine. Maybe it was, but— later. She would deal with it later. It'd lasted this long, right? Right.

Ugh! Then why did she still feel like a jerk? She didn't have time for this. Eastside. She was going with Felix and Kelsey to Eastside to figure out how to save Chase. The node could wait another day or two, and besides, Chase fixed stuff. Maybe he could figure out what to do with the stupid thing.

She snorted. Yeah, because that was just like remodeling a bathroom.

A wave of Chase's pheromones hit her as she opened her door, and Jena choked back a sob, pointedly not looking at the still-rumpled bed. How could they just take him like that? He'd been so worried about her, but if it was him that

Malcom had been talking about back at the cabin…God. What a mess.

She grabbed her spellbag from under her desk. Aside from gathering herbs the other day, she hadn't worn it here, but it'd been her constant companion in the city, mainly because the city had been rife with sin. She hadn't expected it in Havers. Well, nothing worse than Harvey Keels cheating on his wife, or Judy Hoil stealing from the tip jar. She definitely hadn't expected to run afoul of Malcom or whatever was up at those ruins. Jena slipped the strap over her head, its reassuring weight settling against her. She could do this.

She headed back to the sitting room. Felix and Kelsey stood by the kitchen talking with Sweets. Jena forced a smile. "Okay, I'm ready." She wasn't, but personal preference didn't seem like something the universe was going to factor in.

"The three of us will stay here until you get back," Sweets said. "We want to strengthen the shop's wards." She glanced at Aggie sitting with her eyes closed in one of the big chairs and lowered her voice. "And I don't like the way she's sounding. I sent Otis for supplies. There's a potion or two I'm planning on pouring down her miserable gullet whether she's willing or no."

"Thank you." Jena choked back tears. That was Sweets's expertise, and the woman brewed up some miraculous things. "She's being awful about going to Klineville General. You're welcome to use whatever you can find here, but I'll warn you, it's slim pickings."

"You don't say." Sweets cocked a brow at the heap of prickly herb dust at the top of the garbage.

"Not for nothing," Kelsey said, "but you wouldn't have been able to get past Fayet. The packs have closed borders, and with Chase's pheromones all over you, there's not a chance they'd let you through."

"There's seriously a were blockade going out of town?" Jena asked.

Kelsey nodded. "Yeah, the Eastside is locked down, too. Some of the younger guys got into it the other day with the Westside pack. Things are tense."

Great. The bell for the door below rang as someone else entered the shop. Footsteps shuffled up the steps, and Mr. Fynbender came in a moment later hefting an overflowing milk crate and a loaded canvas tote slung over his shoulder. He closed the door after himself and threw the deadbolt. Jena's stomach dropped at the look on his face as he turned.

"I don't think they're just after Chase," he said. "Your shop is being watched."

CHASE BUZZED his lips and tossed another stone against the wall. It rebounded and plunked into the steadily rising water. He was freezing, and his skull throbbed with the hum of energy around him—enough that it'd started screwing with his eyes.

Weird flashes of light spiked his vision, and his nausea was worse. Whatever that sound was, it was driving him nuts, and it wasn't the only thing setting him on edge. The small hairs on the back of his neck still prickled with the feeling of being watched, though he was pretty sure whatever that'd been had passed…if it'd ever really been there.

His grasp on reality was slipping, and that scared the shit out of him.

He blew out a breath and tipped his head back, trying to focus on the circle of sky above. It'd gotten darker, another wave of rain rolling in. A lengthening ellipse of faint light had steadily crept down the western side of the hole and made a ninety degree turn as it hit the pool. Noon. It had to be close to noon.

Jena had to be freaking out. God, if she thought he'd abandoned her after last night, she'd never speak to him again. His stomach churned at the possibility, and his wolf whined. Chase chucked another rock, swearing as it plunked below the surface. He wet his lips and frowned at the pool, seriously considering lapping the walls. No way was he drinking the cholera-infested mess he was sitting in, but the fact that it was there was killing him.

What the hell was the point of sticking him down here? It wasn't like Malcom couldn't lock him up somewhere in the pack manor. Chase knew damned well his father'd had a sound-proof room installed in the basement when the house was built.

So did that mean his father didn't know Malcom had taken him? Seemed unlikely…or maybe they were trying to keep it from his mother, but that didn't make sense either. Not with how hot she'd been on planning this stupid wedding. Him disappearing would make her mental.

He clambered to his feet and splashed around the perimeter. A dozen steps. Chase looked up again. He'd already tried to claw up the side and fucked himself up royally. Had to be C40 or the UPHC they used for high compression civil jobs—

Wait a minute.

Absolutely nothing in this town would require concrete with that kind of tensile strength, except those fucking wind turbines they were putting in. Jesus. He had to be stuck at the bottom of one of the deep foundations for the eyesores the mayor was crowing about at the last public hearing. Asshole had been all gung-ho about them making the town energy independent, but the federal grant had dried up, and all he'd done was piss away the surplus the last administration had left him with.

People were livid at staggering amount of bonded debt and the hazard to public safety the unfinished the project represented. The next mayor was gonna have their work cut out for them, unless there were enough idiots in this town to actually reelected Chambers. Unfortunately, that wasn't outside the realm of possibilities, considering how cozy he and Chase's father had been the other night. Chase wouldn't be surprised if Chambers's reelection campaign was getting an abrupt influx of cash with their bullshit agreement.

Asshole should be in jail. That hum…it had to be the leyline, and the coven was spot on about the turbines fucking with it. Nothing about it felt right, and without any magical ability, he shouldn't be feeling it at all. No wonder they'd been so pissed.

Chase ran a shaky hand over his mouth and scratched his stubbled jaw, trying to focus. Damn, he wished he'd thumbed through that portfolio his father had tossed at him. What else had been in there? His father supporting Chambers's reelection would make sense if Chase was married to Crystal, but the bullshit she'd spewed about being handed the pack didn't.

He chewed his lip. The more he thought about it, the more that bothered him. No way would his father give alpha up without being put down. And Wallace's ambition notwithstanding, Chase's mother would slice his father's throat herself before she allowed that to happen. She was way too invested in being the alpha female to step aside for Crystal.

So why did Crystal think she was getting handed the pack?

Chase swore, kicking himself again for not reading the damned thing.

It didn't matter. Jena. He had to get back to Jena.

Chase's anxiety ticked up, his heart rate increasing with his nausea. If he was right about where he was, he'd also been right about no one stumbling over him. The entire hillside had been clearcut and gated off with an eight-foot chain-link fence. The nearest neighborhood was Sunnyside, and no one was gonna be out this way for a stroll.

Fuck, fuck, fuck—move, he had to move. He began pacing again, pushing his nausea down, the lack of anything to occupy him steadily chipping away at his composure. A laugh burbled up his throat, fur sprouting and retracting, way too close to losing his shit.

The reno, think about the reno…

The fireplace at Jena's shop. He'd need to remove that brass surround first. Probably would have to lube the screws before he messed with them, otherwise the drives would deform. Flathead, 3/16th screwdriver, no—five millimeter. Soak them to clear the threads of gunk and reuse. Then knock what patina he could off the surround with a nylon wire brush. Anything harder might score the metal. A medium fine prep disk, mushroom scuff pad…

He splashed back down to sit, his breath smoothing as he went through the process in his mind, polishing each twist and turn the metal took until it gleamed, bright brass resolving from beneath the dull brown tarnish. By the time he mentally set it aside, his heart rate had returned to normal, and his clammy skin prickled with cold. His anxiety waned, and Chase tipped his head against the wall, exhaustion dragging at him.

His eyelids drooped. The coal basket would be more work. The ash cover was missing a knob, but he could turn a new one easily enough in the shop…

Chase's mind went through the motions, his vision of what the fireplace would look like slowly taking shape, his fingertips and lips tingling as his eyes closed and darkness took him.

Chapter Fourteen

"ARE YOU KIDDING ME?" Jena asked, resisting the urge to march over to the window and look. What the heck did he mean the shop was being watched?

Mr. Fynbender frowned. "Unfortunately, no." He handed Sweets the crate, and Felix took the bag from him, hauling it into the kitchen. "That should be everything you asked for."

"Thank you, Otis." Sweets batted her lashes and followed after Felix.

"My pleasure." Mr. Fynbender smiled, erasing a couple decades from his face.

Jena glanced between the two; he was still chasing after her?

"That's what they call a seasoned romance," Kelsey murmured at Jena's shoulder.

"And you can't beat the flavor." Mr. Fynbender shoved his hands in his pockets and grinned like a schoolboy, rocking back on his heels as Sweets left the room.

O-kay. Jena really didn't want to know what that was all about, but to each their own. "What do you mean the shop is being watched?" she asked.

"Just that." The older warlock shrugged. "On my way here, there had to have been a half-dozen weres loitering around, which I suppose isn't that odd…but all of them being some of the more unsavory Westsiders unduly interested in your storefront certainly is. They were more than a little brazen about it. One of them's right outside on the stoop, just beyond your ward, and he smiled at me as I came in. It wasn't pleasant."

"No, that sounds like they're trying to intimidate us into staying put." Kelsey growled. "Which means this is the last place you should be. We need to get you across the tracks, into Eastsider territory."

"Agreed," Mr. Fynbender said, "but I don't suggest using the front door."

Jena chewed her lip. "No, but Felix can distort us if we go out the coal shoot."

"Aha! I knew that was how you used to sneak out!" Aggie coughed from her chair.

"What? I have no idea what you're talking about," Jena deadpanned, though the older witch was right. It was going to be a tight fit, but she was pretty sure she could still squeeze through. The other two shouldn't have a problem, though you wouldn't know it from the look on Felix's face.

"And miss all this? Not a chance," Aggie fluttered a hand, wheezing. "I'd grab that charm of yours before you head out, if I were you."

Oh crap, right. Jena slipped into the kitchen, her skin prickling at the magic Matilda, Sweets, and Ms. Pao were raising over the cauldron on the stove. Hopefully after they set those wards, they could do something for Aggie, since it didn't sound like Jena taking her to Klineville was an option. Maybe one of them would if whatever Sweets brewed up didn't help.

Jena snagged the dangling charm and slipped it over her head. She tucked it beneath her shirt, the weight of it settled between her breasts as she went back into the other room. It was comforting, even if it was just a pretty hunk of metal at the moment.

"Seriously, the coal shoot?" Felix was still frowning. "You're paying for my dry cleaning."

"It's not that filthy," she lied. He was going to have a fit.

"Ah, before you go…" Mr. Fynbender reached into his pocket. "I hate to ruin the surprise, but after what Kressida said, here." He handed Jena a pair of rings. "When Chase came in the other day, he bought this second set and asked me to hold on to it for him. This purchase he was much more excited about, and I couldn't help but note the disparity in style. I believe he intended them for you."

"For me?" Tears pricked Jena's eyes as she took the intricate bands from him. Was he serious? God, they were beautiful. The blue stone winked up at her from its nest of filigree, and she dashed a hand over her cheek. It was exactly what she would've picked out for herself. How had he known?

Conviction settled in Jena's chest. He'd known because he was her fated mate, damn it, and she was going to get him back.

"What's this I hear?" Ms. Pao came out of the kitchen, shaking sparks of magic from her fingertips onto the rug. She snuffed them out with her orthopedic sneaker. "Sorry, that ward's a stage five clinger. Chase bought Jena a ring? Wonderful. That should help mitigate whatever hold the other has on him. Well, what are you waiting for? Put it on, and let me see."

Jena slipped them onto her finger. They caught at her knuckle for a breath and then slid over it with the faintest prickle of magic to settle on her hand like they belonged there.

"Hmm. I had wondered," Mr. Fynbender murmured. "Interesting."

Ms. Pao frowned, taking Jena's hand in hers and raising her glasses to inspect the set. "Very. Where did you get them?" she asked him.

"Tullamore estate liquidation a few years back."

"Tullamore, Tullamore…" She frowned. "That's not a witch family name."

"No. It's sidhe, ah, seelie, if I'm not mistaken. There's a very faint Gaelic inscription inside the band…something about remaining true."

"Otis," Ms. Pao tsked like she wasn't entirely happy about that. "What have I told you about bringing stray talismans into town? After the havoc that cursed locket caused, you'd think you would've learned your lesson."

He colored, and she shook her head with a long-suffering sigh. "Men. The magic in this is very old and deep, but I haven't a clue what its purpose is." She adjusted her glasses and met Jena's gaze through the thick lenses. "Be careful with them. A sidhe—seelie or unseelie—never gives a token without expecting payment, and I suspect this is no different. There will be a price to balance out any benefit."

Jena bit back a laugh. Great. Just what she needed; cursed rings to add to her collection of fuckery. "Anything else before we leave?"

"Yeah, don't get caught, and take an umbrella. It's really starting to come down out there. Wouldn't want to catch your deaths," Matilda said gleefully from the kitchen's doorway.

"Indeed." Mr. Fynbender frowned as he unbolted the door at the top of the steps and held it open. "I locked the front and drew the curtains before I came up. All I can say is good luck."

Jena glanced over at Aggie. "I'll be back."

"I'll be waiting." The older woman wheezed.

"You better be." Jena bit back a sniffle. *God, please let her be better then…*

The three of them started down the steps. Jena grabbed her raincoat, and Felix snagged a purple polka-dotted umbrella from the stand. She rolled her eyes. "Inconspicuous much?"

He shrugged. "It could've been leopard print."

"Rain doesn't bother me. I'll just shift," Kelsey said.

Because nothing said sly like a party parasol and werewolf trotting down Main Street. Jena shook her head. Whatever. Felix's power could deal with it.

They cut through the shop, then behind the counter, and went into one of the backrooms used for storage. A large section of paneling had been removed, the naked studs stippled and streaked with black mold.

Ew, gross. That must be the water damage from Aggie's bathroom, and all of that funk couldn't be good for her or anyone else. Maybe that really was why she was so sick. Jena turned away, fighting back tears again. One more problem to deal with when this one was taken care of.

She led Felix and Kelsey to a door just past the mess and down into the basement. It was even danker, and more fans had been set up in the tiny windows blowing out into the alley beside the shop. Jena stopped in front of a wooden hopper with a slanted ramp set into the stone foundation. Above it, a cast iron hatch festooned with cobwebs was latched shut. Crap. It was smaller than Jena remembered…or maybe she was just that much wider.

"Not that filthy, huh?" Felix muttered, the drone of the fans muddling his voice.

"You'll be fine," she said, hefting herself into the hopper and reaching up to unlatch the little door. They all winced at the scrape of metal, holding their breaths and waiting for the sound of the weres outside coming to investigate. After a solid minute of nothing, Jena wet her lips and swept a hand around the opening—

Ouch! She flinched back. Damn. The iron had started to spall, and the frame set into the wall was rusty and jagged. She looked at Felix and flicked the accumulation of webs and bits of rust to the floor.

"You should go first," she said, wiping her scraped fingers against her jeans.

He rolled his eyes. "Fine, but in all honesty, I'm only going to be able to distort us for five, ten minutes max. Jena knows how this works, but you'll need to stay close," he said to Kelsey. "And the less noise you make, the better."

Kelsey nodded and helped him into the hopper. Jena raised up the hatch, and he glowered at her before the tingle of him pulling his power washed over her, raising the small hairs on her arms.

He scrambled up the chute and through the hole. Something splashed.

"Goddamn it!" His voice hissed back at them. "Mind the puddle."

"You next," Jena said to Kelsey, ignoring his grumbling. The lithe were scrambled through, her form wavering as her head cleared the hatch. Her muffled laughter followed.

Jena frowned, more worried about how she was going to fit through the hatch than whatever was going on beyond it. She hefted herself up and tossed her raincoat through, bulky enough as it was. Damn it. Here goes. She sent her arms past the jagged frame like she was diving, and her hands splashed wrist-deep into Felix's mucky puddle. Ugh, that was gross. She pulled herself forward, trying to wriggle the rest of herself through—

And got stuck.

Shit. Her frickin' hips... She sucked in her gut and strained, rocking—*think skinny, think skinny*—Damn it, she winced, iron jabbing her side. She couldn't get enough leverage—"A little help?"

A very wet and bedraggled Felix set aside his umbrella to take one arm, and Kelsey took the other. Jena bit back a smile despite her predicament. Had he fallen into the puddle face first? Her amusement was cut short as they glanced at each other and heaved—

Jena bit back a scream as she scraped past the hatch's metal frame and fell chest first into Felix's puddle. Ugh, she pushed up to sit, dripping, her side on fire.

"Sucks, doesn't it?" he asked.

His suit was smeared with rust and his button-down translucent and spattered with alley gunk. The rain pouring down wasn't doing him any favors, either. He could probably ditch the umbrella at this point. It sure wasn't worth putting her raincoat on. She scowled and shoved it back through the hole.

"If it makes you feel any better, it was deeper when I went in," Felix said, stubbornly gripping his umbrella.

It didn't, but at least her shirt was black…unfortunately, it had one hell of a tear in it now. She lifted it and eased down the waistband of her jeans. A long, jagged gash bled down her side. Christ, that was deep. No wonder it'd hurt so bad.

Kelsey's head lifted, scenting the air. "You're bleeding," she muttered, glancing down the alleyway. Before Jena could protest, she'd crouched beside her, and Kelsey's mouth was on the wound—and then she was thudding into the wall across the alley, the ring on Jena's finger buzzing like an angry bee.

Guess it didn't like that.

"What the hell?" Kelsey asked dazed, shaking her head as she got to her feet. The were worked her tongue in her mouth, scowling. "That was like licking a cattle prod."

"You do that enough to compare?" Felix asked, his curls dripping.

"Once was enough," she shot back.

Jena glanced between them and then down at gash. It looked the same as it had, and she no idea why Kelsey had gotten shocked, but she was pretty sure she'd just discovered what the ring did. Whether that was the carrot or the stick though…

"Figure it out later, we need to go," Felix said, flicking a sodden curl from his brow. "The rain helps, but all this is burning through my karma faster than I'd like."

Jena pulled herself out of the puddle and reached in to lower the hatch, making sure it didn't clang as it closed. A bright smear of her blood stained the metal. She tossed a handful of water over it. "Are we going down Cross, or cutting through—"

"Can't you smell it?" A massive were growled, stepping into the alley and raising his nose to sniff. "It's fresh."

"I can, but between the rain and all these fans blowing, I don't know where it's coming from," said another doing the same as he followed him.

Felix and Kelsey moved to stand by Jena, and he raised his hand making a scissors motion. Cutting through the cemetery it was. They slowly backed out of the alley. The weres' voices followed them.

"Maybe they're upstairs killing chickens or whatever witches do."

The first were grunted. "Whatever keeps them busy. Malcom didn't seem to care about what they did, as long as they stayed put...but this don't smell like chicken blood..."

Jena stopped short at the name, and Kelsey bumped into her.

Felix glanced over his shoulder at them. "Come on!" he mouthed, tapping his wrist.

Right, karma. They hurried to catch up with him.

The row of shops on Cross backed up to a municipal parking lot bracketed by an L-shaped, chest-high, cement retaining wall. Virginia creeper gone scarlet and yellow clusters of bittersweet berries spilled over the top, the vines lacing through the chain-link fence above. Beyond it was the churchyard and the cemetery, then the tracks were another two blocks past a residential neighborhood and a stretch of pasture.

They headed to the far corner of the lot where the

retaining wall had crumbled, and the fencing curled away from the post. Felix scrambled through the muddy gap, dropping his power as soon as they joined him behind the leafy blind. "Next bit's all you, I'm saving the rest of my karma for an emergency," he panted, plucking at his suit. "One that's not related to fashion. God, this is disgusting. My tie is ruined."

The entire outfit was gonna have to get tossed if Jena was any judge. "I'll buy you another, and I'm not so sure you're off the hook." She frowned, looking past the crooked stone markers of the town's founding members.

The main cemetery was through the hedge opposite them and a completely open stretch, aside from the few tombs dotting the grounds. A chill mist grayed the distance, but they were gonna stick out like sore thumbs. She put a hand to her still-bleeding side. God, it throbbed. Kelsey's spit was definitely not as effective as Chase's. "Where's your car?"

Felix shot her a look. "Parked outside of town hall. There's no way we're going to be able to get it without being noticed. Especially not looking like this," he said, frowning at his suit.

"I walked," Kelsey said. "It's not that far."

Because of course she had, and yeah, it was. Damn it. Felix was right. They weren't going to be able to make it across town without someone spotting them. Jena chewed her lip, but maybe…

"How much karma would you need to distort us enough not to be immediately recognizable?" she asked Felix.

He raised a brow. "A lot less than I just burned though, especially if Kelsey doesn't mind shifting. A random couple with a dog in the rain is a lot easier to pull off than nobody there. Why, what are you thinking?"

Jena sighed. "I'm thinking desperate times call for desperate measures." And that karma had the tendency to linger. "Do you mind shifting?" she asked Kelsey.

The were was already half out of her clothes. "Nope, but

whatever you do, make it quick," she said glancing through a gap in the mess of weeds hiding them from the parking lot. "You reek like wounded prey, and those two weres just came around the back of your shop. You got room in your bag for these?" Jena gave a reluctant nod, squeezing them out before packing them away. Kelsey finished stripping and shifted into a sleek red wolf easily twice the size of anything you'd find in nature.

Jena blew out a breath. Damn it, now it was her turn.

"What do I need to do?" Felix asked.

"Just be ready to take it."

He fluttered his lashes. "God, I love it when you talk dirty to me."

Jena snorted and ran a hand over her face before placing her palms against the ground. She hated eating sin. Yes, the power boost was amazing, but you saw all of it. Every detail of how a person had accrued the shadow upon their soul. That was the universe's price for clearing someone's karmic scales, and as far as she was concerned, it wasn't worth it.

But if they were going to get through town...she took another breath and called up her power. These graves were hundreds of years old, how bad could their sins be? It was probably stuff like showing their ankles and snacking on the sabbath.

Her stomach lurched as the first wave hit her. Shit, that'd been wishful thinking. Slavery, sexual assault...damn it. The times may change, but shitty people didn't. Karma strained through her, the shadows sloughing off and dissipating into the aether as she channeled pure power to Felix. He gasped, the houndstooth of his suit muddling to solid gray joggers and his hair becoming a mousy brown. The umbrella turned solid purple, and beside him, Kelsey's fur darkened, her form shrinking to a medium size dog's. Jena's hair lightened out of the corner of her eye—

"We're good," Felix said.

Jena wasn't after being privy to that. So much for the good old days. She gratefully dropped her power, her hands trembling. Lord. When people talked about the sins of their forefathers, they weren't kidding. Felix helped her up, and they started across the churchyard hand in hand. Kelsey glanced back at the lot then trotted after them.

"The distortion won't be enough to pass close inspection, but as long as no one comes within ten feet, we should be okay," Felix murmured, holding open the cemetery gate for them.

They made their way through without incident, and fifteen minutes later they were cutting across someone's backyard into the residential neighborhood. Quaint gingerbread houses studded the treelined streets behind low stone walls and wrought iron fences. Jena kicked through a pile of dappled leaves, her footsteps slowing at children's excited screams from the next street over.

"Shit, I forgot about the trunk-or-treat," Felix murmured.

Jena glanced at him askance. "The what?"

"Trunk-or-treat. Instead of letting the little urchins run around unsupervised to cause havoc after dark, parents sit by their cars in the driveway, decorate the trunks, and let the kids have at whatever candy's inside."

Was he serious? "In this weather?"

"Town hall lent them those big canopies for the main drag," he said. "Wouldn't want the little blighters to get wet."

She shook her head. "Doesn't gentrifying the holiday defeat the entire purpose?"

"Not if your purpose is to get stupid amounts of candy with basically no effort." He craned his neck. "Unfortunately, my sister said the whole neighborhood was participating, and it's gonna be mobbed. Someone will definitely get close enough to recognize us."

Kelsey whined, pressing against Jena's knee. She was

looking back the way they'd—shit. "Keep walking. I'm pretty sure someone already has."

Felix's gaze snapped to the two weres that had been outside the shop crossing the backyard they'd just cut through. "No..." he said, his hand tightening on hers as one of the weres pointed at them. Felix tossed his umbrella. "Now we run."

They turned and sprinted to the next street, bursting out into a crowd of costumed revelers. Damn, Felix was right, it was packed. Tarps and canopies had been set up across the entire street. Jena caught herself as she tripped over a guide line and almost took out a table of goodie bags. Kelsey yipped and changed direction, bowling people over. A man yelled, and people turned to stare.

Shit, shit, shit! Nothing for it—Jena and Felix sprinted after her, running past blinged out trunks and through mobs of trick-or-treaters. Another person yelled behind them, and a woman screamed as something crashed in their wake. The shrill screeches of kids sliced through the air, and Jena's stomach churned, terrified to look back.

Felix dropped his spell, and Jena pushed herself to go faster, lagging behind them. The pain in her side was awful, and a stitch was setting in beside it. God, she was not physically equipped for this shit...

Kelsey changed direction again at a privacy fence, and they raced across someone's side yard. The pasture where the tracks cut through was just beyond. A were howled behind Jena as Felix and Kelsey disappeared down the embankment at the edge of the lawn. Damn it—Jena bit back a ragged sob, her chest burning. She clutched her side, cramping up, and trying not to break her neck as she fled pell-mell down the slope to the pasture.

Felix waited for her on the other side of a split rail fence. Kelsey was nowhere in sight. Another howl sounded at Jena's back, and he stared, pale and wide-eyed at something behind her. Oh, Jesus. That couldn't be good. Her feet pounded over the bumpy turf—*too slow, too slow, too slow*—and a manic laugh burbled up her throat. There was no fricking way she was gonna make it—a growl and the thud of paws closed in on her—

Felix drew a glyph in the air, then slammed his wrists together over his head as a hot wash of breath hit the back of her neck. A wave of force rippled over her, and a wolf howled in pain—

Others answered it.

A half-dozen massive red weres bounded over the pasture's fence.

"Get on!" Felix screamed, climbing onto a wolf's back as another brushed up beside her.

What? Was he—the were turned to her, his eyes amused as he lowered himself to the ground, then huffed. Shit. Jena swallowed her protests and threw a leaden leg over his broad back. She leaned forward and buried her hands in his ruff— then screamed, plastering herself to him as he rose and was off and running in one smooth—*airborne, holy shit, they were fucking airborne*—the breath went out of her as they cleared the fence and landed.

Jena squeezed her eyes shut, focusing on not falling off, and the were was off and running again.

"HOW WE DOING IN THERE?" Patrick's voice echoed down into the deep foundation.

At least Chase thought it was Patrick.

Chase cracked an eye against the rain beating down on him. Between that, the head injury, and the hum of the leyline rattling through his skull, he wasn't thinking very clearly. The curve of an umbrella's shadow sliced over the hole above.

"Peachy," Chase rasped, still not entirely sure he wasn't

hallucinating, but either way…"I'm assuming you're not here to help me out."

"No." Patrick laughed. "Not after all the trouble Malcom went to making you disappear."

Chase gritted his teeth, not about to give Patrick the satisfaction of asking why. Chase also wasn't sure he could coherently string that many words together.

"Here." Something plummeted down the shaft and splashed into the water. A bottle bobbed up, and a plastic sandwich baggie floated beside it. "Wouldn't want you to get piqued while you wait."

Asshole. "Dad's gonna kill the both of you," Chase growled up at him, squinting against the rain.

"Doubtful. He's got bigger problems than you going feral again and vanishing into the woods."

"What?" Chase staggered to his feet. "Are you fucking kidding me? Everyone thinks I'm feral?"

"Why wouldn't they?" Patrick snorted. "You've been giving quite a performance lately, stalking around like you want to rip everyone's heads off. Sprouting fur at dinner was a nice touch. I couldn't have scripted it better."

That goddamn, slimy—Chase's hands fisted at his sides. "All this bullshit with Crystal was your idea?"

"No, but it didn't take a rocket scientist to figure out how you were gonna react to it." Patrick's shadow shrugged beneath the umbrella. "Dad should've seen the writing on the wall, but I'm pretty sure he's beyond regrets by now. It's a good thing there's contingencies in place."

Contingencies? Chase pinched the bridge of his nose, light-headed. Christ, he wasn't in any condition to try and figure out Patrick's squirrel's nest of logic. "The fuck are you talking about?"

"Not your problem. You know, you and Dad are just alike. He didn't read through the agreement either. But then, why would he with me acting as his legal council?" Patrick laughed again. "Eat up, Chase-y. You don't look so good, and you're gonna need your strength."

The umbrella pulled back and he was gone.

Fucking hell. Chase leaned forward to snag the bottle of water and almost went ass over teakettle, the pool at least two inches deeper than it had been. He splashed back down to sit and glowered at the bottle. The seal was broken, and Chase wouldn't put it past the prick to poison him. Patrick was definitely trying to do that with the sandwich. It was tuna, and unless Chase wanted to go into anaphylactic shock, he wouldn't touch it with a ten-foot pole.

How sweet of his brother to give him an out.

Chase tossed the bottle back, letting it float and scowled, his skull throbbing so hard it threatened to split. Contingencies. Great. So Patrick was using this to get him out of the way. No surprise there, but it was surprising that Malcom had broken faith with their father to co-sign whatever the hell Patrick had cooked up...and that they hadn't just killed him. Not that he wasn't grateful, but it bothered Chase—a lot.

He huffed out a breath, his stomach clenching and his skin pebbled with cold. Christ, he was freezing. Chase's brow furrowed, everything Patrick had just said preying on his mind. What the hell could've made Malcom turncoat? He was stupidly loyal to Chase's father and had seemed just as invested in this sham of a wedding as the rest of them.

Chase winced, his head pounding in time to the hum around him. Speculation wasn't gonna do him any good; he couldn't think clearly enough to follow a solid train of thought. He closed his eyes and leaned back again, flexing a hand. Sooner or later, they'd let him out, and when they did, there was gonna be hell to pay.

"JENA, honey, you can let go now."

Her eyes flicked open at Felix's voice, then narrowed. The wolf she'd been straddling stared at her, his tongue lolling like it was laughing

"I knew that," she muttered, weakly pushing off the were to roll to one side and flop onto her back. Chainsaws rumbled in the distance, despite rain misting down through the thick pine boughs above.

"You okay?" Felix asked, his brow knit.

"Yep. Just gonna lay here." Fuck it. She was done.

Beside her, the were's form shimmered, and Kelsey's twin brother Liam abruptly grinned down at her. Oh, God. It would be him. "Looking good, Jena."

She slapped a hand over her eyes. "Please go put on pants."

He laughed and jogged toward a trailer raised up on blocks, then disappeared inside. Three more of the things stood in close proximity, set at angles between the massive pines. Looked like they'd officially made it to the other side of the tracks.

She shot Felix a look. "Tell me you didn't know."

"Oh, I totally knew," he said. "But I'll take dealing with Liam over your bloody remains any day of the week. Those Westside weres were not messing around."

Jena winced, a hand on her side as she struggled to sit. "Yeah, I got that impression." She raised the edge of her shirt. The angry red gash hadn't stopped bleeding. Damn. She gingerly touched the bruising that had set in. Ugh, it was swollen and hot.

Felix hissed air through his teeth. "That looks like it hurts."

"It does. I probably contracted gangrene or something from that hatch."

"Pretty sure that's not how it works, but it could be tetanus, hepatitis, or—"

"Thanks." She glowered, dropping her shirt as she cut him off. "I don't understand why Kelsey's saliva didn't heal it."

"Need me to try?" Liam asked, puffing his dark curls aside, his stupid grin too wide as he came over, pulling on a tee. He wasn't quite as buff as Chase, but he came close, and he was a thousand times more trouble.

"No," Jena and Felix said together. God, the last thing they needed to do was to encourage Liam Montgomery to get physical.

He put a hand to his chest. "I'm hurt, guys. I thought we were friends."

Felix rolled his eyes. "Don't we have somewhere to be, *friend*?"

"Oh, yeah," Liam brightened up, like he'd totally forgotten about why they were there. "My dad wants to see you. I'm sure Kelsey's already filling him in." He turned, waving a hand over his shoulder and started past the trailers.

Jena groaned, her thigh muscles pinging and twitching. Felix reached down to help her up. "Come on, it's not like you have to go to the prom with him."

"No, you did that." She cocked a brow, brushing clumps of damp pine needles off herself. Ugh. They were all in her hair.

A chainsaw cut out, and a yell split the air. Jena glanced

deeper into the forest at a sharp crack and the sound of branches snapping, followed by a *whump* that went right through the soles of her shoes. Jesus.

"Don't remind me," Felix muttered, peering in the same direction before heading after Liam. Jena limped along, taking up the rear. "Worst decision ever."

Yep. That it had been. She couldn't help but scowl remembering talking Felix down from the "polycule proposal" after he found Liam canoodling with Jenny Rys. Felix had been crushed.

"You know he married her," he said a moment later, like he'd been thinking about the same thing. He slowed his steps to match her pace.

"Who, Jenny?"

"Mmm. They had four kids, and then she left him for Pete Randall. That was five or six years ago. Someone said Liam headed out west after, but I didn't hear anything about him being back."

"That's shocking," she said, still picking needles out of her hair. "You'd think they would've flagged him at the edge of town and sent out an emergency broadcast like they did for me."

"True, the gossip dost flow," Felix allowed. "But trust me, there were no broadcasts when you came back, emergency or otherwise. I'm in charge of issuing those for the town. There were, however, a flurry of posts on the church message board." He frowned, trying to smooth his ruined tie.

"Like that's any better." Jena grumbled, glancing toward the sound of a chainsaw starting up again. "Have you ever met his dad?"

Felix shook his head as they picked down the rutted path after Liam. Some kind of big equipment had recently driven through here. "No. Our relationship was more of the 'let's hook-up under the bridge outside of town' kind of romance.

You know how things were back then. No one aside from the pack was allowed into their territory and fraternizing frowned upon. His dad's still a recluse, but I did meet his mother at a bake sale once. She seemed nice."

"Mmm." Jena hummed. She did know how it'd been, which made all of this so much weirder. The only reason they knew any of the Eastside weres was from school. In theory, the town itself was neutral territory between the two packs, but they hadn't lingered after class. Kelsey working at Cups never would've happened back in the day.

Ahead, Liam had stopped by two massive pines. "Dad's down in the hollow," he said when they got close, the smell of a campfire teasing their noses. "It takes a day to get the bed of coals hot enough for the pig roast, and all this rain isn't helping. You guys coming to that?"

Felix just looked at him, and Liam had the decency to blush. "Right…" He rubbed the back of his neck and started down the rocky slope.

They followed after, and Jena shivered as they stepped past the trees, a faint sense of magic prickling over her skin. "Did you feel that?"

"Feel what?"

"A ward." It was old, and oddly similar to the ones at the ruins. This one wasn't keyed to ill-intent though…invitation only, maybe?

"No. I don't feel anything except filthy and annoyed." Felix shook his head, his ginger brows furrowed. "Come on, Liam isn't waiting for us. Not like that's a surprise."

No, but feeling her mother's magic here was, and now that she thought about it, she was pretty sure there'd been another, fainter ward as they'd crossed over the tracks into Eastsider territory. Of course, she'd been hanging on to stupid Liam for dear life at the time, so who knew for sure.

God, all of this was so weird. Jena took a deep breath as

they hurried to catch up. The trees here were set farther apart, but the canopy was somehow thicker. Stumps dotted the spaces between them, and the forest floor was pristine. A stream trickled down the hillside paralleling them as they got farther along the path, ferns and thick lichen decorating the stones. Naiads turned to watch them pass, poking their sharp little faces around the greenery.

"Pretty," Felix murmured, glancing from the idyllic scene toward a series of regular thumps punctuating the stillness.

It was pretty, and someone had roped solar lights through the lowest branches above. They passed a smattering of damp picnic tables, and the smell of wood smoke got thicker. A plume wafted up from behind an outcropping of boulders ahead. Liam disappeared behind them. Guess that's where they were headed.

Jena trailed a hand over the rough granite as they passed, a faint prickle of magic beneath her fingertips. She chewed her lip, the faint regard of the node teasing her consciousness. Granted, it was the same kind of stone that the pillars on the tor were made of, but it shouldn't be resonating with them this far out.

Beyond the outcropping was a smoldering pit with tarps strung up around it. Liam leaned against more of the stones, and Kelsey sat on a rock feeding the low fire. A massive were in flannel was chopping seasoned logs into slats of kindling nearby. He turned as they approached, and Jena sucked in a breath.

Her heart about stopped. It was Chase's father—no, it couldn't be, but...

"Ah, there you are," he said. His smile was genuine as he set his axe down and held out a hand to Jena. "Phil Montgomery. Nice to see you again, though I doubt you remember me."

She raised hers to meet it in a daze. "You're a twin?"

He scowled as they shook, his palm callused and rough. "Don't remind me."

"Sorry?" Jena winced.

Phil grunted and nodded toward a picnic table away from the billowing smoke. "Have a seat, we need to talk." He raised his face to sniff the air. "You're hurt?"

"It's nothing," Jena murmured, her side throbbing. They went over to the table, and she gratefully sat, her legs officially jelly. Crampy, tingling, pinging jelly. Ugh. "Why is there a ward around the hollow?"

"Felt that, did you? I'm not surprised. Your mother spent a lot of time on it, here," he said wistfully looking around. He ran a hand over his dark beard. "Damn. This is going to be harder than I thought. Where to start…"

"How about with the silence between the packs, otherwise none of this will make sense," Kelsey said, handing them each a bottle of water with a chiding look at her father.

Phil frowned. "Yeah…that." He sat across from them and buzzed his lips.

"He doesn't talk about it," Kelsey stage-whispered.

"Don't you have coals to tend?" her father asked. "Tell Liam to keep chopping."

She huffed at him and meandered to the fire. A moment later the rhythmic fall of an axe picked up.

"The silence came about because after the last alpha passed, Wallace and I had very different visions for the Montgomery pack. Mine looks like this and his looks like Sunnyside." He frowned like he wanted to spit. "And that's entirely thanks to that piece of shit beta of his. I wish to God they'd never met. Wally wasn't always such a prick, but once he and Malcom started hanging out, he changed, and not for the better."

No surprise there. Jena cracked her water bottle and took a sip. God, that was good. Felix did the same, his eyes drifting back to the fire pit.

"In a perfect world, one of us would've taken alpha and the other beta. Suffice to say, Malcom's influence screwed that up and put us at loggerheads. Neither one of us was backing down. That usually calls for—well, never mind what it calls for, it wasn't happening."

"Killing your twin curses your line," Felix murmured.

Phil's gaze flicked to him. "Yeah. So we split the pack. His vision in the west, mine in the east, and the town itself to remain neutral...except thanks to Malcom and that rabid bitch Wally ended up marrying, it didn't, which is why we instituted the silence and closed borders. The wards you passed are part of that."

"Wait." Jena pinched the bridge of her nose, agreeing with the bitch part of that statement, but... "Rabid? Are we talking about the same Mary Montgomery? The one in 24/7 pastel pants suits and kitten heels?"

Phil snorted. "Yeah, and pray that you never see the side of her your mother did. That outer ward slices across this entire part of the peninsula for a reason, and she's it."

Mary Montgomery? Really? Goddamn, all this was wild. "Why did she hate my mom so much?" Jena asked. "Ms. Matilda said Mrs. Montgomery was jealous."

"That's as likely reason as any." The big were shrugged. "When Mary transferred into our pack, Wally and I were at college. I got the impression she'd suffered a personal tragedy and needed a fresh start. Whatever the circumstances, she definitely did not come from any kind of means. I remember my mother saying Mary showed up with everything she owned in a garbage bag and a wicked case of fleas."

"Now there's a visual," Felix murmured.

Phil grunted. "Rebecca took Mary under her wing, and she practically lived up there on the tor for the first handful of years she was here. Then everything went to hell. The old alpha passed, and I had so much of my own shit to deal with,

I'm not sure what happened between the two of them. Rebecca wouldn't talk about it, and the slander that flew out of Mary's mouth I never believed and won't repeat."

Well, that sounded on brand. "So, you were friends with my mom?" Jena asked, rubbing her still pinging thighs.

Phil nodded. "She was like a sister to me. Whatever she needed, I was happy to oblige, and vice versa. She warded our territory, and the pack and I helped take care of the manor and surrounding property. After your grandparents' accident, we were both orphans of a sort and looked after each other…" his voice petered off, and his eyes grew hard.

"And then your father rolled into town. I hated that sack of shit, and after I'd made that plain, he made sure I wasn't welcome. I'll spare you the details, but what he put her through—if he wasn't already dead, I'd hunt him down and kill him just for the pleasure of doing it."

He shook his head and pulled a beat-up leather satchel from under the table and slid it toward her. "Thank God she finally wised up to his bullshit. Everything in there she left for you."

Jena's brow furrowed as she flipped it open. What the hell? A half-dozen legal briefs, deeds, something had been incorporated—"I don't understand."

Phil ran a hand over his beard again. "After your grandparents passed, your mom created a series of trusts to protect their land and holdings. Right bit of luck there, considering William burned through everything that wasn't nailed to the floor."

"You're talking about the trust the ruins and the surrounding property are included in," Jena said, slowly flipping through the pages of legalese.

"Yes," he nodded, "but there was another trust that she made me the beneficiary of with the understanding that it would transfer to you when the time was right. That's what I used to buy the land you sold, then leased it to my pack." He tapped the articles of incorporation. "You've been making a pretty penny on the harvested timber and the mineral deposits we've found."

"Isn't it illegal to sell yourself your own property?" Felix asked.

"Technically she didn't, she sold it to me," Phil said. "Don't you work in government?"

"Okay, yeah, that's fair," Felix agreed, taking another sip of water.

Jena glanced between them, slack-jawed. "I don't believe it."

"I figured you would say that, which is why I brought this, too." Phil pulled out a slim volume wrapped in dark silk from the bag that she hadn't seen against its lining. He handed it to her, and her fingers tingled as she took it, the magic within resonating and making her bones hum.

"Holy shit," Felix swore, flipping a leg over the picnic table's bench to face her. "Is that—"

Jena nodded, her heart in her throat as she nudged the silk aside. It was her mother's grimoire, or part of it. It seemed too slim to hold everything she would've chronicled before she'd died.

"I can't help but think that somehow, she knew what was coming and did what she could to preserve your family's legacy. I'll give you some time," Phil said, standing. "We can talk more over dinner. There's a couple of guest trailers you're welcome to use if you want to clean up and get some rest. Kelsey can take you back up, but we're gonna need to move onto current events sooner than not, especially if that young man of yours is missing."

"What do you know about that?" Jena asked, tearing her gaze from the leather cover.

"What I know and what I suspect are two totally different things."

"They're saying he went feral again," Kelsey said, handing Jena her phone.

She scanned the screen, her stomach in knots. A public safety bulletin had been sent out asking everyone to keep indoors while the Western pack looked for him. What? They said he was dangerous…her brow furrowed as she read…use extreme caution…no. She didn't believe it.

Jena handed the phone back. "This is all a lie."

"Shit," Felix said at her side, scanning his. "So much for Mayor Chamber's fundraising meeting. I'm gonna catch hell for not being there to send that alert out."

"Regardless of whether it's true or not, the real shit won't hit the fan until tomorrow's full moon. Wherever they have him, he should be safe until then." Phil nodded at the grimoire. "And it's probably best to hear what I have to say after you thumb through that."

"Then I vote for clean clothes," Felix said, getting up. "And you need to take care of that that gash. I wasn't kidding about tetanus."

Yeah, that was probably a good plan, except the part where they had to hike back to those trailers. Jena frowned as she clambered to her feet, and Felix steadied her as she swayed.

"Need another ride?" Liam asked, ambling over.

Oh good Lord, he'd taken his shirt off and glistened with sweat from chopping wood. Felix made a pained noise.

"No," Jena said, glaring at Liam. "I'm fine."

She wasn't and the walk back to the guest trailers was miserable. The shower was painful as hell made marginally better once she gave up, sat down in the little stall, and cried. She didn't quite collapse onto the bed after, but it was close. Her legs were killing her, and the gash at her hip had become agony.

Jena winced, calculating her karma. She'd tried taking the rings off, and—surprise, but it wasn't really a surprise—they hadn't budged, which meant were spit was out. That left magic, but unfortunately, she was gonna need to rescue a busload of kindergarteners from a typhoon to even her scales if she healed herself.

Unless she ate sin to do it.

Damn it. If she wanted to be able to function, she didn't have a choice. She could hardly move, and the gash on her side was deep enough to need stitches. She reluctantly opened herself up to that awful part of her power—

And beside her, the grimoire shone like a beacon.

What the hell? Her brows furrowed. Granted, ritualistic implements like an athame, caldrons, or alters absorbed karma from the practitioner using them if their intent was consistent enough, but grimoires were more like a mash up of a recipe book and a diary. What could've possibly left that much residue?

Jena chewed her lip, not sure she wanted to find out, and pretty positive she didn't have a choice. She reached out with a trembling hand, her palm sliding over the grimoire's embossed cover, and an all too familiar roil of nausea churned through her stomach. Then her gut dropped.

Magic prickled around her as a spell took hold.

JENA WAS IN A MEMORY, trapped in someone else's body—a woman's—as they stole down a hillside toward a dark wood. A waning crescent moon shone bright above. The woman glanced over her shoulder, the scent of bergamot in her hair. Behind her, a stately manor stood upon a hilltop, its windows black, and the sound of night creatures all around. A silver trail marked her path through the damp grass, leading from a garden with seven standing stones at its center.

Jena started, positive she was in her mother's memory.

She took in the house where she'd been born as it had been, her heart in her throat. The few photos of it hadn't done it justice—

The node stirred beneath her mother's feet, uneasy. A whisper of warning went through her, with a sense of intrusion. Something at the border of this realm and the next was amiss.

Her mother turned away and continued on, into the forest, silent as she moved through the bracken, and Jena a passenger as the scene played out. A murmur of voices came from farther on. Her mother's steps slowed, and she wiped her damp palms against her sundress, creeping closer.

There, through a break in the trees was a pond. Across its mirror surface upon a rise, a circle of birch graced the shore. Her mother frowned at the tingle of magic spicing the air. No wonder the node had been alarmed. A gateway had been opened between their dappled trunks leading from this realm to that of the sidhe.

Two of the creatures stood beneath the crowning limbs in shadow, their furious whispers carrying clearly over the still waters.

"…don't care," the shorter of them hissed. "I told you, the witch knows and has taken precautions. The node is beyond my reach, which is why I called you." He jabbed a finger into the taller man's chest. "And you owe me."

"Would that I didn't, but I'll allow that I do, and you're just as much of a fool for getting caught. Gods, they can't even do colors right here," the taller man muttered, plucking a leaf to inspect, then let it flitter to the ground. "It serves you right getting banished to this shit realm and shackled in that pathetic form. Are you enjoying being a beast?"

"Hardly. It chafes, and you're going to release me of it."

The taller man pulled a dagger. "That's an easy enough request."

"You'd like that, wouldn't you?"

He shrugged, flipping the blade into the air and catching it. "It doesn't matter to me either way, but it might be easier. This 'favor' will put you perilously close to being back in *my* debt. I'll allow she's toothsome, but from what I've seen, Rebecca is cagier than a witch has any right to be."

Jena's mother tensed, sinking lower into the bracken.

"You do this for me, and I'll gladly owe you in turn."

The taller man snorted. "By all that's dark, you must be desperate to offer that up. Are you truly that keen to return to court? Moghaied's still livid you got a bastard on that were-bitch," he said, his scorn ringing through the night.

"What bargains I make should be none of Her Dark Majesty's concern—" The shorter man growled, then waved a hand. "No matter. When I deliver the node, she'll take me back."

The taller man snorted. "Good luck with that."

"I don't need luck, I have you, and I swear on all the old Gods, Brizathilis, if you fuck this up…"

He laughed. "If *I* fuck this up? You seem to be doing a proper job of that yourself. That 'accident' was a botched job, and I still can't believe you wasted your firstborn on one of those beasts."

"That's not a waste, that's to plan," the shorter of the two scoffed. "Mongrel or no, once he comes into his power, the boy's blood is blue enough to sever the witch's bond along with the wards around the node and transfer its allegiance to me and mine."

"Mmm. Yes. I saw just how blue it is…sidhe-blue, in fact. But you'll need more than the bastard's blood to pull that off—"

"I'm well aware of what will be required, and I've plenty of time to accomplish it."

"More like you'll be cutting it rather close. Three decades, four, until the proper alignment of the seasons and the moon? You won't last here long enough to try twice—" The taller man paused. "How do you plan on nesting the cuckoo until then?"

"The boy's coloring was easy enough to explain away with the were bitch's mongrel pedigree, and besides, the last time anyone made that connection, these hills were still beneath the sea. There hasn't been a mound in this part of the country in centuries—unseelie or otherwise."

The taller man tapped his lip. "Creating one would win you points…"

"No, it will win me Moghaied's hand and a consort's crown, but I can't do that with a damned sin-eater squatting on what should rightfully be mine."

"Pity you didn't kill her with the rest of them."

Jena's mother's breath caught.

"I'll agree it was an unfortunate oversight on my part, but how was I to know the witch wouldn't be in the car?"

"Maybe because they only seat five?" The taller man sniffed. "I'll do what I can to bind her to me," he tapped his lip, "but it won't be easy…"

"Perhaps she'd be more inclined to trust you if you acted worthy of it."

The tall man laughed. "You do recall my nature, don't you? Chaos is my bread and butter, and this town's far too tempting for mischief." He clasped the other man's shoulder. "Not to worry, I'll shatter her wards along with her heart, and take all she holds dear as my prize."

"As long as the node is mine." The shorter of the two stepped a pace from him and turned, his hands on his hips. He looked up, and the moonlight played over Malcom's sharp features.

Jena's stomach clenched, and her mother put her hand to her abdomen.

"As you say, and a favor—along with all the witch owns—belongs to me."

"It's agreed. Take what you like. You rid me of her, and I owe you in turn."

The slice of the taller man's smile flashed in the shadows, and he held out his hand, then drew his dagger across his palm. Malcom did the same, and they clasped hands, intoning as one.

"So mote it be."

Chapter Sixteen

JENA'S EYES snapped open as the spell from her mother's grimoire released her. She stared at the shadowed, water-stained ceiling, moonlight spilling across her face, and faintest whisper of bergamot still teasing her nose. Her body thrummed with power from the sin she'd just eaten, and she fought to calm the pounding of her heart. Flickery amber lights were on around the outside of the trailer, and the rain sounded like it'd abated…how long had she been trapped in that spell?

She put a hand to her head, her mouth gummy. Ugh. What the hell was going on? If her mother had known her father was unseelie, and he and Malcom were after the node, why would she get involved with him?

Jena pinched across her temples. Guess she didn't need that genealogy test, damn it. And God, Chase…did he have any idea? She'd known her father was a piece of shit, but Malcom? Well, everyone knew he was a piece of shit, but he was supposed to be a were piece of shit, not an unseelie one.

She gingerly sat up, wincing, and drew a glyph to heal her side. It knitted together with a flash of purple light, and the ache in her legs faded away, along with the power thrumming through her. God, that was better. She sighed, running her palm over the smooth flesh, and did a double take at the grimoire. It'd opened to a page with an ink drawing of a tall, slim man, his face occluded by sharp pen strokes, and an inscription beside him. Whoever it was, it wasn't Malcom. Her dad? She held the book up to the light.

Beware Brizathilis and mark his name. Changeling, trickster, scion of the unseelie court. He arrives in darkness and chaos follows in his wake.

A symbol for the rule of three was below it, drawn and underlined in dark red ink. Jena frowned. Well, wasn't that just tits. She scrubbed her face. Thanks, Mom. She'd remember to floss, too. How was pointing out that any intent you sent out came back threefold going to help her? An actual spell would've been nice—or hey, how about a primer on what had actually gone down between them?

Aggie said her father left town, but Phil seemed pretty convinced he was dead, so which was it? A better question was if it even mattered anymore. Seemed like her priorities should be on other things.

Like maybe dropping a dime on fucking Malcom for murdering her family.

Jena flicked the grimoire closed and buzzed her lips. Stupid node. If the unseelie court wanted it that bad, she'd sign the damned thing over just to be rid of it—okay, maybe not, but how was this even a thing? All she'd wanted to do was make Aggie's last days comfortable and settle her affairs, but nooo. Let's dive right into an insidious plot to upset the magical balance in this crap town.

Christ. *Calm down and think...* Jena scrubbed her still-damp hair with a towel and sighed at the yoga pants and 80s hairband tee that'd been left for her. Couldn't wait to squeeze her ass into those. Whatever. At least there was a hoodie. She started pulling them on, wracking her memory.

Right, supe history 101. The grid of nodes and leylines crisscrossing the country had been established way back in the day by taming wild magic specifically to prevent mounds from forming. Those were caused by the sidhe realm intruding into this one, kind of like a zit. But instead of too much pizza, they required a metric shit ton of wild magic to form, which also rendered the surrounding land uninhabitable for everyone else. The sidhe thrived in that kind of chaos, but they had their own lands full of crazy beyond the veil. The grid guaranteed the magic here stayed tame, and they stayed put.

Which they did, for the most part. Sure, there were some sidhe on this side of the veil, but their magic seriously suffered. And without that constant influx of wild magic, they also deteriorated physically, got sick, and died after a century or so. For beings with typical lifespans long enough to mark continental drift, that wasn't exactly a selling point. All of them here were basically exiles under a death sentence and needed to carry government issued visas.

She pulled on the tee, not particularly thrilled that all of that tracked with what she'd just seen, and it didn't sound like Malcom had gotten his green card. But if her mother had known about him—about him murdering their family—why hadn't she flagged his ass to the feds? That should've been a no-brainer. They would've picked him up and her dad, and they'd both be rotting in some detention site right now instead making her life miserable. Calling them in was sounding better and better…

She paused, looking out the window at the pixies catching bugs beneath the lights. No. There had to be a reason. It was probably a good one, too. Jena eyed the grimoire like a snake. If the answers were in there, did she want them? Technically, she should be on a registry if she was half-sidhe, and since her father had been unseelie, chances were high she'd be detained.

She'd also probably be ousted from this realm into the next along with Malcom and Chase when they found him. She snorted. Like she needed to be part of that relocation program.

The trailer door rattled as someone knocked on it.

"Just a sec," she called, dumping Kelsey's soggy clothes out of her spellbag and scooping up the stupid book. Shit. Everything in there was damp now…whatever. She shoved the grimoire back into the leather satchel with the rest of the papers Phil had given her and crammed it into her spellbag. She looped it over her shoulder and toed back into her soggy sneakers, glad for the reprieve as she answered the door.

Whoa. Felix stood there in a borrowed tracksuit two sizes too big that actually matched.

"Looking good, Felix."

"Ha ha." He frowned down at himself. "More like boring. But it's not like I had options." He tugged up the collar and sniffed it. "Trust me, I would've taken them. This cologne is so senior year."

Ouch. "Liam's?"

"Mmm." He scowled, flipping a lock of hair from his eyes. "Come on, they're setting up a late dinner. Phil wanted to give you time to do whatever you needed to do with your mom's grimoire," he said, waggling his upraised fingers. "I hope you took care of that gash while you were at it."

"I did," she said, falling in step with him as they followed the lighted path back down into the hollow. The rain had stopped, but by the clouds it wasn't done, and the ground was super muddy.

He glanced at her askance. "Okay, spill. I know that look."

"What look?"

"Like you're on info overload. You read it?"

"Sort of," she said, hopping over a rut.

"And…"

"And I need time to process."

Felix stopped with a dramatic huff. "You know, you'd think we were dating the way you're constantly edging me. 'Just wait, Felix. It will be worth it, Felix. I need to process, a cone of silence, and a margarita, Felix,'" he said in a high falsetto, a hand on his chest.

"Shut up, I do not sound like that." She laughed.

"You do, and you're lucky I'm a masochist, otherwise I would've dumped your ass years ago." He started back down the path, fiddling with the drawstring on his borrowed pants as they slipped. "Though a margarita does sound good. At least give me something…was banging Chase all that you imagined?"

Jena bit back a smile. "Better."

"Did he make you call him Daddy?" Felix asked, a hand on her arm. "He totally gives me Daddy vibes."

"Ew! No." She laughed again, trailing her fingers over one of the sentinel pines as they entered the hollow. The magic from the ward rose up again to meet her. Yeah, it was definitely invitation only.

"Don't you yuck my yum." Felix tsked.

"Me? Never, but he's more of a 'sir' kind of guy."

Felix fanned himself. "Okay, you're forgiven. That's hot. Bossy boys are the best."

Jena smiled wider. He wasn't wrong.

The solar lights in the trees above had come on, twinkling above the picnic tables. A canopy stood above one set up with a red-and-white checkered tablecloth, and Kelsey was helping an older, curvy woman put out place settings.

"Hey, guys!" she called, waving. "Hope burgers are okay. This week everyone usually has to fend for themselves since mom's cooking so much for Saturday."

The older woman tsked. "Kelsey Ann, that's not true. I made macaroni salad not a half hour ago for this." She turned to them with a wide smile. "Tess Montgomery," she said, wiping her hands on a towel before reaching for Jena's to shake. "My, last time I saw you, you were knee high to a dragonfly, and didn't you just grow up pretty as your mama?"

"Um, thanks," Jena said, releasing the woman's hand and rubbing hers together awkwardly. "Can we help?"

"What? No! You're guests, sit, sit." She ushered them to the table and a woof came from beneath it as Jena took a seat. A fuzzy muzzle pushed into her lap. "Don't mind Nana, she's just looking for love."

"Nana…" Jena's brows knit as she stroked a hand over the dog's wiry gray coat, an odd sense of déjà vu stealing over her. "I feel like…what kind of dog is she?"

"Irish wolfhound," Kelsey said. "Dad breeds them special."

Felix edged away from it, the struggle on his face real. He was one hundred percent a cat person, and dogs freaked him out, especially big dogs. "Um, isn't that a little…odd?"

"I suppose that all depends on which wolves they're trained to hunt," Phil said, rounding the stones to join them with a platter of burgers. "Nana and her litter are primed to go after Westsiders crossing into our territory. Believe me when I say it doesn't happen often."

Jena's hand stilled behind the dog's ear. Well, that wasn't particularly reassuring considering she smelled like one. Nana huffed, looking up at her with big liquid brown eyes, and Phil chuckled.

"Don't worry. I let her and the rest of them know you were coming."

"Um…okay?" Jena gingerly resumed her scritches, and the dog's eyes closed in bliss.

"They've got pack memory Dad can access. It's way cool," Kelsey added, doling out condiments from a picnic basket. "She probably remembers you."

"She seems really familiar…did my mom have a dog like this?" Jena asked.

"No," Phil said, setting the platter of burgers on the table and sitting across from her. "But I did. That's actually Nana Four. They're beautiful dogs, but they don't live very long.

You probably remember Nana One. The two of you were inseparable whenever we brought her over to the manor, and she stayed up there more often than not after her own pups were grown. In fact, that's how her line got their names, after that dog in *Peter Pan*. Your mother couldn't ask for a better babysitter."

"I think I remember…" Jena murmured, a vague recollection of being dragged out of the house by the back of her shirt. Around her, the smell of smoke intensified.

The alpha grunted. "Well, dig in while it's hot," he said, motioning toward the platter. "You eat while I talk. I'm gonna assume you had a look at your mother's grimoire?"

Jena nodded, waiting for Felix to pass the mayo and not meeting Phil's eyes.

"Good, because some things can't be spoken about without drawing attention." Jena did look up at that, and Phil nodded at whatever he saw on her face. "I'd suggest you keep it close for now."

"Why do I abruptly feel like the cool kids have a secret, and I'm not one of them?" Felix asked, his eyes narrowed above his burger.

Phil snorted. "Because we do, and you're not, but for better or worse, it's about to come out," he said, ignoring Felix's irate glare.

"If you tell me to wait for it, I'm going to scream," he muttered.

"Why didn't she call the feds?" Jena asked over his grumbling.

The alpha pushed back, buzzing his lips. "You don't ease into things, do you? You get that from her, you know. Rebecca was always direct."

"You know you're killing me, right? I'm so dumping you," Felix groused, biting into his burger. Kelsey's mom sat beside him and patted his arm.

"It has to do with the sidhe," Kelsey stage-whispered.

"Oh no," Felix dropped his burger on his plate. "Now you've really got to spill."

Phil shot Kelsey a look, and she shrugged. "We didn't get the feds involved because if they sent one of their inquisitors out here, that wouldn't have been the only *irregularity* they found." He smeared his burger with mustard and slapped a bun on top with another warning look at Kelsey. "And that's all that's gonna be said about that."

Jena fished a pickle out of the jar, her mind racing. Who else in town had sidhe blood? It had to be someone still established here if they'd been worried about it back then and hadn't squealed since…It also had to be someone who wasn't a dick, otherwise they wouldn't care if they got picked up.

A plop of macaroni salad landed on her plate, and she jumped. "Oh look, your favorite," Felix gushed, knowing full well she hated the stuff. He smirked as she bit back a scowl at the sacrilege. Pasta was not meant to be served cold in dressing; it belonged in sauce with ungodly amounts of pipping hot cheese.

"Is it?" Tess asked, her face brightening. "Oh, I'm so glad! It's my mama's recipe; everyone raves about it."

"Awesome." Jena smiled back. Crap. Now she had to eat it.

Felix stabbed a noodle and popped it into his mouth. "Mmm, delish."

"So's the burger," Jena said, trying not to gag at the pile on her plate. "I hope I have room."

Tess beamed. "Oh, don't worry, honey, I'll send you home with some."

Great. Maybe Aggie would eat it.

"So why the big to-do about this wedding?" Felix asked all chipper, apparently satisfied he'd gotten his revenge. "Which is totally a lie, by the way. Chase said it's some scheme his father and the mayor cooked up. Why break the silence between the packs now?"

Phil put a napkin over his mouth and finished chewing. He cleared his throat. "Two reasons. First, Chambers is an idiot, and those turbine foundations need to be dismantled. It shouldn't be happening, but ever since they went in, all the power that's supposed to be streaming to the next node is backfeeding into this one and leaking out into the reserve nexus." He glanced at the outcropping of granite. "Even I can feel it building up out here."

Jena frowned, not happy that the coven had been right about that.

"Second reason is that if Wallace cedes alpha to one of his sons, they can declare open season on the Eastside pack without fear of invoking that curse Felix mentioned," Kelsey added, apparently immune to her father's stink eye.

Jena shook her head. "Chase would never do that." Beneath the table, Nana stirred, wriggling out from underneath to stand. She shook herself and scented the air, facing west.

"No, but Patrick would," Kelsey said, pulling out her phone as it chimed. "The papers said he's best man."

"So?"

Tess gave a soft cough. "In were culture, that's not just an honor reserved for your friend. The best man and the maid of honor are obligated to take the groom or bride's place if anything happens to either of them."

And Chase was missing, which meant Patrick would end up marrying Crystal. Jena cocked her head. Sucked for the Westsiders having that dynamic duo in charge, but it wasn't the worst news she'd heard today. Well, aside from the potential for a were blood-feud kicking off in their midst. That was pretty bad—Wait a minute…

"But those weres outside my shop—they said Malcom wanted to keep us there. Why would he—"

"Because if you don't claim guardianship of the node and our pack is out of the way, there's nothing but a couple of old, worn-out wards between the node and him." Phil frowned at the faint shrill of a siren squealing through the trees.

And the node just happened to be full of a metric shit ton of pissy magic, right before Samhain when the veil between realms was the thinnest, and Malcom had abducted Chase, who was conveniently his first born.

Jena felt herself pale. He really was going to try to turn the node into an unseelie mound, and he had everything he needed to do it by the full moon.

Which was tomorrow.

"I see you've grasped the seriousness of the situation," Phil said, tossing his napkin aside and eyeing the dog as its ruff rose. "Nana, come."

The dog gave a low growl and padded farther up the hill from them.

"Yeah. I think I do," Jena said, her burger threatening to make a reappearance.

"Oh, it gets worse," Kelsey said. Her throat bobbed as she tore her wide-eyed gaze from her phone. "That siren? They just found Wallace Montgomery's body out by the tracks. He's dead, and they're giving even odds on whether the Eastsiders or Chase did it."

CHASE STAGGERED around the bottom of the pitch-black pit, trying to focus on faint circle of night above, and his wolf going mental. Either half the town was burning down or somebody had died. There wasn't any other reason the sirens above would be blaring like that. *God, please, please, please let Jena be okay...*

He threw his head back, the howl that'd been building in his chest all day tearing from his throat and echoing up the tube. He panted, fists clenched, faced raised to the heavens as it faded, his anxiety on overdrive—

Move, he had to move. He willed his sluggish body around the pit again, his feet dragging and kicking up stones. He stumbled, splashing to his knees, sharp gravel cutting into his palms as he caught himself. Chase panted, mania creeping up his throat in a deranged chuckle. He fell onto his side with a splash, his shoulders hitting the wall, and his head lolling as he laughed. Fucked, he was fucked—

The siren above cut out, silence humming in its absence.

Jesus, stop it. Pull your shit together, Chase. He ran a wet hand over his face. This place was screwing with him way too much. The leyline's fucking hum that'd been plaguing him all day reverberated through his bones, filling him with a prickling anxiety, the need to *do* something—

Water sloshed against him from the other side of the pool.

Chase froze. His throat bobbed, his breath too loud in his ears. The fuck? He must've imagined—

A ripple tided against him again.

Fuck. He hadn't imagined it. What the hell was in here with him?

Chase strained his ears, the hum rising up in response and growing louder. It broke apart, changing and flowing into a low murmur, then individual threads…conversations…

Swirls of color formed in the darkness, misty shades of blue and green coalescing into shapes…forms…he shook his head and pressed the heels of his hands against his eyes.

No. Not this. Not again. He wasn't losing it, damn it, he was sane—

Water splashed by his feet, and he flinched back, plastering himself against the wall, and holding his breath. The fuck?

The hum dropped an octave.

His eyes sprang open, the small hairs on his body rising as a low chuckle resonated through the darkness.

A specter of ghastly green stood with its back to him. Wavering. Flickering like the end of a reel of film as it laughed. Chase pushed back against the wall, his breath huffing out in a thick cloud, the temperature abruptly frigid. The creature's shoulders straightened. Ice-rimed water lapped along the sides of the concrete tube as it shuffled, turning.

Chase fought down a surge of bile as it stared blankly ahead, wearing his father's face. The specter's throat was torn out and gaping claw wounds shredded its torso and ripped through its prodigious gut. Loops of intestine dangled from the wound, fatty flesh hanging in tattered curtains swaying against the creature's thighs.

Chase stared in horror as the specter became aware of itself. It looked down and put a ghostly hand to its belly, marveling at the slick of spectral gore coating its palm. Its fingertips slid together, and confusion marred its brow—

Its eyes flicked up to Chase.

Ire burned in their cold, dead depths, and a macabre expulsion of air rasped out as it tried to speak, the ruined flesh at its throat rattling in a death keel. It raised an accusatory finger at him and opened its mouth. The creature's fangs extended, and it lunged at him in a blur.

Chase shouted, throwing his arms over his head as an icy blast went through him, and he seized, choking on cigar smoke and brandy.

Chapter Seventeen

JENA STARED at Kelsey in shock as Phil sprang to his feet, dark hair sprouting over his body and his bones cracking and shifting. Fabric tore as his form exploded outward, and a great wolf stood where he'd been only a moment before. He lifted his head and howled, the answering calls of his pack reverberating through the night.

Tess stood with Kelsey and hurried to clear the table.

"What's going on?" Jena asked, her pulse racing.

"The Westsiders are coming for us," Kelsey said with no small amount of relish.

Her mother tsked. "Hell's bells, you're just as bloodthirsty as your brothers. No, don't—this lid goes on that," she chided, handing her a different top. "That one'll make it spill."

Jena and Felix exchanged glances. "What do we do?"

"Stay here," the older woman said. "The ward around the fire pit should slow them down if they get this far, but the others are too far gone to make much of a difference if their blood is up." Her brow furrowed, and she ran a hand over the lines, smoothing them as she forced a smile. "But don't you worry. Phil and the rest of the boys will take care of things. And while they do, you'll stay here with them, Kelsey Ann. I need to get back to the rest of the pack. Your Aunt Selma doesn't have a lick of sense and will just sit up there howling while Rome burns down around her."

"Fine." Kelsey scowled. Her mother hurried off, the picnic basket in tow.

"How the hell can she stay so calm?" Jena asked as Nana came back to their side with a whining huff, not seeming excited about babysitting them either.

"It's her superpower." Kelsey shrugged, then turned to the dog. "Aww. Did Dad send you back? Don't worry, if any of them get through, I'll let you have first dibs." The dog's tongue lolled in a goofy canine smile like it'd understood her, then faced west again.

"I feel like I'm in a weird B-movie, and a tornado of sharks is about to descend," Felix muttered, looking between the two, then swore at his borrowed tracksuit. "God, I cannot die in this. Promise that if I don't make it out, you'll bury me in Burberry."

"Do you own any Burberry?" Jena asked, her eyes glued to the crest of the hollow. Had that been a snarl? She'd definitely heard a snarl.

"No, but you'd think you could splurge a little to honor my dying wish. Their plaid is on point, and I saw those numbers Phil gave you, you're loaded." Felix chewed a nail. "I might have a parking ticket or two you can take care of while you're at it."

"God, you're not dying and neither am I." She also couldn't just sit around doing nothing. Jena shook herself and looked around, her financial situation the last thing on her mind for once. "We can help by strengthening the wards." She didn't have enough karma to do it, but sin...she opened herself up to her power again—

Crap. A big fat nothing...but if they could use the power leaking from the node... She stood and grabbed Felix's sleeve, hauling him over to the outcropping of granite and slapped her hand on it. Power lapped between her fingers. "You feel that?"

Felix frowned as he put his hand beside hers, then snatched it away with a little yelp like he'd been zapped. "Yes, and no thank you. Whatever power's there is ornery, and I don't think it likes me."

Great. Looked like she was doing this alone. Jena huffed, raking her hair back and stood for a moment, her hands on her head. "Do you have something I can use as a cauldron?" she asked Kelsey.

"Um…" The were pursed her lips and glanced around. "No…wait, maybe. Would a dog bowl work? I think there's one under the picnic table."

"I'm on it," Felix said, jogging away from the fire pit to snag it and heading toward the stream.

Jena blew out her cheeks. Okay…how was she going to do this? There was zero chance of her having all the spell components for an invitation only ward, but a straight-up intent one? That she could probably pull off—

A pained yip and a shriek came from beyond the hollow, and a snarling wolf appeared at its crest. Nana lowered her head at the beast, growling, but before she could meet it, another wolf came out of nowhere, bowling the intruder over in a cacophony of furious snapping.

Jena's throat bobbed as she lost sight of them. Or she could just attempt to shove as much raw power into what was left of the existing ward and hope for the best.

She rummaged through her spellbag. Come on, come on… she knew she had—yes! Salt, black Tourmaline, amethyst, and citrine…check. Damn it, she didn't have any—her gaze fell on a bundle of greenery and jars on the picnic table by the fire. "What's all that?"

"Hmm?" Kelsey glanced from the crest of the hollow to look at her blankly for a breath. "Oh. Herbs and seasonings to dress the pig with. The guys were about to bring it down and start cooking," she said, edging farther from the fire pit, a hand on the clasp to her overalls.

Jena parsed through the herbs. More salt, rosemary, sage… the rest wouldn't help with what she had in mind, but that was definitely more than she'd hoped for, and she might even be able to draw a passible circle to do it in.

Which by the distant baying coming closer, and Kelsey stripping down again, Jena needed to do, like, now.

"Dog bowl cleaned and filled with spring water," Felix said, running over with it.

"Draw me a circle?" she asked, handing him the container of salt and going back to pinching herbs from their stems.

"Deosil?" His head snapped up at another yelp just past the crest of the hollow. Nana growled, her hackles raised, and Kelsey shifted, joining the dog.

"Yes." Jena said. Clockwise. They needed the power to rise like the sun. She shook out her hands and closed her eyes, trying to center herself. Felix completed the circle and nodded at her, stepping to the side. *Right, deep breath, Jena.* She could do this. It was just like strengthening the wards around the shop.

Okay, it was nothing like that, but still. Piece of cake.

Jena bit back a manic laugh and brought the bowl over to the smoldering coals with one more deep breath. She set the bowl on the grill Phil had used for the burgers, an incantation rolling off her tongue to call the corners and set her sacred space.

Blue flame sprang up, licking the bowl as she added the stones and herbs, chanting, and let herself fall into the magic—

The power of the node rose around her, swirling, sparks tripping across her skin like laughter, flowing into her and filling her, waiting for her intent.

*No, I don't mean to, I just wanted…*Jena faltered, and it caught her.

Our service for yours.

Fuck. Her throat bobbed at the seductive croon. *I-I'm just visiting...*

A wash of annoyance rolled through her, and the flames tinged purply red.

NO. OUR SERVICE FOR YOURS.

God, if the node had a foot, it would've stomped it. Enraged growls sounded, closer, the baying at the rim of the hollow. Nana took off, and the shriek and howl of dogs fighting shot through the night.

"Jena, whatever you're doing, you need to hurry!" Felix yelled.

Damn it! She'd just wanted to cast a frickin' ward—

A vision of Chase slumped at the bottom of a well, his lips blue and his skin gray as he struggled to breathe flashed across her mind's eye. Then another, Aggie prone, Sweets and Matilda above her while Ms. Pao gave her CPR...

Jena blinked them away, her heart in her throat. What? No! She couldn't lose them, no. No! Not the both of them—

OUR SERVICE FOR YOURS.

Jena trembled. Fuck, she didn't have a choice, if she—if the node—could help them..."My service for yours," she sobbed. "But you have to save them, please—"

Power hissed around her, wrapping her in its coils like a serpent. *Swear it...*

"I swear! I swear! My service for yours!"

Bubbles of jubilant laughter prickled around her, and Jena's body went rigid, channeling the node's power.

Magic rose up in a flash of violet sparks, a ring of warding flaring, encircling the stones and crazing outward in a web, crackling from the circle and running through the hollow like ground fire. Another bright flash of light illuminated the crest of the hollow, and then a second lit the horizon a handful of heartbeats later. Shrieking yelps of wolves pealed from the surrounding forest, chorusing through the night and grew faint.

Jena staggered, the flames beneath her bowl flickering and gutting as she fell to her knees, her vision graying.

Words to vow spoken, the blood of thy veins to bind. Seven stones to witness thy oath. Our service for thine…

An image of the ruined basement on the tor and the circle at the center of the garden flashed through Jena's mind. The scent of bergamot thick in her nose, darkness claimed her.

CHASE SHOT upright with a heaving gasp, the taste of alcohol and tobacco cloying upon his tongue. He coughed, doubling over and retched, spitting into the icy water surrounding him, a weird tingle running through his body.

Jena.

He'd seen her, surrounded by violet flame, her eyes emerald fire, hair twisting in an ethereal wind, like some kind of goddess. Jesus. The amount of power she'd called…but why? What the fuck was happening up there? He rubbed his chest, eyes straining into the darkness, listening, but there was only silence from above.

And whatever that thing had been was gone.

Around him, the icy chill of its presence had dissipated, and the leyline's hum resonated differently. It'd morphed into something that felt…appeased somehow. The pain in his head had receded too, and he didn't feel like he wanted to throw up anymore. Unfortunately, that itching need to do something was still there. He snorted. All things considered, he'd gladly deal with that instead of that…that thing.

God. What had Jena done? He crossed himself and ran a hand over his throat, shivering with more than cold. Above, the quality of the light had changed. The rain had abated, and a circle from the gibbous moon crept down the eastern wall of the pit. He tipped his head back, staring past it, his breath a stream of chill fog.

Those colors…the sounds…the last time he'd seen that—had heard those voices—he'd been stark raving mad, caught in a shift somewhere between wolf and man.

But even out of his goddamned mind, he'd never seen anything like that thing that'd been in here with him. Chase ran a pruned hand over his face. Fuck. The more he thought about it, the more he was positive it'd been his father. The way he'd looked at him at the end…

Yeah. He'd seen that hatred in the old man's eyes before, and Patrick said Wallace Montgomery was past having any regrets—not that he'd had many in life. Had that little fucker actually killed him? No. It had to have been Malcom. Patrick was a sneaky piece of shit, but he wasn't capable of that kind of savagery. He preferred to eviscerate his enemies with his legal briefs.

And if their father was dead, that meant Chase was alpha by default, unless someone stepped up to challenge him… except everyone thought he was feral. That would nix that, and he was sure Patrick had just been tickled to step into the position. If Malcom was backing him, he might even manage to hold it. Hell, their dad had for close to four decades, and there was more than one were in the pack that could've bested him physically.

It also meant that Patrick would step up as Chase's best man and marry Crystal. He snorted. The motherfucker could have her, and Chase wished them the joy of each other. Damn. Now wasn't that just pat, both him and the venomous bitch getting everything they'd ever wanted. He scratched his stubble, positive Chambers would too, with his reelection campaign funding secured.

But that still didn't explain what the hell Malcom got out of it.

Chase watched the circle of moonlight slip farther down

the wall, his mind going back to the voices, the forms in the colors. He didn't feel like he was crazy. Of course, he wasn't sure he had when he was. Going feral...he didn't remember a lot about it, and that was probably for the best.

That dream he'd had when he was, though...that he remembered with crystalline clarity. It'd been about Jena. About them. He'd been walking up the tor toward the manor. It'd been rebuilt, and kids—two little girls—had run down to meet him. He'd picked up the smaller of them. She had his caramel waves and Jena's green eyes, and the elder, her hair long and dark, had taken his hand, leading him up the hill.

And then she'd been there. Jena. A hand on her round belly, another baby on the way, and a wide smile on her face. She'd risen up on her toes to kiss his cheek, then snuggled close. *"I'm so happy you're back..."*

Chase dashed a hand across his eyes. That was *why* he'd come back. For that. For her. He looked up at the cloud covered moon. It was real. It would be real.

And as soon as he got out of here, he'd burn the world down to get it.

Chapter Eighteen

"JENA. Say something. I'm gonna be super pissed if you're dead."

Jena's brow furrowed at Felix's voice, his sweaty hand holding hers. She worked her tongue around her mouth, tasting sulfur. "I dunno, am I?" she murmured, feeling bad enough to wish she was. A motor was running somewhere, and its discordant drone was sawing through her head. Ugh. Magic hangovers were seriously the worst, and this one was a doozy.

"Oh my God—finally!" Felix squealed.

Whatever she was on bounced, and her brow furrowed, pain shooting through her temples. She slapped her palm over her eyes, squeezing them shut. "No, no bouncing, ow…"

"You're fine," he tsked, dropping her other hand. "Stop being a baby. You're not allowed to die. Like, ever. Well, not before I do. I don't even know what you'd want to be buried in, but after that whole wolf-ageddon thing, I been thinking about it. If you left the choice up to me—"

Jena's eyes snapped open. "No."

"Bodycon," he whispered dramatically.

"Oh my God, ow, no, don't make me laugh," she winced, looking around. The clock below the bedside light said it wasn't quite four-thirty in the morning. She was tucked into a fluffy, pillow-heaped bed, and the dimly lit room was totally unfamiliar. It looked like someone had vomited LL Bauer, Eddie Bean—ugh, whatever that company was—all over the place. Everything was green and blue plaid, and the silhouettes of moose were sprinkled liberally about. Christ, were those vintage snow shoes tacked up on the wall?

"What? You'd be uber hot in one of those bandage dresses, and it would be like a whole mummy homage," Felix said, gesturing at her vaguely.

She rolled her eyes. More like a homage to a pastry-wrapped sausage. Speaking of which, she sniffed, smelling breakfast. No, she had to be crazy. Who was up this early, never mind cooking already? Her stomach rumbled, adamant somebody was. "What happened?"

Felix abruptly became serious. "You passed out and totally crapped your pants."

"What?" She shot up, clutching the comforter to her chest and put a hand to her head, wincing. Ow…

He nodded. "It was disgusting—Oh wait, no, that was me. You reestablished the pack's wards and then some, and now everyone thinks you're amazing, which I already knew. We even get house privileges," he said, looking around. "Such that they are…"

"I hate you so much," she grumbled, falling back against the pillows. Her gaze flicked to him. "Did you seriously shit yourself?"

"Little bit." He held his fingers up, not quite touching. "But in my defense, the Westside pack had breached the outer ward at the tracks and were tearing things up. All that bullshit about the Eastside killing Wallace Montgomery made them mental. They were in full-on revenge mode."

Jena fought to swallow the lump in her throat. "He's really dead?"

"Oh yeah." Felix looked queasy. "I saw them bag up what was left, and it wasn't pretty. One of the Eastsiders said they saw Westsiders dump him out of a van and take off. I heard the sheriff say there were tire tracks supporting that when Phil was giving his statement, so, hello, smear job. I told them I bet it was the same van they took Chase in. A missing persons has been filed, FYI, and you're welcome."

Chase. Jena's breath caught. That vision—

Aggie.

"Where's my phone?" she asked, anxiety tightening her voice.

"Drying out, along with everything else in your bag, and before you ask for it, little Miss EMP, it's dead along with the rest of the peninsula's technology. The compound is running on generators, and I don't even want to know what's going on in town."

Was that what that godawful sound was? "What? No, I have to call the shop. I saw—I saw her dying, Felix. Her and Chase. That's why I promised the node—"

Her stomach dropped, and she choked back a surge of bile.

Oh, God. She'd promised the node.

"Keep going," Felix said, a finger spinning for her to keep talking. "You promised the node…"

"My service for theirs," she muttered.

Felix's brow knit. "Theirs?"

"Yeah, there's voices—it doesn't matter," she said, shaking her head and regretting the motion. "I just wanted to reinforce the old wards, but it wouldn't let me, got all pissy, then showed me Aggie and Chase dying and…I promised."

"Oh, well, then you're screwed."

She glared at him and scowled.

"What?" He put a hand to his chest, like he was offended. "Don't kill the messenger. And I call bullshit. Don't you think it a little odd that right at that exact moment both of them were in mortal danger?"

Goddamn it, he had a point, but—

Jena brightened. But maybe they weren't dead. "Do you

think it lied?" Could it lie? She chewed her lip. Regardless, she needed to get back to the shop and check in. She didn't like leaving Aggie for this long. The coven members would probably try to keep tabs on the older witch, but Jena was all too aware of how Aggie got when she thought people were babysitting her. The woman turned into pure, unhinged misery.

"I hate to break it to you, but whatever you tapped into out there was wild magic, and it isn't exactly known to 'follow the rules,'" Felix finger quoted, "and not for nothing, but the node's been holding out for you to come back for a long time. I wouldn't be surprised if it kicked you when you were down to get what it wanted. What I'm more curious about is who exactly you agreed to serve. It might be pissy, but last I knew, magic wasn't sentient enough to speak, and that 'theirs' bothers me."

Jena frowned. How the hell had she channeled wild magic? He had to be wrong. "You and me both, but I can't stay here, Felix—"

"You might want to rethink that, considering how badly you fucked up the Westside pack. I can't imagine you're their favorite person right about now. Staying's probably for the best. The coven will make sure Aggie's okay."

Jena groaned, pushing farther back into the pillows and terrified of what her scales looked like. Even if she hadn't used it to power the spell, she'd still accrue its karmic weight. "I-I didn't kill anyone, did I?"

"Not that I know of, but a few of them probably wish you had. That ward of yours hit them with the equivalent of Kelsey's cattle prod until they crossed back to their side of the tracks."

Jena gave a huge sigh of relief. "What about the Eastsiders, was anyone hurt?"

"A couple of them." He frowned and then forced a smile. "But weres heal quick. Last I heard, the sheriff's department was rounding up every Westsider they could find for questioning and charges will be filed. Meanwhile, none of the Eastside pack is leaving the protection of the ward, and they've officially locked their borders down. No one in, and no one out."

"I don't care," she said, fighting with the blankets to get up. "I have to go back to the shop. I-I saw Ms. Pao giving Aggie CPR." Jena's eyes welled up, oh God, what if she—what if Chase—really was dead? She couldn't take that chance.

"Knock, knock," Kelsey's mom, Tess, said sing-song, hipping open the door and carrying in a loaded tray. She brought it over to the bed, and Jena froze, her mouth watering. "Oh, don't get up, honey. I'm bringing it to you. I wasn't sure what you liked, so there's pancakes, scrambled eggs, sausage, bacon, and a blueberry muffin. Plenty to share." She winked at Felix.

Jena rescued one of the sloshing cups of coffee as Tess set the tray across her lap. "Thank you, but you didn't have to do all this."

"Oh, please. This is nothing. You should see the lumberjack's breakfast I pull together every morning for the pack," the older were said. "That ward going up when it did saved our boys' bacon. Least I could do was make you a serving of your own."

Jena looked down at the spread and grabbed a fork, too hungry to argue. Felix had already helped himself to the muffin, damn him. She stabbed a sausage, her stomach not about to let her go anywhere until she put something in it. "Is it true the border's closed? I need to get back to my shop. I-I think something happened to my aunt last night…she's been really sick."

"It is," Tess's brow furrowed, "but let me see if I can work something out while you eat. This pack owes you a sight more than breakfast. Go on, dig in while it's hot, and I'll be back."

Jena blinked back tears as Tess left the room, and Felix handed her half the muffin, buttered.

"God, you're always so dramatic." He huffed. "You don't have to cry about it, I was going to share."

She sniffled, laughing. "Thanks."

"And we'll figure something out even if she doesn't," he said, glancing at the door. "I mean, it's your ward, it's not like you can't get past it."

Jena gave a little nod, not entirely sure that was true. The boundary by the tracks encompassed the same swath of land the node was on, and it'd been pretty adamant about her heading there next—not in the opposite direction.

CHASE PACED the pitch-black perimeter of the tube, his body thrumming with energy. The leyline didn't sound appeased anymore. Its hum had ticked up, waking him from a troubled sleep. It'd started as anticipatory, but damn, if it didn't feel impatient now.

Shit, maybe that was just him. He was itching to get the hell out of here, and it was just a dumb magical current, right? He muttered to himself, trailing a hand over the damp concrete as he walked, the water-swollen pads of his fingers worn raw.

The hum reminded him of standing in the middle of the substation where he'd done part of his electrical engineering internship, back before he'd decided he hated playing with high voltage. There, the sound was caused by a transformer's core windings vibrating in response to alternating magnetic fields. What the hell would do that out here? None of the turbine components had been installed yet; the civil side of the project hadn't even been completed.

He rested his palms flat against the shaft's gritty surface and frowned, a discernible difference between the two. His left hand trembled, the turbulence beneath it coming from beyond. On the right, the flow was dampened, like there was an obstruction.

His brow furrowed as he slid his hands along the wall. The turbulence in his right hand kicked up, then muted beneath his left hand after about eighteen inches.

He slid his palms up, and they both hit a dead spot. He traced along it, out and then down, the area forming a grid. That had to be from the rebar embedded in the precast. Chase stepped back, picking his lip. From what he remembered, that was supposed to be a composite fiber, but if Chambers had cut corners, and they'd used carbon steel on the sly—

Christ. Carbon steel was like ninety-eight percent iron. What a fucking idiot. If Chambers had planted a shit ton of that smack dab in the middle of the leyline—iron repelled magic. No wonder the coven was losing its shit.

And no wonder the leyline's hum was pissy as fuck. Iron was supposed to be to magic what silver was to weres. Going through a sieve of something that felt like taking an acid bath wouldn't be his first choice either.

No way would Chambers get reelected if it got out that he'd signed off on this. The town would lynch him. God, was he actually that stupid? Chase snorted. More like greedy, and the coven was right. There was no way the leyline was flowing to Fayet like it was supposed to be.

Jesus, what if that's why relations with their pack were so bad? If Havers was starving out their practitioners, it was a distinct possibility, and the more he thought about it, the more it sounded like Chambers wasn't the only asshole. Chase's father had probably been whispering in the mayor's ear, turning this bullshit to his advantage. Well, him or Patrick. What a goddamned clusterfuck.

Chase scrubbed his face, no idea how you would even go

about putting something of this magnitude to rights. At least not without one hell of a crane and bankrupting the town in the process.

He sighed and sat back down, his sodden jeans chafing and his stomach rumbling. Chase stared into the darkness, his brain going reno on him. The cement tubes didn't actually matter, but how would you get rid of all that encased metal, short of ripping everything out? The only things he could think of that broke down iron were time, oxygen, and water.

Although…electricity might be able to do it. He scratched his jaw, his stubble officially edging in on beard territory. The hum around him ticked up as he settled back against the wall, the lines of rebar glowing in his mind's eye. The concrete was already wet, dampness permeating the structure. A charge—electrodes positioned at the top to create a battery—could work as an electron pump to degrade the metal…

Too bad the lines for the substation hadn't been run yet. There wasn't a chance of getting enough voltage out here to do a damned thing. Chase reached down and picked up a handful of gravel, chucking rocks and listening to them plink and plop as it began to rain again. Much more of that, and he'd be in here up to his waist—

He flinched as something slapped down against the wall from above. His pulse surged. What the fuck was that? He stared into the darkness for a good minute before getting up and tentatively reaching out—

A thick, knotted rope hung against the side of the tube. His fingers closed around damp nylon, and he wet his lips, squinting up into the darkness. "Hello?"

No one answered.

Well, then it hadn't been Patrick. Shithead would've definitely felt the need to run his mouth. Malcom on the other hand…did he trust it? Chase reached up and tugged, then leaned back and yanked on the rope with all his weight. Seemed secure. He ran a hand over his face. If it wasn't and let go after the halfway point, there was a really good chance he wouldn't be getting out at all.

But staying here when he had an out wasn't an option. He began to climb, weaker than he'd like after being at the bottom of this fucking pit for almost a day. By the time he hit the foundation's rim, his arms were shaking and his legs were on fire. The extra weight from his soaked clothes dragged at him, and his palms and the inside of his knees where he'd shinnied up were raw. He gritted his teeth and hefted himself up and over the concrete lip, collapsing into the mud.

Fuck, that'd hurt. Chase panted, cold rain pelting down on him. The sky was just beginning to lighten in the east. He flexed his hands, the mangled flesh taking its sweet time to knit together. Combating hypothermia and whatever funk was festering in the water down there was probably taking up what little resources he had. He needed to find shelter and something to eat—preferably a steak—to kickstart his metabolism.

His wolf whined, and Chase clambered to his feet, glancing at where the rope had been secured. Shit, that was a bowline knot, and there was only one person he knew that could pull something like that out of his back pocket. Chase raised his head, scanning the landscape for his younger brother, Luke. Didn't look like he'd stuck around, and Chase couldn't blame him. He untied it and let it drop into the shaft. Kid had taken a huge risk coming out here, Chase didn't need to leave the evidence for Malcom to find.

Damn. Chase dashed the rain from his eyes, looking toward town.

Jena. He needed to get to Jena.

Chase staggered toward the fence's gate and shouldered through, the padlock gone. He stumbled, falling against the chain-link, the hum of generators coming from Sunnyside. A laugh burbled up his throat. His mother was gonna be pissed about that. She had a fit whenever they lost power and not having it to get ready for the festival? Her and Sue had to be having a bird.

He started down the far side of the hill, staggering away from the bougie neighborhood and toward town at a slow jog, trying not to smack into anything. His wolf was oddly subdued, and after what he'd seen in the bottom of the tube, he didn't trust himself to shift. Luckily, there was only about a mile and a half of woods, and then he'd hit the residential neighborhood outside of town. Twenty minutes—His boots slipped out from under him, and he stumbled to his knees, his shoulder slamming into a tree. He yelped, seeing stars as it about dislocated. Christ, that'd hurt—okay thirty...ish... maybe forty minutes.

Fuck, he'd be lucky to get there in an hour, but he would, damn it.

He blew out a breath and grimaced, gripping his shoulder as he got to his feet and headed for town.

JENA PUT a hand on her stomach and sat back from the decimated breakfast tray. Man, that'd been good. All those calories had helped temper her magical hangover, and she almost felt human again. Well, half-human at least. She had no idea how a sidhe felt, but guessed it couldn't be that different—

She glanced over at a quick knock on the door, and Tess pushed through with Liam trailing in her wake. Felix scowled, rolling his eyes and put his back to the were. Tess smiled at them, oblivious. She clasped a bundle of laundered clothes to her breast.

"I spoke with Phil, and Liam's offered to drive you both into town. With him being gone for so long, he's the farthest removed from all this drama between our packs and we'd both feel better knowing he'll be with you," she said, setting the bundle down on the bed, then gathering up the breakfast tray.

"Drive us?" Jena narrowed her eyes at Felix. "I thought I fried everything."

"You did, dear, but Liam's Jeep isn't one of those new ones with all the gadgets—"

"You're still driving that piece of crap?" Felix asked, cutting Tess off.

Liam pulled back like he was offended. "It's not a piece of

crap; it's a classic, and aside from needing a jump, we're good to go."

"Great," Felix muttered.

Jena wasn't thrilled either. Last she remembered that "classic" was open to the elements and about ninety percent rust, but him driving was definitely preferable to them hoofing it back to the shop on foot. She blew out her cheeks. "When can we leave?"

"As soon as you're ready," Liam said, his expression tight as he glanced at Felix, who was pointedly not looking at him. Liam turned away with a frown. "I'll be waiting downstairs."

Jena's brow quirked as he left. Huh. Wonder what that was about? Whatever. On the off chance he actually felt bad about what he'd done, it was way too late. Felix might seem all easy-breezy, but he could hold a grudge like nobody's business.

Tess rested the tray on her hip and reached for the door. "Well then, I'll see you two before you go, and don't think I forgot." She beamed as she left. "I've got that container of macaroni salad waiting for you."

"Fantastic." Jena dropped her smile as the door clicked shut. She flopped back on the pillows. "You gonna be able to deal?" she asked Felix.

He scrubbed his hands over his face, then scratched his stubble. "If it means being able to get this thing off my face and out of these clothes, then yes. I'm borrowing your razor and call dibs on that blue jumpsuit I know is still hanging in your closet."

The razor she understood, Felix was one of those guys whose beard grew in like he had mange, but the jumpsuit? "The one from the seventies cosplay?"

He cocked his brow. "Do you own any other jumpsuits I don't know about?"

"Nope." Jena snorted. "And it's all yours." She hadn't been able to squeeze into that since high school, not that she would've worn it again if she could. She pulled over the pile of laundered clothes. Thankfully, it was all her stuff, and she didn't have to stretch out anyone else's yoga pants. She didn't quite roll her eyes at the neat little stitches mending her tee. Aggie would've stapled it.

Aggie.

Jena hurried to get dressed and made a face as she slid her feet back into her still-damp sneakers. Gross, but at least she wasn't in borrowed clothes anymore. She eyed Felix scowling at the pair of Liam's sweats he was wearing. "Your suit didn't make it?"

"No, but I fully expect it to be reborn as a throw pillow," Felix said, glancing at a flannel one with shirt buttons on a chair across the room. He opened the door and held it for her.

"Houndstooth doesn't exactly match the decor," she said as she stepped into the hall.

"What are you talking about? I would be a statement piece."

"Okay, maybe, but the statement would be 'what the fuck?'"

"Har har," Felix muttered, following her.

Beyond the doorway was a long railed hallway overlooking a great room below, the blazing fieldstone fireplace flickering light throughout the space. Jena headed for the stairs, pretty sure she'd never seen so much finished timber in her entire life. It even smelled like cedar beneath the remnants of breakfast flavoring the air.

Phil and Tess were waiting for them by the front door, and she had a frickin' gallon container of macaroni salad. She held it out with a wide smile, and Jena forced herself to take it with one of her own.

"Thank you." Jeez, it had to weigh five pounds. How much did this woman think she ate?

"Of course!" Tess waved like it was no big deal. "Hopefully, all this blows by quickly, and you're able to make the pig roast tomorrow, but I wanted you and your aunt to have enough for a meal just in case. You're both welcome this side of the tracks any time."

"I appreciate that," Jena murmured, Tess's sincerity tugging at her heart.

"You ready?" Felix asked, one hand on the door knob.

"Almost." Jena turned to Phil. "You said earlier that my dad was dead, but Aggie told me he skipped town after he hexed everyone."

"He did." Phil and Tess exchanged a look. "But then about four years later, he came back."

Jena's stomach cramped. "Then that last spell my mom cast…" She swallowed, feeling sick. "It was to banish him, wasn't it?"

"Could've been." Phil blew out his cheeks. "I wasn't there, but Nana One was. She's the reason you got out of the house when you did. Their pack memory doesn't work like ours, but from what I could piece together, William and Rebecca had one hell of a fight. Once Nana had gotten you out of harm's way, she went back and saw your mom blast that sack of shit into a million pieces before she crumpled," he said, putting an arm around Tess. His voice thickened. "By the time I got there, she was gone."

Shit. Jena put a shaking hand to her lips. Blasted into a million pieces or not, she was pretty sure her father wasn't. Her mother might've vaporized his body, but sidhe were harder to kill than that. Jesus. All that sin up in the ruins was from him? She swallowed the lump in her throat, the entity outing itself to her making a lot more sense. "And you never said anything."

"No. If I had, we'd be hip-deep in inquisitors, and you'd suffered enough."

She nodded, swallowing as her breakfast threatened to reappear. Yeah. They definitely would've taken her into custody after that. Her gaze met Felix's. "I'm ready to go now."

He opened the door for her, and they exited the house onto a wide, covered porch. Jena hugged the vat of leftovers to her chest wishing it was lasagna as the cold hit her. Comfort food. She needed hot comfort food after that. Damn. It figured the weather would wait until now to turn seasonable, and it was raw.

"You okay?" Felix asked, putting his arm around her.

"No, but—"

The two of them stopped short. Whoa. They both stared at the Jeep idling in front of the steps, mist raining through the beams from its headlight.

"Wow. Is that seriously Liam's Jeep?" she asked.

"Yeah," Liam said, pushing away from the shadows close to the house to join them with a wide grin on his face. He flipped his cherry-cola curls from his eyes. "I told you she was gonna fix up nice."

Nice? That was an understatement. The rusted-out frame on wheels Jena remembered had somehow become a showpiece of a vehicle. Its paint job was a flawless matte gray with charcoal trim, and the undercarriage was the same flat black as the soft top. Fixing it up had to have cost a mint. What had he been doing while he was away?

Liam opened the driver's side door that definitely hadn't existed back in the day and flashed another smile over his shoulder. "Hop in."

Jena and Felix exchanged a glance. "Shotgun."

"It's all yours." Felix snorted as they rounded the back of the Jeep to the passenger side. Rain misted, pearling down the thick plastic windows. "Guess we know where those child support payments his ex has been bitching about never getting went to." He sniffed.

"Meow," Jena said, holding the door open for him, though he could be right. Damn, those were nice leather seats.

"Oh please, like you weren't thinking it," he muttered, getting in the back.

She climbed in after him and did a double-take at Kelsey crouched low behind the driver's seat. She put her finger to her lips. Great, they had a stow away.

Before Jena could say anything, Liam put the Jeep in gear, bumping down the tracks leading away from the Eastside weres' compound.

"I'm assuming you're not supposed to be here?" Felix asked.

"Nope." Kelsey grinned from the floorboards. "But this is the most exciting thing that's happened in Havers in forever, and somebody's got to help you guys keep Liam in line."

And there wasn't really any good argument against that bit. Jena sat back against the butter-soft leather and tried not to groan. Man, this was a step up from her car. Unfortunately, being chauffeured around in luxury left her with nothing to complain about and plenty to piece together.

Could that really be her father up there in the ruins? The odds were better than she liked. Like, pretty much a thousand percent, but that resolved, it only left her with more questions. Why had he come back? And still, the better question was why the hell had her mother gotten involved with him in the first place knowing what she did?

Jena's fingers tightened on the grimoire in her bag. She might not want to know the answers, but it was pretty apparent that she needed them. Ugh. Nothing was ever frickin' easy. She stared out the window into the pre-dawn fog, the headache from her magic hangover slowly creeping in again.

"So. You're back," Liam said after a solid five minutes of bumping along the forest track and listening to his wipers sweep across the windshield.

"Yeah. You too." Jena nodded, the rain pattering down louder on the Jeep's soft top. Geri was definitely going to be dealing with grass stains on wet tulle. The sky had lightened enough to make out the cold drizzle soaking everything and a thick ground fog hung between the trees.

"Yeah. I went out west for a while," he said, his thumb tapping against the steering wheel. "You?"

"South."

"You like it there?" Liam asked.

Jena shrugged. "It was okay. How about you?"

"I loved the desert, but it wasn't ever really home." His eyes flicked to the rearview mirror. "There were a lot of things in Havers I missed."

"Like your kids?" Felix pipped up from the backseat. Kelsey smacked his thigh, and Jena winced at the pained look that flitted over Liam's face.

"Jury's still out on that," he muttered.

Ouch. Guess it was a sore subject. They drove in silence again, then bumped onto the main road, and across the tracks—

A wash of power caught Jena, along with the distinct impression of annoyance. The Jeep slowed to a crawl, and Liam swore, downshifting.

I'll be back, I swear, Jena thought at the node. *Just let me see Aggie…*

Words to vow spoken, the blood of thy veins to bind. Seven stones to witness thy oath. Our service for thine…

Yes! I remember, I do. I'll be there—

Before the moon rises, the rite must complete. He's here, he's here, HE'S HERE…

Shit, Okay, that was new, and she had a really bad feeling the "he" the node was talking about wasn't Chase. The node's annoyance shot through her again, and she flinched. *Yes, fine! I'll be there! I swear.*

A distinct harumph went through her mind, and whatever was slowing the Jeep let go, the vehicle gunning forward. Behind her, Felix yelped. She turned to look at him.

He smoothed his frazzled curls. "Getting zapped like that is getting really old," he said, glaring at her. "As soon as we make sure Aggie's all right, we're heading to the ruins. E-stim is definitely not my kink."

Jena's brow furrowed. "E-stim?"

"Erotic electrostimulation," Kelsey supplied. "It's an acquired taste."

Okay, then. Jena looked between them. "That's a kink? Being shocked?"

"Oh, please," Felix rolled his eyes, "Everything's a kink if you do it right."

Kelsey laughed. "And sometimes when you don't."

Jena opened her mouth and then closed it again, wondering if that was why Kelsey was licking—nope. Never mind. She did not want to know what the freaky little were was into.

"What the heck did I get hung up on?" Liam asked, slowing the Jeep as he looked in the rearview.

"The node," Jena muttered, her conscience pricking her as they drove farther from it. "I have to be at the ruins before moonrise to finish the rite to claim guardianship."

"Nice," Kelsey fist pumped. "We'll get you there way before then, right Liam?"

"Yeah, sure," he said, glancing at Felix in the rearview.

Outside, the rattle and hum of generators slowly overtook the thickening silence inside the Jeep. People were already milling along the sidewalks carrying boxes and bags, heading to and from town hall. A bevy of big white tents were set up on its front lawn and the green across the street. A billowing cloud of steam came from the back of one of them.

"Looks like the pancake breakfast is still a go," Felix murmured, chewing his lip as he looked out the window at the "No Parking" cones dotting the gutters. "That means they're going to be closing down the streets. God, I'm so fired. You frying the town has got to have the organizers panicking. The mayor's phone must be ringing off the hook."

"Want me to let you out?" Liam asked, slowing as a sheriff held up a hand for the car in front of them to let a group of pedestrians cross. A couple of deputies dragged a sawhorse to the curb with a big "Road Closed" sign on it. Damn. Felix was right, and it looked like they were already getting ready to shut down traffic.

Jena whipped around to glare at him. "Don't even think about abandoning me."

"Too late," he muttered, then louder, "nope, I'm good, just about to be unemployed. Your shop hiring?" He batted his lashes at Jena.

She snorted as the sheriff let the line of traffic through. "Aggie does enough napping behind the register." Or she did. Jena wiped her palms against her jeans. God. Please let her be okay…

Liam turned onto Cross Street, and Jena chewed her lip, not entirely sure going in the front was the best idea. "Drive around to the lot by the church. We can go in the back."

"By back, you better not mean the coal shoot." Felix glowered.

Jena put a hand to her side. That wasn't happening again. "No, I'm talking about the door we used to take deliveries at." She didn't think there was too much crap piled in front of it to push through.

Liam pulled up behind the shop, and Jena whipped off her seat belt. His arm slapped across her chest, pinning her. "Wait a sec. You don't know who's out there." He glanced in the rearview at Kelsey, and she squeezed past Felix and out Jena's door.

They all watched her as she sniffed the air, then ducked into the alley. A breath or two later, she popped back out with the all clear. Jena jumped out of the Jeep and ran to the back door, the ward prickling across her skin as she spoke the incantation to unlock the deadbolts. She shivered, Matilda had definitely contributed to it. The spell was nasty. Whoever tried to cross it with ill intent better have friends around, because they were not walking away by themselves. Jena's gaze fell on a black mark by the step that hadn't been there before.

Good. Served them right.

The deadbolts clacked open, and she turned the knob, shouldering the door wide enough to slip through. Behind her, Liam pulled out of the lot.

"He's going to park on the other side of town hall and walk back," Kelsey said, squeezing through the crack. "Otherwise, once they close the roads, we won't be able to get out."

Jena frowned. In theory that was a good plan, but it meant that they would have to go through the festival on foot. She had no desire to relive the trick-or-treat debacle, but it didn't sound like they'd have much choice. Jena buzzed her lips. Guess they'd deal with that when it happened.

Felix squeezed through next, and Jena closed the door behind him. Her fingers hovered by the deadbolt—no, Liam needed to get in, and that ward would take care of anyone that shouldn't. The shop was silent as she headed out of the back and up the stairs, Felix and Kelsey trailing in her wake.

"Aggie?" she called, opening the door.

"Shh!" Sweets hissed, bustling in from the kitchen. "She's in her room, resting."

Jena's knees buckled, and Felix caught her. "S-she's okay? I-I saw…" she bit her lips, overcome as her vision swam. Felix steered her to the couch, and she collapsed onto it. Across the room, Ms. Pao's soft snoring hitched, and she turned to snuggle deeper into one of the overstuffed chairs.

"Aggie's really okay?" Jena whispered, her voice shaking.

"Woman's better than she's got any right to be after the fright she gave us." Sweets huffed out her cheeks. "Kressida was up all night sitting with her, and Matilda's in there now. I'm more concerned about what happened on the Eastside. There's no mistaking that was the node's magic that rolled through town causing havoc."

"It was," Jena said, wiping her eyes. "I saw Ms. Pao giving Aggie CPR—"

"Did you now?" Sweets's eyebrow rose, and she crossed her arms over her breasts. "I didn't think true-seeing was in your line…but I do remember the node showing your mama glimpses of what it thought she needed to know. Have you finally stopped your nonsense and taken it in hand?"

"Kind of." Jena's stomach churned. If she'd truly seen that, what about Chase? She took a deep breath, calming herself. If the node had really shown him, it had to know where he was, and she was positive there was only one way it would tell her. "I have to go back and finish the rite, but I needed to see Aggie first."

"Thank God," Matilda said, coming down the hall. "She's up, ornery, and is itching to see you, too. How you stand living with someone so miserable—" Sweets snorted, and Matilda glowered back. "You have something to say?"

"Not a word," Sweets said.

"Well, that's a load of crap." Matilda shook her head, her springy curls bouncing as she disappeared into the kitchen.

If Sweets did say something else, Jena didn't hear it, already out of the room and pushing through Aggie's door. Her aunt was propped up in bed, running a hand over a haze of steel gray fuzz on her scalp that hadn't been there yesterday.

She turned from the window as Jena came in. "It's about time you showed up."

"Sorry." Jena sat on the bed beside her, tears pricking her eyes again.

"Stop that," Aggie chided. "I'm not dead yet, and I know damned well that's because the node brought me back. All

Kressida managed to do was slobber all over me and crack a bunch of ribs." She grimaced. "Woman about burnt herself out healing them after the fact. Now you wanna tell me what part you played in the first part of that equation?"

Jena sniffled. "The node made me promise my service for theirs, and then showed me you and Chase, hurt…I asked it to save you when I did."

"Well, that was fucking sneaky, but par for the course. Alive or dead, sidhe don't have a real firm grasp on ethics," she muttered. "And if you promised them your service, you need to be out at the ruins finishing the rite, not here, blubbering at my bedside."

"I have until moonrise." Jena's brow furrowed. "But I don't understand. How are the node's voices sidhe?"

"Moonrise strikes me as cutting it a little close." Aggie pursed her lips. "And you know magic is made up of the life-force of all things. Well, when those things die, their energy has to go somewhere, and on this side of the veil, that's a leyline or a node. Most beings fade pretty quickly, but sidhe live so damned long, their consciousnesses tend to linger."

Jena blinked at her. "Why am I just finding that out now?"

"Maybe because you just joined the damned coven, and extra bit's next-level witchery," Aggie snapped.

"Okay," Jena huffed, wondering what else she only knew part of. "But if they're sidhe, wouldn't they want a mound on this side of the veil?"

Aggie tapped the side of her nose. "Ah…but for a mound to form there has to be wild magic, which means no node. Their energy wouldn't go into a collective, it would be scattered all over the place."

"So, you're essentially telling me that if a mound forms, it ruins their afterlife."

"Bingo."

Jena rubbed her face. "Great, so I'm the caretaker at the Stanley," she muttered.

"Nothing's shining, but it is backing up, and you need to figure out why."

"Sure. I'll add that to the list of everything else I should be doing."

Aggie frowned at her. "Since we're talking about Coven 101, you remember that photo album of mine with the gold-and-ivory-papered cover?"

"I think so. The one with all those old family photos?" Jena asked.

"Yeah. Get it for me. It's in one of the boxes upstairs." Jena paused, and Aggie shooed her. "Scram. I'm not getting any younger. You got time, moonrise girl, and we need to get some things straight before you head up there. Here, don't forget to take a flashlight," she said, snagging the one from her bedside. "Not a damn thing's working. Make sure you bring it back so I can find the crapper."

Jena took it and stood. She glanced at Aggie again, and the older woman waggled her fingers at her to go. Jena sighed, not in the mood to argue, and technically she did have most of the day to kill. It wasn't even seven a.m. yet, and the ruins were only a twenty-minute drive.

Jena sighed. Fine. Guess she was rooting through boxes. She went to the double doors down the hall and yanked one open. Ugh. It was musty and smelled a lot wetter than it should. She clicked on the flashlight. A trail of footsteps went through the dust.

Her stomach churned as she followed them. They had to be from when Chase looked at the roof. Jena's heart hurt thinking about him. If what she'd seen had been true…No. The node had saved Aggie, it would've saved him too, right? That was the bargain she'd made with it, and if they were sidhe, they couldn't go back on their word. God, she had to believe that. Besides, if Malcom was planning on making it a mound, he'd have to bring Chase there to do it.

All she had to do was finish the rite and wait for them to show up.

She shivered. Somehow, that plan didn't feel like it was gonna work out so hot. Jena stepped onto the landing, cringing at the sound of water pattering on wood. A steady stream pissed down from the bowed ceiling at the far end of the room into a growing puddle. Great. Right over the kitchen.

She looked around. Didn't they have a couple of those big garbage barrels up here—

Her flashlight glinted off metal as it swept past the boxes and stacks of crap. What the heck? She swung the beam back and slowly walked forward, entranced.

The fireplace had been restored—well not all of it, but the metal cage thing was a brilliant brass, and a shiny little knob was on the ash door. When had Chase had the time to do that? She reached out to touch it, and a tingle of magic flitted against her fingertips.

Jena's stomach sank, not sure if it was a new development, but it was proof positive that he'd come into whatever power Malcom had been waiting for. She frowned, turning to run her flashlight over the moldering boxes. Damn, it looked like a couple of them had split, and the contents were stacked in a haphazard pile, way too close to a puddle forming on the floor.

That had to be moved or it would all be ruined. She swung her flashlight around—ah, there was one of the garbage barrels she'd been looking for, and it looked pretty dry, well, drier, over by that wall.

Jena glanced at the rain lashing down the big floor to ceiling windows. Moving everything was going to take a good half hour, but she didn't want to lose what little she had left of her mom. She didn't want to lose anything from Aggie's life before Havers, either, and the rain didn't look like it was going to do them a solid and let up anytime soon.

She huffed out a breath, set the flashlight down, and started moving boxes.

~

CHASE CROUCHED behind a parked car in the lot in back of Jena's shop, catching his breath. Almost there. He'd had to make a loop around town to avoid all of the festival preparations, and that hour he'd figured on had been more like two. He winced, gingerly flexing his shredded hands, his socks sticky with blood. The wet fabric from his jeans was tearing up his injured legs, and he still wasn't healing like he—

One of the Eastside weres darted out from the alley and headed for the back door. Holy shit, was that Kelsey's brother, Liam? When did he get back into town? His stride hitched as he reached for the door knob, and he glanced in Chase's direction, snuffing—

Chase growled. Fuck this and the silence. If Kelsey had wanted him to talk to Phil, chances were Liam was on board.

"Hey!" Chase called, pushing to his feet with a strangled groan. "Liam!"

The were's spine straightened as he squinted at him. "Who—"

"Chase," he said, flicking his wet hair from his eyes.

"Jesus, I didn't recognize you. Where's your hat?"

"Gone. Little help?" He winced again as the Eastsider hurried over and steadied him. The two glanced at each other, and Liam's eyes widened as their gazes met. Damn it. Chase looked away, ducking his head.

Liam broke the uncomfortable silence first. "Jeez, man, what happened? You stink like prey."

"Malcom and a deep pit."

Liam grunted. "Sounds on point. Come on, let's get you inside. Kelsey says Jena's going apeshit you're missing." He threw Chase's arm over his shoulder, and they slowly made their way to the back door. A prickle of magic went over Chase as he ascended the step. Damn, if he could feel that, it must be a serious spell.

"She's okay? What the hell's been going on? I heard the sirens…"

"Yeah, she's fine, and dude, I hate to break it to you, but your pops is dead." Liam said, shouldering open the door so they could get through. "The rest of your pack went mental and came at the Eastside. Jena made some deal with the node and sent them packing, but it fried everything in town. We're here to make sure her aunt's okay, but then she's got to go back to the ruins to finish some witch thing."

Chase frowned, but none of that was a surprise after what he'd seen. "So, Patrick's in charge?"

Liam shrugged and swiped the rain from his eyes. "I dunno. We just rolled into town. Your pack's keeping a low profile. I didn't see any of them when I passed through just now, and there's no one watching the shop that I could scent, well, except you."

Chase grunted, thankful for small favors, but his entire pack being incognito might not bode as well as Liam seemed to think. If Patrick couldn't hold alpha, shit was gonna hit the fan.

Liam frowned, edging past the piles of dusty inventory. "Christ, this place is a dump."

"It just needs some work," Chase shot back defensively.

"Preach, brother." Liam grinned, helping him through the clutter. "I heard you were a reno man. Cars are my thing. My baby's a '72 Jeep I restored. Labor of love right there."

"Those are the best kind."

"Facts," Liam said, moving behind Chase as they wended through the shop to the back steps. "You got that?"

"Yeah." He might have to go up on hands and knees, but he'd get there.

It was close, but he made it to the top standing. Liam knocked on the door, and Kelsey answered it. Her eyes bugged out.

"Holy shit, where did you come from? Never mind, let me grab some towels." She disappeared down the hall and was back before Chase had made it all the way into the room.

"Lawd, if you two don't look like drowned rats," Sweets McConnely said, bustling in from the kitchen. "Kelsey, grab some blankets from the hall closet. Both you boys need to get out of those wet clothes and wrap up in something warm."

"I agree," Matilda Hanson said in the kitchen doorway around a forkful of something. "Get to stripping and don't mind me."

"Where's Jena?" Chase asked, his stomach growling.

"With Aggie," the sour little witch said, stepping in front of him. "And they have witchery they need to discuss, so you're gonna sit your ass down and wait for them to do it."

He went to open his mouth and Matilda smirked like she was hoping he'd argue. Fuck, he was too damned beat up to deal with this. "Yes, ma'am." He frowned, shucking off his shirt.

"We'll give you two some privacy," Sweets said, eyeing Matilda leering at them. She huffed as Sweets herded her back into the kitchen. Kelsey dropped off the blankets and followed them.

Chase kicked off his boots, his skin pimpling with cold as he peeled off his jeans. He was gonna have to do something about all the drafts in here—

"Good Lord!" A woman squeaked from across the room.

He grabbed a towel and threw it around his waist. Shit. "Ms. Pao?"

The librarian's bulbous eyes blinked behind her thick glasses, looking between him and a very naked Liam, a hand on her heaving breast. She wet her lips. "Boys. That was... was..."

"Totally wasted on you," Matilda groused, back at the kitchen doorway. Liam laughed, plopping his bare ass onto the couch.

Chase chucked a blanket at him. "Dude."

"Oh. Right." The were covered himself up.

Chase sighed as he sat, pulling another blanket over his shoulders. Damn, his legs were shredded. He glanced down the hallway towards Aggie's room, not rushing in there to see Jena was killing him.

"Is there anything to eat?" If he had to wait, getting something in his stomach would go a long way toward helping his healing ability along.

"Yeah," Matilda said, her eyes on the wounds like she was thinking the same thing. "About a gallon of macaroni salad. Hey, Sweets," she called over her shoulder, "I think we're gonna need that potion after all."

Kelsey came back into the room and bounced onto the other end of the couch next to her brother. She sucked in a breath. "Oh, yuck. Yeah. You need to eat."

Chase ran a hand over his jaw. Macaroni salad wasn't his favorite, but beggars couldn't be choosers. "There tuna in it?"

"Nope," Kelsey said. "Chicken. The canned kind."

That didn't make it sound anymore appetizing. "Can I have a bowl?" he asked.

"I dunno, can you?" Matilda shot back.

"Oh, enough of you," Sweets said, bustling out with a heaping portion and handed it to him along with a glass of something foul. "Can't you see the poor man's been through enough. Kelsey, go hang those wet things over the tub. I've got a cantrip that will dry them out in no time." She turned to Chase, her hands on her wide hips. "Well, don't sit there screwing up your face—drink it."

"What is it?" he asked, frowning as he tipped the glass. The viscous brown goo made a slow slide to the opposite rim.

Sweets huffed, crossing her arms. "A restorative brew. I

made it for Aggie, but after she got hit with that jolt from the node, I was leery of giving it to her. It should fix you right up."

Chase's throat bobbed, everyone's gaze on him as he put it to his lips, trying not to gag at the smell…he held his breath and started chugging. The way it tingled going down his throat didn't help to settle his stomach. Neither did the urge to chew it.

But about halfway through, he had to admit he was feeling better.

A *whump* came from above their heads as he finished the glass, and Chase looked up as he set it on the coffee table. Shit. Was that the roof?

"So, where'd Malcom have you hidden away, and does he know you're out?" Sweets asked, taking a seat in one of the overstuffed chairs by the window, one eye on Kelsey hauling the wet clothes from the room.

"Ah…I don't know, but he had me at the bottom of one of those turbine foundations," Chase said around forkfuls of macaroni salad. "You're right about them messing with the leyline. They didn't use the composite fiber rebar the mayor said they were going to. It's all iron—"

"Ah! I knew it!" Matilda crowed, her expression pure, malevolent glee. She rubbed her hands together. "And I know just the spell to even his scales…"

"Oh no." Ms. Pao bolted upright like she'd been goosed. "Not after what happened the last time we let you turn someone into a frog."

"What? No one told him to hop into traffic."

"No, but you didn't do anything to stop it either," Ms. Pao scolded. "Poor Otis had to deliver that man's flattened remains to his family in a manilla envelope. Can you imagine? Saddest funeral I've ever been to." She sniffed.

Chase tuned the witches' banter out as another *whump* came from above. His eyes flicked to the ceiling again. Not the roof, though all this rain couldn't be doing the building any favors. Someone was up there. He frowned, finishing what was in his bowl and considering a second. The *whump* came again. Was that Jena?

He stood, his legs protesting as newly formed scabs stretched. "I'm gonna go see what that is—"

"Hey, you're back!" Felix said, coming into the room, freshly shaven, in a short-sleeved powder blue jumpsuit straight out of the seventies.

"I—yeah." Wasn't the craziest thing Chase had seen Felix in, but damn. "Where the hell did you get that?"

"Oh, this?" Felix asked, plucking at the ridiculously wide collar with a self-satisfied smile. "Jena's closet. She owed me, and this suit has been calling my name since she bought it."

Chase's eyebrow quirked. "That was Jena's?"

"Mmm. Yes, *was*. I left a pair of sweats on her bed that will probably fit you." Felix glanced over at Liam's growl of protest and rolled his eyes with a dismissive huff. "She's upstairs, getting something for Aggie."

Okay then. Chase glanced between the two and shuffled past the slim warlock, going into Jena's room. He glowered at the vanity's mirror. That was gonna have to go, or Jena was gonna have to get some window treatments in here. He considered moving it for all of a breath, then tossed his towel over the glass, covering it up.

Damn. He sat on the bed. Long swaths of scabbed-over skin bled down his legs from where the seams of his jeans had rubbed, and around them it was puffy and red. He winced, his palms in the same condition. Sweets's brew had helped, but he was far from healed. Sitting in all that water for so long had fucked him up royal, and marinating in a leyline couldn't have helped.

Chase snagged the sweats Felix had left, that term not giving him warm fuzzies.

He pulled on the tee and zipped up the hoodie, smelling

Liam. Were those mating pheromones? Chase sniffed the collar. Yeah, they were faint, but they were there. His brow furrowed, vaguely recalling Felix and Liam dating at one point, but Felix didn't seem very into Liam now… Whatever, Chase was more concerned his wolf didn't seem to care that he was wearing another were's scent. *You okay, buddy?* He got a distant sense of reassurance, like that part of him had been weakened somehow.

Which wasn't reassuring at all.

What the hell had Malcom throwing him in that foundation done to him? Chase stretched out his shoulders, the fabric protesting—

Another thump came from above.

Jena. She might know.

He just had to climb another set of stairs to get to her.

Fuck.

Chapter Twenty

JENA HUFFED the hair from her eyes as she lugged the largest garbage barrel over to the most egregious of the leaks. She'd found smaller containers for some of the others, but it was a losing battle. Chase was right, the roof was in sad shape, and it wasn't going to last much longer.

At least the stuff the puddle was threatening was safe—unless the ceiling caved in—which is why she'd ended up hauling the entire mess of accumulated crap at the top of the stairs into one of the back rooms. It'd been dry in there, at least for now.

She positioned the barrel beneath the stream, and it immediately started to fill up. How she was going to haul all of this water out of here…her fingers tightened on the barrel's lip as she hung her head, sniffling. *I will not cry, I will not cry…*

"Hey, we'll take care of it," Chase murmured into her hair, his arms wrapping around her waist.

Jena shrieked, jumping as she turned. "Chase! I didn't even hear—where did you—you're okay!" She sobbed, her arms around his neck.

He held her tight as she cried, his lips at the top of her head. "I was worried about you too, but it sounds like everyone else should've been. Liam said you kicked some serious ass."

"That was the node, not me." She laughed, wiping her

eyes. "But the jerks deserved it. God, you're really here. I was so worried when Kelsey said Malcom had you—" Her lip trembled as she teared up again.

"Shh…it's okay. I'm here now." He frowned, eyeing the leaking roof. "Damn. That greenhouse needs to go, and I have to get staging in here a-sap. Come on, there's nothing else you can do right now, and I don't like standing under this. We can talk downstairs." He turned toward the steps and stumbled, biting back a cry.

She pulled away to look at him. "You're hurt? Where? What's wrong?"

"It's my frickin' legs," he said, picking the fabric of the joggers away from his thighs and grimacing as he hobbled across the room. "Sweets dosed me with one of her brews, but I'm still not healing like I should. Long story short, Malcom stuck me in a leyline. I think all that magic did something to me."

Jena glanced at him askance, pretty sure he was right, and she didn't think that messing with his ability to heal was all of it. "How bad are they?"

He held out his hands, his palms scabby and swollen. "Like this, but worse."

Gross. Jena drew a glyph over them, speaking an incantation to heal him without thinking twice about it. Magic flared, and the swelling and scabs faded, leaving unmarred, pink skin. It also left her karmic scales at a serious deficit. Crap.

"No kidding. I didn't know you could do that." He made a fist, then ran a thumb over his palm. "Why didn't you use your magic when you sprained your ankle at the falls?"

Her mouth opened and then closed, heat rising to her cheeks. "You didn't give me the chance—How did you get out of the foundation?"

"Luke dropped a rope." Chase laughed, a sly grin on his

face. "And don't change the subject. I think you wanted me to rescue you. Admit it."

"What? Are you—no!" She glowered at his chuckle. "Keep it up, Montgomery."

"For you? All night, baby," he said, wincing as he changed his stance to cop a feel and kiss her.

God, his lips...but she was pretty sure this was a classic case of the mind being willing, and the flesh being weak. His body was going to have other plans, and her heart hurt that he was in so much pain.

"Hold on. Let me see what I can do..." She took a deep breath and closed her eyes, centering herself.

The node was a bare brush against her consciousness, but there wasn't a chance she was getting an influx of power from there. Not until she finished the rite. It felt even more agitated than it had earlier. Damn it. She needed to deliver that photo album to Aggie and get on the road.

But first she needed to heal Chase, and if karma and the node were out, that left her with sin-eating. She wasn't certain there would be any collective karma hanging around the shop, but the building was old. It was more likely than not, and if she could use it to help him... Yeah. No decision necessary. She opened her senses to that side of her power and dark tendrils immediately cloyed at her.

Ugh. Lucky her, she had plenty to choose from. She turned toward the nearest mess of dark energy, and opened her eyes. They landed on Aggie's frickin' photo album. Seriously? Jena blew out a breath, feeling a stronger pull from one of the backrooms and quashing it. That was danker than she wanted to deal with, and if she had to eat-sin, whatever was in the album would be a more digestible bite.

Okay, maybe not, considering the last Easter egg her mother had left for her, and Jena had no doubt this was another. She glanced at Chase—

He was staring at the fireplace, his face white. "D-did you…"

"What? No. I didn't do anything…but I'm pretty sure you did," she said, a hand on his back.

He bit his lips and gave a slow nod. "When I was down in that foundation…I don't…I can't…" He huffed out a breath. "Being in my own head isn't great. Thinking about stuff—projects—how to do them, all the little steps. It helps. But how…" He turned to look at her, his big sidhe-blue eyes wide. "I don't get it, Jena. I'm a were. I don't have magic, not like that."

Crap. How the heck did she tell him? She reached up to play with the zipper on his hoodie. "Let's sit for a minute."

She kept pace with him as he shuffled back to the landing and gingerly lowered himself onto the top step. "Why do I feel like you're breaking up with me?"

"That might be easier to hear." She snorted out a laugh at his expression and sat beside him, pulling the album into her lap. Her fingers drummed over its cover. "Chase…Wallace Montgomery isn't your father."

He ran a hand over his face. "Christ. Is it shitty that my knee-jerk reaction to that is 'good?'"

"All things considered, no, but you don't seem surprised."

"He said something once." Chase shook his head, staring into the shadows. "After my…lapse…and the way he looked at me…there's no way you could look at your own flesh and blood like that, Jena. I knew the man never liked me, but after that…the color of my eyes…no. I'm not surprised."

She hugged his arm and rested her head against his shoulder. "I'm sorry."

He snorted. "I'm not. It's a relief. That means I don't have to play along with any of this pack bullshit." He kissed the top of her head and grinned. "And hell, if I'm mixed, I don't even have to affiliate. I'm fucking free. Patrick, my mom…

damn, I'm glad she banged someone else. I'm done with the pack and all the rest of it."

"Not quite..." Jena winced. He'd taken that way better than she expected, but was pretty sure this next part would not go over as well.

Chase frowned. "What do you mean?"

"My mom was friends with the Eastside's alpha. Your uncle, Phil—he had her grimoire. She left a spell on it, and I saw my dad and yours. They're both unseelie." She cringed, waiting for him to say something about that.

His brows knit. "Okay...so we have to register and probably get an immigration lawyer—"

"Malcom. Your dad is Malcom," she blurted and slapped a hand over her mouth.

Chase stared at her, then laughed, shaking his head. "That motherfucker."

"It's not funny, Chase, the entire reason he knocked up your mom is so he'd have a first born he can sacrifice to the frickin' node tonight and create an unseelie mound."

Chase laughed harder. Shit—was this what happened when weres went feral? No. It was just the shock, right? Jena chewed her lip. She would've definitely lost her shit if she'd found out Malcom was her dad. Not that hers wasn't crappy enough.

"Are you all right?"

"Peachy," he said. "I am so out of my fucking depth here, Jena. I don't know how to even begin wrapping my head around that. Goddamn, and I thought figuring out how to zap enough voltage into those turbine foundations was an impossible task."

"Why would you want to do that?" she asked, her brows knit.

"The rebar in them's iron. They're screwing with the leyline and short of yanking the damned things out, the only other solution I can think of is to hit them with enough voltage to degrade the metal in place."

What? "That's why it isn't flowing?" How stupid were they?

"Yeah." He frowned, any levity gone. "And all that magic's really not happy about it."

"No, they wouldn't be," Jena murmured, and she needed to get out there. She blew out her cheeks. *Right, priorities, Jena.* Chase, Aggie, then the node. She flipped open the album, whatever her power was pinging on, it was coming from inside. "Okay, first things first, let's heal those legs…"

"Damn, those are really old," Chase said, putting an arm behind her. She nestled against his shoulder. "How's looking through these going to help?"

"There's a pocket of sin somewhere in here…" she murmured. "Witches can't just cast spells, they use their karma to 'pay' for them, I guess you could say. If I cast too many, or if my intent is ill, my scales would tilt to the deficit, and magic would stop answering when I called. Taking care of your hands just tapped mine."

She chewed her lip, that whole exchange made a lot more sense now that she knew sidhe shades had their hands on the magical spigot. In life they were notorious for bargaining. It made total sense that they'd want something for their frickin' services in death and would cut a practitioner off if they didn't get it. Which begged the question, what were they doing with all that accrued karma?

"I don't understand, what does sin have to do with it?" Chase asked, squinting at a blurry sepia image.

"My family can eat it," she muttered, setting her question aside for Aggie to answer later. Jena puffed out her cheeks at his side-eyed glance. "I can sense bad karma—sin—and pull it through me. The negativity gets sloughed off, and I get access to all that power after I sift through it."

"Where does the bad stuff go?"

Jena glanced up at him, surprised that he actually sounded interested. She shrugged. "I dunno, it evaporates, I guess. My mom died before she could teach me how it works."

His brow furrowed. "Aggie doesn't know? I thought she was your aunt."

"No. I've just always called her that. She was my mom's best friend, but we're not blood related. Her line's power is divination," Jena said, turning the page. "Technically, I think she's my godmother."

"Wait a sec. Can I take this out?" He pointed to one of those insta-film photos.

She shrugged. "Yeah, sure. Why?"

He held the photo up to the light. "Because my mom's been in all the pictures on the last three pages, and I swear I know where this was taken."

The photo was of Jena's mom and another girl. They were in their mid-to-late teens, and the two of them had wide smiles on their faces, their arms around each other's shoulders as they stood at the end of a dock. Damn. They had been friends. "Really? Where?"

"A cove on the south side of the bay. My brother Luke keeps his boat there." He flipped the page. "And now she's not in any of these...but this..." he pulled out an odd photo of trailhead with a path leading into the woods. All the other photos had had people in them. "This is on pack territory. It leads into a nasty track of swamp bordering Fayet. Why would there be a picture of this in there?"

Jena wasn't sure, but it glowed with sin in her mind's eye. "I don't know, but I have a bad feeling I'm about to find out." She took a deep breath and reached for it, her fingers trembling—

A wave of nausea rolled over her, and magic prickled over her as a spell took hold.

~

JENA WAS IN ANOTHER MEMORY, trapped in another woman's body—not her mom's this time—and whoever she was, she was filled with terrified anticipation. She stood naked at the fringes of a flooded woodland. Her breath came too quick as she stared out at the diseased and dying trees listing from the algae-choked waters. She forced a deep breath and spun on her heel, cold mud squishing between her toes.

A low fire burned within a circle of toppled stones. Jena's stomach roiled at the sin rolling off it. Oh God, there'd been a dark altar, here, in Havers?

The woman retrieved a cage with a rabbit in it, and brought the frantic beast to the blood-stained slab of stone. Jena fought to close her eyes, knowing what was coming—

She couldn't, and the rabbit's end was not quick. The woman chanted as she splayed the poor beast's entrails, and the flames behind her begrudgingly burned blue. Whoever she was, she wasn't a true practitioner, but the dark side of the art wasn't picky. Enough blood in a place of power with strong enough intent would be enough to cancel out a lack of inborn ability. The woman spun at the flames crackle, a gust of wind howling through the circle with the parting of the veil.

A sidhe stepped through, and Jena's breath caught.

Tall, broad, and blond, there was no question that it was Chase's father in his true form. The sidhe stepped forward, a golden circlet of elder leaves rested against his brow, and a kilt rode low upon his slim hips. A torc of antlers encircled his throat. His azure eyes narrowed and a wide smile slid across his face. "Are you ready to fulfill the next part of our bargain, my vengeful one?"

The woman trembled, falling to her knees. Her breast

heaved as she nodded, and he reached forward, tipping up her chin. His long nails bit into her flesh, and she whimpered.

The sidhe snuffed at her, sucking in a great chestful of air. His kilt strained against his growing erection. "So full of fear. You should be. I will not be gentle."

"But I'll have my prize in return?" she gasped, clutching at his wrist and meeting his gaze.

"Greedy thing." He chuckled, grabbing her throat and raising her to her feet. He walked her backwards, butting her against the altar. "Did I not deliver all that I promised before? All those who wronged you, writhing beneath your teeth and claws. A new life in exchange for the old—"

"But she saw it. All of it. Everything I've done—I want her dead and everything she has!"

Jena started at the woman's shrill. Holy shit, she knew that screech. She'd been on its receiving end at Sal's right before she'd gotten fired.

"Shh...I hear you, little serpent. Save your cries," he murmured, lifting a much younger Ms. Montgomery onto the altar and laying her down amongst the viscera. "It is of no import, and her fate has already been written, as has yours. Deliver me a child and queen of this dunghill you shall be..."

OH GOD. Jena's eyes snapped open as the spell from the photograph released her with a puff of bergamot. She wrapped her arms around her clenching stomach, willing herself not to vomit.

Beside her Chase panted. "What the fuck was that?"

She whipped her head around to look at him. "You saw?" How was that possible? But the expression on his face was all the confirmation Jena needed. She wet her lips, her stomach roiling. "I'm pretty sure that was your mother screwing around with dark magic to summon an unseelie prince into this realm, and I don't think it was her first rodeo."

All of which qualified as some major sin. Never mind whatever her mother had seen that Ms. Montgomery had been freaking out about. Jesus. That woman's karma had to be blacker than the devil's asshole.

"Is that all?" Chase barked out a laugh. "And here I was, hung up on being conceived in a bunch of rabbit guts. What the fuck, Jena? I thought you said Malcom was my father."

She winced at Chase's indignation. "Yeah, he is. Apparently knocking up your mom up pissed off some unseelie queen, she cursed him into his current form, and then exiled him here for the duration."

Chase just stared at her.

"Look, I don't make the sin, I just eat it. You want your

legs healed or not?" Jena scowled when he didn't answer and drew a stupid glyph over them anyway, her head buzzing with the power she'd gotten from that little trip down memory lane. Magic flared purple, and that was enough of that, thank you very much.

Chase closed his eyes with a groan of relief. "Yeah, thanks…and I'm sorry. That was just…a lot." He pulled her against him and kissed her temple. "My mom's a bitch, but damn. I didn't know she was evil."

"I did," Jena muttered. Well, maybe not that evil, but still. She snorted, things clicking into place. If Mary Montgomery had hated Jena's mom because she'd known what her sins were, it stood to reason she'd be worried Jena could figure them out, too. Ugh. She shivered. After what she'd just seen? Chase's mom could keep them to herself.

He chewed his lip. "So…does this change things?"

Jena's brow furrowed. "What do you mean?"

Chase shrugged, dusting his knuckles against his palm. "I dunno. How do you feel about us? You know, now that you know what shitty stock I come from."

"What?" She laughed. "Trust me, your family wasn't exactly a selling point before. What about you, now that you know about my dad and how sin-eating works?"

He pulled her close. "Baby, I already knew he was a piece of shit, and it's going to take a lot more than you seeing someone else's skeletons to get rid of me."

"Oh. Then I guess I have to try harder," she teased.

Chase chuckled, skating his nose against hers. "You need a reminder of who you belong to? Because if you keep talking like that, you're gonna get one."

Jena's gaze drifted to his lips. "Maybe?"

He grinned and kissed her softly, then with more passion. Lord, she wanted nothing more than to drag him back into her bedroom. But if that happened, neither of them was coming up for air, and she had a needy node to deal with. Damn it. The sooner she did, the better.

Jena reluctantly broke away from his embrace and stood, holding out a hand for him. "Let's go down. I need to drop this with Aggie and get back to the ruins."

"You mean we need to—hey." He caught her hand, staring at the rings on her finger. "You're wearing the set I bought."

Jena's cheeks heated and she looked away. "I—Mr. Fynbender gave them to me. H-he said he thought—that ring you gave Crystal binds you to her, whether you meant it or not. He and Ms. Pao think me wearing this might mitigate whatever hold it will have on you—but if they're not—"

"What? No. I-I got them for you, I just…" Chase's throat bobbed. He wet his lips. "Does that mean yes? T-to me, to all of it?"

Jena's mouth went dry her gaze searching his. "I dunno. What are you asking me?"

"Marry me, Jena," he rasped. "Be my mate, my love, the mother to my children."

"I…" She swallowed the lump in her throat, her joyful disbelief tempered by the thought of kids—but with him…? Jesus Christ, she was seriously considering an addendum. "H-how about yes to you, and the possibility of continuing negotiations on the rest?"

Chase laughed, his dimples studding his cheeks. "Fuck, baby, I'll take it," he said, pulling her down onto his lap to kiss her. She wound her arms around his neck, stupidly happy, his mouth on hers—

"Since you're already kissing the bride, I suppose I should pronounce you man and wife," Sweets declared, sweeping a quick sign of the cross through the air as they sprang apart. "May no man tear asunder what's been ascribed by fate."

"Oh my God, I love weddings." Felix sniffed from behind her.

Jena blinked at them. "Excuse me?"

"You just got hitched. Mazel tov," Matilda said, toasting them with a teacup. "Sweets is an ordained minister and like she said, it's fated, no point in waiting."

Jena gaped at them. Were they serious?

"Works for me," Chase said, grinning ear to ear. "Now you can't change your mind."

"What? I wouldn't—" Jena huffed at him then turned to stare at them. They had to be kidding. "How long have you three been standing there?"

"What you should be figuring out is how much longer you're going to be," Felix said. God, he was wearing her jumpsuit, and damn him for looking better in it than she ever had. "I need to get to work, and you need to get back to the node. The streets are already filling with people."

"You're going in?" she asked.

"Yeah. I should at least make an attempt at damage control." He frowned, glancing back at the other room where Kelsey and Liam were. "And five of us will be a little too cozy in Liam's Jeep."

He had a point. "Okay. We'll head out as soon as I get this to Aggie," she said, gripping the album as she stood. "Stay safe."

"Same. You better take care of her," he said to Chase.

He put his arm around her. "Trust me, that's all I want to do."

Felix grunted as they parted ways, and she and Chase went to Aggie's room. Jena rapped on the door before she opened it.

"Well, well. It's about damned time." Aggie smirked from her pillows as they stepped inside. "Congratulations. I expect you to name your firstborn after me. Now where's my damned tea?"

Chase froze. "Uh…"

Jena rolled her eyes. "Oh my God, leave him alone, and what do you mean congratulations? Your door was closed, how did you—wait a minute, our firstborn?" Her gaze narrowed at the older witch. "Tell me you didn't see that in one of your visions."

"I'm not telling you anything with that attitude." Aggie huffed.

Jena gritted her teeth. "How long, Aggie?"

Chase glanced between them. "How long what?"

"I wanna know how long she's known about us, and I'm not giving her this until she fesses up," Jena said, tapping the album.

"Don't you threaten me," Aggie shook her finger at Jena. "You already saw what was most important. Now close the door and sit your asses down for a hot minute so I can fill you in on the rest."

"You know, you're awfully feisty for someone who almost died a couple of hours ago," Jena grumbled, tossing the album onto Aggie's bed. Whatever the node had done to save her, Aggie sounded suspiciously like her old self, and that wasn't particularly helpful.

"And you're awfully mouthy, period." The witch narrowed her eyes at Jena, and she rolled hers in turn. Chase found a chair. "See? Him, I like." Aggie sniffed, pulling the album over and flipping through it. "Maybe even more than you. Now, why did you huff in here like we've got rats again?"

Jena scowled and perched on Chase's knee. "There's no rats, but the roof's leaking like a sieve, Wallace Montgomery is dead, Chase and I are both half-unseelie, his real dad is Malcom who *is* trying to create a mound, the entity haunting the garden is my father—Oh, and Mary Montgomery practices dark magic naked at an altar out in the southwestern swamp." Jena said, ticking off her fingers. She frowned at Aggie's lack of reaction. "And you don't look surprised…" Wait. That conversation they'd had when Aggie was drunk… "Shit. You knew about my dad, didn't you?"

"Not looking surprised is easy to do when you don't have eyebrows," Aggie murmured, slowly turning the pages and squinting at the images like she was looking for something. "And yes. I knew about your father. Tell me more about Malcom. You're positive he's unseelie?"

"Yes," Jena said, trying to rein in her temper. God! Aggie had known all this frickin'—Why hadn't she—Ugh! Jena huffed out a breath, fighting for calm. The rotten woman would totally clam up otherwise. "Phil had my mom's grimoire. She spelled a memory in there of a meeting between him and my father talking about how Malcom had been banished here by some dark queen for knocking up Chase's mom. I think her name was Mogha—"

"Pst!" Aggie interrupted holding up a hand. "Don't say it. Especially not today. Last thing we need is that rabid bitch showing up in a flaming chariot of skulls."

"Seriously?" Chase asked.

"Mmm. And if you wanna see some rats, the ones that pull it are the size of clydesdales."

"You know who she is?" Jena blinked at Aggie's scowl. Wait a minute…

"Unfortunately." Aggie frowned, glancing askance at Jena. She bit back the accusation at the tip of her tongue, and Aggie sniffed, flipping through photos again. "Now, what were you saying about Malcom?"

Jena took a slow breath, attempting to swallow her indignation. Aggie was the other sidhe in town. She had to be. Damn it. No wonder no one had called the feds. "He wants to turn the node into a mound to impress her and get back into the sidhe realm."

Aggie snorted. "Like that would ever happen."

"Apparently it will if I don't claim the node," Jena said, throwing up her hands.

"Nope. Not even then. Her Dark Majesty doesn't forgive, never forgets, and is one hell of a hand at transmogrifying.

No wonder I couldn't sense him. Bastard's no more sidhe than Matilda at this point, but you're right, the node needs to be taken in hand, and Chase needs to be there when you do it."

"What? No!" Jena went to stand and Chase's arm caged her waist, keeping her on his knee. "He's the only thing Malcom doesn't have right now—"

"You're right, but I'm betting he's got that ring of Crystal's, and if you make him tug on that leash, the only thing that's going to happen is people are going to get hurt."

"And there's no way I'm letting you go out there alone," Chase growled.

Goddamn it. Jena slumped against him. Stupid frickin' men.

"The two of you need to cross the bridge in the garden before the sun sets," Aggie said.

Jena's eyes flicked up to hers. "You saw it?"

Aggie shrugged. "I saw something, and knowing that it's William up there, it makes a lot more sense now. Regardless, I can guarantee that if you're both not there at moonrise, shit is gonna hit the fan." She stopped leafing through the album and pulled it close, then removed a photo from behind the crinkly cellophane. "Here."

Jena leaned forward to take a photo of a very tall, very handsome man with raven black hair and startling green eyes. They were wide, like the photographer had caught him off guard doing something he shouldn't be. "That's my dad, isn't it?"

Aggie's mouth screwed up like she wanted to spit. "Yeah. His name's on the back, and you'd do well to remember it. If your mother had bothered to tell me what she was doing, it might've put an end to this already."

"You never told me I looked like him."

"You don't. You look like you."

Jena huffed and flipped the photo over. Her brow quirked. "This isn't what Malcom called him."

"Of course it isn't," Aggie snapped. "You think sidhe just bandy their true names around like everyone else out here?"

"Then how do you just happen to have it?" Jena asked, batting her lashes.

Aggie batted hers right back. "Wouldn't you like to know?"

"I would, which is why I asked. God, I really hate you sometimes," Jena muttered as she stood, slipping the photo into her back pocket.

"Good, it would be weird if you didn't. Now scram," Aggie said, waving them away. "You've got places to be, nodes to claim, and lingering assholes to banish." Her gaze fell on Chase. "And you better come back with that cup of tea and my scone."

"YES, MA'AM," Chase said as he stood, taking Jena's hand. He didn't understand all of the subtext to the conversation they'd just had, but something had royally pissed Jena off—

She stopped abruptly and turned back to Aggie. "Why did she do it? My mom knew what he was and what he wanted. Why in God's name would she sign up for that?"

"Because if she hadn't, there would be no you, and Havers would already be on the bottom of the sea. Fun fact, all the nodes' guardians have to have a certain percentage of sidhe blood, and the Seymores were due for an infusion."

"And I'll just bet you saw that too, didn't you?" Jena spat.

"Come on," Chase said, after the two of them had glowered at each other for a solid minute. He put an arm around Jena's shoulders and steered her from Aggie's room, back into hers. "You wanna talk about it?" he asked as the door closed behind him.

"No." Jena seethed, dumping a messenger bag out on her bed and rooting through a bunch of witchy stuff.

Okay then. Chase frowned, but didn't say anything, heading for the pile of his clothes at the foot of the mattress. Looked like Sweets had been able to dry them out. He raked Liam's hoodie and tee up over his head and picked up his shirt. Huh. He sniffed it. Wasn't great, but it was better than smelling another were on him—

"You know, she did the same damned thing with her diagnosis. She knew she was sick before I left for college and didn't say a goddamned thing," Jena blurted, jamming things back into her bag and trading others for stuff inside an inscribed box. "I didn't even know she was going for treatments until collections came after me." She ran a hand over her brow and hung her head. "God, why she can't just tell me things…"

Chase dropped his shirt and pulled her into his arms. "Pretty sure that's not how it works. I mean, if she really is a sidhe, aren't they supposed to speak in riddles?"

"Yeah, that and bargain for your soul, steal babies…" Jena buried her face against his chest. "Please, please tell me you didn't know she was unseelie. God, I feel so stupid," she murmured with a half-sob.

"How do you know she's not part of the bright court?"

"You've met her right?"

Chase laughed. "She's crabby, but she's not evil, Jena. She wouldn't even let me kill the spider I found in her bathtub." He stroked her hair, smiling as she calmed at his touch. "And no, I didn't know. I mean, not until she was talking about your dad and recognizing the dark queen you were talking about. Pretty sure regular witches aren't rubbing elbows with any kind of sidhe, royalty or otherwise."

"Okay, you have a point." Jena sighed, leaning back to meet his gaze. "But how screwed up is it that Aggie's my literal fairy godmother? I thought they were supposed to be all bibbity boppity."

"Maybe you just got the boo." He smiled at Jena's scowl. "You have everything you need?" he asked, glancing at her bag.

"No, but it is what it is." She flopped down to sit on the bed, chewing her lip. "How the hell am I going to do this, Chase?"

"I dunno," he said, putting his arm around her as he sat beside her. "But you are, and I'm gonna be there to help you."

She leaned against him, raising her chin to be kissed, and he slid his hand up her back to her nape—

"Shit!" He flinched back, his fingertips blistered. "You're wearing silver?"

Her brow furrowed, then guilt stole over her face as she pulled a necklace from her shirt. "It's a were-b-gone charm."

He eyed it, sucking on his fingers. "Were-b-gone?"

"What? I was mad at you, and it's not activated yet…"

"Baby, silver is always active, and you just fried my fine-motor skills."

"Sorry," she said sheepishly, then laughed. "But, at least it didn't zap you into a wall." His brow furrowed, and she held up the hand with the rings he'd given her. "Kelsey tried to lick me, and they sent her flying. Ms. Pao says they're sidhe rings."

Chase growled. "You were hurt?"

"I'm fine now." Jena laughed. "But Kelsey said it was like licking a cattle prod. The inscription has something about remaining true."

Chase ran his knuckles down the side of Jena's face. "You think they'll do that if I try to lick you?" he murmured.

Jena wet her lips, her eyes searching his face. "Um… probably not. I mean you were kissing me earlier so…"

"Yeah, but I wasn't *licking* you. Doesn't seem like

something we should leave to chance. I think you should take off that necklace and come sit on my lap."

"What about your fine-motor skills?" she asked, dropping it to the floor and straddling him.

He leaned back against the pillows, bringing her with him. "Guess you're gonna have to do all the work."

She bit back a smile. "We don't have time for this."

"Sunset, right? There's plenty of time for this, it's not even noon. I missed you, baby, lemme show you how much," he murmured, teasing her lips with his and sliding his good hand over the curve of her ass. He rocked his hips against hers, swallowing her groan.

Jena pulled back, biting her lip. She skated her hands over his chest. "We'd need to be quick…"

"Then I suggest you get naked."

She pulled her shirt up, along with her sports bra, her nipples pearling as her clothes joined the necklace on the floor. Chase wet his lips. "Good girl. Push your tits together for me…yeah, like that. Now tug…" Fuck, that was hot. "Come here, baby. Lemme taste."

Jena crawled forward, and he lapped around her nipple before drawing it into his mouth, sucking as it tightened between his lips. He groaned, his dick throbbing as she wriggled out of her pants, and the scent of her arousal hit him, heavy and sweet. He slid his hand between her thighs, rumbling his approval as her wetness coated his fingers.

She rocked against them, needy. "Oh God, Chase…"

He pulled his hand away, and chuckled at her cry of dismay, licking her desire off his fingers. Damn, she was delicious. Next time he'd feast. "You said quick, right?"

"Maybe not that quick," she huffed.

Chase grinned, his dimples studding his cheeks. "Mmm. I like it when you're needy. Take my dick out," he rumbled, kissing up her throat, the room dense with pheromones. His canines elongated as her fingers slipped into his sweats and pulled him free, his tip slick with need. "Now be a good girl and look at me when you sit on it."

She raised herself up and slicked his cock across her slit, positioning him at her entrance. Her gaze met his, her big green eyes widening and her lips an 'o' as she slowly took every inch.

Jesus fuck, the feel of her velvet walls clamping around him—he fisted the hair at the nape of her neck, pulling her down to him and claiming her lips, bottoming out deep inside her. Her smell—Chase moaned. Sweet, she was so damned sweet—a tremor went through him, his dick stone. "Jesus, you're ripe, Jena."

Her eyes went wide. "I'm not—"

"Soon." Damn, so fucking soon. His hand tightened on her hip, sweeping his thumb over her belly. Mmm…

She arched against him. "You're not getting me pregnant." Her hips rocked with his, her body saying something totally different.

"Yeah, I am." He nuzzled beneath her ear, their bodies undulating, her riding him as he pressed up, thrusting in long, strong strokes. "Jesus, I wanna sink my fangs into you so goddamned bad."

She panted, her nipples diamond points, baring her throat. "Oh God, Chase…"

"Is that a yes?" He traced his nose down her jugular. "You want my bite, baby?"

"Yes…" she breathed.

His chest rumbled, pulling her close again and sweeping her hair to the side, already on the brink of spending himself. "Touch yourself, Jena. I want to feel you come when I finish claiming you."

Her fingers dropped to his slick cock as it pumped into where their bodies connected, then rose to circle her clit. He licked up her throat, sucking and nibbling, humming in pleasure. She shivered with a little cry. Beneath his lips her pulse sped, tiny tremors building around his dick, an answering tingle at the base of his spine.

Her head dropped back, nipples pearled to points against his chest. "I'm close, so close…"

Chase nuzzled at the nape of her neck, running his fangs over her skin, his breath coming fast in anticipation. "Christ, you take my dick so good, Jena. Such a good girl—"

She gasped, her pussy clamping around his cock, and Chase bit down as he thrust into her. She cried out, her blood coating his tongue, her passion running over his sac. He groaned, his eyes rolling up in head as he came, the base of his cock expanding and long ropes of his searing desire spurting, filling her with his seed—his hand tightened on her ass, driving himself deeper as she came again, grinding against her until she stilled and went lax, the two of them replete.

His fangs retracted, and he lapped over the punctures, sealing them, his scent a permanent part of her now. "Mine," he rumbled, kissing the tiny marks.

"Yours," she murmured, collapsing onto his chest. "And now I don't want to do anything."

Chase laughed, his knot still keeping them close. He stroked her hair. "You don't have to for a while."

"Mmm." She rubbed her cheek against his pec. "Waiting for your knot won't take long enough for a nap."

Chase swallowed his smile. "No, no time for a nap." He glanced out the window, savoring the few moments he had with her like this as it dissipated. "Come on, it looks like the rain's let up. We should go."

Jena nodded and stood with a sigh, sweeping up her necklace and putting it back on. Chase didn't like it, but had to admit, it wasn't the worst idea if they ran into trouble.

They cleaned up then dressed, and he took her hand and paused before he opened the door. "You don't have a ball cap I can borrow, do you?"

She shook her head. "No, sorry. I can't stand anything on my head."

Shit. He frowned, mussing his hair over his eyes.

"Why do you do that?"

"Do what?"

"Hide."

He opened his mouth and then closed it again with a soft laugh. "Guess I don't have to anymore, do I?"

Her eyes flashed. "You never did."

Chase brought her hand to his lips and kissed her knuckles as he opened the door. "Thanks for that."

Kelsey and Liam's laughter came from the other end of the apartment. Chase's joined theirs as they walked into the sitting room. The two of them were swathed ornate robes—

"What are you doing?" Jena gasped. "Do you have any idea how expensive those are?"

"They feel it." Liam grinned, the wide, belled-sleeves dusting his knuckles as he rolled his shoulders beneath the heavy fabric. "These things have got to weigh twenty pounds, but if you've got a better idea of how we're gonna walk down Main Street incognito during the festival, I'm all ears."

Jena looked between them. "What? Why wouldn't we just cut through the cemetery again?"

"Because of all the security," Kelsey said. "Anyone who gets caught on private property gets arrested. No exceptions."

"And everyone's going to be dressed up in their cross quarter day garb," Chase said, catching on to their line of thinking. "We go out there as is, we'll stick out like sore thumbs."

"But if we wear these, we'll fit right in," Kelsey said, smoothing a hand over the embroidered moons on the amethyst velvet robe she was wearing. "Plus, we can keep the hoods up. If Malcom and the rest of the Westside pack is out there, none of them are going to be looking for us decked out as witches." Her nose wrinkled. "We'll smell like them, too."

Jena frowned. "Okay, but as soon as we get to the Jeep, they go in the back. Those are like five hundred bucks a pop, wholesale."

Kelsey clapped her hands, bouncing on the balls of her feet. "Yay, this is so exciting! We brought these two up for you." She pointed at one in midnight blue and another in emerald draped over one of the chairs.

"No, I have my own." Jena sighed. "I'll kill myself tripping over the hem in one of those. Gimme a sec." She headed back to her room, and Chase took the one Kelsey handed him.

"That blue's gonna look great with your eyes."

His stomach flipped. Goddamn, he missed his hat. "Yeah...thanks," he muttered slipping on the robe. Damn, Liam hadn't been kidding, it weighed a ton.

"Well, look at you three," Matilda said, leaning in the kitchen doorway. Behind her, Sweets and Ms. Pao were chanting over the caldron. "Not bad, but you won't fool any of the real witches out there. Try not to insult anyone and get hexed." She held out a credit card between two of her fingers to Chase. "Here, you probably want this back."

"Thanks." He took it from her, not about to ask where she'd gotten it from.

"I'll make sure they behave," Jena grumbled, coming back into the room in something considerably less ornate.

But damn, she looked a hell of a lot more impressive.

Delicate sliver chains pulled back her hair at either side of her temples and crossed her brow like a diadem. She'd put makeup on, darkening her eyes and the dark gray robe, though simple, accentuated her curves. A long leather belt was looped around her waist, and a crescent knife dangled from it along with a bunch of charms and a leather pouch.

"That's what a real witch looks like." Matilda sniffed in approval before going back into the kitchen.

Jena stopped short, staring after her. "Did she just say something nice?"

Liam looked poleaxed, too. "She did."

"Shit, then we better hurry," Kelsey said, making for the door. "Hell is freezing over."

The twins headed out to the landing, and Chase held out his hand for Jena. "You look amazing. How come I've never seen you like this?"

Her cheeks flushed as she looped her messenger bag over her head. "Because it's ceremonial. I think I've worn it like twice before, and it's definitely snugger now than it was." She frowned, tugging the fabric over her hip.

"Then it didn't fit right before." He batted her hand away and smoothed over the curve.

She failed to swallow a smile, then pulled away. "Be careful, all this is silver."

"Totally worth the burn." Chase stooped to kiss her—

"Are you guys coming?" Liam called up the stairs.

"Not soon enough," Chase murmured, his gaze running over her as he held the door. Her cheeks pinked again, and he grinned, following her down the steps.

JENA PULLED the hood of her robe up as they stepped from the alley a few shops down from hers and onto the street. Felix hadn't been kidding, the sidewalks were filled with people, and the majority of them she didn't recognize.

"Is everyone here from Havers?" she asked Kelsey.

"No, people come in from as far away as Galleon Falls. The Samhain festival is one of Haver's biggest tourist attractions, and this is nothing compared to how mobbed the waterfront must be. There's a huge carnival down there, and I think they upped their game this year with a rollercoaster."

Jena could believe it, the distant squeals from people on rides and that ubiquitous crappy carnival music plinking above the hum of the crowd on the street. It was surreal, and as much as she hated to admit it, wearing robes had been a good idea. No one was in regular clothes, but everything else was fair game. Halloween costumes, ballgowns, men in suits, people dressed up as other supes, and easily a dozen variations of robes...

Chase's hand tightened on hers. "You okay?"

"Yeah...I just, wow. I guess now I get why they have security." She'd be pissed if all these people were tramping through her yard, too. It reminded her of the crowds during events in the city...which she'd studiously avoided. Being in the middle of this many people always made her claustrophobic.

"I'm parked over on Merritt if we get separated," Liam called over his shoulder, someone cursing as the big were jostled them.

Jena put her free hand to her stomach, anxiety churning. Right. Okay, that was only like two blocks past town hall. Should only take them another ten, fifteen min—

A sea of people stretched out before her as they rounded the corner onto Main Street.

"Crap," she muttered.

"Agreed, but I don't see or smell any other weres." Chase's brow furrowed like something about that bothered him. "Still, you two should stay between us," he said to Jena and Kelsey, then nodded at Liam. "You got point, and I'll bring up the rear?"

Liam's brow quirked, but gave a thumbs up and started wending through the crowd, people making way as he pushed through. Kelsey followed on his heels, and Jena came after, Chase reassuring her he was still there with a touch whenever they had to pause.

The tops of the tents around town hall poked up above the crowd, and the scent of mulled cider, apple fritters, and exhaust from the generators spiked the air. Jena's stomach rumbled despite the hydrocarbons and the breakfast they'd eaten, her eyes lingering on a line of food trucks over on the green.

"You hungry?" Chase asked, his lips close to her ear.

She jumped. Damn, she needed to put a bell on him. "No, I'm okay—"

"Because I'm starving after being in that hole, and I think I see a food truck with chili dogs."

Jena perked up. God, if they had baked potatoes, it was game over. The node could wait while she scarfed down some broccoli, chili, and cheesy goodness. Besides, they could eat and walk, right? Right. "Okay, I am hungry."

She tugged Kelsey's sleeve to get her attention and pointed to the food truck. The were grinned and poked Liam. He leaned back to hear what she had to say, his eyes darting to chili and cheese paradise, and he changed his route to head in that direction.

A microphone squealed over the grinding hum of generators, and the sounds of someone fumbling it rumbled through speakers. The emcee cleared their throat, and the milling crowd slowed to a standstill, craning their necks to see who was going to speak.

Chase pushed through them and went up to the food truck's counter. "Three chili-cheese dogs, heavy on the chili," he said, then looked at Jena. "What do you want?"

"Ladies and gentlemen!" the mayor cried over the sound system. "Welcome to the eighth annual Havers-by-the-Sea Samhain festival!" The crowd around them clapped and hooted as he began announcements.

Three chili cheese dogs? Wow, Chase must be starving. Liam and Kelsey were hitting up the fried dough vendor. Jena's gaze lingered on the loaded baked potato and then drifted to the Cesar salad with grilled chicken—

"You better get something just as trashy as I did," Chase said.

Jena bit back a smile. "Baked potato with everything, please," she said, not feeling guilty about her order for once. God, that was nice.

"That's my girl." Chase paid, and they stepped to the side to wait. "And for the record, this is not the first date I was envisioning."

Jena laughed as their order came up, and he handed her a dripping white-and-red folded cardboard bowl of caloric delight. "You're in luck. I love these stupid potatoes."

She snagged a wad of napkins and a spork, then another as she watched Chase hold one of the dogs away from himself, trying not to drop the majority of it down the front of the robe as he bit into it. Jena sighed and grabbed another handful. "Spork?"

He looked at her like she was nuts and shoved another massive bite into his mouth. Jena rolled her eyes, oddly impressed he could fit that much in his mouth. That dog had disappeared in a half-dozen bites.

"Actually…" He took Frankenstein'd piece of cutlery and scraped out the container before starting on the next dog.

Jena worked on picking the cheesy bits of broccoli out of hers, having long since perfected the proper way to eat a carnival potato to avoid wearing it.

"Oh my God, I love fried dough," Kelsey said around a mouthful, a slick of sauce down the front of her robe. Liam's was speckled with powdered sugar. Damn it, but it wasn't like the steady mist of rain was doing the velvet any favors, either. They'd need to be dry-cleaned, regardless.

"Right, let's get moving," Chase said, licking chili from demolished dog number two off the side of his hand before the slick of grease ran into his sleeve. He winked at Jena and took a massive bite of the third as Liam stepped back into the crowd. Kelsey dribbled more sauce down her chest ducking past a man dressed as Friar Tuck to catch up to her brother. Jena sighed again and followed with Chase close behind her. The friar stopped after a few steps to join a group of merry men blocking their path, and the crowd hemmed Jena and Chase in.

Well, this was going nowhere fast. She shoved bites of cheesy chili into her mouth, catching glimpses of Mayor Chambers between the bodies in the crowd. He thanked various sponsors as he paced the raised stage in a tuxedo. A tiny pair of horns poked out of his salt-and-pepper hair, and a tail trailed behind him.

Her gaze caught on Felix standing in the shadows beside a

bunch of hay bales and the setup for a band at the far edge of the stage. He was white-knuckling a clipboard, his face a careful blank.

Jena's chewing slowed. Something was up. That wasn't him in his typical blasé, municipal mode, that was him in currently-struggling-not-to-pull-power-and-disappear mode. Shit. What could've happened to freak him out so bad?

"What do you think is wrong with Felix?" Chase asked, wrangling a bunch of napkins from her grip and scrubbing at the chili in his beard. "He smells stressed."

"You can smell that? From this far away?"

Chase shrugged, wiping off his hands. "Weres imprint on the scents of people they care about. Felix is important to you, so he is to me, too. I'd be able to find him or Aggie in a crowd triple this size. Come on, let's go make sure he's okay."

Jena blinked back tears. "Really?"

"Yeah." He turned to her, his brow furrowed. "Why is that so hard for you to believe?"

Maybe because no one had said anything remotely like it to her before. She scraped at her denuded potato and shoved another bite in her mouth so she wouldn't have to answer him.

He sighed and ran a hand down her back. "Come on, Liam's headed in that direction too, and if we cut down the side of town hall, we can probably get to where he's parked quicker."

It wasn't the worst plan. Jena nodded and started forward. All of that was municipal property, and even if the town had it gated off, Felix could get them through.

They slipped through the edges of the audience around the stage as the mayor began to extoll the accomplishments of his administration, people drifting away. Jena couldn't help but note that more than one of them from Havers did so with a frown. Guess Felix was right about the mayor's reelection campaign going poorly, and it served the jerk right. She tossed the soggy potato container into the garbage as she passed and licked the grease from her fingers, then drew a glyph, willing Felix to look at her.

His gaze snapped to hers, and his body slumped as he murmured something at the sky. He jerked his head meaningfully toward the back of the stage.

"Come on, this way," she said, taking Chase's hand and the lead. They slipped past the temporary staging to the area behind it, just in front of town hall's steps. A band decked out as zombies was lounging on them underneath the overhang as they waited to go on. Liam and Kelsey were just past them, and it sounded like she was trying to talk her twin off a ledge.

"No, you cannot," she hissed at him. "Think for once in your freaking life, Liam. If you push—oh!" Kelsey's eyes widened as she caught sight of them, and Liam jammed his hands into his pockets, scowling. "Hey, guys. Um, we were thinking cutting around the back of town hall might be faster than going all the way down the block."

"Yeah, us too, as soon as we make sure Felix is okay," Jena said. Was it her imagination, or did Liam's shoulders relax at that? Damn, if he was still hung up on Felix, he was gonna be in for a world of hurt—

The curtains rustled at the back of the stage as weak applause came from the front. Felix pushed through and gestured for the band. They filed up the short flight of metal steps past him, and Felix dropped the curtain as soon as they cleared, hurrying over. "Where's the Jeep?" he asked without preamble.

"Parked on Merritt," Kelsey said before Liam could answer, "but—"

"Walk now, questions later," Felix said, grabbing Jena's hand and pulling her after him at a jog.

～

CHASE HURRIED after Jena and Felix. Whatever had spooked the spry warlock couldn't be good. They ducked down the side of the building, and Felix broke into a run, dragging her after him. Damn.

"What the hell?" Liam growled, glancing back over his shoulder as he and Kelsey sprinted to catch up.

Chase couldn't help but do the same, but there wasn't anything there as far as he could tell. Regardless, Felix kept running like something was hot on his heels—well, kind of running. After that initial burst of speed, Jena was definitely lagging. He slowed down when they turned the corner onto Helm Street. It was considerably less crowded, everyone milling about occupied with grabbing early seats for the parade.

"Why were we running?" Jena panted, struggling match Felix's pace.

"Because you need to finish that rite, and the sooner the better," he said, glancing back at them. "The Westside weres are imploding. I heard the mayor talking to one of them. No one's seen Malcom, Ms. Montgomery, or Crystal since the pack went after the Eastside last night. The mayor and his wife are freaking out, and someone beat the shit out of Patrick when he tried to claim alpha. You're lucky the sheriff hasn't already hauled you all in for questioning."

"Are they blaming us for that, too?" Kelsey spat, stepping around a group of kids drawing on the sidewalk outside of the municipal playground. They squealed, holding up gummy chunks of chalk slowly dissolving in the crappy weather.

"Let's just say they're not *not* blaming you."

"Yeah, but the Eastside grabbing them isn't fricking likely." Chase's brow furrowed as they skirted the chain-link fence, his hand on Jena's back. Malcom had probably been out there, but there was no way his mother or Sue had been involved in the raid.

Chase swallowed the lump of dread rising to choke him as they wove through a gaggle staking out the next corner with lawn chairs. They rounded onto Merritt and the lights on a gray jeep flashed as with a soft beep as it unlocked. Chase headed toward it on autopilot.

With Wallace dead and Malcom missing, alpha was up for grabs, and it was gonna be chaos until someone claimed it. No wonder Patrick had gotten his ass beat. Hopefully their mom, Sue, and Luke had made it to the sailboat and were riding things out on the bay. Otherwise, best case they were hostages, and worst case, they were dead. Crystal would be on that list, too, with the bullshit engagement.

Chase chewed his lip, pinging through the handful of weres that would be gunning for the position. None of them were an ideal candidate. Christ, far from it, and if the Fayet pack had heard the territory in Havers was no longer affiliated under an alpha—Shit.

Felix was right, Jena needed to do what she needed to do up at the ruins, and then they had to find someplace to hunker down. Things were about to get ugly, if they hadn't already. Chase ran a hand across his brow, glancing at Kelsey and Liam. "You think your dad's gonna throw his hat into the ring?" Chase asked. If Phil had been waiting for an opportunity to reclaim the rest of the Montgomery pack, this was it.

The two exchanged a glance. "I don't know," Kelsey said, tipping the seat forward for Jena and Felix to climb in, then joined them in the back, stripping out of her robe. "He might. Either way, he needs to know what's happening."

"I'll drop you at the tracks." Liam frowned. "I'm not getting involved."

Fucking hell. Liam started the engine as Chase got in with a bad feeling he wasn't going to be able to do the same.

JENA BREATHED a sigh of relief as the Jeep finally broke free of the pedestrian traffic strangling the town and pulled onto the state road. It wouldn't be long now. She took a calming breath, her knee jiggling as they crossed the first ward and went over the tracks. A sense of urgency washed over her, her anxiety ticking up with the node's plaintive cry into her psyche.

He's here, he's here, HE'S HERE…

Ugh. What the heck had happened to having until moonrise? Jena put a hand to her stomach, the baked potato abruptly not sitting very well. The energy plucking at her felt wrong, like it'd been tainted somehow, and the acrid flavor of sin coated the back of her throat.

Felix put a hand on her knee. "You're vibrating. That's usually not a good sign. You okay?"

She nodded, forcing a smile as Liam pulled to the side of the road, and Kelsey squeezed out. Jena avoided Felix's eyes, watching the were lope across the field toward the Eastside's compound. "Yeah, why wouldn't I be?"

"Seriously? You know it's perfectly acceptable to be losing your shit, right? I mean, I'm losing my shit. Like, on a scale of one to ten, I'm at 'tell me that was not the finale to GoT' levels. How about you, Chase?" Felix asked as Liam got back on the road.

"Country chic." He passed his robe back, nicely folded as opposed to the stained wad of stupidly expensive fabric Kelsey had left.

Jena snorted. "Country chic?"

"Yeah. That white, chippy worn crap puts me through the roof." He reached up like he was going to adjust his hat and frowned, dropping his hand to rub his chest. "How about you, Liam?"

"Big ass spoilers on shitty cars." He flicked the wipers on, the mist officially a light drizzle.

"See?" Felix said. "Everyone's freaking out."

Yeah, that didn't make her feel much better. Neither did the odd shifting hues outside the window. She hadn't been sure at first, but the closer they got to the ruins, the more vibrant everything—

The Jeep swerved, and Liam swore, trying to keep it on the pavement. "Did you see that?" He swallowed heavily, wide-eyed. "A fucking satyr just bolted across the road."

"Are you sure?" Felix asked, paling at his nod. Jena didn't blame him. Satyrs weren't considered lesser fae and, as a general rule, didn't do well on this side of the veil. For one to be over here, a constraint on the node had to have broken, and wild magic from the sidhe realm was officially bleeding over into this one.

"Yeah, I saw it, too," Chase said. He winced, his hand at his chest again.

"Are you okay?" she asked.

"No," he rumbled, fur sprouting over his knuckles. "I think Malcom's using the ring on me. I'm all fucking tingly, and my wolf is going batshit."

She swore. "Can we go any faster?"

Liam floored it.

Ten more minutes...*I'm coming, I'm coming...*she thought at the node.

It didn't reply, and that was somehow worse than it talking to her.

By the time they pulled up to where the gates had stood, the forest had morphed into a weird Technicolor version of itself. Everything was too vibrant, resonating at a pitch at the edge of Jena's hearing. She pinched the bridge of her nose as she got out of the Jeep and stumbled. Ugh. The dimensions of everything were wrong, the autumn foliage crystalline and every grain of sand beneath her feet in high definition. No wonder people couldn't survive where there was a node. Even the precursor to it was awful.

Chase steadied her, the strain on his face evident.

Jena's brows furrowed. "Are you—"

"I'm fine," he snapped, scrubbing a hand over his chest. "Sorry. It's like I have something under my skin, pulling me that way." He nodded down the drive then turned to Liam as Felix joined them. "You heading back?"

The were killed the engine. "No. I don't feel good about leaving you guys stranded out here. Place looks like one too many buttons of peyote." He shook his head, a hand at his temple. "Feels like it, too."

"It's definitely a bad trip," Felix muttered, toeing what was left of the gates. They'd been ripped from the stone posts at either side of the drive, and one of them had been dragged a good hundred feet before it'd fallen into the bracken.

If that was a reflection of the ward's condition...Jena closed her eyes, reaching out with her power—

Sin, sin, sin, sin...

Her knees buckled, and the potato threatened to make a reappearance. The ward was still there, but an ugly ruddy brown hole pulsed where it'd been breached. Magic fizzled around the ragged space, unable to fill the void. Jena shivered. The only thing that left a stain like that was the dark side of the art, and with the amount of sin lighting up her mind's eye...

She choked back a sob, not wanting to see anymore. God, why did she have to—Ugh. What she wanted didn't matter, and feeling guilty about not doing something sooner wasn't going to fix this—but owning her power would go a long way toward that end.

Whether she wanted to admit it or not, the stupid node and what was in that garden were her responsibility. And if this ward had been breached, the rest of them were in danger of falling—if they hadn't already—which wouldn't just take away the node's constraints. It would open the way for Malcom's unseelie mound and release what was left of her father.

And the town wouldn't survive either one.

She couldn't let that happen. It was time to adult, damn it. Jena stepped past where the gate had stood, sin raising her hackles. She pulled the container of salt from her bag with trembling fingers. *Shit, big girl panties, Jena. You got this.*

"You want us in or out?" Felix asked.

"That depends," she said, her voice surprisingly calm. "I'm sealing the circle. If you're in, you're in. If you're not..." She blew out a long breath. "I don't blame you."

Felix rolled his eyes and joined her. "Please. You know you're my ride or die."

"And I already told you that you're not doing this without me," Chase growled, doing the same.

"Ditto," Liam pulled a knapsack from the back of the Jeep and grinned as he stepped past the posts. "Kelsey's gonna be sooo pissed she missed this."

Jena snorted. She didn't doubt it, his sister's taste was suspect at best. "You might want to give me some room."

If this worked anything like it had the last time she'd channeled the node's power, it wasn't going to be subtle, and she wouldn't need extraneous spell components other than a focus. She trailed a line of salt across the drive, linking the two ends of the stone wall encircling the property, and pulled a tumbled piece of onyx from her spellbag. She began an incantation, and a sluggish pulse answered her call instead of the bright flash she'd expected.

Her brow furrowed at the node's lack of response, and she knelt at the center of the drive, rubbing the stone with her thumb. Her vision fuzzed as she inspected the damage. Why wouldn't it—sin. The node's power was weighed down by sin, damn it. That hole, the ruddy pulse…Malcom hadn't just breeched the ward, he'd used the dark side of the art to force the magic from its natural path and make its flow erratic.

The taint needed to go.

She gritted her teeth and opened herself up to that side of her power. Oh God—It hadn't just been Malcom. A torrent of darkness poured into her along with the too vivid details of Wallace Montgomery's murder at his wife's hands. Jena's breath caught, fighting not to focus on the images staining her psyche, the dark arts and depravity…*Holy shit, holy shit, holy shit—Chase's mom had done that?! No. Later.* Jena panted, struggling to calm down. She could freak out about it later—

Chase's hand settled against the small of her back, and she leaned against it, drawing on his strength. *You're not alone, now, focus, Jena.* Her breath slowly evened out. Right. She needed to cleanse the karma and use it to make sure the node's tainted energies didn't spread any farther than they already had.

Jena took a deep breath and pulled the sin through herself, whimpering at the influx of evil. She gagged, graveyard midden and rot flooding her mouth and nose, bile rising at the corruption sloughing off into the aether around her in a dark mist. She forced her leaden tongue to speak an incantation, the words passing through her lips like treacle. Her vision grayed, and she fell forward, slamming the bit of onyx to the ground.

Power erupted in a wave, shooting up and outward, flooding past the original bounds of the ward and doubling back upon itself, sealing the breech with a flash of brilliant violet power and encompassing the tor.

Words to vow spoken, the blood of thy veins to bind. Seven stones to witness thy oath. Our service for thine...before the moon rises, the circle must complete...

I'm trying... she thought back at it, muzzy.

The node murmured and hissed, urging her on, to hurry... *he's here...*

Chase's arms were around her as her own gave out, and he picked her up, holding her against him. "You gonna let me carry you this time?"

Jena nodded, her lids drooping, totally spent. The faint scent of bergamot swept over her. "Just for...just for a little while...he's here, Chase..."

CHASE FROWNED as Jena's head lolled against his shoulder, the rain coming down harder than it had before. He stared at the long crystalline droplets falling like shooting stars around them, that tugging in his chest driving him apeshit. Christ, this was getting weird. He cradled Jena against him and turned to the others.

Liam sucked a breath through his teeth, his gaze fixed on the violet boundary streaming across the drive and through the woods at either side of them. He reached out to the swirling opalescence, the small hairs on his arms rising as he got within a few feet of it.

"I wouldn't do that if I were you," Felix said. Liam jumped at the warlock's voice and shoved his hands into his pockets.

"What next?" Chase asked Felix.

His eyes rounded. "You're asking me? I don't know the

specifics, but I'm pretty sure whatever has to happen next, she needs to be at the ruins for."

Chase grunted and hefted Jena higher, her face pressing against his neck. "Then let's go."

He started down the tree-lined drive, the tugging easing now that he was headed where it wanted him to go. That didn't make him feel any better. Neither did the scenery. Chase warily eyed the trees as he made his way down the muddy, gravel drive. Their limbs were too sharp, subtly shifting independently of each other, the tips glinting.

Beneath the menacing branches, things flitted at the corners of his eyes and the surrounding forest smelled wrong. At the gate, there'd been the distinct odor of fresh blood, but here, the air was threaded with a subtle tinge of corruption. Meat left out to spoil, a fresh kill bloated by the sun until it'd split...the unclean sweetness of death teased his nose and raised the hair at the nape of his neck.

And, save for the rain, it was silent; the woods around them completely still. Not a breath of air stirred the oddly prismatic leaves, no small animals rustled over the forest floor or birds in the trees. Only the ever-present patter of rain.

He blinked it away as it ran into his eyes, his breath fogging and his clothes sodden, dragging at him. Christ. He was so fucking sick of being wet—

The woods abruptly opened up, and a nightmarish version of the tor he'd seen in his dream was before him. Last night's frost had blasted the landscape, wild flowers rain-beaten and jumbled into rapidly decaying mounds tangled into treacherous heaps.

Ruins crowned the top of the hill, fire scarred stones stabbing out from the vines and brambles strangling them. Above, the sun was on its descent, occluded by ominous swirling thunderclouds. Bursts of lightning flashed in the distance, too far away to hear the rumble of thunder.

"Welcome to the house of Usher," Felix murmured.

"Jesus Christ, we've got to go up there?"

Felix turned to Liam. "You're welcome to wait for us," he said, flipping a dripping curl from his eyes. There was definitely a challenge in them.

"No," Chase said. "We need to stay together. Jena said he was here."

Felix paled. "Malcom?"

"I'm assuming." And he'd be able to see them coming as soon as they left the trees. Aside from the rain, there was zero coverage out there. Unless…Chase turned to Felix. "Can you—"

He shook his head. "Not without going into a deficit. My karma hasn't recovered from yesterday. I'm not sure I'd even be able to distort myself for more than minute or two."

Chase frowned "Then there's nothing for it. Let's get it done." He started forward, the other two trailing behind him.

The footing was even worse than it'd looked. He swore, stumbling over rocks and into rabbit holes opening up in his path, the crystalline rain lashing down. Halfway up, Felix cried out, limping. He scowled as Liam shouldered under his arm, steadying him, then begrudgingly let the were help him.

They hit what was left of a stone patio in front of the ruins, and Chase took a knee, dashing the rain from his eyes. His clouded breath spiraled away, the temperature at least ten degrees colder up here than it'd been at the base of the hill. They needed to find cover. Being in the open like this was just asking for trouble, if it hadn't already found them. He smoothed Jena's wet hair from her face as Felix and Liam joined him—

A long, low howl echoed in the distance.

"Was that from town?" Felix asked, all of them looking in that direction.

"Yeah," Liam said grimly at an answering cry. "My dad just challenged for alpha, and it sounds like Fayet answered."

Christ. Shit had officially hit the fan back in Havers, and Chase was pretty sure whatever was going to happen here wasn't far behind. "We need to find some shelter."

"I think there's an overhang around the side," Felix said, chewing his lip.

Chase hefted Jena back up, his legs burning and that tugging in his chest abruptly worse. He carried her around to the side of the ruins, stumbling over the canted pavers. There wasn't an overhang exactly, but the remains of the chimney had listed and crumbled, creating a low arch of stone that didn't look like it was going anywhere. Vines of withered bittersweet and brambles hung around it in a veil. He ducked through, and settled Jena on the ground against the stones. It wasn't much drier, but at least it was out of the driving rain.

"Here," Liam said, handing him a crinkling packet from his knapsack. "It's one of those space blankets. She needs to stay warm."

"Thanks," Chase gratefully took it and tucked it around her. His brow furrowed when she didn't stir.

"You don't happen to have another one of those, do you?" Felix asked, favoring one leg, arms around himself and his teeth chattering.

"Yeah, if you don't mind sharing," the were said, not meeting his eyes as he took another crinkly silver packet from his bag—

"Well now, if this isn't just precious."

Felix yelped, and Chase's head jerked up at Malcom's dry rattle. The son of a bitch had his claws around the warlock's throat, and a bright line of blood dripped from his grip. Chase growled, crouching in front of Jena. If Malcom thought he was getting his hands on her—

"Don't hurt him!" Liam growled, springing to his feet.

Malcom laughed, taking a step back as two other burly weres came into view. "Hurt him? I wouldn't dream of it," he said, his gaze squarely on Chase. "Not as long as you cooperate."

Liam screamed, a flash of silver around his throat. He fell backwards, scrabbling at it, his flesh smoking as a third were with heavy gloves hauled him into the rain, thrashing. Felix cried out in horror, and Malcom's claws tightened, digging into his jugular.

He tsked. "I wouldn't struggle too much, boy. More you do, the deeper you're gonna drive that chain—"

"Leave them alone, you sack of shit!" Chase spat, fighting the urge to lunge at him.

A wide grin split Malcom's face. "There's my boy. Why don't you and that whore of yours come on out? We've got things to talk about, like how you managed to extract yourself from your previous predicament. I was almost impressed until you delivered yourself here, not that I don't appreciate it."

Like he'd had a choice. Chase glowered at him, pain blooming through his chest. "Fuck you."

The trickle of blood at Felix's throat widened. "You sure that's what you want to lead with?" Malcom rasped.

Chase's gaze met Felix's. An odd determination had bloomed in the warlock's eyes. He glanced down, his fingers moving in a deliberate pattern—

"She's not in there with him anymore," the were crouching over Liam's convulsing body growled.

Malcom's eyes narrowed, and Chase's gaze flicked back to Felix. He shot him a pointed look. Shit. The warlock had to be using his power to hide her, but after what he'd said, he wouldn't be able to do it for long.

"Where'd she go?" Malcom growled, Felix rising onto his toes with a pained cry.

"To claim the node," Chase lied, his wolf frantic as he crawled out from the overhang, leaving her unprotected.

"And I'm pretty sure you being here's bought her enough time to do it."

Malcom's grin got wider as the two weres beside him moved to flank Chase. "Is that right? Then how about we go wait for her in the garden? There's someone there that's eager to meet the both of you."

Chapter Twenty-Four

JENA GROGGILY CAME TO, an angry buzzing in her ears and tiny stinging slaps pattering over her cheeks. She waved a hand, and her brow furrowed as something crinkled—

"Ow!" She flinched back, her eyes flying open at a sharp bite of pain on her lip. "What the hell?!"

"Kissed-her-awake-he-kissed-her-awake!" A flurry of wings beat the air around her with a rapid buzz of gleeful little voices.

Pixies? God, her head…she moaned. That wasn't a frickin' kiss, one of the little shits had taken a chunk out of her. She put a hand to her lip, the damned bite already swollen and itching. She winced as a weird silver sheet crinkled around her with the motion. Why the hell was she wrapped up like a potato, on the ground, and shoved up against a bunch of stones?

Oh, Jesus. Was this another weird food dream? Where…?

"Jena-Jena-Jena!" The harem squealed, two dozen plus pixies filtering about in a softly glowing cloud before settling on the stones around her.

No. She sneezed, waving away the dust. She was way too uncomfortable and annoyed for this not to be real. Jena struggled to sit, clutching her head. Everything spun, and her stomach lurched, the power from the node thumping through the ground in time with the agony between her temples. Fuck. What did she remember? The ward. She'd sealed the perimeter of the node, and then Chase had been carrying her.

Chase. Shit. She glanced around the shadowed space, then through a veil of bracken. Beyond, it was pouring, the low wall of the garden barely visible. Okay, she'd somehow gotten to the ruins, but where was everyone? Her vision fuzzed in and out as she started forward—

A pixie wearing a mouse skull as a cap zipped in front of her, a smear of her blood on his chin and his hands on his hips as he hovered, shaking his head. Her fingers rose to the welt on her lip, and she just stopped herself from scratching it. Ugh, it was double the size it should be. Little bastard.

He was saying something, his words too quick to follow, and the deluge coming down didn't help. Lightning flickered and a roll of thunder came from directly overhead. She stared at the pixie blankly, and he threw up his hands and pointed through the dripping vines at the garden. *"Thumps!"*

Jena blinked at him. "What?"

Another pixie zipped over, shouldering him out of the way in a cloud of dust to land on Jena's shoulder. *"Bad-thumps-looking-for-you!"* she pipped into her ear.

God, she was not in any condition to translate pixie. "Thumps?"

Mr. Mouse Skull scowled, pointed at her again, and mimed stomping around. *"Thump-thump-thump!"*

Oh. Big people. Shit, no. *Bad* big people. "Malcom's looking for me?" The harem nodded as a collective, and Jena scooted back into the shadows. Great. She rested her throbbing head against the chill stones, her mouth gummy. "Is that what happened to Chase and the others? Does Malcom have them?"

More nods.

Double shit. That wasn't good. Jena closed her hand around the pendant beneath her shirt and peeked out at the clouds blackening the flickering sky. With the storm raging, it was hard to tell, but it had to be close to sunset. Unfortunately, close only counted in horseshoes and hand-grenades and anything less than the full moon wouldn't activate her stupid were-b-gone charm. Damn it. Why hadn't she done that last night? She needed to stop procrastinating like, tomorrow.

"How many are out there?" she asked the harem.

The pixies exchanged glances. One held up four fingers, and another nine. A third just shrugged. Okay. Guess math wasn't their strong suit, but either way, it was more than Jena could handle, especially right now. She pinched her eyes shut. Crap. She felt like absolute crap and couldn't afford to.

Okay…think, Jena. You're here for the node. The moon hadn't risen yet, she still had time, and Chase should be relatively safe until it did. She needed to get down to the basement.

"What's the easiest way to get to the well from here?" she asked the harem.

One of the pixies perked up, jumping off a stone to zip over. *"Easy-easy-easy!"* She flew past Jena's shoulder and disappeared into the bracken. Behind it was a pixie-sized hole, and a faint glow came from beyond.

Yeah, that wasn't gonna help her get down there, but what the heck was glowing? Jena put an eye to the hole, and her stomach sank. Shit. The pixie's hole did lead to the basement, and at its center, the well cast a soft blue light around the ruined space, just bright enough to highlight the three massive weres skulking in the shadows. Two of them were the same Westsiders that'd stalked her across town the other day, and none of them looked happy. Jena fell back to sit. There was no way she wanted to tangle with them.

Okay, inventory, Jena. What have you got to work with? Her karma was spent, if she ate sin chances were good Malcom would know exactly where she was since it belonged to him, and the node…she sighed, her stomach churning at the power coming from it. That dankness she'd sensed down at the gate had only grown. Sin striated through it, the magic erratic, pulsing and spiraling off into wild mercurial tangents and completely ignoring her call.

Wild. The node was going wild, and she had bupkis. Jena gritted her teeth. No, it wasn't. It wasn't wild, it was just… agitated. She could fix this. She just needed to bind herself to the well before she spoke the vow at the stones, and it would settle down. Right? Yeah, right. Easy.

Or it would've been, yesterday. Damn it. How the hell was she going to bleed into the stupid well now? She picked at her crusty, swollen lip. Ugh, she was screwed and itchy on top of it. God, pixie bites were the freaking worst. Miserable little carnivores—

A really bad idea pinged into her brain as her gaze lit on Mr. Mouse Skull and the rest of the harem. "Hey…do you want to play a game?"

His face contorted, suspicious. *"A-game?"*

"Yeah…" she licked the bite on her lip before she'd thought better of it. Ugh, it was sour. "It-it would be like a—a favor."

"A-favor?-What-kind-of-favor?-What-do-we-get?" he asked, suddenly way too eager. The rest of them crowded in on her, their voices buzzing in kind.

God, this was gonna bite her in the ass, but she was already missing one chunk of her… "Whatever you want, as long as it's in my power to grant, and won't stain my karma."

Mr. Mouse Skull looked intrigued. *"For?"*

Jena took a deep breath, pretty sure this was either gonna be genius or one of the dumbest things she'd ever suggested. *God, please let me be able to do this by proxy…* "I need you to bite me and spit my blood into the well. Whoever gets a whole mouthful in there, earns a favor."

His severe little eyebrows rose. *"We-bite-you-and-we-get-whatever-we-want?"*

"Only if a whole mouthful of my blood goes in the water down there. And then, yes, you get to pick a favor."

"*Game-game-it's-a-game!*" Another pixie clapped.

They congregated, their rapid little voices increasing in speed until it became a shrill hum, then it dropped off and Mr. Mouse Skull nodded. "*Coconuts.*" He held up all his fingers. "*This-many-each.*"

Well, that was random. What the hell would pixies want with coconuts? Whatever. She didn't care. "Um…okay. Deal."

The harem was on Jena before all the words were out of her mouth, their sharp, stabbing teeth at her neck and wrists, pain blooming a hundred times worse than wasp stings—

And then they were through the hole like bees returning to their hive.

"What the fuck?!" A were yelled from the basement, the sounds of a scramble ensuing.

Jena bit back a sob, the horrible bites already swelling as she put her eye to the hole. The harem zipped around the three burly weres, taking turns hawking bright red mouthfuls of gore into the azure water. It pulsed, a purple glow slowly rising from the depths along with the distinct scent of bergamot.

"Hope you're happy, Mom," Jena muttered, scratching.

A tinkling laugh and a wash of power crested through Jena, clearing her head and settling her stomach. The harem returned through the hole in a rush and she stumbled back onto her rear, her palms splaying on the ground as she caught herself.

Her mind's eye opened at the contact, the constraints around the node laid bare. Instinctively, she re-channeled its energy, strengthening the existing wards—

It wasn't going to be enough. The backup of power was reaching a critical mass, and she couldn't reroute it without having full access to the node's power and the leylines that fed it. Jena looked out at the driving rain, conviction settling in her belly as lightning flickered through the clouds and the sky rumbled ominously.

She needed to finish the rite, and she had to get to the center of the garden to do it.

~

CHASE SAT CHAINED to an iron loop set into one of the seven standing stones in the garden, his face tipped up to the rain, and his eyes closed, biding his time. At either side of him was a bare monolith, and then past those, Felix was to his right and Liam to his left, both strung up against the next stones in the circle by their ankles.

Felix shivered beneath the deluge, coughing at odd intervals, and his lips blue. Liam didn't move. They'd taken off the silver chains, but the damage had been done. He dangled, his hands brushing the tip of the inverted pentagram that'd been drawn across the circle of stones, his face an unhealthy gray and his breathing shallow.

The fire beneath the caldron at the center of the circle crackled azure, leaping in defiance of the storm, and beyond it, Malcom—

His stomach clenched. He didn't want to think about what Malcom was doing.

Chase seethed. Patience. He had to have patience...a muscle in his jaw jumped, his knuckles white at the small of his back. Fuck, he knew that, but sitting here trying to buy time for Jena to do whatever she had to—if she even *could* do what she had to after sending up that ward at the gate—was trying him in ways he hadn't thought possible.

He rolled around the image of the manacles they'd fastened around his wrists, walking through the steps to release the chain between them...feeling the tumblers of the lock shift in his mind...he stopped before the last fell into place.

No. Not yet. Jena would come through. He had to believe—

A tremor swept through the tor and across the circle, the fire momentarily gutting. Malcom gave a low growl, his gaze snapping towards the ruins.

Chase didn't bother to swallow his smile. *That's my girl…*

Malcom thumbed the pommel of the blade in his hand, then grunted, sinking back into a crouch, his attention on the corpse he was in the midst of mutilating. Chase swallowed raggedly, forcing himself not to gag at the visceral reek of offal and burning flesh despite the pouring rain.

Trying to convince himself that what was left of it hadn't been his mother, despite the string of blood-stained pearls still dangling around her ravaged throat. Jesus, if he dwelled on what Malcom had done to her…fuck. That'd been his mom.

Mary Montgomery had been strung her up by her ankles and hung splayed against one of the seven standing stones then disemboweled, her abdominal cavity stuffed with hot coals. A single loop of intestine had caught against her chin, and the rest lay in a steaming pile beneath her head. Her eyes, wide and unseeing, had filmed over gray; her face a rictus of macabre surprise.

Malcom had gleefully prodded her to describe in horrific detail what she'd done to Wallace as she alternately screamed and sobbed about their deal. Jena was right, his mom was evil, but reconciling her confession with the woman who'd raised him…what he'd seen in that vision of Jena's…Karma might be the bigger bitch, but God only knew what else his mother had done to deserve an end like that.

Later. He'd deal with it later.

If there was a later.

Chase closed his eyes again, breathing deep. No. There would be. He had to believe that.

Malcom stepped back to inspect the arcane symbols he'd

carved into her chest and thighs, then flipped the knife in his hand, chanting.

A ruddy bubble of power flared from the corpse, encompassing the circle of stones and diverting the driving rain around them. Dark tendrils of mist gathered, swirling above the cauldron, and Felix began to sob softly.

Malcom ignored him, turning toward his next victim.

Lashed upright to the stone at the fifth point of the pentagram, Crystal cringed from him, a gag cutting into the sides of her mouth. He rested an arm above her head and ran the flat of his blade down her cheek, following the dark streaks of makeup streaming from around her eyes.

"You're so much prettier when you cry," he murmured, softly kissing her forehead. She cowered back. "Don't worry, beauty. Your part will play out soon enough."

Behind him the mist coalesced, and the shadowy form of a tall man stepped from the flames. "She comes."

Chase flinched at the obscene anticipation dripping from the entity's lips.

Malcom turned toward it. "She does, and our bargain is now complete. Do with her what you will, the node is mine."

The entity gave a low chuckle, solidifying as it slowly paced around the circle to stop in front of Chase. Shit. It was the man from the picture—Jena's father. He was very tall, his hair a dark shock of raven and handsome in the way only a sidhe could be. He wet his lips, and stared down at Chase with the same emerald-green eyes as Jena. The entity lowered himself to a knee and grasped Chase's face, sniffing as he turned it this way and that.

Chase jerked free. "Don't fucking touch me."

Jena's father chuckled again. "Well, aren't you a surprise." A cruel smile flitted across his face. "Your line ran truer than I'd have thought," he said over his shoulder, a hit of glee in his voice. "A manifester. How frustrating that must be for you."

Malcom scowled. "Leave him be, we are quits, and it's of no matter."

"So you hope." Her father stood, looking back toward the ruins. Another cruel smile stole across his lips, and he was gone.

Chase stared at the space he'd been, his pulse pounding in his ears. A manifester? What the hell did that mean? A vision of the repaired fireplace flashed across his mind's eye. He'd done that...moved the tumblers in the lock keeping him chained...had willed it to happen. Was that what he'd been doing? Manifesting his will? He glanced at Malcom and his jaw set, concentrating on exactly how he was going to kill him.

Chapter Twenty-Five

JENA TOOK a deep breath and darted out into the rain toward the shadowed garden, lightning flashing and bringing the landscape into stark relief. The deluge hit her like a fist, her robes plastering to her, wrapping around her legs and threatening to trip her. Damn it. She crouched beneath the trees by the reflecting pool and wrenched the sodden fabric aside, letting it hang open.

A ruddy glow sprang up at the center of the garden, lighting her way like a beacon as a wave of sin rolled out from it. She hunched over gagging. Oh God, whatever Malcom was doing in there, it was pure evil. Her temper flared, the feel of it far too similar to what'd been coming off the dark altar in the vision her mother had left.

Jena ran the back of her hand over her mouth. The bite on her lip throbbed and the rest of them were a study in frickin' misery, but she needed to save what karma she had. She crept through the garden's entrance, taking the same path she had not three days past. A thrumming anticipation resonated through the stones at her feet, fractured power bleeding up from the earth, along with a creeping sense of being watched.

The space between her shoulder blades pricked, and this time she wasn't even going to try to pretend it was her imagination. Something was definitely aware of her presence. She passed the tumbled urns and long stone planters, rainwater overflowing and splashing down onto the cobbled path. Her pulse sped, the weight of regard increasing with every step.

Jena bit back a sob as the twisted, overgrown limbs of the ornamental trees caught at her, as if to hold her back. Like the dryads that'd once inhabited them knew something bad was about to happen—no. She couldn't stop. Her chin trembled. She had to do this. *You can do this...*Jena pushed through the branches, hurrying past the drowned pocket gardens—

And then there it was. The stone bridge.

She shivered, scratching a wrist, her nightmares coming back full force, the darkness of the entity she'd sensed...*One step at a time, Jena, you've got to get across that mess first.* Below the bridge, the stream had filled, straining its banks and washing over the stone footings. The last three feet of the path lay beneath a rising stretch of swirling water. What was in the fountain's basin sloshed onto the path around it with each gust of rain. Jena's skin prickled with wild magic. At its center, the statue of Hecate stood heedless of the storm, its eyes somehow more seeing than they had been.

Fuck...If you're there, please, please, please lend me your favor...

She swallowed the lump of fear threatening to choke her as she approached the flooded portion of the path, and jumped to the bridge just as a slim, gray-green pair of hands darted from the pool. She slipped, falling to a knee as she landed. Ugh! Frickin' naiads! She scrambled back onto her feet, pulling her dragging robe from their reach, and turning as she swept the rain from her face.

The massive stone urn stood just across the way, daring her to cross.

The creeping sense of being watched increased a hundred fold. That darkness, the entity—her father—was waiting for her.

And so was the node.

The storm raged around her as she stepped forward, wild magic lashing at her, the stones of the bridge shimmering, caught somewhere between this world and the next. Reality deepened, gaining another dimension and rendering everything crystalline. The taint of rot seared her nostrils.

She paused, her toes at the edge of the containment circle, and raised her chin with a deep breath. *Here goes...* "Hi, Dad."

A deep chuckle resonated around her, and a shadowy form took shape by the urn. "Jena. So nice of you to come and see me after all this time. And my, haven't you grown, though you're looking a bit worse for the wear."

She shivered, his voice rolling over her like a cloud of carrion. "Why did you come back?" God the sins of this creature...how could her mother have stood to be close to him?

"Why, for you, my child." He smiled, and it was more endearing than it should've been. "But alas, your mother wasn't amiable to me taking custody, and I'm afraid our discourse became...heated."

Jena gritted her teeth, absently scratching her neck before she caught herself. Frickin' pixies... "You don't say."

"But it's not too late," he said, extending a long-fingered hand, the ruddy light from whatever Malcom was doing playing over it. "And I'd very much like to get to know you."

She stared at his outstretched palm, a tattoo of a pentagram writing against his skin. A sick certainty rose in her throat, choking her. "You're not unseelie."

He chuckled again. "Seelie, unseelie, sidhe. They're such broad terms. Let's just say I've enough to qualify, and as to the rest...well, that's a bit murkier." His fingers undulated, hypnotic, urging her closer.

Jena closed her eyes, her lips and fingertips tingling with intent. "You killed her. Blackened her name and ruined my life. You took everything from me," she rasped, glad the rain was hiding her tears.

"Now that's not true," he crooned. "I've a sneaking suspicion there's somethings very dear to you at the center of this garden, and whether or not they remain on this plane of existence is entirely up to you."

Jena's breath caught, her magic dying as his smile widened, those long fingers beckoning her again. Behind him, the sun had just set, its last rays barely visible through a break in the distant clouds.

"Come child, it's time."

It was. Jena blew out a shaky breath, swallowed her fear, and stepped into the circle.

~

CHASE STARED AT MALCOM, vividly imagining clawing through his guts and feel of viscera slipping through his fingers. The sadistic asshole paused carving another symbol into Crystal's flesh, her screams already devolved into low, sobbing moans. He glared over his shoulder at Chase and growled, a hand on his stomach.

"Well, aren't you a prodigy," he spat out a gob of crimson and reached up, deboning the ring finger from Crysta's hand with a gristly pop. "Fortunately, there's a cure for that." He pulled the engagement ring from it and slipped it onto his pinky. "You need to come to heel, *son*."

Another weird tug went through Chase, and whatever power he'd been accessing dropped away. Goddamn it. "It's true?" he asked, fumbling for whatever he'd been tapping into as the son of a bitch turned back to Crystal. Jena said the ring he'd given her could mitigate the hold it would have on him…yes, there. Thank God, she was right. He latched on to a tiny thread of power and focused on the last tumbler in the lock at his wrists.

Malcom laughed, then grimaced, spitting out another gob

of gore before going back to his gristly task. "That you're mine? In every sense of the word."

"Why are you doing this? What the fuck is the point?"

"The point," Malcom said, gouging out another chunk of Crystal's flesh, "is for me to return to the realm and reclaim my throne." He flicked his knife around the circle in disdain, a hand on his gut as he grimaced. "This pale reflection is an anathema…as are you."

The tumbler clicked, and Chase caught the cuff as it fell from his wrist, slowly working the chain still attached to the other through the iron loop at the base of the stone. "Guess you shouldn't have fucked my mom in a bunch of rabbit guts then. You had to know that wasn't gonna turn out well."

Malcom's spine straightened as he turned, coming closer. "On the contrary, that turned out exactly as I expected…but what would you know about that?" he asked, stopping just in front of him.

"Way more than I want to." Christ, the chain was almost free, he needed to keep the shithead talking. Hopefully, whatever he'd done to the asshole's insides would slow him down. "So what, you were some kind of prince? Of what? Ill-laid plans? Must be, if you were slumming over here. It must suck to lose your crown over a piece of tail."

Malcom narrowed his eyes at him and spat another crimson gob to the side. "Sidhe royalty is bestowed based on power, not birthright, and only the strongest have a claim on consort. Of those, only the cleverest ascend to Her Dark Majesty's side."

The end of the chain slipped free. "Shit, then you didn't have a chance." *Come on, just a little closer, you motherfucker…*

Malcom took one more step and grinned down at him, his teeth flecked with blood and the scent of viscera on his breath. "I'm going to enjoy killing you. Maybe I'll fuck that whore witch in *your* guts."

Chase exploded forward, wrapping the chain around

Malcom's throat and driving his knee into the were's stomach. Malcom screamed and a burning slice flared across Chase's abdomen as they fell. Fuck, he'd forgotten about the goddamned knife—His muscles strained against the thrashing man, trying to keep his grip on the links—A jab of agony lanced through his flank, and he rolled, pinning Malcom's hand with the knife to the ground beneath him.

The motherfucker started to shift, raking at Chase with his claws. Chase's fangs elongated, and he lunged at Malcom's throat, biting into the soft flesh beneath his jaw.

Malcom howled, a wash of briny copper pulsing over Chase's chin. He shook his head and it surged, spurting crimson. Beneath him, Malcom went limp, and Chase fell back panting, a hand over the gnarly slice across his abdomen. He spat the taste of the man from his mouth. Asshole had just about gutted him. Fuck, that needed stitches, and who the hell knew what the stab to his back had hit. If it was a kidney—

"You need to finish it," Felix rasped weakly. "Sidhe don't die easy."

Chase stared blankly at the dangling warlock.

"You need to cut off his head."

Chapter Twenty-six

JENA TOOK her father's hand, and he smiled, tucking her arm through his as they strolled toward the standing stones at the center of the garden. Sin wrapped around them, sheltering them from the deluge and turning her stomach as it picked at her. The air vibrated with wild magic, infusing and altering the landscape, the stones wavered—breathing—like they were alive.

Beneath her feet, the node pulsed, as angry as the storm above their heads. The wards constraining it screamed at her, ready to burst at their seams. Sweat trickled down her back. Jena bit back a sob, at a total loss. God, what would Aggie do? Oh, that's right. She'd tell her to claim the damned node and banish the asshole.

Easier said than frickin' done.

"This is nice, isn't it?" her father asked, patting her hand genially. "You, me. Look how lovely we're getting on. I didn't think I'd fancy being a father, but here you are, proving me wrong."

Jena just looked at him, and his grin widened.

"Ah. You're a stoic like your mother. Very well then, why don't we see how Malcom's fairing? We should be just in time to say our goodbyes. If I'm not mistaken, the realm is about to open to us, and we can get on to business."

"Business?" Jena asked, scratching the bites at her throat.

"Mmm. Yes. My affairs must be quite out of order. There will be plenty to do, things to see, people to kill—debts to claim." He smiled at her again. Christ, Aggie hadn't been kidding. Despite the horrible things coming out of his mouth, he was stupidly charming. "Here now, darling, no need to suffer…"

He ran his fingers over her throat, and the bites wriggled, like worms were being expelled before a ruddy light flared beneath her chin. She raised a hand to the smooth skin, her pulse coming way too fast.

"Yes. That's better. You're much more appealing now. Say thank you."

"T-thank you."

He patted her arm again. "That a girl. See, we're friends."

She choked back a surge of bile. They were most definitely not friends. The path before them opened up, a dome of sickly, red light capped the garden's center. Her breath sped as they approached, a body lay prone on the ground before the bubbling cauldron, and hanging against the standing stones, Liam, Crystal, and—

Jena turned away, heaving. *Oh God…*

"Mmm. We will have to work on that," her father tsked, then clapped his hands together. "Ah! Chase, is it? Marvelous job, my boy!"

Jena glanced up, her stomach threatening to rebel again. What the fuck? Felix dangled from his ankles against another of the stones, and Chase slumped below him, covered in blood with Malcom's severed head at his feet. Her father swept it up, holding it at eye level.

"Alas, poor Yorick! I knew him, a fellow of infinite jest and most excellent fancy—well, no, I can't say that. I'm afraid outside of this little grift, he was quite dull." He tossed the head over his shoulder and dusted off his hands. It bounced across the flagstones and came to a stop beside Liam. Oh God, he didn't even twitch.

"Now, where were we…ah, yes." Her father snapped his fingers. "The node. Do take that in hand, darling, it's what you're here for, isn't it?"

Jena ran the back of her hand over her mouth, lightning crackling through the sky as the storm outside the dome intensified. Yes, but why would he want her to do that? She glanced at Felix and Chase, but neither of them returned it.

"Yes? Yes. Chop, chop." Her father tapped his wrist. "It's not going to wait much longer."

He was right but…shit. She didn't know what else to do. "I-I pledge myself as guardian of the node," Jena stammered. "M-my service for yours—" A tide of power surged from the ground to engulf her, stars exploding across her vision as the leylines and the node were laid bare to her psyche, the obstruction at Sunnyside a blackened void cutting into the line.

Words to vow have been spoken, the blood of thy veins has bound. Seven stones witnessed thy oath. Our service for thine…

Save them, she thought back, *and I'll try…*

The voices rose in pitch, pleading and warning—

Sin washed over her drowning them out.

"Now, now, that's quite enough of that," her father scoffed. "No need for all that doom and gloom when we're getting on so well."

"No…" Jena panted, her lips and fingertips crackling with intent. "This needs to be put right, and that's enough of you."

A brilliant smile slicked across her father's face. "Oh, how lovely. You're about to become a problem, aren't you?" he asked gleefully. "Fabulous. You know, you get that from me." He shook out his arms and adjusted the cuffs of his jacket. "How would you like to begin?"

Jena closed her eyes and opened herself to the power of the node. It shot through her like a geyser, atomizing the dome and erupting into the clouds, brilliant violet sparks and bursts of power exploding through the heavens.

"Huh," her father huffed as if puzzled. "Not what I would have led with, but I suspect that's not something you see every day."

Jena turned to face him, power crackling around her. "You haven't seen anything yet."

~

CHASE'S EYES SNAPPED OPEN, his gut and back itching as they healed. The same weird tingle from after Wallace's shade attacked him ran through his body. Fuck. Chase shivered. That had to be the node bringing him back again—

The node. He sucked in a breath as the scene before him registered, his fingers tightening around the sticky dagger still in his hand. The ground shook as if it were about to erupt —Jesus, the node had to be at capacity—before him, Jena faced her father, surrounded by violet flame again, her eyes emerald fire, and her hair twisting in that weird, ethereal wind. A column of energy shot up from the ground around her, into the clouds, lightning crazing around manic bursts of magic. Goddamn, the voltage up there must be insane—his eyes went wide.

It was voltage.

He clambered forward on his hands and knees across the flagstones, trying to stay out of the entity's sight. If he could get to her—the ground heaved, and he lurched forward, and then back, massive spiders materializing from the cracks between the pavers. Jena shrieked as they converged upon her, and her father laughed.

"Is there an issue?" His eyes were alight with malevolence, great horns and wings streaming from the shadow he threw against the stone pillar behind him. "I thought that was a challenge. Eat up, little girl, there's plenty more sin where that came from."

Jena drew a glyph, still channeling power from the node up into the clouds like an arcane pressure relief valve. The spiders erupted into flames, their bodies hissing and popping as they exploded in bursts of foul green ichor.

"Not to be dissuaded, hmm?" Her father grinned. "I do like your grit. Something a bit more loathsome then." He made a gesture, and dark tendrils of sin sped from him, reassembling their corpses into gruesome caricatures of knee-high rats.

Chase shouldered one aside, and it plowed into another feasting on what was left of Malcom. Chase's stomach lurched. God, this was so fucked up...head down, he was almost there...his fingers brushed the hem of Jena's robe, and he sent out a massive wave of his will—

"Oh no you don't," the entity growled, projecting a nasty, pulsing orb at him.

"Right back at you!" she cried, drawing a glyph in the air, her eyes blazing with emerald fire. A name burst from her lips, and her father's face contorted in fury. "Take all of it, you son of a bitch, and fucking choke on it, times three!"

A tsunami of power whipped out from her as Chase's will was swept up the column of power and into the clouds—

A shock wave blasted them back against a standing stone, lightning jagging above. An epic boom cracked apart the heavens, purple light searing across his vision, and a massive detonation in the distance rendering everything else silent. The ground heaved and vibrated, roiling with a muffled roar like freight train, felt more than heard, streaming west beneath their feet.

And then all was still, dust shimmering down around them, a fine gray pall setting over the circle—

Along with a smattering of tiny purple flowers perfuming the air.

The hell? Chase shook his head, blinking the spots from

his vision. Jena lay across him, blood running from her ears. He pulled her into his lap, and her lids fluttered.

"Did I get him?" she murmured, the scrapes and scratches from the explosion disappearing before Chase's eyes. How were they not dead?

*Our service for yours...*a chorus of voices whispered through his mind.

His throat bobbed as he glanced around the circle. Malcom and his mother's bodies were gone, along with any trace of Jena's father. Crystal and Liam both sat at the bases of the stones they'd been chained to, whole in body, though by the way Crystal was rocking, her mind might be another story.

"I dunno," Chase said, his voice ragged. He turned to Felix, sprawled out beside them. "Did you see what happened?"

"I don't know what I saw, but I know I don't want to see it again." He glanced at Jena and then up at the clear night sky, the moon just cresting the tree line. Sirens sounded in the distance and the baying of wolves came from closer by. "Boomerang hex?"

She nodded, smiling softly as she held one of the tiny blooms to her nose. "Boomerang hex."

Chase hugged her tightly and kissed her temple. "If those sirens are for us, you're gonna have to let them in."

Jena nodded, closing her eyes. "Kelsey and your dad are here," she said to Liam after a moment. Liam bit back a sob and buried his face against his bent knees. Felix made like he was going to get up, and then sat back as a pair of weres bounded into the circle.

The smaller of the two bowled into Liam licking his face. He threw his arms around its neck, his shoulders shaking as he sobbed.

"Shit," Kelsey's dad murmured as he regained human form. Jesus. One of his eyes had been gouged from the socket and livid, half-healed claw marks raked over his torso. "Is everyone all right?"

"Physically," Chase said. "You?"

"I've been better," he murmured, his gaze lingering on Liam and Kelsey as the sirens grew louder, then died by the base of the tor. "But Havers is united under one alpha again, and Fayet got sent packing, though that won't be the end of it. Assholes made off with your sister."

Shit, that wasn't good, though Sue being Sue, Chase wouldn't be surprised if they sent her back instead of claiming her. It was a problem for another day. "You hear anything about Luke?"

Phil shook his head. "No, but that boat of his isn't at the dock. I'm assuming he's out on it, and Patrick is in traction at Klineville General. The only Montgomery not accounted for is your mother."

Chase swallowed, his eyes flicking to one of the standing stones. "You don't have to worry about her."

Phil grunted, toeing one of the purple blooms. "Malcom?"

"Same."

The alpha blew out his cheeks, turning at the sound of boots on stone. Two pairs of wide-eyed EMTs carrying stretchers appeared. One set hurried over to triage Crystal and the other to Liam.

"This is gonna kill her mother. The mayor didn't do so hot in the turn-over," Phil murmured as the first pair carted Crystal away, catatonic. "Remind me never to piss off Matilda Hanson."

"Oh God, she didn't turn him into a frog, did she?" Jena asked.

"No, but he's the sleekest weasel I've ever seen." Phil's gaze went to Felix. "And from what I understand, you're mayor for the foreseeable future."

"Me?" Felix squeaked.

"You," Phil said. "No one else seems to know how to get

anything done, and the town's a fucking mess. Between the power outage, the stampeding crowds, and Sunnyside being flattened after that freak lightning strike, you're the one everyone's looking to get direction from."

Jena laughed as Felix stared at the alpha in absolute bewilderment. "That's what you get for being competent, but at least your new salary should cover those parking tickets."

"You make a valid point." He rose shakily to his feet and flicked a bedraggled curl from his eyes. "But fuck salary, I'm approving overtime for this."

Kelsey came over with a sheet draped around her. She handed another to her father, and the keys to Liam's Jeep chimed in her hand. "They're taking Liam to the hospital for observation. He asked me to drive you guys back to town."

"He okay?" Chase glanced over at the were. He'd laid down on the stretcher with his back to them, and one of the EMTs was talking to him softly.

"I don't know," she said, biting a nail. "Liam's...he gets in his head a lot."

Phil sighed, wrapping the sheet around his waist. "I'll stay with him."

Kelsey forced a smile as her dad kissed her forehead and went to join him. "Did you want that ride?" she asked.

Chase glanced at Jena. "We done here, baby?"

"For tonight," she said as she stood, cradling one of the blooms. "But I'm pretty sure this is only the beginning."

Three months later

JENA LOOKED up from The Witchery's register at the pause in hammering from above. Was that Chase wrapping things up for the day? Ever since he'd moved in with her and Aggie, he'd been a man on a mission.

The final repairs to the roof would have to wait until spring, though he'd done what he could before the snow had flown. The greenhouse had been taken down and meticulously laid out in pieces in one of the rooms below, and a super structure of scaffolding, tarps, and temporary sheeting had been put up in its place, waiting for spring.

But meanwhile, everything else was fair game, and what that man could accomplish when he put his mind to it…Jena shook her head. He'd told her that her father had called him a manifester, and there wasn't any question in her mind that it was true. Chase definitely had the uncanny ability to make things happen.

She put a hand on the small rise of her abdomen and sighed, reconciling the cash register drawer with a soft smile. They'd had another good day. A few more months of this, and the shop might even be solidly in the black. With the leyline flowing the way it should, practitioners had started to drift back to Havers and Fayet, and The Witchery was the only legitimate supplier to the occult community in the county.

It had also gained more than a little notoriety after a video of the column of power from the node shooting into the clouds had gone viral. Not that many people knew the whole story behind that, and if they did, they weren't talking—despite the swarm of inquisitors that'd descended after the fact. All of which had only served to feed speculation and make the town even more of a tourist destination.

Being a Seymore wasn't such a bad thing anymore.

But being an unregistered sidhe was still a big fat no. Luckily, Aggie had been strong enough to make herself scarce while the feds were in town, and no one had any cause to suspect Jena and Chase were anything other than what they said they were.

Which was pretty much just deliriously, stupidly happy.

His boot falls descended the stairs, and Jena hurried to finish up.

"Hey, mama," he murmured in her ear a moment later, wrapping his arms around her and sliding a palm over her abdomen. "You calling it a day?"

"Mmm, that depends, are you?" she asked, closing the till and leaning back against him.

"I am, and Aggie says she's making lasagna."

Jena laughed. "She can cook whatever she wants, but we're not naming our kid after her."

"I'm not sure it's entirely for you," he said, kissing her neck. "When I got the preliminary approvals for the new manor this morning, Gorman said something about seeing me later at dinner."

Jena looked over her shoulder at him, incredulous. "She's got a date?"

Chase shrugged. "Sounds that way."

Holy crap. Jena turned and laced her arms around his

neck. "I guess I don't have to worry about her being here by herself once we move out to the tor…but Gorman Howe?"

"He's not a bad guy."

Jena cocked a brow. "You complain about him at least twice a week."

"Which is a hell of a lot less than you complain about Aggie."

Okay, he had a point, but still. "Well, if she's making lasagna, I'm inviting Felix over—"

"I already took care of it. He'll be here after the zoning meeting."

"Sunnyside?" she asked.

"Yeah. I'm hoping they're gonna nix the plan for the industrial park, but if they don't, I'm putting in that bid we talked about for a new lumberyard. Fayet's still stonewalling."

Chase frowned, and Jena didn't press him, knowing he was thinking about his sister. They hadn't heard anything from Sue since she'd been claimed by the other pack. That wasn't that strange in were culture, but it bothered him, a lot. Apparently, she hadn't always been a miserable bitch, but Jena'd be damned if she'd ever seen an inkling of that.

"Ready to go up?" he asked.

"I don't know," she teased, taking his hand. "Do I have a workable shower?"

Chase grinned at her, dimples studding his cheeks. "You say that like you didn't enjoy the sponge baths."

"Oh, I did, but somehow I always ended up filthier afterwards."

"Mmm. I like you filthy, but yes, the shower is working, and so is clawfoot tub." He opened the door on the landing, and Jena groaned as a wave of garlic-y Italian decadence rolled over her. "Is that in anticipation of dinner, or of the bath I drew for you?"

She paused, honestly not sure. "You drew me a bath?"

His sidhe-blue eyes sparkled as he led her down the hall, and she smiled, following him.

In an ocean of small towns, Havers-by-the-Sea had officially become home, and Jena hadn't just learned to swim, she was sailing.

THE END

Karma can kiss it.

WHEN FELIX SIMMS took over the position of mayor in the small town of Havers-by-the-Sea, he had no idea he'd inherit so many problems. Between the town of Fayet suing them for magical appropriation, a looming budget crisis, and the butt cheek bandit's reign of terror, the last thing Felix needs is to be saddled with his delinquent sister's urchins over the holidays. And he certainly doesn't have time to deal with Liam Montgomery trying to make amends for suggesting the disastrous "polycule proposal" that broke Felix's heart senior year.

But Liam is desperate to prove he and Felix are meant to be together. Unfortunately, Liam's pending divorce has taken a nasty turn, and juggling that and the Havers's rumor mill is seriously affecting his mental health.

Meanwhile, a new threat is rising, putting all of Havers in danger. To face it, Felix and Liam have to put their differences aside. Because if they can't, it's not just the town that's in jeopardy, it's everyone they love, and Jena and Chase will be the first to fall.

Magic happens and sparks fly in the small town of Havers-By-the-Sea when a sassy warlock with oodles of style crosses paths with an angsty shifter. WARDS AND WARLOCKS, a spicy standalone slow burn M/M paranormal romance novel in the Star-Crossed Chronicles series by AK Nevermore.

This book was weird. I got the idea from a call for anthology stories. The first scene in the book popped into my head when I read the description, and then it went way the hell over the word count they were looking for. Whoops.

I had thoughts of shopping it out to agents and publishers, but then decided I didn't want to wait 12-18 months to see it in print, and hey, it's almost Halloween. I wondered if I could get it out by then…and yes, these are the things I do to myself…and my team.

So thank you first and foremost to Nancy at NN Light's Book Heaven for squeezing me into her editing schedule. This book would not be out right now if it weren't for you humoring me and doing a meticulous job in the process.

It also wouldn't have a cover, associated graphics, or any of the PR buzz with out Jena working her highly-caffeinated fingers to the bone for me. She's amazing at what she does, and I would be a mess without her.

But before any of the above could happen, thank you to all my beta readers with extra hugs to JJ Graham, who flags all of my misspellings, plot holes, and when things just flat-out don't make sense or aren't consistent. Your input is what tells me if something is ready to publish or not.

And last but not least, thanks, Mom. Here's another volume to add to your shelf.

THE DAE DIARIES - URBAN FANTASY WITH SPICE

One Night in Bliss — Flame & Shadow — Air & Darkness — Playing with Fire

THE PRICE OF TALENT - SPICY DYSTOPIAN ROMANCE

*Breeder — Breaker — Destroyer — Binder — Conspirator — Split Overlord — Exile — Dyad **

THE MAW OF MAYHEM - PRN MC EROTIC ROMANCE

*Bites of Mayhem — The Maw of Mayhem — Grimdarke Darker — Kit-Kat — Katherine — Deuce **

STAR-CROSSED CHRONICLES

Weres and Witchery — Wards and Warlocks — Vampires and Vendettas

ANTHOLOGIES & STANDALONES

Secrets We Keep — Sense, Sensibility, & Shifters — Fairytale

**Forthcoming*

ABOUT THE AUTHOR

AK Nevermore is a bestselling author of paranormal, dystopian science fiction, and urban fantasy romance. She enjoys operating heavy machinery, freebases coffee, and gives up sarcasm for Lent every year.

A Jane-of-all-trades, she's a certified chef, restores antiques, and dabbles in beekeeping when she's not reading voraciously or running down the dream in her beat-up camo Chucks.

Unable to ignore the voices in her head, and unwilling to become medicated, she writes full time. Her books explore dark worlds, perversely irreverent and profound, and always entertaining.

Want more Nevermore?
Sign up for her newsletter and never miss a release!

aknevermore.com